W9-AMJ-294

THE VIRTUOUS CON

a novel

Maren Foster

TWO TAILS PRESS

CHICAGO

This is a work of fiction. All characters, organizations, situations, and events portrayed are a product of the author's imagination. Any similarity to real people, living or dead, or events are entirely coincidental.

THE VIRTUOUS CON Copyright © 2021 by Maren Foster

All rights reserved. Except as permitted under the U.S. Copyright Act of 1976, no part of this publication may be reproduced, distributed, or transmitted in any form or by any means, or stored in a database or retrieval system, without prior written permission of the publisher.

TWO TAILS PRESS
Chicago, IL
www.twotailspress.com

First published in June 2021.
All inquiries contact info@twotailspress.com

Library of Congress control number: 2021910620

ISBN 978-1-7373082-0-1 (trade paperback)

Book and cover design by Karen Magnuson

For Victoria Solomon and all of the other bad ass women in this world who are an inspiration

"The confidence game starts with basic human psychology. From the artist's perspective, it's a question of identifying the victim (THE PUT-UP): who is he, what does he want, and how can I play on that desire to achieve what I want? It requires the creation of empathy and rapport (THE PLAY): an emotional foundation must be laid before any scheme is proposed, any game set in motion. Only then does it move to logic and persuasion (THE ROPE); the scheme (THE TALE), the evidence and the way it will work to your benefit (THE CONVINCER), the show of actual profits. And like a fly caught in a spider's web, the more we struggle, the less able to extricate ourselves we become (THE BREAKDOWN). By the time things begin to look dicey, we tend to be so invested, emotionally and often physically, that we do most of the persuasion ourselves. We may even choose to up our involvement ourselves, even as things turn south (THE SEND), so that by the time we're completely fleeced (THE TOUCH), we don't quite know what hit us. The con artist may not even need to convince us to stay quiet (THE BLOW-OFF AND FIX); we are more likely than not to do so ourselves. We are, after all, the best deceivers of our own minds."

-Maria Konnikova, THE CONFIDENCE GAME

PART 1: THE PUT-UP & THE PLAY
February 2015 to October 2016

THE PUT-UP

Friday, February 20, 2015
Evanston, Illinois

Staring at the list of entry level jobs on the student services webpage, I filtered by location: New York, NY. The list shrunk to only a handful of positions.

I thought about my future, which meant I thought about him, remembering, years earlier, when he told me that he was from New York, loved the City, and would definitely move back after graduation. He was a few years older than me. *Does he still live there?* I googled his name and clicked on news. A number of different stories popped up; there were a handful of Nathan Ellises in the New York area. Based on the news articles, one was middle aged and had coached his son's little league team to a state championship in 2010. Another was an investment banker in Manhattan. The most recent news about *my* Nate was a celebratory article in the Westport Gazette about the twenty-something, who had started his own business while in college and was on his way to prodigious success after recently founding a second company. There was a photo of Nate shaking hands with an older guy, both wearing dark, tailored business suits, smiling for the camera. The date on the article was February 3, 2015. *That's less than a month ago. So he is still in New York.*

I stared at his Facebook profile: a professional headshot of him above his name and location, New York City, NY. One mutual friend. I clicked to reveal our mutual connection, expecting it to be my roommate from freshman year of college or her boyfriend. Instead, the name beside the picture read "Adam Hart." *My Adam?* Next to Adam's name, it read "53 mutual friends." *Nate knows Adam? They did go to the same Ivy League school, but I thought they were in different frats.*

Are they actually friends? A mutual friend could give me away. Just to be safe I unfriended Adam. *He won't notice, he's hardly ever on Facebook and I can't risk Nate connecting the dots.*

Nate's Facebook account was set to the strictest security settings; I couldn't see anything else. I need to see what he's been up to. I'll have to send him a friend request, but he can't know it's me.

I grabbed my laptop, pulled up my Facebook profile, and clicked on personal information. I changed my name from Freddie Laurent to Wyn RL. *So long to the naïve young woman that Nate once knew.* I edited the rest of my profile.

Works at	*Blank (well, TBD really)*
Studied at	*I deleted the name of my alma mater and left it blank*
Lives in	New York City *(not yet, but soon enough)*
From	*Blank*
Gender	Female
Birthday	February 15, 1993
Political Views	Traditional
Interested	In Men
Relationship	Single

I snapped a quick selfie, applied a soft filter, and uploaded "Wyn". I waited until after midnight to "friend" Nate, hoping he was out partying and would think I was a friend of a friend or someone he'd struck up a drunk conversation with at a bar or club. *Fingers crossed.*

Three months later, after the barrage of interviews and testing that comprise the modern job search, I accepted an entry-level position with an up-and-coming marketing firm in Manhattan. My mother, Vivienne (Vi for short), had generously saved for undergrad, but made it clear that despite her lawyer's salary, she wouldn't support me or my sister after college graduation. She raised us on her own and never hid her belief that women should be self-sufficient first, and wives and mothers second. I'd realized as I watched my college classmates and sorority sisters compete for the best grades, the best internships, and the best job offers that I just didn't have the same drive. It wasn't that I thought I was too good for work, I just lacked their passion for any specific vocation, or for money, prestige, or power. I couldn't see the allure of having a career. For me working was a means, not an end; a matter of necessity (for the time being at least), not a calling. I'd be making just enough money to survive in New York City, just long enough hopefully to be married, have children, and if I was lucky, get to stay home with the kids.

I packed up my things and Vi drove me to the airport on a Thursday morning in late June. I was a little surprised to see her tear up when we hugged in the departures level. She caught me off guard, handing me a personal check just as I turned toward security.

"Call me when you get there," she yelled after me. "Love you, Freddie." I kept walking as if I didn't hear her.

"Freddie" was short for Wynafreda, which my mom staunchly defended throughout my formative years. *Ugh, Wyn-a-fred-a, yuck!* Every time I pestered her about what on Earth had led her to name her daughter Wynafreda, she maintained that she thought it was pretty, but she only invoked its complete ugliness when she wanted to get my attention, knowing full well that I hate it.

As I waited to board my flight to New York City I checked Facebook again. Nate still hadn't accepted my friend request. I'd done a thorough online search for any insights into his life, habits, or routine, but there was nothing of note. *Come on, accept my request!*

I boarded my flight with the basics I would need for my new, adult life: a few brand new business suits, a cluttered make-up bag, and my three favorite pairs of heels. Awaiting me in New York City was a room in a three-bedroom apartment with two girls from my sorority, and my best friend and almost high school sweetheart, Adam Hart.

The squat 1960s faded-tan-brick building paled in comparison to its more mature red-brick neighbors. My roommates were both out of town when I arrived, so the building manager agreed to let me in. As instructed, I met him at the main entrance. Rather squirrely looking, the manager gave me a set of keys, warned me not to make copies, and showed me inside. The apartment was in Hell's Kitchen, on the second floor of a four-story walk-up, with a tiny galley kitchen, no dishwasher or washing machine. My bedroom barely fit a single bed and a child-sized dresser, but it did have a tiny closet, which I knew was a luxury. I could just barely afford the rent. I'd be living in the shabbiest building on a very respectable block. I sent Vi a few pictures of the apartment and she seemed pleased. Perhaps, to her surprise, I'd become the independent woman she had always hoped I would.

I cashed Vi's check and went to the corner store to buy the basics: a carton of eggs, loaf of bread, box of cereal, and milk. I'd use the rest of her gift to take the sting off first month's rent.

The next day I woke up early and ate in silence, staring out the window at an overcast sky. *Three more days until I start work, and just one more thing I have to do: my transformation.* I ventured out for a walk and to find a pharmacy. I'd been to New York City once when I was young and then again in high school, but each of those times I had been with Vi and my older sister Alicia, following their lead. I remembered Vi taking us on long walks through offbeat neighborhoods. She always seemed to know someone to stop in on and visit: former colleagues or classmates from law school.

It was unseasonably cool for late June, but New Yorkers were out walking, carrying groceries, pushing strollers, determined to enjoy a long-overdue summer. I wandered the crowded streets, acutely aware that I was alone.

I texted Adam, "I'm here!"

His response came moments later, "Show you around tomorrow?"

"Yeah, sounds like fun," I replied.

Adam and I grew up together. Our moms were best friends from college and had conspired at every opportunity to set us up. Photo albums documented shared family vacation and complementary Halloween costumes. From a young age we were enrolled in nearly all the same extracurriculars, save football and ballet. In high school Adam was tall, lean, and athletic. I was 5'4", petite, and first chair in the orchestra. We were fourteen the first time he tried to kiss me. I remember it clearly. I pulled away awkwardly, thinking that a failed romance with my best friend might rob me of the extended family that Vi had worked so hard to cultivate. In response Adam ignored me for weeks, but eventually he gave up and we fell back into our usual routine.

After our senior prom, laying together on a blanket at the beach he kissed me and I let him, but when he began to pull at the zipper on my dress I told him to stop. It was exactly what I'd been trying to avoid. I knew I wasn't ready for a serious relationship and we would be going separate ways to colleges in different states. The odds of

4

us working out were slim and I didn't want to ruin our friendship. Instead we fell asleep in each other's arms.

Three years later, in the summer between our junior and senior years of college, we traveled around Europe together. At the end of the trip, as we sat sipping drinks, the sun setting behind the Basilica di San Marco, he mused that if we were both single at thirty we should get married, have kids, and live next door to our parents. Thirty was still a ways off, but it didn't stop me from dreaming about a fairytale life with him, raising a few kids with the help of our parents. Despite my hesitations in the past, somewhere deep inside, I truly believed that we belonged together and would end up together eventually.

On my way back to the apartment I stopped at a pharmacy and bought a box of hair dye. My light auburn hair was the kind of reddish-blonde that looked unnatural. It wasn't uncommon for people to accuse me of lying when I said it was real. Vi and Ali both had rich, chestnut brown hair. Growing up, I felt like the odd one out, which at times was uncomfortable, but also garnered me a lot of attention. I chose a box called "Mocha" and paid the cashier.

Back in my room I massaged the harsh-smelling mixture onto my scalp and down the length of my long hair. I twisted it into a pile on top of my head, set a timer, and used a Q-tip to apply a few drops to my eyebrows. I washed out the chemicals and towel dried my hair, examining the result in the dull, scratched up mirror above the bathroom sink. I nodded. My skin was less olive-colored than Vi's and Ali's, but the dark brown tone worked well with my fair coloring

THE PUT-UP

Saturday, June 27, 2015
Hudson Yards

Adam told me to meet him in the park outside the 34th St – Hudson Yards station. I snuck up behind him and wrapped my arms around his waist. He turned and looked at me.

"Who the hell are you?" he teased.

"You don't like it?" I asked, flipping my long brown hair from one shoulder to the other.

"Why? I like your real hair."

"I needed a change." *So that Nate won't recognize me.*

"I don't get it."

"New city, new look!"

"Whatever."

"So, where are you taking me today?" I asked.

"Can't tell you. It's a secret," he said as he took my hand and pulled me behind him.

He walked quickly down 34th Street and I struggled to keep up. I clasped his hand tightly as we passed run-down food carts and a line of beleaguered travelers waiting to board inter-city buses. Half way down the block, Adam pulled me through an open gate onto a walkway where beautiful foliage partially blocked the view of a sprawling truck yard.

"Slow down! You forget how short I am sometimes," I said. "What is this place?"

"It's the High Line," he said.

"Some view," I teased, observing the parking lot below us.

"This is just the start. It gets better. I promise."

"Uh huh, hopefully."

"It opened a few years ago. I think trains used to run up here," he said, pointing to the steel tracks still embedded in the foot bridge. "Anyhow, I thought we could walk the whole thing with a couple of stops along the way."

"Okay, sure, but please slow down."

"Yeah, sure."

We walked over the parking lot to the first real viewpoint. I leaned against the railing. "What the heck is that?" I pointed to what looked like a woven vase rising out of a lush, green oasis.

"Oh, that's The Vessel. I don't think it has a purpose. It's just a tourist attraction. The views from the top must be nice, but I'm sure it costs an arm and a leg."

"Whoa, look at all the trains right there." I pointed down, below the trail to the underbelly of the city. Adam had come up close to me, leaning against the railing on his forearms.

"Yeah, crazy, right?"

We watched as a passenger train pulled out and rolled down the tracks below us. I turned to look at him and our eyes met. He smiled and leaned a little closer as if he might kiss me. I smiled back and closed my eyes in anticipation.

"Come on. We'll never get to the stops along the way if you're gonna be such a gaping tourist," he teased.

"Oh, yeah, sorry. I'm just in awe of this city."

"You and everyone else. Come on."

We continued around the rail yard, weaving past families with children, couples embracing, and inspired amateur photographers. As we continued on toward Chelsea I wondered at the mix of historic and modern; the vintage brick warehouse buildings and garages amidst a maze of rooftop ducts and faded grey concrete. Invigorated by the possibilities inherent in the unknown I grabbed Adam's hand.

"So, when do you start your job?" he asked.

"On Monday."

"You nervous?"

"Nah, it's just a job."

"Yeah, I guess."

"But I'm excited to experience New York City with you," I said.

"Yeah, please don't think you're going to drag me to every museum in the City though. Museums are boring!"

"Mmmm, maybe just the most important ones," I teased.

"You wish," he said. "Oh wait, we need to go down there." He pulled me toward an elevator and a sign for 16th Street. We snuck in just as the doors were closing, to disapproving looks from those inside.

"Where are we going?" I asked as we emerged onto 16th Street.

"You'll see," he said, crossing the street ahead of me.

We walked into a stately brick building with an ornate, illuminated arch for an entrance. "Chelsea Market" was painted on the brick wall followed by a listing of epicurean experiences.

We stopped at a spice shop and I asked for a sample of turmeric. I enticed Adam to smell it. He leaned in and inhaled, then drew back, surprised by the pungent fragrance and let out a forceful sneezed.

I laughed and he laughed with me, poking his fingers into my ribs and then pulling me toward him playfully.

"Gotcha!"

"You did," he agreed.

I smiled at the girl behind the counter and we moved on to the next attraction.

At a jewelry stand on the second floor he tried to guess which of the sparkly pieces was my favorite. When he finally got one right: a gold necklace with delicate iridescent beads strung haphazardly, he fastened the clasp behind my neck and admired the way it fell just above my neckline.

"I'm buying this for you," he insisted.

"You can't."

"Think of it as a 'welcome to New York City' present," he said. "Something to remember this day."

Eventually I let him buy it and wore it as we walked back out into the bright summer sun.

We followed the rest of the High Line to Gansevoort Street and then took Washington to one of the piers that jutted out into the Hudson River. Brave New Yorkers were sunning themselves on the raised green space in the center of the pier. Adam pulled me to the end of the pier and we turned to admire the view of the New York skyline.

"Pretty great, isn't it?" he said.

"It is."

He put his arm over my shoulders.

"It's good to have you in New York," he said.

"I'm excited to be here."

He leaned forward and kissed me. At first I couldn't help myself. It had been a long time since we had let ourselves get swept up in the romance of a new place or the creation of a beautiful memory, and even longer since he'd tried to kiss me. It just felt right. *I can't do this, not right now. I can't have any distractions right now, and getting romantically involved with Adam would be a major distraction. I have to stay focused on Nate.*

I pulled away.

"What now?" he asked.

"I can't."

"Of course." His disappointment was obvious.

I turned away. "I'm sorry."

"Are you dating someone?" he asked.

"No, but there's something I need to do first. I came to New York for something and I can't be with anyone until it's done."

"What are you talking about? I thought you gave up on being a dancer a while ago." He squinted in the bright summer sun.

"It's not that. Four years ago something unforgiveable was done. A life was ruined and a life was taken, and it's up to me to make sure that the person responsible pays."

"Freddie, what are you talking about?" he said, using my nickname from childhood. *Ugh, call me 'Wyn'!*

"I can't tell you right now."

"Are you ever going to be honest with me? If you're not interested, just tell me."

"It's not about that. I am."

"Then what? What are we waiting for?"

"This isn't how I want it to be. I've tried everything else." A tear ran down my cheek and Adam pulled me toward him. "It's just, there's no other way. I have no choice. There's no justice in the right way. There's only one thing to do and it's up to me to make sure it's settled."

He looked confused. "I have no idea what you're talking about."

"Eventually you'll understand."

"Eventually. Always eventually."

"I don't want you to be complicit. It's better if you don't know." *I can't tell him about Nate. I have to deal with this on my own.*

Maren Foster

"Should I be worried about you?"

"No, at least not yet."

"Okay. Well, you know how I feel, but I'm here for you if you need me."

I squeezed him tight. "Thank you."

THE PUT-UP

Sunday, June 28, 2015

Hell's Kitchen

Sunday morning I woke up early, tossed and turned for a bit, but despite my best efforts, couldn't fall back asleep. I wandered out for a walk. Turning down a side street, I watched an assortment of families and older couples flowing into a stately old church. *Just what I need, perhaps.* I watched from down the block until the last of the parishioners was inside. As I walked up to the front steps I saw a plaque that read, "United Church of Christ". *I'm a little underdressed but at least I'm not wearing jeans.* I snuck in quietly and took a seat at the end of the very last pew. The cream-colored walls of the chapel were bathed in blue light. The mustard-colored marble columns that punctuated the pews glowed, and the cerulean blue ceiling was as bright as the cloudless summer sky outside.

My mind wandered through the early formalities but I listened intently as the pastor began her sermon; "We've all read the verse in Exodus, 'But if there is harm, then you shall pay life for life, eye for eye, tooth for tooth, hand for hand, foot for foot, burn for burn, wound for wound, stripe for stripe.' And we have all surely read the passage in Matthew, 'You have heard that it was said, 'An eye for an eye and a tooth for a tooth.' But I say to you, do not resist the one who is evil. But if anyone slaps you on the right cheek, turn to him the other also', but what else does Jesus teach us about forgiveness?" she asked rhetorically. "You may also be familiar with the passage in Matthew, where Jesus instructs his disciples to forgive 'seventy times seven times'. I don't know about you, but that seems like a lot of forgiveness to me."

The congregation let out a muffled approval.

I tried to distract myself but the memories flooded back: his strong hands around my wrists, the smell of his overpowering cologne, the abrasiveness of the cheap bedsheet against my face. *How to forgive such a violation?*

She continued, "Then in Luke, Jesus says that, 'If there is repentance, you must forgive.' As Christians, we know that we are called to turn the other cheek, but what should we do if we have been truly harmed. Now, I'm not talking about when someone cuts you off in traffic, or makes fun of your eclectic fashion sense." She paused as the parishioners let out a self-conscious laugh.

"I'm talking about real harm. Intent to harm. We know that despite our devotion to God and to our savior, Jesus Christ, there are times in life when we may be vulnerable. Our Faith cannot protect us from all evil. How should we respond when we find ourselves in this situation? What should we do if the person who has harmed us does not repent? Will not repent? Are we called to forgive in the absence of repentance? Let us look to the Bible for our answer," she proclaimed.

"During the crucifixion, Jesus does not forgive his unrepentant attackers. The man who embraced sinners and healed the sick with his bare hands prays to God to forgive his attackers. In this moment, when he is tested, he asks for forgiveness for those who hurt him, but he does not forgive them unconditionally. In fact, look again and you will see that Jesus never says that unconditional forgiveness is a virtue or a requirement of Christians. He does, however, in that very same Gospel of Luke, instruct his followers to 'bless those who curse you [and] pray for those who abuse you'. So we can see through his example that we are called to pray for those who have sinned against us, but we are not expected to be tolerant of their abuse."

She paused for effect.

"And so I say to you, good men and women of God, if you know someone who is being harmed, or if you yourself have been harmed, remember this, in the absence of authentic repentance and reform, we are called to pray for our abusers and to support victims, nothing more. Let us pray."

I bowed my head to pray. *Dear God, please show him the error of his ways, open his heart to you, help him to repent and to become a better man so that he may not hurt another person the way he hurt me. But please, also grant me the strength and courage to seek justice and peace so that I too may someday live free from the weight of his sins. Bless both of our souls so that we may be healed, and so that we may know your love.*

I waited and listened, hoping for some indication that I should keep going or turn back, but I was left with only silence and the insistent reverberations of my thoughts; *an eye for an eye...wound for wound...he must pay for what he did.*

I stepped outside and was invigorated by conviction. *I will never find peace without justice.*

Back at the apartment, I used my roommates hand steamer to prep my best suit for my first day of work, and set three alarms before finally falling asleep.

The first alarm woke me just after six-thirty, giving me plenty of time for the sixteen block walk to my new office. I checked in at the front desk and waited until a woman in her mid-thirties from Human Resources waved me back.

"Wynafreda, welcome." She held out her hand.

"Call me Wyn please," I said.

"This will be your desk." She motioned to a small white cubicle barely separated from the desks on either side by a short white partition.

"Thanks."

She handed me a piece of paper. "Here is your login information and the url for the training program that you'll need to complete today. Ladies' is down the hall, also coffee and tea. Let me know if you have any questions or need anything. Ethan will be by shortly to welcome you."

"Great, thanks!" I said.

The woman sitting just a few feet in front of me looked up. "You won't be so enthusiastic once you start the online training program," she said.

She was slightly chubby with jet black hair and a few magenta streaks. She looked like she was in her late twenties or early thirties. She stood up to reveal black skinny jeans, high heels, and an oversized sweater.

"Noreen." She held her hand out.

"Wyn."

13

"Nice to meet you. Tell me to fuck off if I'm being too nosy. As you can see, it's pretty hard to get any privacy around here."

"Nice to meet you too," I said.

She went back to typing for a minute and then looked up again.

"Have you met Ethan before?" she asked.

"At my interview, yes."

"He has no budget and no real authority. He just assigns and checks our work for Alan."

"Who?"

"Alan Donovan, head of marketing for the Northeast."

"Oh."

She lowered her voice, "Classic douchebag."

I nodded. "Good to know."

A woman in her late thirties or early forties and well-dressed walked toward us. She had that mom look which made it hard to tell exactly how old she was.

"Oh, you should meet Natalie." Noreen's tone was loud and exuberant again. "She's great! She's worked here forever and knows everything you'll need to know to survive."

"Jeez, you'd think I was a dinosaur," Natalie said. "Nice to meet you." She extended her hand. "And welcome."

"Wyn," I said. "Thank you."

The rest of the day was uneventful. My boss, Ethan, introduced himself again and then disappeared. The online training was about process, procedure, and ethics, and by the end of the day I was jittery from all the coffee I'd consumed to stay awake.

Back at the apartment I opened Facebook on my phone and scrolled through my list of friends. *Shit! Nate still hasn't accepted my request. I need to find another way to get close to him. I need to get close enough to know what makes him tick and what weaknesses I can exploit.*

I rescinded my friend request to Nate and invited myself over to Adam's apartment in Brooklyn. Getting there was a hike, but Adam had a tiny studio to himself, so visiting him was also a nice escape from my roommates.

Just like old times, we turned on bad t.v. and lounged on his tiny couch.

"Do you remember this guy from Penn?" I said, holding up a

picture of Nate on my cell phone.

"Don't think so. Why?"

"No reason, just curious. He was in some 40 under 40 list recently."

"Oh."

"It says you are Facebook friends with him. Do you mind?"

"You're the nosiest woman ever," he said as he handed his cell phone to me. I typed in the month and day of his birth to unlock his phone, and then looked for the app.

"You don't have Facebook on your phone."

"No, I don't. That shit is a waste of time."

"Yeah, yeah. You say that, but where do you go when you want to know if some girl is single," I teased.

I downloaded the app and put in his email address and his usual password as a first guess. *Bingo!*

Sure enough, Nate appeared alphabetically in the list of Adam's friends. I pulled up Nate's profile, and clicked on "About".

Works at	Ellis Enterprises, Inc.
Studied at	University of Pennsylvania
Lives in	New York
From	Westport, CT
Gender	Male
Birthday	July 29, 1990
Political Views	Conservative
Interested In	Women
Relationship	Single

I scrolled through the photos of Nate: with his buddies at a golf outing, with his mom at his college graduation, with his sister in Europe. Then a few photos from a weekend in the Hamptons with friends. A photo of him at a black tie event, accompanied by a slender (to be honest, anorexic) young woman. Her arm wrapped around his.

The next woman was bustier than the first, followed by a series of women, each rivalling the next in beauty, bustiness, and thinness. *There's no question he has a type.*

The majority of the photos and posts documented a wealthy partying lifestyle, but about six months earlier the nature of his posts had changed, dramatically. Instead of pictures of him partying with beautiful women, the more recent photos were of particularly gorgeous sunrises over the Upper Bay or artistic shots of the City.

There was a photo of the Hudson Bay on a clear day with a line of cargo ships stretching into the distance, and another one of the Brooklyn Bridge lit up at night. *Hobby photographer?* There was a post a few months earlier from a conservative leaning magazine that I skimmed and found to be relatively intellectual, titled, "The spiritual dearth of modern life." *Maybe he's changed? Yeah right!*

I perused the various Facebook locations where Nate had checked-in over the past year. There were the expected local, regional, and international tourist attractions, like the Empire State Building, restaurants and bars in the Hamptons, and a beach on Nantucket Island. There was also a cluster of check-ins at bars and restaurants on the Upper West Side, and a fancy gym that was a few blocks from my apartment.

He's clearly in good shape based on his photos. Maybe I should join that gym. If I'm lucky, I'll run into him there and can make small talk. Then again, I don't have money for a gym membership and what if he doesn't actually belong there. The idea of working out was completely off-putting, but I needed to see him, meet him, get his attention, capture his interest.

A few days later I went to the swanky gym that he'd checked-in at and told the receptionist that my boyfriend had left his membership fob in the locker room earlier and asked if she could check to see if anyone had turned it in. She looked up Nathan Ellis in her system and said that she could see that he'd checked in earlier that morning but no fobs had been turned in for his account. *He is a member!* I thanked her for checking and headed to the membership office.

I signed a contract for a membership that amounted to essentially all of the money I had budgeted for clothes and other unnecessary items, but it would be worth it if it meant an opportunity to meet him, seemingly by chance.

THE PUT-UP

Saturday, July 25, 2015
Upper West Side

The summer days were warm and bright. It had been a few weeks since I'd joined the gym and despite the occasional early morning workout, going back after work, and spending far more time at the gym on weekends than I'd have liked, I hadn't seen Nate. I was about to give up and had thought about cancelling my membership when I caught a promising glimpse. It was a Saturday morning, not too early but not late either. He was dressed in mesh basketball shorts, a worn-out cotton t-shirt, and running shoes. He had earbuds in and walked past the elliptical on which I was struggling to find a rhythm. I couldn't believe it at first and did a double-take. I hadn't seen him in more than three years; *what if I don't recognize him.* My heart began to beat faster. For a moment I wasn't sure, but then he turned to fill up his water bottle and I saw the back of his t-shirt, which read:

Westport High School
Class of 2008

Yep, that's him. He turned toward me and I instinctively looked away.
    I struggled to catch my breath. I looked down and noticed that my hand was shaking. As he walked right past me again, it felt like something heavy fell on my chest. *Oh God!* A sense of intense weakness washed over me. My head suddenly felt as light as air, like it was floating, disconnected high above my shoulders. *I don't feel well. Is this how it feels before you faint?* I managed to hold it together until he was out of the room. I grabbed my stuff and ran to the single stall bathroom behind the check-in desk, locking the door behind me. *Calm*

down! I just need to relax. I sat on the toilet and leaned back, closing my eyes. *Breathe!* I clasped my hands together to keep from shaking.

Awhile passed before someone knocked on the door. "Anyone in there?" A woman's voice called with concern.

"Yeah, one minute." I splashed cold water on my face before opening the door.

"Are you okay?" A woman wearing the all-black staff uniform asked.

"Yeah, I'm fine," I said. "Thanks."

She smiled and turned around. I followed her as she walked away.

Holy shit. What was that? I tried to forget about it, but couldn't. I'd never felt anything like it before. When I got home from the gym, I pulled out my laptop and typed into Google, "trouble breathing, dizzy". Among the top results were, of course, "Heart attacks in Women". *I'm too young to have a heart attack, right? Crap.* I tried not to worry about it. *I'll be fine. What am I going to do now? I have to see him again. What if that happens every time I see him?* I would have to get to the gym more regularly, which I told myself would be good for my health too, but the more I thought about going back to the gym the more anxious I became. *I have no choice. I have to see him if this is going to work.*

I took a week off and then started going to the gym early, choosing cardio machines with a full view of the reception desk and main floor, which were also close to the women's locker room so I could make a quick escape if needed. I watched for Nate incessantly. As I watched, I worried about what would happen when I saw him. *Will my body freak out again like last time? Will I make a scene? Will I have a heart attack? What if he recognizes me?* I tried to reassure myself. *He won't. I look so different now. There's no way he'll recognize me.*

It was early on a Tuesday morning and I'd timed my half hour of cardio (all I could handle before I was bored out of my mind) to be over when all the morning classes ended. I put a towel down and began to stretch, lifting my head to switch positions when I saw him approaching in the reflection of the wall-to-wall mirror. *Don't stare. Don't panic!* He sat down a few feet away from me and began stretching. He wore exactly the same overpowering deodorant that he had in college. *That's how he smelled that night!* My heart beat rapidly. The memories came rushing back: the thumping bass from the dancefloor, the panic as I realized I was trapped, the pain of every ensuing violation. *Stay calm! He can't hurt me now.* I felt the pressure begin to build on my chest. I felt his gaze. I looked up and forced a smile. He was staring right at me and smiled back. *Oh my God, it's happening again!* My hands began to shake. I jumped up. *So much for meeting him casually at the gym! I can't do this!* Beads of sweat formed above my brow. I was sweating more now than I ever did on the elliptical. I ran to the women's locker room and collapsed into a corner at the end of a row of lockers. Closing my eyes, I tried to relax. *I'm fine. Nothing bad happened. It's okay. Breathe.*

"Are you alright?"

I opened my eyes. A woman in her forties was standing over me. The look of concern on her face scared me a little.

"I don't know," I said.

"I'm a doctor."

I nodded. *Okay.*

She kneeled down next to me. "What's going on?"

"I don't know. I just got really dizzy. I couldn't breathe."

She took my forearm gently in her hand, held her fingers against my wrist, and stared into the distance.

"Pulse is fine. Are you starting to feel any better?"

"A little, yeah."

"Did I have a heart attack?"

"I don't think so. Have you ever had a panic attack?"

I shook my head. "I don't know."

"I think you'll be okay now, but you should follow up with a doctor as soon as you can."

I knew this was going to be hard, but I'd underestimated the physical reaction I would have to seeing him. *How on Earth am I gonna be able to go through with this? How will I ever be able to execute my plan if I can't even get close to him?*

On my lunch break, I snuck out to an urgent care clinic around the corner that took walk-ins. I waited for half an hour and was taken to a tiny closet of a room. A nurse asked me to describe my symptoms.

"I don't think it was a heart attack," she said, "but we'll do an EKG just to make sure."

"How long will that take?"

"Not long, maybe five or ten minutes."

"Okay."

"Wait here," she said and disappeared.

She came back with a handful of wires and applied cold round sticky patches to my chest. I tried to relax as I stared up at the fluorescent light on the ceiling. Within seconds, a printer began churning out results next to the bed.

"Your EKG looks fine to me," she said.

"Oh, good."

"I'm going to show the results to the doctor just to be sure. Wait here."

She returned a few minutes later with a referral to a psychiatrist and a local phone number in large, swooping feminine print.

"You most likely had a panic attack, but you'll need to see a psychiatrist to confirm the diagnosis. Call this number to schedule your appointment."

I don't have time for this!

She also handed me a script for a medication, scribbled in a man's tidy handwriting. "In the meantime, this will help," she said.

"What is flu-ox-etine?" I asked.

"It's Prozac," she said. "The generic form."

"Oh." *Whatever it takes to control this crazy physical reaction I have every time I get close to him. There's no hope if I can't stand being close to him.*

"Make sure you follow the instructions very carefully. You'll need to increase your dosage slowly."

"Okay, thank you."

"Please call if you have any problems. Strange behavior, uncharacteristic feelings, extreme emotions as you start this. Also, this is only for one refill. You'll have to see the psychiatrist for a full prescription."

I nodded.

I filled the script on my way home from work and took the first dose right away.

The gym was the most boring place on Earth, and yet I forced myself to go. Although I was slowly getting into better shape, I was also growing impatient. I saw Nate almost weekly, and the medication seemed to be working, but then the closest I'd managed to get was the other end of a stretching mat, and despite my best efforts to impress, he usually seemed lost in thought. *Turns out the gym is an awkward place to strike up a random conversation with a stranger.*

My appointment with the psychiatrist was on a Wednesday afternoon. I left work and took the subway to an outdated high rise in Lenox Hill that housed outpatient medical offices.

I waited on the couch until a middle-aged woman dressed in a white smock opened another door and welcomed me back through a long hallway to her office. She leafed through a file and asked a litany of questions, making notes and checking off boxes on various questionnaires on a clipboard in front of her.

The official diagnosis was panic attacks. She provided another limited script, on the condition that I see a therapist as well. I left her office with a list of names.

I'd seen a therapist briefly after the incident. I hadn't been impressed but had been overwhelmed by the pain and shame of trying to talk about what had happened. I didn't want to go to therapy, but I knew I needed a refill of that medication. It was the only thing that would enable me to continue. I called and made an appointment with a woman whose office was not far from my apartment.

A week later, I waited on an austere couch before a casually dressed, young woman welcomed me back to her office.

"My name is Doctor Sanderson. Pleased to meet you, Wynafreda."

"Please call me Wyn."

"Sure."

She talked briefly about her background and experience, before explaining her approach, and the style of therapy that she would employ.

"Let's get started," she said. "Why don't you tell me about why you are here?"

"I was told I had a panic attack. I think I had more than one actually."

I told her about my symptoms and she nodded in agreement.

"And what was happening when you began to feel dizzy? Where were you? What were you doing?"

"I was at the gym, on an elliptical."

"What were you thinking about?"

"I'm not sure," I lied.

"Do you exercise frequently?"

"Yes."

"And had you ever had anything like that happen at the gym before?"

"No, never."

"Wyn, I need you to try to remember what you were thinking about when you began having the panic attack."

"I guess I was thinking about him."

"Who?"

I shook my head.

"Was he a stranger or someone you trusted?"

"Both," I whispered. "I had only just met him but I trusted him anyways. Stupid."

"No, it's not."

I shook my head. "He ruined my life." A tear rolled down my cheek, and she handed me a box of tissue.

"How? What did he do?"

I shook my head.

"Can you tell me anything about him?"

"I met him in college. It was the end of my freshman year."

"How did you meet?"

"We met at a party. He knew my roommate's boyfriend."

"What happened?"

I shook my head and fought back tears.

"He hurt you."

I nodded.

"Physically?"

"Yes."

"Can you tell me what happened?"

I hesitated. "I don't think so."

"It's okay. I would like you to try writing about what he did to you. It's been shown to really help survivors to write about their experience and the trauma they've been through. Start from the beginning."

I nodded and promised to try.

A few hours later I sat on my bed staring at a blank laptop screen. I'd taken two creative writing classes in college, which I'd actually enjoyed, once I learned to stick to the recipe that our frumpy instructor pedaled. I remembered just a few bits of the cliché advice: show don't tell; every good story has a beginning, a middle and an end; and give the reader at least one character to root for. *I can manage the first and third, but it's still unclear, even to me, where exactly the story began, and only time will tell how it will end.*

I thought back to what seemed like the beginning, and began to write, filling in details as my memory allowed and recreating dialogue as accurately as I could. *After all, it has been three years already.*

Friday, June 8, 2012

It was the weekend before finals and tough to find an open seat in the library or at one of the coffee shops around campus, so I was studying in our dorm room. It was unseasonably hot and oppressively humid for early June in Chicago and the old dorm air conditioner was running constantly, emitting a low hum that made it difficult to concentrate.

"What're you gonna wear tonight?" my roommate Krista asked, as she rummaged through her makeup bag.

"I don't know, it's so hot, maybe a swimsuit," I joked.

I looked up in the mirror and watched as she applied eye make-up at her little desk directly across from mine. She didn't even react to my ridiculous suggestion about the swimsuit. Then again, I had seen sorority pledges wearing little more than a swimsuit at parties all spring.

For nine months Krista and I had lived together in the largest co-ed dorm on campus, a non-descript orange brick building that was incongruous with the historic stone and brick buildings that comprised the rest of the campus. Krista grew up in the west suburbs of Chicago, about an hour drive from the university. She didn't have a car, so she hardly ever went home. She was relatively plain looking with regular features and eyebrows that nearly disappeared on her face, a bit like a blank canvas. She had light brown hair that she frequently highlighted blonde. She spent more time every day than I did in a week applying, reapplying, and perfecting her make-up. Her artistic ability had improved perceptibly since we had moved into our little room, although she had begun to look more and more like a stage actress that had wandered off set. I finished applying a sheer eyeshadow and some black mascara and glanced at her as she reapplied and extended her eyeliner from the corners of her eyes.

"Do you mind if I borrow your black mini dress tonight?" she asked. "I like how short it is on me and it's so hot out."

We were conveniently, although sometimes annoyingly, the exact same size and build, except for the four inches of height she had on me, which meant all of my clothes were shorter on her.

"Okay, but I'm wearing your Pocahontas dress then," I said. She had a tan leather dress with a fringe skirt that fit me perfectly and came in handy as a conversation starter in those awkward moments waiting for a drink refill in the basement of some frat house. I tied a bright blue headband around the center of my forehead and grabbed the only exotic make-up item I owned: bright blue eyeliner.

"Alright, let's go."

I put my wallet, cell phone, and lip gloss into the nicest purse I had and ran my finger over the pepper spray that my mom insisted I keep with me at all times. I had never needed it and frankly it scared me. I couldn't help but wonder, *What if I deploy it by accident? What if I do need it and I'm not able to get the safety thing into the right position?* Seeing it and thinking about it stressed me out. I made sure the safety latch was engaged and put it in my purse.

We walked from our dorm, across the quad, past Evers College of Commerce and Industry, toward the Phi Psi house.

"Oh, hey," she said. "Some guy from Jake's frat is visiting from Penn. He's single and from what Jake said about him, I think he might even be *your* type." Jake was Krista's serious boyfriend of about six months.

"Gee thanks. What the heck do you think my type is anyway?"

Krista and I had been living together for almost a year now and she was beyond hiding her disappointment about my enduring virginity. Before she started dating Jake, she had slept with at least ten different guys, and the idea that I was still (voluntarily) a virgin at the end of my freshman year of college confused and annoyed her.

So far, I had dutifully rejected a handful of would-be suitors who had each professed their unrequited love for me within a week of a first date, if you could even call a beer at a grimy bar a date. The few times I had been genuinely smitten and thought for a brief moment that perhaps it was love, I was reminded unequivocally of the truth by the (at least weekly) meltdown in our dorm of yet another freshman girl who had been lied to, slept with, and then quickly tossed aside. As I watched the drama unfold each week from the threshold of our room, I felt a bit of pride in my ability to see through the unoriginal lines and hasty professions of love that frat boys, bookworms, and soulful artist types all seemed to employ with similar ease. I found that if I resisted even the most convincing suitor's advances for about a month, they disappeared without word, and never to call again.

"I guess he's a rower at one of the Ivy League schools and is going to graduate at the top of his class from a prestigious business school this year. He's already started some business out of his frat and he's not hideous or socially awkward. Could be good enough to meet even *your* impossible standards," Krista said.

"If he's so amazing why is he still single?"

"He's twenty-two! Why do you have to be such a pessimist? Maybe he just hasn't found the right girl yet. It's not like he's forty and single."

"You know I'm a closet romantic. I want to find my soulmate. I'm just skeptical that he is a visiting frat boy, in town for only the weekend, but I guess anything's possible."

I wasn't raised in a religious house, but Vi had routinely warned us, as we hit puberty, about the one thing that most men were after. For her part, my sister Ali came home after her freshman year of college telling me story after story of friends devastated by co-ed "players" who professed their love quickly to get a girl in bed, only to move on days later to the next conquest. I looked up to Ali, so it was her advice and warnings that really led me to promise myself that I would be smart and avoid sex until I was sure I had found love. Throughout my freshman year, it became almost a personal challenge as I watched other young women succumb: I would not lose my virginity in a way that I might regret.

"I think you're just a prude," Krista said with a bit of sarcasm to veil what she thought was an uncomfortable truth.

I didn't hesitate; "I'd rather be a prude than a slut."

Silence permeated the oppressive summer heat as we walked past Robb Hall.

It was relatively early still and our entrance at the party was met with one or two nods of acknowledgement. The old Tudor's glory days were long past and the inside of the frat house was where the decades of abuse showed the most, despite the efforts of the Chapter Supervisor. The original molding and wood framed windows had been patched endlessly and the patches had been stained to match with little success. The lower half of the walls were marked by grease, oil, and beer, which only further robbed the former mansion of any remaining shred of dignity. A group of guys were sitting around the living room drinking beer and watching a cult classic. Jake was sitting on the long couch and got up when he heard the clicking of high heels on the worn wood floor.

"Hey baby," he said and kissed Krista on the mouth.

Another guy, dressed measurably better than the rest of the guys in the house, in a pair of khaki shorts and a collared t-shirt, stood up.

He smiled at me and said hi.

"Hey." I smiled back.

"Nate."

"Freddie."

He was tall, almost a foot taller than me and I had on heels. His hair was dark chestnut brown and curled just above his ears. "Not hideous" certainly wasn't an accurate description, he was gorgeous. His eyes were brown and filled with intensity, which reminded me of what Krista had said on the way over about the business he'd already started.

"You two hungry?" Jake asked.

"We ate at the dorm, but thanks."

A big group of Theta sophomores that always hung around walked in through the open front door. The self-anointed leader of their group, Jamie, barged past us and yelled to the guys strewn around the living room, "Let's get this party started!" Behind her, six transfers, who were renting rooms in the frat house over the summer and were already posturing to be pledges the next fall, struggled to haul three kegs of beer up the short staircase to the front porch. One of the guys walked over and turned on an old hi-fi system, plugged in his iPod and selected a playlist that I later saw was called "clothes off!" It was a little aggressive for the hour, but Jamie and the other sophomores obliged and danced toward the middle of the room. Within half an hour the house was full and what was already a hot, humid evening, became an unbearably sweaty dance party. As I edged my way toward the front door, Jake's friend appeared.

26

"Where're you off to so quickly?" he asked.

"It's hot. I need to get out of here."

"Mind if I join you?"

I shook my head and he followed me out.

We sat on the front steps of the old house, the bass thumped aggressively behind us. He took a tin of strong mints out of his pocket and offered me one before popping a couple into his mouth.

"What are you studying?" he asked.

"Communications with a minor in French."

"What about you?"

"Business. I graduate next week."

"What then?"

"I'll probably move to New York City. It's the best place to raise capital in my industry."

"I love New York. Maybe we'll meet again someday in New York!"

"Maybe," he said, and I cringed as I realized how uncool it was that it sounded like I was already planning a future life that included him.

"I mean, I have no idea where I'll be three years from now, but New York sounds cool," I said.

Nate smiled and leaned toward me. He didn't hesitate and kissed my lips, passionately, pushing his tongue inside my mouth. His mouth was warm, wet, and tasted sharply of mint. He held me tight and for a moment, I gave in and enjoyed the decisiveness of it. I liked how certain he was of himself. The feeling of his tongue in my mouth began to turn me on and I pulled away.

"Something wrong?" he asked.

"It's just, I'm waiting."

"Waiting for what?" He seemed genuinely confused.

"For the right person."

"The right person for what?"

Oh, God, how awkward, I thought.

"I'm a virgin," I said quietly.

From only inches away he stared at me blankly. I was surprised to not immediately hear one of the moronic lines I had grown so accustomed to: *that's the way I like 'em; I can solve that problem for you right now;* and the worst I'd ever heard, *"Hy-men!"* That was the moment I usually bolted, quite literally.

Instead he said, "I didn't think we were having sex on the porch right now."

Oh God, of course not! I'm such an idiot. "No, that's not what I meant," I said.

"Uh, what did you mean?" he said. "I shouldn't kiss you? Are you Mormon or something?"

"No. You can kiss me. Please do," I added. "I just don't want to have sex. I thought you should know before things got too heavy, that's all."

"Hmmm, okay."

Oh my God, what a dork! He must think I'm such a freak now.

In the silence that followed I felt the need to explain myself. "It's just, I'm sort of waiting to be in love first. You know?"

"Sure, whatever."

"I didn't mean to make that awkward. I was having fun," I said.

He nodded. "It's fine," he said.

THE PUT-UP

Saturday, August 22, 2015

Manhattan

I texted Adam, hoping he might take me on another romantic walk around New York City, but he responded that he was having a few friends over to watch a college preseason football game. I showed up anyhow with a six pack of cheap beer and a bag of chips, and squeezed in next to Adam on the couch. As the game apparently became more exciting, evidenced by the silence between plays and how everyone else in the room had slowly inched closer and closer to the t.v., I picked up Adam's phone and opened Facebook.

Nate's most recent post was a link to an article about the challenges and frustrations of online dating, particularly for people of faith. The article highlighted the rise of faith-based online dating platforms and discussed the pros and cons of each. *That's it! If we match on a dating site he'll never suspect it's me. I haven't had much luck at the gym anyhow. It's time for a new approach.*

Back at my apartment, I logged on to the leading Christian dating website. "Love is Patient. Love is Kind. Find Love Here." It said on the landing page in a scrawling gold script. I created an account.

Wyn L., 24
New York, NY
Evangelical, Marketing

Tell us about you: I selected activities which I knew, based on my initial Facebook stalking, would be best bets for a match.

Sports and Fitness: I selected golf, weight training, and sailing (not that I'd ever done any of those activities, but I could be aspirational. Besides, there were a few photos of him on Instagram, on a very nice looking yacht in Upper Bay).

Activities: This was the most difficult, as nothing seemed quite right. I knew that bridge, activism, and meditation were dead wrong but none of the other options seemed to fit either. I picked entertaining (there were a couple photos of him amidst impressive looking table spreads, surrounded by magazine-ready guests. Below one photo he'd boasted about his original recipe for a rub for short ribs, of course sourced locally from some farm in upstate New York, and the undisputed success of the evening). I selected stock trading and motorcycle riding to round out my list.

Arts and Entertainment: Easy. Horror movies (according to Facebook his favorite movie was *Saw*), mysteries and thrillers beat out antiquing, poetry, and Origami. *Seriously, origami is an option?*

I specified that I was seeking men between the ages of 24 to 26, within 10 miles of New York, NY. *That should narrow it down a little bit.* From a long list of denominations I selected Evangelical and Catholic. *That should cover the possible spectrum.* I put on the small gold cross that Adam's mother had given me for my sixteenth birthday. It hung just above my cleavage. I unbuttoned the top two buttons of my faux silk shirt, held my cell phone up, looked toward the light on the ceiling, and smiled. The lighting wasn't great, but the photo wasn't bad. I applied a soft filter and admired the result. I still had some make-up on from work, but not too much. It didn't look like I was trying too hard, which was important. I looked relaxed but put together. Below my neckline the small golden cross was understated, but reflected the light slightly. *Perfect.* I hit upload.

I clicked on the thumbnail of my profile picture in the top corner. It was live. I read through the details in the About Me section and admired 'Wyn L.' There were already some suggested matches. I scrolled through the first ten or fifteen profiles that were already in my queue, but his wasn't among them.

I woke up early the next morning: 23 unread emails. I clicked on the mail icon. In just twelve hours I'd been inundated by Christian dating spam.

> Someone's checking you out! – Wow, look at you! No really, click here to see who's been viewing your profile.

> Someone just winked at you! – **RunNYC** just winked at you. Log in to return the gesture.

> You've got a message! – **SeoulMate** sent you a message. Log in and read your messages – love may be a click away!

The list continued, full of abbreviated names and bad monikers. I logged in and scanned the profiles looking for his image. *Bust.* There were a few of the same guys from the day before so I swiped to the right to remove them. I started swiping from the top of the list downward, leaving one or two handsome guys at the top of the queue. As I did so, it replenished with a new, never ending list of names and pictures.

There were personalized messages from a few guys. Two were particularly good looking. I clicked a link to read a message and received a prompt, "Upgrade Your Account". *Ugh! $25 a month. Never mind.* I put the phone down and got ready for work.

Later in the week, back at the apartment after work, my roommates tried to convince me to go out to some bar in Tribeca with them, but all I could think about was the story that was beginning to take shape in my mind. The details that kept coming back to me, flooding my consciousness with the painful minutiae that had been repressed, packed away for the past three years so that I could function, so that I had the strength to move forward day by day, to set my plan in motion. I told my roommates that I didn't feel well and was staying in. Once they left, I grabbed my laptop and began to write.

Friday, June 8, 2012

Inside the frat house, Nate led me toward the faded, yellow kitchen, pushing past the line of twenty-somethings holding red solo cups, and pulling me back to a dimly lit corner. Nearly every girl we passed stared at him and then at me. *Are they wondering why he's with me? Are they jealous?* I wondered. He opened a cabinet door that I would have needed a stool to reach, and brought down a bottle of whiskey. He held it out to me first. *Hmmm, what is a gentleman!*

The buzz from the beer had almost worn off, so I thought, *what the heck?* and tipped the bottle back. The whiskey burned as it went down. It was exciting to be taking shots with the best looking guy at the party. Nate took a long swig and handed the bottle back to me. I took a small sip and gave it back to him. A doey-eyed freshman standing next to him eyed the bottle. He shook his head. She pouted her lips and he shook his head again as if to say, *get lost.* She disappeared. I was in awe of the effect he had on women. *Why does he want me? He could have any girl here.* He took another swig and put the bottle back.

"Let's dance," he said and grabbed my hand.

We pushed our way back past the bathroom line which now snaked all the way down the hallway to the kitchen. The bass was thumping in the living room, so loud I was surprised the cops hadn't shown up yet. Nate led me to the middle of the dance floor and we began moving back and forth to the beat. He faced me and leaned forward as he danced, smiling. There was no mistaking that he was into me, and I could feel people watching us. I caught the eye of one of my would-be-suitors who had prematurely professed his love for me during fall quarter. I smiled and looked back at my dance partner, excited by the prospect of real love. I smiled and made eyes at him as I moved closer and then further away teasing him. Making a game of it, I turned my back to him and danced away as if rejecting him. He followed me, grabbed me around the waist, and pulled me back to the middle of the dance floor, leaned down and kissed me passionately. He spun me around and pulled me close to him, my back against his chest. As we moved back and forth to the beat I could feel his hard on grow against my lower back. *Whoa Buddy!*

I glanced at my watch: quarter past ten, it was still early but I was getting a little tired and I didn't want him to get the wrong idea. He was clearly turned on. I looked at him, fanned my face dramatically, and motioned toward the kitchen.

"Hot!" I yelled over the bass.

"You are!" he yelled back.

I smiled and then pushed my way back to the kitchen. He followed me.

Out on the back deck I watched as he went to fetch the bottle of whiskey. As I waited, I couldn't help daydreaming about a future in which I would be waiting for him to come home from work, to a big house in the suburbs, a young girl with blonde pigtails running across the room to greet him. He would lift her up above his head and plant a kiss on her forehead.

Nate held the whiskey out to me, and I shook my head. He took a few more swigs from the bottle, which by now looked suspiciously empty.

"So you're a virgin?"

"Yeah, why?" I turned toward him.

"Because that just makes me want you even more," he said with a sly smile.

"Well, you'll just have to fall madly in love and marry me then, won't you?"

"I guess I will," he said and pulled me toward him. He leaned down and kissed me again. It was only the third time, but it felt wonderfully familiar already. I looked up and smiled and he smiled back.

"Come on, let's go," he said and took my hand, leading me back into the house.

On our way back toward the dance floor he pushed open one of the doors in the long hallway and pulled me into a room. It was a tiny room with a single bed, a dresser, a closet door, and one window. He shut the door behind him and pulled me close. He kissed me again, massaging my tongue and biting my lip gently.

"You're incredible," he said.

I looked at him eagerly and smiled.

"You're incredible," I repeated, believing every syllable. *Is this what love feels like?* I was so excited I could feel my heart beating with wild anticipation.

Nate put his hands on my butt and held me tight. His hard-on beat in time with the rhythmic pounding of his heart.

He began kissing my neck and then reached down and grabbed the hem of my dress. *Really, slow down. This is what I meant earlier.* I brushed his hand away and pushed gently against his chest.

"Playing hard to get. I love it. Look how much it turns me on." He took my hand and pressed it against the bulge in his pants.

I shook my head.

"I need to go," I said, and took a step toward the door.

Nate quickly picked up a belt that was lying on the bed, grabbed my arm as I tried to pull away, and wrapped the belt tightly around my wrists. His strength surprised me.

"Stop. This isn't sexy," I said. "Besides, I told you, I'm a virgin. I'm waiting."

He looked me in the eyes and a large grin crossed his face. "I know. That will make it even better," he said.

There was something about the way he said it. His intent was unmistakable.

Oh my God. Scream. I opened my mouth but before I could make any noise he shoved a pair of balled-up socks into my mouth. He spun me around and pushed me down onto the bed. I tried to move my legs in a way that would restore me to an upright position, but he pushed me down and forced my legs apart. He ripped off my underwear, and then I heard him spit as he pushed his hard dick in between my legs.

The first pain was the unmistakable tearing as he pushed himself into my dry vagina. With every clumsy thrust he tried to get deeper and with every penetration my body tightened up a little more. I began to feel the thumping of my heartbeat in my torn up vagina, syncing with the thumping bass blasting two walls away, punctuated by the rhythmic shocks of pain he inflicted. I buried my face in the bed.

Think! Where is that pepper spray when I finally need it? It was in my purse tucked behind a chair in the living room. *Shit.*

Hadn't I heard before that if you were being raped you should pee on your rapist because that would turn them off and get them off of you? *Worth a try.* I tried to pee but he had picked up his pace, and the few seconds that passed between each thrust didn't give me enough time to relax, my body was instinctively rigid as I braced for each sequential assault. *Holy shit.* I realized that I could do nothing to stop the pain and then it hit me; what was really happening. This asshole, who I had just met and who had probably never been told no before, was violently stealing my virginity because he was bigger and stronger than me. I tightened up even more, every muscle in my body contracted in defiance of what was happening. Finally I felt something I had only heard about before. His rhythm began to slow and he came inside my body. I felt him convulse a few times before he finally pulled out.

I figured the worst was over. Nate grabbed my arms and rolled me onto my side.

"Not bad for your first time."

Motherfucker. I felt him lay down on the bed next to me.

"Being tied up really suits you."

You fucking asshole. You'll pay for this someday.

"I know what you're thinking," he said. "Eventually, I'll untie you and you'll go running out of here screaming. You'll go home and tell everyone you know that I raped you. Maybe you're even thinking that you'll go to the police. But you won't, and here's why."

Nate got up and walked over to the dresser which was about the height of the bed. He rubbed his finger over the mouse pad and the screen lit up. On the screen was the reverse image of my face, my eyes empty and hollow.

"If you even think about telling anyone about what just happened, this video will be all over the internet with your smiling face, a porn-star soundtrack, and your full name. Do you want everyone to think you're a slut?" he asked rhetorically as he tapped at the keyboard a few times.

"Think about your family, your future. You think people want to hire a dirty slut, who gets off by being tied up?" He shook his head. "They won't be able to take you seriously. Every time you open your mouth, they will hear moans of pleasure. You don't want that," he said, and walked back over to the bed.

Oh god, now what?

"Plus, it's already backed up in three different places, so don't bother taking the computer when you leave," he warned. "If you ever tell anyone about this I'll ruin you."

Then he shocked me by climbing back in the bed. He was still naked and he pushed his naked, sweaty body against my bare skin. I laid there awake while he began to breathe deeply and eventually even began to snore a little.

It played over and over in my mind: the pain of the first violation, the second, and each successive assault that followed. I laid there in silence, staring at the ceiling, unable to process or accept what had just happened.

I awoke to the sound of the zipper on a pair of jeans. His jeans. Nate pulled his dress shirt on over his head without bothering to undo the buttons. He was dressed and looked just as good as he had the night before. He walked out of the room without a word and closed the door. *Wait, my hands!* I began to panic, but as I moved I realized that they were already untied. I slowly pulled my arms forward and wrapped them around my knees. It was light outside.

I looked down and for the first time, I saw the drops of blood. He must have seen it hours earlier. He had even laid on it as he slept next to me. There it was. The proof of my stolen virginity and his despicable deed. *Monster!*

I stood up slowly and got dressed. His laptop was still sitting on top of the desk. His words echoed in my head; *already backed up, don't bother taking the computer when you leave.* I left the room. As I took the first few steps down the hall, the sharp pain between my legs alerted me to the severity of my injuries. My heart raced. *I have to get out of here.* The house was eerily quiet. I didn't see a single person as I walked down the hall and out the front door.

Out of the house and into the calm suburban surroundings, my mind wandered to the image of the little girl with blonde pigtails but this time she wasn't smiling. We were alone and she was crying. *That monster has to pay!*

Saturday, June 9, 2012

I walked across campus thinking I would get some breakfast, or lunch. The further I walked the more intense the throbbing became. *Jesus, how bad can it be?* I hadn't actually checked, I didn't really want to know.

The pain only grew as I walked. About three blocks from the frat house I saw a large hedge and snuck behind it. Safely out of view of passing cars, I pulled my skirt up and spread my legs. I couldn't see much, but what I could see was bruised and bloody. It reminded me of the swollen, broken face of a boxer who'd just been badly beaten. *I'm hurt. I need help. Think clearly. What to do? I need to see a doctor, but where?* My thoughts were scrambled. I was in shock. *Just think. Hospital.* I turned right and walked toward the University Hospital on Lake Street. As I walked the world spun around me. Cars whizzed by faster than before. A young guy yelled across the street to his friend and I jumped a little. A woman walked by with a canvas shopping bag. I watched them in awe, going about their normal lives, like everything was just fine, while my world was upside down.

My dorm was on the way to the hospital and I really wanted to wash my face and brush my hair. *What if someone sees me like this, what will they think? Do I look as bad as I feel?* I walked around the back side of the building where there were loading docks for the dining service. A service door was propped open. I went in and up a back staircase. Relief poured over me when I walked into our room and discovered Krista wasn't there. As I took off Krista's dress and folded it, I realized that there was blood on it too, my blood. *Oh my God, Krista's gonna kill me!* I took off my bra and underwear and put everything I had been wearing into a plastic grocery bag. *These clothes are evidence now.* I pulled on a clean V-neck t-shirt and a pair of loose black dance pants. I grabbed my toiletry bag and peered out into the hallway. *Clear.* I made it to the bathroom without seeing anyone.

I stood in front of the long row of sinks and stared at my reflection in the mirror, barely recognizing the exhausted young woman staring back at me. I removed the make-up from my eyes and cheeks and washed my face. I brushed my hair. *That's a little better.* I thought as I tried to force a smile. *I'll be okay.*

Back in our room, I put the plastic bag, my wallet, and cell phone into a small backpack. I was about to leave when I heard a key in the lock. *Fuck!* Our door opened and Krista came in. She had headphones on and was singing out loud and out of tune, "because, I'm happy..."

"Oh, hey. How was the rest of your night?" she asked as she took her earbuds off and threw her stuff onto the bed. "You two were so hot together on the dance floor! And then you just disappeared. Did you finally get lucky?"

"Um..." I hesitated. *Should I tell her what happened?* I wondered. "I was raped," I blurted out.

She stared at me and smiled. "What? You mean you finally did it! I thought so!"

"I said I was raped."

She shot me a look of disbelief.

"I didn't have sex, I was raped."

"Oh my God. By who?"

"Nate. That friend of Jake's."

"What do you mean?"

"I told him 'no'."

"You two had massive chemistry. Of course you had sex with him." She looked up at me, and then it was as if what I'd said finally registered.

"What do you mean, you were raped? Freddie, nobody waits 'til they're married anymore. Loosen up. Just because you wanted to wait 'til you were in married doesn't mean having sex with Nate was wrong. Nobody cares about that these days. There's nothing wrong with sex."

"It's not about any of that. I didn't *want* to have sex with him. He *raped* me."

"Oh come on. He could have had any girl at that party. You should have seen the way they were all flirting with him the moment you were out of sight. Why would he rape anyone?"

"I don't know." I realized how naïve I sounded, like a five year old tattling on their sibling after they'd clearly started a fight. *I could show her the bloody dress and my bloody underwear. Then she'd have to believe me.* The thought of showing her my underwear and her ruined dress made me sick to my stomach.

"Yeah, exactly," she said.

So that's how it's going to be. My own roommate doesn't believe me, and the thought of showing her the evidence makes me ill.

"I'm going out. See ya later," I said.

If Krista doesn't believe me, who will? I mulled it over as I walked across the quad. Then I remembered something. As part of our initiation into the sorority we'd had mandatory sessions at the house that were like mini lectures given by the upperclasswomen. After one about the rules of the house and expectations about behavior and grades, three seniors gave an emotional talk about the time each of them had been raped. One had been gang raped by her three male college roommates in a room she was subletting one summer off campus. Another had been date raped by an older guy she'd been casually dating during a party at his house, and the last had been raped by her boyfriend one night when he was drunk and she had her period and told him she didn't want to have sex. Their stories were meant as a warning and had made quite the impression on most of us, although, there was no denying that even after hearing the stories we all still clung firmly to the belief that it would never happen to us. *If anyone will be able to help me it should be one of them.*

I walked across campus to the sorority house and knocked on Elisa's door.

"Come in!" she yelled. I opened the door.

"Hey. Do you have a minute?" She was laying on her bed with a textbook open.

"Yeah, sure, what's up?"

"I need some advice," I said.

"Of course. Shoot."

"Remember that talk you and Jessie and Megan gave last fall?" I didn't wait for a response. "I was raped."

She jumped off the bed and wrapped her arms around me. I began to cry. It felt incredible to be believed. We didn't know each other very well but I fell apart in her arms. I shook as I sobbed and she just held me. When I was finally exhausted and too tired to cry anymore, she let me go.

"I'm so stupid," I said. "I should have been more careful."

"This was not your fault. Do you hear me? He's a monster. He made a choice. It was not your fault."

I shook my head. "What should I do?"

"Did you shower?" she asked.

"No, not yet."

"Great. Go have a rape kit done," she said, "at the hospital."

"I was on my way there now."

"Good. Do you want me to go with you?"

"Thank you, but no, I think I'll be okay."

"You sure?"

I nodded.

"Then comes the really tough decision," she continued. "His DNA probably isn't in their system yet, so there won't be a match when they run it. You'll have to file a police report too. I did all of that and the DNA wasn't a perfect match. They said the DNA sample wasn't great, but none of that really mattered in the end. The guys admitted to having sex with me, but they said it was consensual. They said I asked for it and called me a slut. They called me worse things too." A tear crested her eyelid.

She continued, "They said I wanted it and it wasn't rape. They all defended each other. It was three of them against me. My word against theirs'. They started telling people about all of the men I'd ever hooked up with. First it was just embellishments of the truth, but then rumors began to spread and grow. It got really ugly. One day I was early to my chemistry lab and my T.A. made a joke while we were waiting for the earlier class to get out. Something about how does a slut know when she should start asking for money? The punchline was something about, when she has to start accusing guys she hooked up with of rape to cover her slutty trail. I couldn't believe it. I wouldn't wish that on anybody."

"What did you do?"

"I reported it to the professor and the administration."

"What did they do?"

"Nothing. They asked if there had been any arrests connected to my report. When I said no, they told me they would look into it."

"And?"

"Nothing. I haven't heard anything. I did get the worst grade I've had in four years in that lab. He said I didn't turn in homework that I know I did turn in."

"Oh my God."

"Oh, and I went and talked to a lawyer at one point and he

warned me that if I filed a civil suit and lost I would probably be ordered to pay their legal costs."

I shook my head. "I'm so sorry."

"Get the rape kit done, just in case," she said. "But my advice would be that if there's any way you can fuck him personally, without involving the university or the police or a lawyer, do it. You won't get any justice through the system," she paused. "No one in a position of authority around here is going to be much help. None of them want to rock the boat. When I went back to follow-up after a few months they basically told me they had better things to do."

I thanked her and left.

How could this happen and there's nothing I can do about it? What is the justice system for, if not to protect victims? What a cruel absurdity. If they won't make him pay then I will. I'll take the thing that's most important to him, the way he took what was so important to me. If there's no justice, how can I make him pay?

THE PUT-UP

Monday, August 31, 2015
Manhattan

My alarm went off early on Monday. I rolled over and picked up my phone. There was a text message from Vi checking in, plus a few new emails in my work inbox. I'd turned off notifications for the dating app because the number of messages was stifling. Out of curiosity I opened the app: 30 unread messages. *God, how would anyone find "the one" on this thing?*

Scrolling down through the messages I saw it. His photo was in the left corner and next to it was the sender name, "NateNYC". I practically screamed out of excitement.

I clicked the link to view the message. Below his name it said "Subscribe to view message." *Ugh, fine! Worth it for this one!*

I got up and ran to the little dining room table, turned on my laptop, and grabbed my wallet. I upgraded my account and then went back to my inbox. Below his username the subject read, "What's up, Wyn?" I clicked on the message:

Wyn,

How long have you lived in New York? Do you actually live in the city? Are you from New York?

Nate

And if I have prophetic powers, and understand all mysteries and all knowledge, and if I have all faith, so as to remove mountains, but have not love, I am nothing. 1 Corinthians 13:2

As I reread it, a large smile crossed my face, but at the same time I worried. *Will the medication be enough to get me through a date with him? I have no choice. I have to get close to him. I have to figure out what makes him tick.*

By noon I'd deleted the dating app from my phone, to keep myself from replying to Nate's message. *I don't want to seem too eager.*

At work I had trouble focusing. I still hadn't responded to Nate's message on the dating app but I couldn't stop thinking about it. *This is my chance! Things are finally coming together. All of the dreaming and planning will finally pay off.* On Tuesday morning I couldn't resist any longer. I logged on to my account and responded:

> Hey Nate,
>
> I do live in the City. It is overwhelming sometimes, but I do love the energy here. Nothing beats a late afternoon run through Central Park or discovering a new gem of a restaurant! What's your favorite thing to do in New York?
>
> Wyn

You see that a person is justified by works and not by faith alone. James 2:24

I scrolled through some of the other messages in my inbox. Now that I was a paying member, it occurred to me that perhaps I should recruit some competition. The appearance of options couldn't hurt my chances with Nate.

I messaged three guys, all attractive and relatively successful for their ages (determined by some light internet stalking).

Nate's reply came in just as I was about to log off. *Wow that was fast!*

> Wyn,
>
> Mine would have to be riding the tram to Roosevelt Island for a picnic. Sound like fun?

Nate

And if I have prophetic powers, and understand all mysteries and all knowledge, and if I have all faith, so as to remove mountains, but have not love, I am nothing. 1 Corinthians 13:2

I was determined not to reply immediately, and waited until I got home:

Nate,

Sounds amazing. Something to look forward to. How about dinner in the city first?

Wyn

You see that a person is justified by works and not by faith alone. James 2:24

I had the evening to myself, so I pulled out my laptop and continued working on the assignment from my therapist.

Saturday, June 9, 2012

I walked out of the house and turned right toward the hospital. It was only a few blocks away and as I got closer I noticed the sign near the large driveway that read "Emergency" in large red block letters. *I have an EMERGENCY! Fuck!* My heart began to race and a tear rolled down my cheek. I walked down the wide driveway and wandered through the automatic sliding doors into a large white reception area.

A man sitting behind a large desk looked up at me. "Can I help you?" he said.

I walked over and stood near the desk, as close to him as I could get.

"I was raped this morning," I whispered.

"What?" he said and squinted as if he was staring directly at the sun.

"I was raped," I said, a little louder. My eyes began to well up with tears. With my back to the waiting area, I couldn't see anyone else in the room, but I could feel their eyes on my back.

He picked up the phone in front of him and dialed. "We have a rape victim," he said into the receiver. "Great, thanks."

He hung up and looked at me. "They'll be right down. Just wait over there please." He motioned to a spartan seating area. I complied and waited near the door. A few minutes went by and a woman dressed in scrubs came through the door.

She looked at me and asked compassionately, "You need a Sexual Assault Forensic Exam?"

Oh my God, this is so embarrassing. How on Earth did I end up here? I nodded.

"This way," she said.

I followed her through the swinging door down a long hallway. She showed me into an examination room.

"Please have a seat. I have a few questions I have to ask first," she said.

"I can't sit." I motioned toward my injuries. "I'll stand."

I stood in between the chairs and the table, as the barrage of questions began: Name? Date of birth? Date of last menstruation?

"How many sexual partners have you had?" She asked.

"None. Unless you count my rapist. Then one."

She saw my teary eyes and shook her head. "I'm so sorry."

I nodded. "Thanks."

"Which clothes were you wearing when the rape occurred?" she asked.

I put my backpack on the table and pulled out the plastic bag. "These," I said.

"Did he penetrate you?"

I nodded.

"Where? Your mouth? Vagina? Anus?"

It was the way she said anus, so matter of fact, as if she had said fork or spoon instead. I pointed to my vagina.

"He penetrated your vagina?"

"Yes," I said.

"Anywhere else?"

"Not that I remember."

"Please undress and put on this gown. Underwear off too." She placed a large plastic bag with "Evidence" printed across the front on the exam table. "Put all of the clothes you were wearing into this bag. I'll be back in a minute."

She closed the door and I began to undress.

There was a stain of pink-colored fluid on my clean underwear. I wrapped the paper sheet around my naked body, and placed my soiled clothes into the bag marked EVIDENCE.

At the end of the exam table, I turned around and sat down. *Ouch.* I stood back up and set about maneuvering my body clumsily up onto the exam table. As I lay there waiting I began to shiver.

A knock came at the door.

"Yes," I said.

The nurse came in followed by a younger man in a white coat.

"Is it okay if Doctor Nelson observes? He is training as a resident?" she added.

I didn't like the idea of a guy who didn't look much older than me watching the exam, but I was tired, cold, on the verge of tears again, and wanted the whole thing to be over as quickly as possible.

"Fine," I said.

They washed their hands, opened a plastic box that looked like a large red lunchbox, and began removing an assortment of swabs, plastic tools, and bags. She walked to the end of the table and extended two metal stirrups for my feet.

My feet rested against the cold metal; there was no protection of any kind from the sheet dress which she lifted up and piled around my waist. I was exposed, spread eagle on the table, with nowhere to hide from the shame and embarrassment of what he had done to me. Tears began to stream down my cheeks. I turned my head away so the nurse and doctor wouldn't see, and cried softly as they carried out the exam.

"Scoot down to the end of the table," she said. "We will need to take photos as we do the rape kit, for evidence."

"Um, okay."

"Are you sure?" she asked.

Whatever it takes to make sure that bastard can be held responsible someday. "Yes, it's fine," I said

She slowly inserted a cold metal object inside me. I winced in pain as she began to pry me open, exposing my insides to the cold, hospital air. The nurse and the resident were both standing at the end of the table, peering into me. She was explaining what she saw and the significance of it all to the younger doctor.

45

"Severe hemorrhaging of the labia minora, Fourchette, Bartholin glands. Laceration of the Fourchette. Hand me a ten millimeter, suchers, and ten milligrams of Novocain."

She turned toward me and in a much softer voice said, "I'm going to give you a local anesthetic. You need a few stitches. They will dissolve after about ten days, so you won't have to come back to have them removed. Refrain from any sexual activity during that time." *Is she kidding? I was just raped. I might never have sex again.*

I focused on controlling the rise and fall of my chest as she shot Novocain into my swollen tissue. The sharp pain that followed was like salt in an open wound. She kept busy preparing her tools while we waited for the drug to take effect. She warned me before she went to work and the resident snapped successive photos up close, from multiple angles.

She expertly swabbed and plucked and pulled evidence from inside me, and opened and closed plastic tubes and baggies of all sizes and shapes. When she was done she removed the speculum.

"Ice," she directed and the young doctor left the room.

"The police will be here in a few minutes," she said.

"Oh, do I have to talk to them now?" I asked.

"Yes, they'll at least want to take a statement while things are still fresh in your memory."

"Oh, yeah."

I hadn't thought about any of that yet. About pressing charges or filing a criminal complaint. Getting caught up in a legal battle with someone who didn't live in the state and who seemingly had the means to mount a strong defense, did not sound appealing. *But he has to pay.* Krista hadn't believed me. Sure, I could hope that they found some of his DNA inside me, but what if it wasn't enough? And even if they did, like Elisa said, wouldn't he just say it was consensual sex? Everyone saw me with him, dancing, groping, kissing. All of a sudden everything felt futile. *What's the point? Why subject myself to all of this?*

"Get dressed and when they get here I'll knock again," the nurse warned before leaving.

I waited, all alone in the cold, white room, remembering the stories I'd heard about women who were raped, only to hear later that charges had been dropped and nothing had been done. I was beginning to understand how the uphill battle of providing evidence, pressing charges, and going to court on top of the overwhelming guilt and embarrassment of being a victim could keep a woman silent. And how much courage must be summoned to take the opposite route; to go public, to make noise, to demand attention and justice. *Easier to just move on and try to forget? But will I ever actually forget or be able to forgive, or will this trauma fester inside me, growing like a cancer until it has consumed the hope and optimism that is required to live?*

If Elisa is right and I won't get justice through the legal system, then what? How can a petite nobody like me get retribution against a big, strong, confident guy like him? I'm no match for him physically or financially. Each time I'd heard whispers of an alleged rape, my first thought had been that I would try to forgive and forget. I'd never understood the women who were willing to go public and fight, only to be embarrassed and publicly humiliated. *Now it's my turn. Now I have to decide. Do I fight or do I walk away? Do I expose him or do I disappear?*

A loud knock startled me. A few seconds passed and the door opened for two uniformed officers, guns visible in holsters at their waists. They followed the nurse into the room. The older of the two looked like he could be my father. The younger was maybe in his mid-forties. They introduced themselves as Detectives Johnston and Cowell and each took a turn shaking my hand.

"We understand that you say you've been raped."

The nurse interjected, "Her injuries are consistent with aggravated rape."

I smiled at her, *thanks*. She looked back at me with a somewhat detached expression, as if this was all business for her and she had seen it all before.

"Tell us what happened. Start at the beginning, please," the officer said.

Nate's warning reverberated in my head: *If you even think about telling anyone about what just happened...I'll ruin you. Think about your family, your future...dirty slut who gets off by being tied up...it's already backed up.*

I took a deep breath. "I went to a party last night at the Phi Psi house with my roommate, Krista Jacobsen."

The younger officer interrupted, "Were you drinking? Taking drugs?"

"We were drinking. First beer and then whiskey," I said. "No drugs. I don't do drugs."

He scribbled on a pad of paper in a metal portfolio.

"Weed?" he said.

I shook my head. "Like I said, I don't do drugs."

"What happened at the party?"

If I tell them the truth and Nate finds out, he'll ruin me. "We were drinking and dancing. The last thing I remember is going out onto the back porch to get some air? I woke up alone in a twin bed in the house," I lied. "I was in pain and there was blood on the sheets."

"Are you saying that you were unconscious for the entire rape?" he asked.

"Yes."

"Do you remember any of it?"

"No," I lied.

"Well, that's good," the younger officer said. By the look on his face I gathered that he was being sincere, but the suggestion that anything about losing consciousness and getting raped could be good made me furious. *The throbbing pain in my vagina disagrees.*

"Do you know who raped you?" he asked.

"No," I lied.

"Was anyone acting differently or strangely before you blacked out? Did you leave your drink unattended at all?"

"I don't think so," I said. "I don't remember."

"Is it possible that you gave someone the wrong idea when you were drunk?"

"I'm not a tease. I was a virgin," I said quietly.

They bombarded me with additional questions about Krista and the other women at the party. They asked about how I was dressed and if I'd ever been on a date with anyone at the party before. After about ten minutes of giving them just enough detail, but not too much, I was exhausted.

"We will need a list of all of the men at the party," the younger officer said as he handed me a pad of paper and pencil.

"I didn't know all of the men at the party last night. It wasn't my party," I said.

"Then please give us the names of everyone you knew."

I tried to remember who I'd seen. There were all the regulars, and a few people I hadn't recognized. I put down all of the names I could remember, including Jake, but excluding Nate.

They told me they would be in touch once they had DNA

results from the rape kit, and that I should stop by the station later that week to review the police report and sign a witness statement.

"Do you have any questions before we leave?" the older officer asked.

"What happens if there is a good DNA sample from the rape kit?"

"It will get entered into the State's DNA database and if there's a hit, then we'll follow protocol to verify that it is a true match, and issue a warrant for arrest."

"What if there isn't a match?" I said.

"If he's not in the system, which he probably isn't given his age, we could still interview people at the party and review any security footage that the fraternity or surrounding buildings might have."

"Oh, okay. What happens to the DNA sample from the rape kit if there is no match?"

"It stays in the database in case there is ever a future match."

I nodded.

"And if you do figure out who did it, what will happen then?" I asked.

"We would arrest him and then you would have to confirm whether you want to press charges."

"If I want to press charges will I have to testify in court in front of a jury?"

"We're not lawyers, Miss., but there would be more questions. The prosecutor and the defense attorney will want all the details you've given us today and more. The defense will get all of the evidence, including the statement you just gave us, before any trial."

I imagined trying to recount the rape in front of a jury and a judge. Elisa's words of warning ran through my head. *Said it was completely consensual...called me a slut and worse things... said I wanted it...spread rumors...got really ugly.* I thought about the video that Nate had threatened to put online. *What would Vi think? What would my teachers, my friends, my acquaintances think? What would potential employers think?* Every time I met someone I would wonder whether they knew, if they had seen the video, and if so, what they thought about me. His defense would say that it was consensual and might even fabricate lies to destroy my reputation. *No, that is not the kind of attention that a young woman needs.* The thought of sitting on a witness stand, telling the whole world the minute details about the most painful experience of my life in order to assuage the doubts they might have that I am the victim made my stomach turn. I felt physically ill.

"I understand. Thanks," I said.

"Yep. Take care."

They left and the nurse came back in. She handed me a prescription for strong painkillers. "If you have additional bleeding, please go to your gynecologist," she said. "You'll want to get a check-up in two to three weeks either way to make sure that everything is healing properly."

"Thank you."

I left the hospital and filled the prescription on my way back to the dorm.

I sat on my bed and tried to focus on studying for my upcoming exams, but my mind wandered as I read through my lecture notes. *He never even told me his last name. I don't even know his last name!* I grabbed my laptop and pretty quickly found his player bio on the university athletics website: Nathan P. Ellis, 22, from Westport, CT. Seven seat in the varsity eight. Studying Business with a minor in Economics. There was a brief Q and A section below his headshot, which I skimmed. The last question was, "What sets you apart?" His answer, "I want to be the best at everything I do. I don't accept failure." *Even when it comes to having your way with women! Motherfucking prick! This guy has to pay.*

THE PUT-UP

Friday, September 4, 2015

Manhattan

At work on Friday, my nerves were hard to hide. Nate still hadn't responded to my message on the dating app and I was getting nervous. *It's been almost a week since I replied. Maybe I responded too quickly and scared him off. Damn it.*

My co-workers, Natalie and Noreen, could sense something was up and kept asking if I was okay. Eventually I gave in and told them about the date I was hoping to land with Nate.

"How'd you meet?" Noreen asked.

"On that Christian dating app."

"ChristianMix!" she exclaimed.

I looked around to see most of our co-workers staring at her.

"Could you *please!*" I implored.

"Since when are you on ChristianMix?"

"Whatever."

"You know, I heard that JewsDate is the place to go to meet successful men who are looking for more than just a fuck." She glanced around the office with a devilish smile on her face.

"You're the worst!" I said under my breath. "Maybe I am just looking for a good fuck!"

"Haha, come on! You'll be fine. I'm sure he's a real gentleman."

"Let's hope." *No chance.*

It was Friday afternoon before Nate finally replied:

Wyn,

How about tomorrow night? I made a reservation at

Bianchi's. 8pm. Hopefully, I'll see you then. I'll be wearing pink.

Nate

And if I have prophetic powers, and understand all mysteries and all knowledge, and if I have all faith, so as to remove mountains, but have not love, I am nothing. 1 Corinthians 13:2

Yes! Thank God! I have to get close to him to learn his weaknesses and how to ruin him. I managed to wait a few hours before responding:

Nate,

Sure. See you there.

Wyn

You see that a person is justified by works and not by faith alone. James 2:24

I was up early on Saturday, too excited and nervous about my date with Nate to sleep in. I'd been on the anti-anxiety med for a while, but couldn't honestly tell if it was working. I realized that I might not really know until I was face to face with him. Just in case, I'd been upping my dose slowly since his first message in hopes and preparation for a date. I took even more with breakfast, and then went to a yoga class. I ran a few errands and spent the afternoon lounging on a blanket in the park, reading the newest Vogue and watching tourists and locals stroll past.

I went in to brush my teeth again and check my face in the mirror just as the late summer sun disappeared behind the New York City skyline. I second guessed myself and applied a little more eye liner before heading out.

The city was awash in an evening glow as I walked to Bianchi's. I found him tucked away in a booth behind the bar. He was wearing a light pink dress shirt and stood up as I approached the table, "Wyn?"

I nodded and smiled. *Oh my God, this is it.*

"Nice to meet you," he said.

"Nice to meet you," I said. *Stay calm. Here we go.*

I climbed up into the small wooden booth. It was the old-fashioned, uncomfortable type, whether or not it was actually old. I looked up and met his gaze. *Holy shit! Face to face again.* He was staring at me confidently.

I leaned forward and rested my hands on the table in front of me, inches from his. They weren't shaking. *I'm okay! The medication is working.*

"Wyn," he said again, "Or should I call you Wynnie?"

"Definitely Wyn please." I smiled. "So, is it Nate or Nathan?"

"Nate."

"Got it."

"You look really familiar. Do we know each other from somewhere?"

Shit! My heart raced. "Um, not that I'm aware. You said you live in Manhattan, right? Which neighborhood?"

"Upper West Side," he said.

"Oh, me too. Maybe we've run into each other before in the neighborhood."

"Maybe, but I don't think that's it. I feel like I know you," he said.

Holy shit! Think.

"Hmmm, I don't think so. I go to the gym on Broadway, near 96th."

"Oh me too."

"That must be it then."

"Maybe, but I have this weird feeling, like we've dated before, years ago maybe."

Oh God. "Can't be. I just moved to New York a few months ago. We must have run into each other at the gym, that's all."

"Really? I never forget a beautiful woman."

I blushed, worried that he had figured it out, but he misread the source of my nerves and smiled reassuringly.

"Doesn't matter," he said. "I'm just glad to be here with you now."

Phew. Close call. Keep it together.

The waitress appeared before us, her slim figure illuminated against the dark room by the light above our table.

"My name is Kate. I'll be your server tonight. What can I get you to drink?"

He looked at me quizzically and then looked at the drink menu.

I nodded.

"Your best whiskey, on the rocks please," he said.

"Manhattan," I said.

"She'll have a Rob Roy."

"Straight or on the rocks?" the waitress asked me.

"Straight," I said.

The waitress nodded and turned to leave. I watched his eyes follow her as she disappeared.

He turned toward me. "It's the whiskey lovers Manhattan."

"What if I want a Manhattan?"

"Oh come on. Give it a try. You might love it."

Still won't take no for an answer I see.

He took his phone out of his pocket and put it down on the table face up, as if he might be expecting an important call. He looked up and stared at me with the same intensity as when I first met him at the frat house three years earlier.

"So you drink?" he asked.

"So do you," I said.

"Yes."

"Not very Christianly," I teased.

"Yeah, well, here's the thing. I know we've just met, and I know we met on a Christian dating app, but I want to be totally honest with you."

Wow, where is this going?

He continued, "I am a Christian. A practicing one, sort of, lately at least. I was raised Evangelical, Grandpa was a minister. Mom ran off and married a Catholic in New York. Had two kids. Then things sort of fell apart. Anyhow, I wasn't so sure for a while, ya know? I went off to college, lived a little." He took a sip of whiskey. "Lived a lot actually, but lately something just hasn't felt right about it, things started to feel empty, I guess. I sort of hit rock bottom about six or seven months ago and decided to recommit myself. Faith has always worked for my family, so I figure maybe it can work for me too."

I nodded and he continued.

"I mean, I'm definitely not as conservative as most Christians, I've seen a little too much of the world, but I do want to rediscover faith, and I want to be with someone who is on a similar path. I've made some mistakes in the past," he paused. "A couple of DUIs and the accusations. I want to do better. I'm ready to do better. I need to settle down."

"Accusations?" I had no idea what he was talking about. *Why hadn't I seen anything on the web about his indiscretions?*

"Yeah, you know, the kinds of things women say when they resent a guy just for being a guy."

"What do you mean? What accusations would they make?"

"Sexual harassment, assault, even rape. The lies that promiscuous women tell when they regret a choice they've made, especially if a rich, powerful man is involved and they realize he's beyond their control."

Has he been accused of rape by someone else? Is he testing me? Does he know who I am or is he just trying to see if I would support him through something like that? "Oh my God. I'm so sorry. I can't believe that's happened to you. That's total bullshit."

He smiled and nodded, seemingly satisfied by my answer.

The waitress put our drinks on the table in front of us. I looked down into my Rob Roy.

"Look, if you're the righteous type who believes that good Christians don't make mistakes, then you should get up right now and walk away." He waited and watched me. I returned his intense stare as confidently as I could.

He continued, "But if you believe in second chances, then great." He picked his whiskey up off the table.

I nodded. "I do."

"Let's have some fun then." He raised his glass.

"Cheers!" I raised my glass to meet his. I put the glass to my lips. *Sweet and strong, a little bitter. Not bad actually.*

"So tell me about you," he said.

"I'm not a prude," I said. "I've been around the block too. My mom ran a tight ship. She was very committed to her faith and expected us to fall in line. I often questioned her beliefs and when I left for college, I wanted to live by my own values, discover the world for myself. I'm not a perfect Christian either. I've struggled too, but I've found renewed purpose in the last few years. A reason to recommit myself and have faith again."

Nate nodded and thumbed his glass. He finished his whiskey, signaled to the waitress to bring another round, and leaned back against the booth.

"Where'd you grow up?" he asked.

"Chicago."

"Do you have any siblings?"

"I have one sister. She's older."

"Are your parents together?"

"No."

"Mine are divorced too."

I didn't correct him.

"Do you see your dad often?"

"Unfortunately, no. We were never close. I hate to say it, but I don't really know him."

"I'm sorry."

I shrugged. "What about you? Your parents, I mean. Siblings?"

"My parents got divorced when I was twelve. It was unexpected, for us at least. My sister was only seven. I know she never really got over it."

"That's tough. Where did you grow up?"

"Westport, Connecticut. Until my mom got custody. After the divorce she moved back to the small town in South Carolina where she grew up. My sister went with her right away. I didn't want to go. I liked my school and my friends in Westport. Eventually, she made me move with them to that small town in the middle of nowhere, and I hated it."

"Hmmmm."

"Eventually I just left. Got on a bus and moved back with my dad. It was probably hard for her. I know it was quite the scandal when the prodigal daughter showed up at home divorced, after having married a Catholic, which her dad never approved of. But it was her fault for running off in the first place."

I nodded in agreement. *Still heartless.*

"You said your mom is faithful, right? What church?" he asked.

"Ah, not like that," I laughed. "I guess it depends on how you define faith. I am pretty traditional. I go to church regularly, but my mom and sister have a different sort of faith," I said. "Feminism. They're a bit fanatical."

"Oh," he looked confused.

"Vi means well, but she can be pushy. I got tired of being told what to do and how to behave. Mostly I just wonder how I'm related to her."

"Who's Vi?"

"My mom."

"Oh, I know how that is."

I raised a brow.

"You clearly aren't very familiar with the Evangelical Church."

I shook my head slowly.

"Didn't your profile say you were Evangelical?"

Shit. "Did it?"

He nodded, "I think so."

I shrugged. "Oh, I don't remember."

"There wasn't any room for debate with my mom and grandma. I got tired of them telling me what to do. Bossing me around. I missed living with my dad. He never did that. He hardly ever asked where I was going or what I was doing. My mom and grandma on the other hand, they were always butting into everything, warning me about what would happen if I did this or that. It was a big deal to them that I chose to go to a non-Evangelical university far from home. They didn't think it was conservative enough."

"I know what you mean about wanting some freedom and privacy." *So that's it. Mind my own business and don't tell him what to do. Don't be like his mom and grandma.*

"Yeah, let's just say, it didn't work. I've seen the real world and I don't need those two or anyone telling me what to do."

"My mom always pushed me to have a real career so that I would be independent. So that I wouldn't need a man to take care of me. She says I shouldn't get married young or have kids right away. Maybe she doesn't want me to repeat her mistakes. I think she means well, but I'm not her. Just because something worked for her, doesn't mean it will work for me."

"Yeah." He took a sip of whiskey.

"I'm tired of her unsolicited advice. I just want to make my own decisions," I said.

He smiled.

"Plus I think it would be nice to be taken care of," I added.

He flashed a charismatic smile.

When dinner arrived and there was finally silence I realized that things were going well. The check came, he didn't hesitate, and I let him pay.

"Can I walk you home?" he asked.

"Maybe next time," I said, and raised my arm to flag a taxi.

"Let me," he said and stepped out into the street to wave one down. A cab pulled over and he opened the back door for me.

"Thanks. And thank you for dinner," I said. I leaned forward and kissed his cheek. He had a short stubble that felt like sandpaper against my lips. Maybe it was the three Rob Roys or maybe it was the thrill of deception, either way, I was elated.

"Looking forward to next time," he said.

"Me too."

"Message me your number, so I can text you," he yelled as the taxi pulled away.

THE PUT-UP

Monday, September 7, 2015
Manhattan

"Clearly it went well!" Noreen said as I dropped my purse on my desk Monday morning.

An immaculate bouquet of assorted roses looked absurd on my small desk.

"Oh jeez!" I said.

"I think you mean 'lucky me!'"

I smiled.

"So it did go well then?"

"Mmm hmmm."

I plucked the card from amongst the buds.

"A rose for each time I thought of you since we parted ways. Nate"

"What does it say?"

"To Wyn, from Nate," I said.

"It does not! Give it to me!" She lunged toward me playfully.

I folded it up and tucked it into my bra.

"Seriously though, who is this guy?" She motioned toward the flowers.

"He's too good to be true," I said. *If you only knew.*

"He might be, but at least he's young, smart, and interested," she said. "Snatch him up while you still can. Otherwise, before you know it, you'll be settling for someone you never would have thought twice about in your twenties."

"Oh stop it," I said.

She shot me a look that said 'grow up'.

"Sorry."

She nodded and looked away.

I decided to mind my own business.

The week passed slowly. Work was a little light and there wasn't much to distract me.

I sent Nate another friend request and this time he accepted. I studied each picture of him on Facebook and Instagram for more clues about his life. *What really makes you tick? Why did you do what you did to me? Was I just one of many and that's why you didn't recognize me?* Based on a few pictures and a Facebook post, it seemed like he had been getting serious with a woman about a year earlier and it had ended right after New Year's. *Did she find out what a monster he really is?*

By Wednesday night I had googled whether someone could tell if you were Facebook-stalking them (turns out not really) and had gone through all of his photos and posts at least three times. *If only Facebook-stalking could will him to text me!* I had messaged him my cell phone number the morning after our date but hadn't heard from him.

Finally on Thursday afternoon while I was working on a proposal for a marketing campaign I got a text from an unknown number, "Picnic Saturday? Noonish?" *Yes, that's him!*

I put the phone down. *Patience is a virtue.* I was so excited I could barely focus until I overheard the newest addition to our marketing team bragging to Noreen about how he had just been assigned to a hot new product campaign. *Of course.* He had joined the company a few months after I did. I felt his eyes on me as he told her about the project. I smiled and picked up my phone. When he was finally gone, Noreen got up and walked toward me.

"Did you hear that?" she said.

I nodded.

"I can't believe they would assign him to that account," she whispered, "that should have been yours."

"I wish."

"I'm sorry."

I shrugged. "Thanks."

"You should complain to Ethan."

My boss, Ethan, was in his early forties, with a wife and three kids. He didn't have a secretary because the company had been restructured a few years before I joined. Management touted the flatter organization as an opportunity for young staff to grow, but I soon figured out it really just meant that there was no one to do any administrative work.

"What good would talking to Ethan do?"

"Yeah, I don't know, crazy idea."

"He'll just make up some excuse why Mike was the right pick for that account. He'll probably just tell me to have some patience."

"Why can't they see how capable you are?"

I shook my head. "It doesn't matter what I do, and it probably never will."

"Have you ever thought about leaving?"

"Let's do this later over a glass of wine. Okay?"

"Deal!" she said.

After work I responded to the anonymous text; "Nate?"

His response came immediately, "Yep."

"Noon this Saturday works for me. What can I bring?"

"Great. Slip 5 at 11:30. Just your lovely self."

I woke up early on Saturday and went to the grocery store. He said not to bring anything but I couldn't help myself. I bought a wedge of smoked Gouda, a mild sheep's milk cheddar, and a round of goat cheese. At home I packed the cheese, crackers, a small jar of raspberry jam, and a butter knife into an insulated bag and threw it in my biggest purse with a book and a pair of headphones.

I rode the No. 1 to South Ferry Station and walked the half block to Slip 5. I didn't see Nate and checked my watch. I was a few minutes early, so I waited on a bench near the ticket booth and watched the ferries and smaller vessels scuttle across the river. The sun was high in the sky and there were almost no clouds in sight; the weather was perfect. I reached into my purse and pulled out my sunglasses.

"Sorry I'm late." I turned and saw him standing behind me with a paper grocery bag in his left hand. "Ready to go?"

I gathered up my bags. "Yep, let's do this."

We boarded the weathered ferry, walked to the front end of the boat, and leaned against the railing, staring out over the water. Another couple stood on the opposite side of the deck. It was cooler than I expected out on the water and I crossed my arms to my chest. Nate startled me draping an arm over my shoulders. *Okay, it's okay. I'm fine. He isn't hurting me. We're in broad daylight. I have to stay calm.*

"So, how was your week?" I asked.

"Not bad." His eyes lit up. "We've finalized a new product that I think will be a real boon to the business," he said. "It will be our first foray into women's beauty products."

"Oh yeah? What type of product?"

"Wrinkle cream."

"Does that stuff actually work?"

"It doesn't matter. Women of a certain age will pay up to a certain price for anything that they believe might minimize or reverse the visible signs of aging."

"Hmmm."

"It's true," he said. "The market research is pretty clear on that. In fact, the higher the price, to a point, the more they believe the product will work, even when there is no evidence."

"Wishful thinking, I guess."

"Hope," he said. "It's a powerful thing."

"It is."

I stared out at the dark water, churning as the ferry spun around toward its destination.

"How was your week?" he asked.

"Not great," I said. "I got passed over for a great assignment at work."

"How come?"

"Not sure. I think I work hard enough, but I'm not willing to be there all the time. I want to have a life too. I need time to date if I'm ever going have the family I want."

"Hmmm. Yeah, it's hard to get ahead these days if you're not willing to sacrifice everything when you're young."

"I guess so. I don't know why I care anyhow, it's just a job."

"If you could do anything, what would you do?" he asked.

I raised my brows.

"I mean what is your dream job?"

"Not sure," I said. "Maybe nothing. I mean who wants to sit at a computer for eight plus hours a day thinking about how to make the next cheap gimmick seem like a must-have?"

"I love my job," he said. "I wouldn't even call it a job really."

"You're lucky. Most people don't feel that way about their work."

"I guess I am. I've never thought about it like that. I just want to be successful at everything I do."

"My mom wanted me to work," I said. "She thinks it's really important that women work."

He nodded.

"She didn't really have a choice, I guess, because she never got married."

"I thought you said your parents were divorced."

"Oh, no, I didn't say that. They were never married, as far as I know."

"Hmmm."

"Anyhow, if I'm ever married and have kids, I think I'll want to stay home and be a full-time mom. That's my dream job, I guess, to be a stay-at-home mom."

He nodded.

I watched seagulls circling above us, white specks soaring against the bright blue sky.

I had gone to college thinking I would be a Fine Arts major. I had always loved dance, art history, and romance languages, but Vi wanted me to study something useful (as she put it) and she was paying my tuition. She wanted me to major in business, or at least be pre-law or pre-med, something that would enable me to be independent and support myself. I pushed back at first but eventually we compromised and I agreed to study Communications with a French minor. I didn't think it mattered. I really wasn't interested in having a career like Vi and Ali. I assumed I would work for a while, which would give me a good excuse to buy some chic clothes. And then, who knew. I would get married, have kids, and stay at home with them. Vi had always looked so stressed when she got home from work. There was one thing that I was sure of: I didn't want her life. But everything had changed that day in June in the frat house, all of my hopes and dreams had been upended and now here I was, on a date with the guy who had ruined my life. *I don't have a dream job because I don't have the luxury to dream. Instead, I obsess about what it would feel like to get justice. Retribution feels like the only job that matters now.*

"Speaking of marriage and kids, is that something you're thinking about already?" he said.

Oh shit. Did I mention kids too soon? I have to be careful to not seem overzealous. "Um, not yet. I'm so young. I guess I've always assumed I'll have kids someday," I said. "How about you?"

"Yeah, I guess I've just taken marriage and kids as a given too. Once I find the right person, of course."

He stared past me, his eyes fixed on the landmass in the distance.

"What do you think about the suburbs?" I asked.

"I grew up in the suburbs. I guess I could move back someday."

"Have you ever been to Greenwich?"

"Of course. That's just down the road from Westport." He poked at me playfully. "I see you have good taste."

"I've only been there once but I loved it! I would love to live there someday." *It has to be Connecticut for my plan to work.* I'd done my research before moving out to New York, and Connecticut was the only state in the area that still considered fault when it came to divorce and awarding alimony. *If I want to be sure he'll pay for what he did when I catch him cheating, then it has to be Connecticut.*

"It is nice." He agreed.

Before I'd even moved to New York I'd heard that Greenwich made the towns on the North Shore of Chicago, where the public schools looked like private colleges, look ordinary.

"A year from now I should be able to buy a house over there," he said, "cash."

What a cocky asshole! "Wow!" I smiled. "I'm impressed." I imagined touring fancy mansions in Greenwich with him, standing in kitchens bigger than a New York City apartment, debating the merits of wine cellars and steam showers. *How far will I have to play this thing out?*

"How many kids do you think you want?" he asked

This is going well. Men like Nate don't ask these questions unless they're really interested.

"At least three," I said confidently. "Probably the first before I turn thirty." I studied his reaction. "What about you?"

"Yeah, two or three would be good I guess. I don't want to be an old dad."

I stared out over the Sound, unable to shake the image of him coming home after work in a business suit and exquisite cologne, to a large suburban house in Greenwich. *Can I really do this? Can I really keep my cool to play him for as long as I might need to?*

He continued, "That way, they are out of the house while you're still young enough to have some fun. I plan to retire early. I'd like to spend my fifties travelling the world, in style of course."

I nodded. "Of course. That sounds incredible."

"Thailand. Japan. Russia. Hong Kong. India."

"Have you been to Asia before?" I asked.

"Of course, but always on business. You never see a new place the way you should when you're traveling for business."

"Hmmm, sure."

The ferry docked with a bit of a thud. After what seemed like a long delay we were allowed off. Nate wrapped his hand around mine, reminding me of the walk down the hallway in the frat house all those years ago. I shivered.

He led me across a field and up a small hill. It was clear he had a specific place in mind. There were only a smattering of people, basking in the fleeting summer sun. He put the grocery bag down and pulled out a blanket. He spread it out on the side of the hill revealing his company's logo in the corner. It was a white circle punctuated by a series of perfect squares set in a pattern with varying opacity. It was strong, clean, and authoritative.

I pulled out a small square, flower-patterned, table cloth and placed white cloth napkins, a small wooden cutting board and cheese knife, and the snacks I'd brought in the center of the blanket.

He pulled out a bottle of champagne, two glasses, and a Swiss Army knife and peeled away the foil wrapper. He held the bottle firmly, followed by a loud pop, and poured two glasses. He laid down next to me on the blanket and raised his glass.

"To the future," he said.

I touched my glass to his, smiled, and repeated, "To the future." We each took a sip and then he leaned in. *Oh God, he's going to kiss me!* I spilled a little champagne as my hand began to shake and I pulled away.

"What's wrong?"

"Oh, nothing. Sorry, I just didn't…"

In his typical, bold manner, he leaned forward and kissed me, as I fumbled for the right words. I was thankful that his unwavering confidence and decisiveness left me no time to avoid his advance. *I have to get used to this if I'm going to succeed.* I could taste him through the sweetness of the wine and the memories of our first kiss flooded back. My mind began to recreate the scene in the dark, humid, frat house all those years ago. I quickly forced myself instead to think about the most awkward kiss I'd ever had with another freshman, before I met Nate, whose sizable nose had pushed against my face to the point of distraction. I nearly began laughing at the memory and began to relax as Nate continued to massage my tongue with his. *I can do this, as difficult and insane as it is.*

We spent the afternoon laying around in the sun. I read my book, he did some work, and then insisted on giving me a back massage. I tried to relax and just as I finally began to, he slipped his hand down under my shirt. I rolled over, sat up, and smiled.

"I'm not a prude, but I do expect some patience. We just met."

"Sure," he said and went back to working.

When we finally got back to the dock he invited me to his place. I definitely wasn't ready to take the next step with him. *I know I can't hold him off for too long or he'll lose interest, but I'm not ready yet. Having sex with him will be the hardest thing I've ever done. I just need a little more time, maybe a little more medication.* I made an excuse and we parted with another kiss.

On the subway back to my apartment I texted Adam, "Whatcha doing tomorrow? Wanna hang?" I hadn't seen him much since moving to New York, and I couldn't help wondering if he was intentionally avoiding me.

Back at the apartment my mind wandered back to Nate. I grabbed my laptop and began to write.

Sunday, June 10, 2012

Back in my dorm room I locked the door, undressed, and wrapped a large, plush bath robe around me. I grabbed the bright pink shower tote stuffed with luxury bath products that Adam's mom, Adrienne, had bought me as a send-off gift. Clearly thoughtful, the five kinds of scented bubble bath were wasted on a communal dorm shower.

I was relieved when I got to the damp shower room and saw that the one stall with a curtain was free. I hung my bathrobe and towel on the nearest hook and let the water run over me. I poured shampoo into my hand until it was overflowing, and then reveled in the feeling of excess soap foaming in my hair and running down my shoulders and my back. I washed and washed my entire body, even as the soap stung where he had forced his way inside me. When I finally got out of the shower, the skin on my fingers and toes was completely shriveled. The wall-to-wall mirrors in the next room were covered in a foggy mist. I walked over to the longest mirror and with my finger wrote, "He must pay!"

I took a step back, looked at the fading words, and just cracked open. I began to heave and tremble as if an earthquake was fomenting deep inside my body. I fell to the floor, overcome, and began to weep.

Two women walked in.

"...I guess he said 'I love you' before they had sex, and then days later he won't even talk to her," one of them said.

"Asshole," the other replied.

Then they saw me. "Oh my God! Are you okay?"

I didn't know what to say. I was curled up in a ball on the tile floor of a dormitory bathroom. I wiped my eyes. "I'll be okay," I mustered.

They gently pulled me up off the floor. They were women I had passed many times in the hallway, been introduced to once in a dimly lit dorm room, but we were not friends.

"Seriously. Are you okay?" she asked again.

"You don't seem okay," the second opined.

I tied my robe closed and they handed me my tote. "Thanks."

I made it back to my room without running into anyone else. *Thank God*, I thought, wrapping another towel around my head and climbing into bed.

I barely made it through finals, every time I sat down to study my mind wandered to the video. I couldn't help Googling my name and holding my breath as I waited for the worst, bracing for that sinking feeling. *So far nothing.* I had kept my end of the deal, well at least I hadn't told the police who he was, so maybe he would keep his.

At the end of finals week, Krista and I packed up our stuff. Krista was moving to the sorority house, but I had agreed to let one of the seniors who wasn't graduating on-time, live in our room with Krista for the summer quarter. I would move back home since it was close by. Given what had just happened, I was grateful to be going home for the summer. I needed a break from campus, and wanted some space.

Vi and Ali drove over on Sunday to help me move. Ali had just graduated from law school and was about to start a new job downtown. She was living at home temporarily while she looked for an apartment in the city.

She gave me a hug. "How are you?"

"I'm fine," I lied, avoiding her gaze. "Thanks so much for coming to help me move."

"Of course. None of the apartments I called about yesterday could be shown today anyhow."

"When do you start your job?" I asked.

"Tomorrow."

"Are you nervous?"

"Looking forward to it, actually. The real deal finally begins."

Ali wanted to be a big time environmental lawyer to save "Gaia", as she put it, "Mother Earth" to the rest of us. She had decided that the best way to do that was to keep her enemies closest. Her goal was to work for some environmental defense organization eventually, but first she would work at a big law firm that was known for representing conventional energy corporations. She figured that if she learned how the enemy approached its defense it would make her a more adept and prepared defender of "Gaia" someday.

We made quick work of loading my boxes into the back of Vi's hatchback, drove to the house, and unpacked just as unceremoniously. Standing in my childhood room where nothing had changed, I felt at odds with the rest of the world. Everything around me marched on exactly as it had before, but I would never be the same. Each small reminder of how carefree my life had been, pulled me deeper into regret and despair. Every moment at home that should have been a comforting reminder of my idyllic childhood, made me sad. Sad that I could never go back. Sad that I might never again wake up in the morning full of hope and optimism about the future. The sadness only continued to grow, until it alienated me from my own life, making me feel like an actor in someone else's story. Over the course of the summer, the sadness would, more and more often turn to anger and I would find myself thinking about him. *I can't let him get away with this. My world is shattered. How can his go on as if nothing has changed?*

I awoke to Vi downstairs making the absurd amount of noise that was typical of her cooking. Pots and pans banging, the coffee pot percolating, cabinet doors reverberating. She was the worst in the morning. She was an early riser and always acted as if once she was up there was no explanation or excuse why anyone else should still be asleep. The consolation was that she was an excellent cook and once you were awake the prospect of her smooth coffee and perfectly cooked eggs was too enticing to stay in bed.

"Morning," she said cheerfully when I got downstairs.

Ali was just finishing a cup of coffee and got up to put her dishes away.

"Eggs are in the pan. Bread is in the box. Coffee on the stove. We should be home around seven." After a graceful flutter through every room on the first floor she was out the back and off to work, with Ali in tow.

I had a week before my summer internship started, and although the time off was welcome I knew I would be desperate for something to do to keep my mind off of him.

I ate breakfast, got dressed, and went for a walk. It was a beautiful day, warm but not too hot, sunny and dry, rare for Chicago in the summer. I lounged around the house for a bit and started reading a novel off the shelf in the living room from Vi's extensive collection. She was an avid reader and somehow managed to find time to read for enjoyment despite working all the time.

I fell asleep on the couch at some point and was woken up by the ping of a text message from Adam: "what up? you around?" It was the first time I'd smiled in a week.

"yep"

A few minutes later he walked into the living room.

"Hey!" He looked tired, but his slightly curly blonde hair was recently cut and he had gained a bit more muscle since I'd seen him over winter break.

He walked over and pulled me into his arms. I buried my nose in his t-shirt and breathed in deeply. *Home.* I tried to shake off the sadness that immediately began to creep in. *Not this too. Don't let what happened corrupt this too.*

Eventually, we went to his house because his parents paid for cable, and laid around all afternoon pretending to watch alternating re-runs of America's Next Top Model and Shark Tank, but really we watched each other. It was a relief to be around someone I could trust.

Vi and Ali were in the kitchen when I walked next door.

"How was your first day?" I asked Ali.

"Mostly paperwork. Lots of compliance. Some HR. No real work." Ali was sitting at the kitchen counter on a bar stool fingering a bottle of Blue Moon while Vi prepped dinner.

"Bummer. Since when do you drink beer?"

"Since Soren asked me if I prefer beer or wine and then teased me when I said wine."

"Who is Soren? What kind of name is that anyhow?"

"He's another clerk who started today. He's Danish."

"Since when do you care what some guy thinks?" I said.

"I don't."

"You do! Are you even allowed to date someone you work with?"

"Yeah, why not?" she said.

"You need to be careful," Vi warned. "I've seen that backfire and ruin a career more than once. And surprise, surprise, it's never the man's!"

Ali nodded, acknowledging that Vi was probably right.

Friday, June 22, 2012

A voicemail from one of the detectives that had interviewed me in the hospital was a reminder to go into the station to sign the statement. I still wasn't sure what to do, so I procrastinated for days. On Friday I finally got up the nerve to go, wanting to get it over with before I started my internship. The police station, just off Main Street, had that late 90s sterile box look and feel. I walked over to the receptionist who was sitting behind a Plexiglas window.

"I need to speak to Detective Cowell," I said. "He called me about signing a victim statement."

"Please have a seat and I will see if he is available."

If I don't tell them it was Nate, then what? I can't let him get away with what he did, but I don't think telling them his name will help right now. He'd find out eventually that I reported him and ruin my life like he promised. I need to make him pay, but not like this, not by exposing myself through the legal system. I'll take matters into my own hands instead. If he's proud of his business and the money he's made then I'll figure out a way to bleed him dry on my own. Shaking a bit as I waited, I told myself that it was just the blasting air conditioning, but I knew it was really nerves about the path to justice I had resolved to take.

"Wynafreda Laurent?" A young woman held open the door. I followed her as she escorted me back to a small conference room. She put a file folder down on the table and handed me a typed document.

"Read this. I'll be back in a few minutes in case you have any questions or corrections to the report."

I pulled it toward me.

EVANSTON POLICE DEPARTMENT
CRIMINAL REPORT

Victim: Wynafreda Laurent
Perpetrator: Unknown male, 22-23 yrs. old, Caucasian,
approx. 6'5", brown hair, brown eyes.
Date: Sunday June 10, 2012
Time: Approx. 1am to 10am
Location: 114 N. Locust, Evanston, IL

Description: Victim met perpetrator at a frat party at the address referenced above. Victim is 19 years old, 5'4" and weighs 110 lbs. Victim admitted to drinking alcohol and estimated that she had six drinks between 7pm and 1am. She did not see anyone put anything in her drinks. Victim was dancing consensually with men at the party and shared several consensual open-mouthed kisses with one of the young men on dance floor. Victim does not remember who she kissed. The last thing victim remembers is going out onto the back porch for some air. Victim alleges that she woke up alone, naked in a twin bed in a room on the first floor of the frat house. Victim said that when she woke up there was blood on the sheets. Victim does not know who raped her.

Physical Evidence Collected: Sexual Assault Forensic Exam (Date of exam: 6/10/2012)

'Victim alleges'. I guess I knew that it would be written that way, but it was still difficult to read. The report made it sound like they questioned everything I'd said. *Have they done any investigation of their own? Do they know that my story isn't 100 percent accurate?*

I looked up. The young woman was standing at the end of the table a few feet away from me, watching my reaction. I hadn't noticed her there.

"Is the report factually correct?"

"Yes," I lied.

"Please sign here," she said and handed me a pen. I signed and dated the report.

"Thanks," she said. "You can go."

"What happens next?"

"This will go into the file. I don't think the DNA results are back yet. When they are, we will reach out if we have a match. If there is no match the case will remain open. Obviously, please come back to the station if you remember any other important details from that day. There is a statute of limitations on these kinds of things," she said.

"Yeah, of course."

"Follow me." She escorted me back out to the lobby. "Thanks again," she said as she opened the door for me.

I replied instinctively, "Thank you."

I got home before Ali and Vi and went straight to the kitchen. Vi had a very modest selection of alcohol in the house but always kept a bottle of her favorite French cognac in the freezer. She cherished it and only brought it out for others to enjoy on holidays or special occasions, so on the rare occasion in high school that I wanted a drink, I knew never to take much. *I need a stiff one after my visit to the station.* I took it out, wrestled with the frozen cap and poured a generous shot into a glass tumbler. I heard the front door and quickly returned the bottle to its place, tipped the glass back and savoring the familiar aftertaste as the cold liquid hit my throat.

Ali walked into the kitchen and went straight to the fridge.

She took out a beer.

"Want one?" she asked. I'd noticed that she was buying a different six-pack of specialty beer each week.

"You really like this guy, huh?"

"You could say that."

"You better be careful or you'll gain the Associate twenty."

"Haha. Not all men like little twig girls like you and your friends."

Ali and I were the same height, but she had been blessed with wide childbearing hips and, for as long I could remember, had struggled a bit to keep weight off. She was by no means fat, but she just didn't have the bone structure to be thin either. In response she had developed a 'don't give a shit what anyone else thinks about me' attitude long ago, but an odd comment here and there made it clear to me that she really did care, and even resented women for whom it seemed easy.

"Actually, I could use one today," I said.

She handed me a butterscotch stout. *Certainly not my first choice, but whatever.*

"Tough day at home?" she teased.

"Just boring," I said, and changed the subject. "When's your first date?"

"Already had it, thought you knew that."

"No, when?"

"Last Sunday morning. We had brunch."

"Lame! I mean a real date."

"Oh, grow up. It's 2012, not 1953. I don't need to be taken out to a four course meal, at an overpriced restaurant to be on a date. And I certainly don't need him to pay either."

I sighed audibly. It was never worth the effort to argue with Ali on any subject where the equality of men and women was concerned.

"Fine. How was the date?"

"Good. As a European, he has some interesting perspectives on the Environmental movement. We seem to have a lot in common."

"Great."

The door creaked again and Vi walked in. "Since when do you think you're allowed to drink in this house? And on a week night?"

"What's the difference between drinking down the street during the school year and drinking here?" I said.

"You're not even twenty-one yet. I'd appreciate if you'd limit it to holidays and special occasions when you're in my house."

"Sure," I said and put the beer down on the counter.

"Oh, chill out. It's one beer," Ali said. She had always been able to banter with Vi and push back in ways that I had never been able to, or at least had never gotten away with. I had been punished for making insubordinate comments that would have been celebrated from Ali; the kind of arguments that would make her a good lawyer someday. Ali and Vi began to debate whether Ali's beer drinking was representative of a desire to conform to the male-centric world around her. I was just glad to be out of Vi's crosshairs.

THE PUT-UP

Sunday, September 13, 2015
Hell's Kitchen

Noreen texted Sunday morning, "How was the date? 2nd right? I wanna hear all about it. Brunch?"

I replied, "Meet me at Sunny Side Up?" It was the kind of familiar neighborhood brunch spot that always had slightly sticky tables and a wait to be seated, despite having average food.

"Half an hour?" she texted.

"Perfect."

We were seated at a small table in the back, and ordered eggs, toast, and mimosas.

"So," she said. "You've seen this guy twice now? What's his name again?"

"Nate."

"So, what's he like?"

"Well, he checks all the boxes. He's handsome and successful, and charismatic. He asked me about marriage and kids on the second date." *He's also a rapist and ruined my life.*

"What!"

"Yeah, he asked whether I want to get married and have a family someday. He said he wants to have at least two or three kids."

"Oh my god, it took my husband six months of dating before he would even respond to my questions about kids. He sounds like a keeper!"

"Yeah, he does, doesn't he?" I paused to take a sip of coffee. "I'm trying to decide how long to wait before..." I made a face. "You know."

"You have sex with him," she said.

"Yes." *And dreading it with every fiber of my being.*

"Well, you're not a virgin, right? So I'd say a month, max."

"You're probably right. I guess I'm just nervous." *God, she's right. I'm gonna have to have sex with him sooner than later if my plan is going to work.*

"How long has it been?" she teased. "You know you can't wait too long these days, he'll lose interest. It is the 21st century."

"Yeah, I know."

"So, there you go."

"Yeah, we'll see. I'll keep you posted."

"I'm excited for you!" She shook my arm gently. "Why don't you seem more excited?"

"Too many disappointments in the past I guess." *One major one.*

"Oh come on, cheer up! Just because you've dated assholes in the past doesn't mean you shouldn't be excited about the prospect of love now!"

"Yeah, you're right."

"Cheers!" she said.

"Cheers," I said as I touched my glass to hers. *I hate lying to her, but this isn't exactly the kind of moment you spring a 'that night a stranger violently raped me' story on someone.*

As difficult as it was, I tried to imagine having sex with him. I would have to convince myself that it wasn't a big deal, otherwise I was sure he would sense my fear and distress. I would have to give my best performance yet. *If I can pull this off, I can pull off anything!*

I managed to hold him off until just about a month after our first date. I could tell he was getting frustrated. He'd invited me back to his place at the end of every date we'd been on and each time I'd made an excuse.

We met for dinner on Saturday night, at a little bistro that almost perfectly split the distance between his condo and my apartment. It was French Moroccan fusion served tapas style. We split a few different dishes including a sweet Seffa dish with meatballs, Kalinti, and kebabs.

After dinner we went for a walk, hand in hand, in the direction of his condo. As we got closer he said, "Come up for a night cap."

I looked up and nodded.

He smiled.

It was my first time inside his house. Everything was classy and high-end, but it was clearly a bachelor pad. The kitchen was very well appointed but small, and way too clean. The countertop, backsplash, and cabinets were various shades of grey: slate, charcoal, and cloud. The living room had a large flat screen t.v. that dwarfed the gas burning fireplace beneath it.

He opened a bottle of champagne, poured two glasses, and handed me one. My hand shook slightly as I took the glass. *Shit. Relax.*

"Cheers!" he said. We touched glasses and I quickly put the glass to my lips and took a large sip.

"You okay?" He asked. *Shit, he can tell I'm nervous.*

"Yeah, great." I forced a smile. *I'm okay, I'm fine. I have to be fine. Just get through this.*

We sat on the couch, my body rigid next to his. Just when I expected him to turn on the t.v. he reached for an envelope on the coffee table. He opened it carefully and pulled out a piece of folded paper. Then without any ceremony he began to read:

> Like dew on the morning buds,
> You are always new to me.
> Like a cool dip in the lake in May,
> You invigorate me.
> Your smile is my happiness,
> Your love, my purpose.

Oh my God, barf! How cliché! He handed me the paper. It was dated September 15, 1915 and the penmanship was nearly indiscernible. In gold lettering at the top of the page it read, Joseph A. Ellis. *Can this be real or is it just some strange ploy he uses to get women in bed?*

"It's a poem that my great grandfather wrote for my great grandmother. When I met you I finally understood what he meant."

I studied the expression on his face looking for sarcasm. *Is this his thing? Does he read this to every naïve woman he brings home? Sick!* He seemed sincere. He leaned over and kissed me, and I let him.

He paused to pull my shirt up over my head and threw it on the end of the couch. He took his off. His chest was strong and tan. He began to kiss me more aggressively. *Oh my God. Can I actually do this?*

Butterflies churned in my stomach. I had been trying to prepare myself for this for so long, telling myself it wasn't a big deal, but it was, and no amount of therapy or medication could prepare me for it. There was no doubt that having consensual sex with *him* would be the hardest thing I'd ever done in my life. *I have no choice now. This is it. This has to work.*

As he began to unhook my bra the panic started building inside me. *What if he tries to handcuff me again? I'll lose my head? I have to stay calm.*

"Hey, I thought you said you weren't a virgin?" he teased.

"I'm not."

"Why are you so nervous then?"

"It's been a while," I said. "A long time actually."

"It's fine," he said calmly, "relax."

He pulled at the button on my jeans as he shoved his tongue in my mouth. He stopped kissing me and stood up, unbuttoned his pants and let them fall to the floor. He wasn't wearing any underwear and his erection was impressive. He raised my legs in the air and then grabbed the hems of each pant leg. I propped myself up on my hands so that he could pull them off. He stepped forward, picked me up off the couch, and held me against him. He pulled my legs around his waist, and as he was kissing me, lowered me down onto him. I was still dry as a bone. *Crap, I'm clearly not turned on. He's gonna think I don't want this.* He lifted me up and spit on himself, then lowered me down again. *He doesn't care?*

"Oh my God," I said, "go slow. You're really big."

He grinned.

Sucker!

"Come on, relax," he said again. "Just enjoy."

With every thrust he pushed himself deeper inside me.

He propped me up on a ledge and thrust his hips back and forth without any attention to what did or didn't work for me.

I closed my eyes and began to moan, loudly. I squeezed the muscles in my abdomen as tight as I could, and he bought it. His motions slowed, and he fell back onto the couch, pulling me on top of him. He shifted his pelvis and lifted me up slightly and off of him. He began rubbing himself and then aimed at me as he ejaculated. He directed his warm cum all over my chest and stomach, and watched himself as he came. When he was done he laid back onto the couch and closed his eyes. Just as I was about to jump up, he sat up and wrapped his arms around me.

"Hey, I'm sorry," he said. "Next time I'll let you do it."

"Yeah, I'm not on birth control right now," I said. "So it's fine. I guess I'll have to go back on it."

"Yeah, I wasn't sure."

I excused myself, ran to the bathroom, and locked the door. I turned the shower on, let the hot water rush over me, and finally lost my composure. *What the fuck am I doing?* I collapsed onto the tile floor. I began to heave. *I can't do this.* I tried to stifle the sounds of my distress. *What was I thinking? I should have just forgotten about him, moved on.* I held my head in my hands, closed my eyes, and sobbed. *I can't do this.*

Eventually I calmed down. *Get it together. He has to pay for what he did.*

I pulled myself up off the shower floor and scrubbed my body with soap, working meticulously over every part me that he had defiled. I scrubbed again and again, until I finally felt clean. I wrapped a towel around my chest, checked my face in the mirror, and opened the bathroom door.

"You okay?" He was still laying on the couch naked, his limp penis hanging against his thigh. "You were in there forever."

"I'm fine," I said. "Just enjoying a long, hot shower."

"Hey, I really am sorry about how that ended."

"It's fine."

I could feel him watching me as I got dressed.

"You aren't gonna stay?"

"No. I have an early morning. Need to get some sleep." *No way I can sleep here.*

"Alright."

"Night."

As I walked home in the cool night air, tears streaming down my cheeks, I tried to focus on the end game. *This is the only way now. It will be worth it eventually.*

I couldn't sleep so I worked on the assignment from my therapist instead.

Friday, July 20, 2012

When I woke up it was far brighter in my room than it should have been for a weekday morning. *Shit, what time is it?* I wondered, looking at my phone: 8:20am. *Crap, I'll be so late to work.*

I didn't have time to shower, so I threw my hair up into a messy bun and put on a loose blouse, a pencil skirt, nude flats and a ton of deodorant. The kind with the toxic chemicals that Vi and Ali were always warning against. I grabbed a banana on my way out the door and fidgeted as I sat on the Purple Line "L" train, which squealed as it rounded each bend on its elevated tracks. My internship at the PR firm downtown was in an old six story brick warehouse building in River North, with exposed brick walls and brightly colored furniture. The dress code was shabby chic and the atmosphere, at least on the surface was laid back, although I sensed that under the chill façade there was stress: grown-up stress.

My job was essentially to make cold calls to potential clients and proofread press releases, which would keep me busy for most of the summer and hopefully keep my mind off of everything else.

I rolled in at nine-thirty, filled a ceramic mug with black coffee, and stared blankly at my computer screen. My boss walked by and asked me to join her at a ten o'clock meeting in the conference room. The meeting was about the marketing strategy for some new laundry detergent and it was a true struggle to look interested for the better part of an hour. Toward the end of the meeting I began to feel nauseous. *Jeez, I didn't have that much to drink last night.* I was the last to get up when the meeting ended, but as I stood up I knew something wasn't right. I tried breathing in through my nose and out through my mouth, like Vi always advised when I thought I might puke. I walked over to the door to leave and then it hit me. I quickly shut the door and vomited into the waste basket. I took a few deep breaths and then looked into the bin. There wasn't too much, it was mostly coffee. I took a few tissues from the box of Kleenex on the table and threw it over the mess. *It doesn't really smell,* I reassured myself. I walked out as if nothing had happened. *That was weird.*

My cell phone rang and I let it go to voicemail. The young detective from the Evanston Police Department had left a message asking me to stop by. *What now? Do they know it was Nate?*

On my way home from work I swung by the Police Station and asked for Detective Cowell. I was shown into an interrogation room. He came in and my first thought was that he looked more serious now than when he had interviewed me in the hospital.

"Wynafreda. How are you doing?"

"Okay, I guess."

"Please sit." He motioned to a straight-backed chair. "Look, I have some bad news," he said. "The DNA from your rape kit did not match any DNA in the system, so we still don't know who did this."

Phew! "Hmmm," I sighed and shook my head.

"I understand that this is very difficult. We'll do our best to determine who did it, but without more information from you or someone at the party, a witness to ID the guy, it's not going to be an easy case to solve."

"I understand." *What now?*

"I'll be in contact if we get any breaks."

"Okay, thank you." *That's it? What about interviewing witnesses, reviewing video footage? I guess a violent rape is a low priority compared to other violent crimes. If they won't do anything about it, I will.*

"Have a good day," he said. "Take care."

"Thank you."

I walked out of the station and again felt my head spin, watching the hum of everyday life going on around me. It was as if nothing had changed, but for me, nothing would ever be the same.

Monday morning I woke up early, wanting to make up for my tardiness on Friday. The sun was low in the sky and cast a familiar glow around my room. I sat up in bed and the moment I did it hit me again. I leaned over and searched frantically for the waste basket under my desk. I found it, and for about a minute I stared blankly into its dirty bottom. It was made of white plastic and had bits of gum and other sticky trash at the bottom which had attracted dust over the years. *Breathe. What the fuck? I didn't have anything to drink last night. Oh shit!* There was one girl in my homeroom in high school who had gotten knocked up and the only thing I remembered about it, besides how cute her kid had been at graduation, was her frequent trips to the bathroom during homeroom. *Morning sickness? Shit.* I curled up in a ball and closed my eyes.

When I finally tried to sit up, I felt it again. I called my boss and got her voicemail.

"Hi, it's Freddie. I'm not feeling well this morning, so I won't be in. If I feel better by noon I will try to make it, but not likely. Will update you later. Thanks."

I fell back asleep. When I woke up again the sun was high in the sky, which helped rouse me. It was warm in my room even though I could hear the air conditioning running.

Now what? I picked up my phone and Googled "puked in the morning". All of the results confirmed my worst fear. The top ten results went something like, "How to alleviate morning sickness during pregnancy." I figured there was only one thing to do. I got up, pulled on shorts and a t-shirt and walked four blocks to the nearest pharmacy. I bought the most expensive pregnancy test on the shelf hoping that accuracy was directly correlated with cost. I figured this wasn't the time to be cheap.

I went home, drank some water, and read the instructions for the test as I waited and wondered, *Am I pregnant with my rapist's baby? What will I do if I am?* I couldn't watch the test as it developed.

I knew that there were girls in my sorority who had gotten abortions, but they never talked about it. On the other hand none of my friends had ever had a baby. Most of the girls in high school who had suffered from morning sickness had suddenly stopped showing up and then never came back. Their best friends wouldn't talk, but there were never a shortage of rumors, that they'd been sent away to some private all-girls school after they'd given birth, far away from the boyfriend that had caused the trouble in the first place.

I walked into the bathroom and stared at two very visible parallel pink lines. *Holy fuck. Now what?* I sat down on the toilet, and held my hand over my abdomen. *He hurt me and this is the result?* The pain of each of his violations came back and my stomach turned. All of a sudden I felt like I was falling. I turned and vomited into the trash can.

What am I going to do? The thing that is meant to be the most beautiful thing in the world, the result of an act of love, has been corrupted. It was one thing to be raped: it would always be a part of me and I would relive it over and over again, but I had started to believe, or at least hope, that eventually I would be able to move on. *They say time heals all. Have "they" been through this?*

Trying to move on was one thing, it was another thing entirely to have a part of him living inside me. A thing that could become a person. A person who I may love, but who may also, first and foremost, remind me of a monster. And now it was up to me, alone, to decide whether to end a life to avoid reliving the pain, humiliation, and guilt that someone else had caused.

I went for a long walk trying to clear my head, but all I could think about was whether or not the test was accurate. I waivered back and forth, at times trying to convince myself that I didn't really feel pregnant and maybe just had a mild flu, all the while, unable to shake the feeling in my gut that I was pregnant. I stopped by a clinic near campus. *I have to know.* They weren't busy since it was an early Friday afternoon in late-June. I peed in a cup, answered a few questions about the last time I'd had sex and told the nurse I would wait for the result when she asked.

I stared at a copy of a celebrity gossip magazine in the waiting room but my mind kept wandering back; *Could I really end a life? That goes against everything I believe in. How could I live with myself knowing that I ended an innocent life?* But I began to imagine giving birth to *his* child, and using my body to nourish and nurture *his* child after what he did to me. I was disgusted. *I can't do it. I can't have his baby.*

"Wynafreda Laurent!" A woman called from an open door. "Follow me".

Oh God, that must mean yes.

She led me back to an exam room and told me to sit down. She examined the paper in her hand again and compared it to the clipboard with my check-in form.

"Your test is positive," she said, trying to sound upbeat.

I shook my head.

"Would you like information about your options?" she asked, handing me a stack of pamphlets.

"No thank you. I don't have a choice. I know what has to be done."

"We have a counselor who you can see to discuss your options and make a follow-up appointment."

She handed me a business card with a woman's name printed above the title MATERNITY ADVOCATE.

I flipped through the pamphlets.

"Is there anything else I can do for you today?" she asked and I got the hint. I got up and shoved the pamphlets into my purse.

"No," I said. "Thank you." I walked back out to the waiting room, made an appointment to see the Maternity Advocate on Monday morning, and headed home.

I put my purse down in the living room, went to the kitchen, and took Vi's cognac out of the freezer. I poured a generous shot and threw it back. The burn of the alcohol was a welcome distraction. I poured another. The second was less surprising and went down a little easier. Like all young women, I knew that pregnant women aren't supposed to drink alcohol, on top of a long list of other dos and don'ts. *It's okay,* I told myself as I tried to numb my pain, *I can't keep you.* I held my hand over my womb and began to cry. *Stop! You have to be strong and figure out how to get through this.* I took a few deep breaths. *This isn't my fault. This isn't my fault. I shouldn't be punished for his sin.*

I checked my make-up and then walked next door. Adam and Colin were watching an old superhero movie. There were empty beer cans on the coffee table and Adam had a can in his hand. I sidled up next to him, took the beer out of his hand, tilted my head back and took a long sip. I laid my head against his chest and felt my breathing sync up with his. I nearly fell asleep when the ping of a new text message woke me up.

The text was from Ali: "Dinner's ready."

Dinner was on the table when I walked in.

"How was your day?" Vi asked.

"Fine. How was yours?"

"Good. Did you go to work?" she asked.

"No, I wasn't feeling very well this morning, but I feel better now."

"You didn't go to work because you didn't feel good, but you put on make-up?" Ali asked critically.

"Yes. I went for a walk once I started to feel better to get out of the house and I needed to run an errand."

She rolled her eyes.

"Sorry, I'm not part of your silent resistance," I said.

"How far would you go to please a man?" she asked.

"Stop it," Vi barked. Vi rarely got involved in our quarrels anymore, and very rarely stood up for me when she did. I caught her eye and smiled. Her timing was impeccable. *I can't let them know what happened. They'd be so disappointed in me, and so angry. They would want me to press charges and then the whole world would know what an idiot I was to fall for his bullshit.*

"So, I was thinking that this summer we could spend a week together up in Door County, just the three of us," Vi said.

"When is it not 'just the three of us'?" I asked.

"I know, isn't it great!" she said. "I thought it would be nice to get away from the city. Spend some time hiking, swimming, enjoying nature."

"Shouldn't you be looking for a man to do those things with?" I asked. "Or a woman, whatever floats your boat."

"I will date when, and if I choose to do so," Vi said, and got up from the table with her plate and empty wine glass.

"Why do you have to be so rude?" Ali asked.

"Me?"

"Yes," she said. "Are you drunk?"

"No. I just feel a little weak still."

"You smell like cheap beer," she said and got up from the table, following Vi to the kitchen.

Thursday morning rolled around and I went to see the Maternity Advocate, who looked to be in her mid to late 30s. She recounted her own experience of having an abortion a decade before, and then showed me pictures of her two young kids. She asked me about my age, occupation, life goals, and what I had heard about abortions. I told her that I did want to have a family when the time was right, but this time it wasn't right.

Then she asked about the father.

"I don't know him," I said.

She stared at me. "What do you mean you don't know him?"

"I was raped. By a stranger."

"I'm so sorry."

"Thank you," I said. "I'm clearly not keeping the child of a monster regardless of the options available, so can we please just get on with this?" My voice quivered.

"When was the start of your last period?" she asked.

I studied the calendar on my cell phone trying to remember. "It must have been around June 22nd."

She counted weeks on a paper calendar. "That's about ten, so you're too far along for a medication-induced abortion. You'd have to have a surgical abortion. We can do those here in the clinic. I'll have to confirm with the doctor, but if she agrees, we can schedule you to have the procedure."

"Okay."

She explained the intricacies of the in-clinic *procedure*, as she started calling it when she noticed that the word abortion made me uncomfortable.

"I want you to understand that you would remain awake throughout the procedure. You'll get an anesthetic, so you won't feel much, but you will be awake. Okay?"

Doesn't she get it...I have no choice. "Yeah, fine. I just want to get it over with, as soon as possible."

"I understand. If the doctor agrees then you'll get a call from our scheduler."

"Okay. Thank you."

I left the clinic and turned to walk home. About a block from the clinic I passed a young woman pushing a baby stroller. I told myself not to look, but as she got closer I couldn't help myself. I stared at the little baby swaddled in a bright pink blanket. The woman made eye contact and smiled proudly. *Oh my God. How can I go through with this?*

I paced around the house. *Maybe I should have gone in to work after the clinic. It would have given me something else to think about.*

A few hours later a woman from the clinic called. "Our first available is next Friday at ten a.m." she said.

I'll have to take the day off work. "Okay," I said.

"We recommend that you bring someone with you for support."

"Okay. Thanks." *I can't bring someone with me because I can't tell anyone what happened.* I thought about telling Adam but then worried that he might not believe me, or worse, he might believe me but think it was my fault. *No, I can't tell anyone. I'll just have to get through this alone.*

Friday, August 3, 2012

I thought about it nearly all day, every day, and dreamt about it at night in the few moments that I actually slept. I woke up early Friday morning and laid in bed, waiting for the existential debate and paralyzing emotions that had consumed me for the past two days to start again, but there was nothing. *I have no choice,* I thought. *It's my only option for survival.* The incongruent images of a beautiful baby that would need me, and the horror of raising *his* child were gone. For the first time since it happened I felt numb. I felt nothing. I got up and put on an old pair of dance pants and a hoodie. They had warned me that I may continue to bleed after the procedure and that I should stock up on thick maxi pads. I had bought the fattest pads I could find at the drug store and threw two into my purse.

A nurse called my name and I was taken back to a sterile exam room. She took my vitals and handed me a paper gown.

I sat on the table, shivering.

"I am going to do an ultrasound and then I will put in the IV. You'll start to feel a little drowsy and it will also reduce any pain you may experience," she said.

She pulled the ultrasound machine over to the table and pulled the paper gown back. Once she had the image up she asked if I wanted to see it.

"No," I said. *I have no choice.*

She put the machine away and hung a bag of fluid on a rack. I never liked needles and began to tremble. She spoke softly and tried to soothe me. She asked about school, what I was studying, and how my finals had gone. I felt the needle as it was forced into my vein. She covered it with tape and advised me to close my eyes and relax, as she placed a heating pad on my stomach. I tried to relax but I couldn't stop thinking about him. *He must pay for this; for everything he's put me through. How? I can't sue him. I declined an investigation. How can I use everything I know about him to my advantage? How can I con him into giving me his money? Women get alimony in a divorce. What if I married him and then got a divorce. That's crazy! It would never work!*

Another young woman came in. She told me that she would stay with me throughout the procedure to ensure that I was okay, and that I could ask her anything I wanted because she'd been through this same procedure herself. My fear and anxiety began to melt away. *The drugs are working.*

An older woman in a white coat came in with the nurse. They asked me to move toward the end of the table and put my feet in the cold metal stirrups. The doctor warned me before inserting the cold metal speculum. I felt a sharp pinch. *How many times do I have to be violated because of him?*

She pulled a machine on a cart over to the side of the bed. It had multiple tubes hanging from it and looked like a vacuum cleaner from the 80s.

Despite the sedative and the local anesthetic I began to feel the pain that I had been warned about. I had never had bad cramps during my period, and for the first time I actually felt genuinely bad for Ali and all of the other women I knew who complained of bad cramps. The vacuum pulled at my insides. I looked around at the other women in the room and then back at the machine. I knew they were there for support, but I was suddenly embarrassed. *This is the kind of thing that no one is supposed to know about and here they are, witnesses to my shame.* I imagined my insides being sucked out and moving through the tubes. My unborn child being sucked into the vacuum. I felt sick. It was as if the young nurse read my mine.

"Shallow breaths," she said calmly. "It will be over soon."

I was grateful that the procedure itself was quick. She couldn't have been digging around in there for more than fifteen minutes. I felt an overwhelming sense of relief when the doctor announced that it was over.

Slowly I started to feel better. The doctor came back in and told me that I'd done well and the procedure was a success. The nurse handed me a packet of papers with instructions on post-recovery.

"You can get dressed now. Please call us if you have any questions or experience excessive bleeding," she said.

They all got up to leave. I touched the young woman's hand. "Thank you," I said, and tears began to well up in my eyes. She smiled. "Of course," she said. "You're welcome."

I swung my legs to the floor and stood up. My head felt like it weighed a thousand pounds, my heart thumped in my chest, and the room was suddenly covered in blurry white dots. I turned to sit back down and saw a few small crimson spots on the white paper where I'd been laying. It reminded me of the stained sheets on the bed in the frat house. My stomach tightened, my chest clenched, and the only trash can in the room was covered with a revolving top. I heaved what little there was in my stomach from the night before into the sink in the corner of the room. As my body wretched the cramps came back, and the pain was more intense than before. That was it, there was nothing left inside me to purge. I laid back down on the bed on top of the blood. *Fuck! Will this ever really be over?*

I was woken up by the nurse touching my arm gently. "How are you feeling now?" she asked. "You did faint so I want you to stay put for a few more minutes."

"I might need some more pain killers," I said.

I laid on the table, staring up at the ceiling tiles, which were old and yellow, waiting for the pain killers to kick in. *What a sad place for life to end.*

As I walked home I wondered at the resolve it would take to suck life out of women all day long. I was equal parts horrified and thankful for the person who could bring themselves to do it. Back at the house, I fell asleep in front of the t.v.

A loud thud, followed by the clang of the metal mail slot woke me up. I had slept longer than I thought, but Vi and Ali wouldn't be back for a while. I took a deep breath, relieved to be alone. Out of nowhere it hit me and I began to cry. Grief consumed me. My body shook and I buried my face in the couch and wailed. I wasn't crying for the fetus that had been pulled from my body, or for the child who I would never know, I was grieving for everything he had put me through. I finally allowed myself to feel the full weight of the pity that had consumed me since that night. I grieved for the young woman who I was, who had lost so much. I grieved because that night had changed everything and I would never be the same. I could no longer go through life, innocently believing that I was safe when I was out. *If this could happen to me, it could happen to anyone, anywhere. If I wasn't safe that night, no woman is ever safe.* The thought was terrifying. *How will I ever feel safe again? How could I bring a child into such a fucked up world? What if I have a baby girl someday and this happens to her?*

The pain in my abdomen came back. I hobbled to the kitchen and took more Ibuprofen and grabbed a heating pad. Back on the couch I fell asleep with a blanket over me.

"Oh Freddie, what's wrong?" Vi said as she walked in and spotted me on the couch. "Are you sick again?"

"Yeah, I wasn't well this morning, but I'm feeling a little better now."

"Do you have the flu?"

"Must be," I lied. *Vi can't know what happened.*

"Is there anything I can get you?" she asked. "Ginger Ale?"

"No. I think I'll just take a warm bath, but thank you."

I pulled myself off the couch and retreated to the bathroom. I washed and rinsed and washed again as steam filled the room. In the shower, my mind wandered back to him: to images of him returning after work to a large suburban house, welcomed by a picture perfect wife and kids, sitting down to dinner. *What if I convince him I'm someone I'm not? Can I make him believe that I love him? Can I survive being close to him again? Can I survive being intimate with him long enough to take everything he values? Will he* recognize me or can I deceive him? Will the end justify the means? Will it be worth it?

THE PLAY

Friday, September 9, 2016
Hell's Kitchen

Nearly a full year had passed since our first date, and I had grown almost comfortable in Nate's company. There were still moments when the memories of that night in the frat house came rushing back, triggered by a song or a whiff of the whiskey we'd been drinking, but by buying him expensive cologne and deodorants as presents I'd gotten him to give up the overpowering scents that triggered my reactions more than anything. Between the medication and systematic desensitization through exposure, I'd managed to be intimate with Nate in ways I'd never imagined possible. I wasn't blind to who he was or what he'd done, and I never allowed myself to slip into love or infatuation despite our intimacy, but I had achieved tolerance. Tolerance that allowed me to put on a convincing performance. A performance that he seemed to enjoy, as long as I minded my own business and didn't ask questions when he worked late or went out with the guys a few nights a month.

Nate texted me around two thirty, "Dinner at Hugo's. 7pm. I'll pick you up."

How did he get a table at Hugo's on a Friday at such short notice? Has he been planning this? For the first time in a while I felt excited, giddy even. Hugo's had always been a bit of a joke between us. Consistently written up as one of the top five restaurants in New York for the last couple of years, I'd never been. It was expensive and almost impossible to get into, especially on weekends. It was where Nate took his most important business partners. He always said it was a bit too conventional to be getting so much attention. Instead, we often went to Deux Cochons, a little French bistro in Seaport that Nate claimed as a hidden gem, every bit as good and never crowded. I'd tease him in response that he must not think I was worth taking to Hugo's. He said he'd take me there when the time was right. I'd been dropping subtle hints over the past month or two about wanting to be engaged. *Is tonight the night?*

I called the blowout salon down the street to see if I could get in last minute. The woman on the phone said they were booked solid, but if I got there soon and waited she might be able to squeeze me in. I told my boss I didn't feel well and went to the salon to take my place in line. After about an hour, a stylist motioned me back to an empty station.

"We had a cancellation," she said. "Must be your lucky day!"

I claimed the empty chair, thrilled that things seemed to be lining up perfectly. As I watched the stylist work, I reassured myself that tonight had to be the night. *I've made so many sacrifices to get to this point. We have to be married for this to work.*

A few blocks away I snuck in for a manicure. *Picture perfect nails for a picture perfect engagement!*

Back at my apartment, I rummaged through my fancy make-up bag. Mostly full of the special giveaway items that came with the high-end make-up I had shelled out for since college. I'd returned the overpriced eye shadows and mascaras, since my savings hardly amounted to more than the price of a round-trip ticket on a budget airline, but kept the free samples for just the right occasion. I applied fake lashes and more eye liner than usual, just enough to look fabulous in case the evening included a photo op. *Tonight has to be the night!*

A pewter, sequined midi skirt I'd gotten at a high end resale shop near my apartment went perfectly with a silk camisole and nude strappy sandals. I put on some diamond studs that I'd gotten at a flea market and grabbed a secondhand designer clutch to match.

We pulled up to Hugo's and Nate tossed his keys to the valet. As I walked around the back of the car I realized how underdressed he seemed for the occasion. Dark jeans, dress shirt, and dinner jacket, but no tie. He looked great, but I immediately felt silly. *Maybe he isn't planning to propose.* Nate opened the door and followed me into the restaurant.

The maître d' nodded and my excitement built as he led us past tables full of finely dressed couples. Eventually, he stopped and motioned toward two seats at the bar. I looked at Nate in disbelief. *He's definitely not proposing. How much longer can I keep this up? Will I ever get justice?*

My frustration must have been unmistakable.

"Oh, come on. Don't be such a princess. What kind of table did you think I could get with a day's notice?" Nate said.

One day's notice isn't how you plan an engagement.

"We are eating here, or we're leaving. Your choice," he said.

I hopped up on the bar stool, pulling at my skirt to avoid an inappropriate reveal, and glanced around the dining room. Admiring eyes watched, and I basked in the adoration.

The bartender smiled as he placed a crystal tea light between us. It sparkled in the dim light and caught the face of Nate's wristwatch. More artwork than machinery, featuring an open face that exposed the complex inner workings of the vintage timepiece.

Nate ordered the most expensive bottle of champagne on the menu, perhaps trying to make amends. The waiter popped the bottle in front of us and made a show of adeptly containing the bubbles. I watched Nate carefully, anticipating each subtle twist of the body, each slight turn of the head, hoping that I was wrong, and any minute he would leap off his chair, get down on one knee, and deliver the kind of proposal worth sharing, but he stayed put. By the second glass of champagne, I had almost forgotten that I was upset that we were sitting at the bar. The bartender kept his distance and we were seated facing each other across the corner. It was almost cozy.

Nate watched as I ate, compelling me to enjoy my share before picking at the food on my plate. After dinner Nate sipped a whiskey and poured the rest of the bottle of champagne into my glass. By the time we left, my head was spinning in that pleasant way, making the lights on the street look brighter and everything sparkle.

As the valet brought Nate's car around, the angel on my shoulder said it was a bad idea to get in. He'd had a few drinks.

"I think I'll take a cab." I said.

"No, come on," he said.

"Thank you for dinner."

"Come on. I'll take you home." He walked toward me. Standing in front of me, he bent forward and took my face in his hands tenderly. *Oh God, not here, not like this, please!*

"Wyn," he said patiently, "I need you to get in the car. I have a surprise. Please don't ruin it."

Tonight is the night!

I got into the car despite my reservations. *I need him to do it tonight.* Nate turned the key in the ignition and revved the engine a little before he popped into first. I put the seat back and closed my eyes.

Nate squeezed my thigh and I realized that I'd started to doze off.

"Wake up," he whispered in my ear, the same way Vi had done at the end of long road trips, when it was time to go into the house and get ready for bed.

"Where are we?" I mumbled.

We were parked in front of a sparkling wall of glass and a doorman held the car door, waiting for me to alight.

I followed Nate into a grand foyer and over to an elevator. He pushed "P" and waited.

"Where are we going?"

"I knew I should have blindfolded you. You're too nosy."

"Sorry."

The elevator doors opened into a large, open living/dining space, punctuated by a large wall of windows with a view of the Empire State Building and Central Park in the distance.

"Wow!"

"I thought you'd like it."

"What is this?"

"Our home."

"You bought a condo for us?"

"Yeah."

"*You* bought *us* a home. I thought that was something couples did together."

"I thought this would be a nice surprise."

Wait, is he finally asking me to move in with him? What's going on?

"It is." I forced a smile. "But you know I don't want to live together until we're engaged."

"Yeah, I know."

Nate opened a door and led me out onto a large balcony with sweeping views of the city. A small, round, bistro table with a bottle of champagne and two long-stemmed glasses looked strangely out of place. All of a sudden, as if it were a movie set, music began playing over outdoor speakers. *My favorite jazz song. The one I learned to play my senior year of high school as a solo for the annual concert.*

Nate took my hand and kneeled down in front of me.

"Wyn Laurent," he said, "you complement me, like no one else ever has. You make me happier than I've ever been before. I would like to build a life with you, here and wherever else life takes us." He paused. "I love you. Will you be my wife?"

Holy shit! That's the first time he's ever used the L-word! In the year I'd known Nate I'd learned how cautiously he approached every decision in his life. I knew that he analyzed every decision and viewed every interaction and commitment as a transaction. *I've got him right where I want him! He's totally committed.*

He waited expectantly and I watched him kneeling in front of me, savoring the fact that I was finally getting what I wanted. *I am in control now. One step closer.*

"Yes," I said, smiling.

He stood up and yelled, "She said yes!"

Raucous cheering erupted and lights flicked on. A group of our closest friends was on the other side of a large glass wall, each with a glass of champagne in hand.

Nate swept me up in his arms and spun around. He kissed me and the cheers grew louder. There was a bright flash, and I instinctively turned toward it. A photographer appeared in front of us and I smiled for the camera.

Nate put me down and grabbed the bottle of champagne off the table. He shook it a bit and pointed it away from us. The loud pop of the bottle echoed off the glass. He held the bottle in the air and let a shower of champagne mist cover us. We were quickly surrounded by friends, mostly our joint friends, which meant Nate's friends and a couple of women I had met since moving to New York. I absorbed the congratulations and accompanying hugs and kisses humbly. As the crowd began to disperse, I looked up and saw Adam standing about ten feet behind everyone else, watching me, smiling, but I knew him well enough to know that his happiness was contrived. I ran toward him and he wrapped his arms around me. As Adam held me, I could feel people watching us.

He whispered in my ear, "Congratulations, if this is what you really want."

My elation vanished. My heart sank. *I can't change what's already happened. I have no choice.*

"Thanks, it is," I lied.

"I'm worried about you," he said, and let go.

I wandered back to the group as nonchalantly as possible. *Nate must have invited him.* As far as Nate was concerned (and he'd never seemed to be too concerned), Adam was simply a really good childhood friend of mine. A welcome reminder of home in an unfamiliar city.

The music transitioned to pop and we danced and drank. After a deluge of congratulations and best wishes, our guests slowly showed themselves out. When the condo was empty, Nate pulled me into the master suite, which had only a large bed with solid metal posts. *What does he have in store for me now?* My heart raced, but he undressed and got in bed without incident.

I got in bed. He pulled me close and quickly fell asleep. I laid next to him, surprised he hadn't wanted to consummate our engagement. I thought back to the very first time we met and how much had changed since then. *I'm finally in control. This is going to work!* I curled up and fell asleep too.

I woke up alone in the large white bedroom, which was empty except for the king-sized bed. There were no shades or curtains to block the morning sun illuminating the cavernous space. It was so bright I wondered how I'd slept in at all.

I took in the sweeping view of Manhattan on my way to the kitchen, where I found Nate propped against the counter reading the morning paper. Coffee and pastries were getting cold. I leafed through the sections that he had pulled out, found *Fashion*, and leaned against the counter next to him, picking sparingly at a blueberry muffin.

"How'd you sleep?" he asked without looking up.

"Fine, you?"

"Great."

We sat next to each other reading. After a while I broke the silence; "I thought we were going to live in Greenwich?"

"And I thought I'd be nice to have a place downtown, since that's where we both work."

"I really don't want to live in the City long-term."

"I didn't say we couldn't have a place in the suburbs too. If that's what you really want."

"It is," I said. "I really like the area around Greenwich. I think we would be really happy there. It seems like a great place to raise a family."

"Yeah, someday."

Crap. I need him to agree to be in Connecticut now, not someday. I'm not sure any of this works or is worth it if we aren't married and domiciled in Connecticut.

A few days later, while Nate was out, I skimmed through the photos from our engagement party. Curled up on the couch with my laptop, I examined each of them carefully, and spent what felt like hours culling the seventy plus images down to the top ten and then finally to my three favorites. I created a Facebook post with the best photos that simply read, "I said 'Yes!'" and hit upload. When I checked half an hour later, I had almost 500 likes.

I called Vi.

"Hey Freddie!"

"Hey Vi."

"How are you? I'm so glad you called," she said.

"I'm fine. How are you?"

"Great. Ali and Soren are over helping me get the early leaves in the yard bagged for pick-up."

"Do you have a minute?"

"Sure. What's up?"

"I'm engaged," I said.

"What? I didn't even know you were dating someone special!"

"Yeah, I didn't want to jinx it," I lied.

"How long have you two been together?"

"It's been about a year now, I guess."

"You've been dating someone for a year and you didn't tell me or your sister?"

"I'm sorry. I kept meaning to tell you, but I didn't want you to get all worked up about it, in case it didn't last," I lied.

"All worked up! Who me? Why would I get worked up?"

"Because I know how you feel about marriage."

"Freddie, just because I'm not married doesn't mean I think you shouldn't get married. You are a little young, but if you are happy and he's the right guy for you, then congratulations," she said. "I'm very happy for you."

"Thank you. I'm sorry I didn't tell you earlier," I said.

Silence permeated the space between us. Finally, she broke it, "What's his name? Where's he from? What does he do?"

"His name is Nate. He's from Connecticut. He has his own business. He's really successful actually."

"Great, I can't wait to hear more about him!"

"Yeah, of course. You'll have to meet him next time you're in New York."

"Of course!"

"How are you? What's going on at home?" I asked.

"I'm thinking I might finally sell the house next spring, so I'm starting to take inventory of what needs to be cleaned up or fixed around here."

"Oh wow. Where do you think you'll move?"

"I'm thinking maybe downtown."

"Chicago?"

"Yeah, I have a few good friends downtown because of work, and I think it might be nice to be downtown before I get too old and you girls stick me in a retirement home in the 'burbs."

"Hah, you're not that old!"

"Not yet, but I will be. Hey, I gotta go, Ali's yelling for me. I'm sorry. Congrats on your engagement, Freddie!"

"Thanks!"

THE PLAY

Saturday, September 17, 2016

Chelsea

Nate was already gone, presumably at his office or the gym, when I woke up on Saturday morning. We'd begun ordering furniture for the condo, but it still wasn't quite ready to be lived in, so most of my stuff was back at the apartment. I ran a few errands on my way back. I hadn't entirely finished putting away my summer wardrobe and the weather had started to change. I pulled two large plastic storage bins out from under my bed and began swapping out summer clothes for soft wool sweaters, long pants, and a variety of colored tights. I got a bar stool from the kitchen and perched myself on top, reaching to carefully swap out the clothes on the top shelf of my tiny closet. I didn't hear the door to my room open as Nate snuck up behind me.

"Irresistible!" he barked from right underneath me.

My heart jumped. The stool jilted. I flew up into the air. He caught me and held on tight. I tried to wriggle free, my adrenaline pumped aggressively. He held me tight and kissed me. When he pulled back, I looked him directly in the eyes. It was clear that he thought he was being romantic. Adrenaline coursed through my body and my heart beat wildly. *Will I ever feel safe again?* I struggled against him and finally wriggled free. I hurried out of the bedroom.

"What's wrong?" he yelled after me.

My roommate, Jordan, was curled up on the couch in our small living room.

"You okay?" she asked as I ran out the front door.

I struggled to breathe. It felt like the wind had been knocked out of me. *I have to get out. I can't do this!*

"Fine," I yelled back, as I ran out the door, down the stairs and out onto the street. I could feel him close behind me.

I kept walking.

"Hey! Stop!" he yelled.

I turned around. "You scared me," I said, crossing my arms to stop them shaking.

He smiled. "Hey, it was nothing. Come here."

He held his arms out.

I have no choice. I have to calm down. I took a deep breath.

"You're stronger than you think," I said.

He nodded and pulled me toward him.

"It's fine. It was nothing." He wrapped his arms around me.

Relax. Breathe.

I let him hold me.

This is it. I can't fuck this up and go back to thinking about him every waking minute, wondering where he is and what he's doing.

After what felt like a long time, I pulled my face away from his chest and looked up. "I've been thinking. I can ask my mom for a loan for the wedding," I said.

The corners of his lips curled slightly. "Don't be silly, my money is your money," he said.

"But the woman's family traditionally pays."

"What is this? 1920? I have more than either of us need."

I smiled. "Okay."

"I'll take care of everything, don't worry." He squeezed me against his chest. "Here. I ordered this for you."

He handed me a black American Express card.

"Oh my gosh! Thank you." I admired my name in embossed silver across the bottom of the card. I leaned forward and planted a soft kiss on his lips.

He held my hand as we walked back to my apartment.

"It's going to be difficult to find a church with a pastor that we both like in time for the wedding," I said. "I've heard that churches book up years in advance in New York City."

"Mmmm hmmm. We'll figure it out."

"There is one thing I've been meaning to talk to you about," he said when we were back in my room.

"Sure. What is it?"

He turned and pulled a legal sized envelope out of his leather shoulder bag.

"Look," he said, "I love you."

That's the second time he's said it! I checked myself and smiled subtly.

He continued, "If you want to quit your job tomorrow, stay home, have kids, and never work again, no problem."

He paused to let me appreciate his generous offer, and then continued, "But, a man has to protect what he has worked hard to earn."

I took the envelope and pulled out a stack of papers. A fancy gold clip held them together. The cover page was almost entirely blank with block lettering in the center that read:

Ellis Prenuptial Agreement
Sterns, Morgan, and Parker, LLC
Esteemed Partners in Law
September 7, 2016

You cheap bastard! I should have known. "Looks like some enthralling bedtime reading," I teased, trying my best to produce a natural, casual smile.

"You'll sign it, right?" he asked.

"Today?"

"Why not?"

Stall. "Because my mom's a lawyer and if there's one extremely boring, but useful lesson I've learned from her, it's that you never know what's hidden in the fine print."

"Don't you trust me?" he asked tenderly.

"Of course I do. I love you. But a woman has to protect herself too. Plus, there are some things that are important to me too."

"Like?"

"Like Greenwich."

"Ugh, what is it with you and Greenwich?"

"I just like it. I thought when we got married we would move there together."

I put my arms around his waist. "Once you sell your condo, maybe we can go look at a few houses over there, together."

"Yeah, I guess."

"Thank you."

I slid the prenup back into the envelope.

"What do you want to do tonight?" he said.

"I don't know. I told Jordan I'd go out with her and the girls tonight."

"I was thinking we could stay in. Watch a movie. You don't need to go out with them again, do you?"

"I haven't been out with them in weeks," I said.

"I thought you wanted to be with me."

Ugh, yes, but does being with you really mean I can't go out with my friends anymore?

"Okay, fine, I'll be back to the condo as soon as I finish up here," I said. *Whatever it takes to seal this deal.*

"Don't be too late. I'm pretty tired from work this week."

"Okay."

He left and I picked up the prenup. *I have to figure this out. Maybe I should get a lawyer, or at least ask Vi to read it.*

I called Vi from my room.

"Hey, Freddie!"

"Hey Vi."

"What's up? How are you?"

"I'm okay, but I actually have a favor to ask."

"Yeah, of course. What is it?"

"Well, Nate surprised me with a prenup. I just started reading it and it's full of lawyer gobbledygook. Can you take a look for me? I know this isn't your area of expertise but you'll at least understand generally what it means. I don't want to sign something that puts me at a significant disadvantage."

"Wow, he must be doing really well already. What does he do?"

"He is, I guess. He owns a supplements business. Will you read it for me?"

"Sure, of course, Freddie. Send it to me and I'll take a look in the next few days."

"Thank you. I will."

Work was slow and I found myself worrying about the prenup. After work I would pick it up and try to make sense of the legalese. I texted Vi, "Any luck with the prenup?"

She called a few days later.

"I read the agreement," Vi said.

"Great! What do you think?"

"Most of it is just legal jargon that doesn't amount to too much. I ran the important stuff by a friend of mine who has written a lot of these."

"Thank you so much. I know how busy you are."

"Freddie, this is important stuff. It's your future."

"It is. Do you think I should sign it?"

"Well, most of it is fine, immaterial, but there's one thing you may want to ask for."

"What?"

"The way this is written, adultery is specifically excluded as grounds for alimony, so if he cheats on you and the relationship ends, you get nothing. Are you sure you want to be married to someone who would include that kind of clause in a prenup?"

"Hmmm. That's not like him," I lied. "I'll ask him about it."

"Well, if you're going to sign this thing, we think it would be in your best interest to ask for a few other clauses to be altered as well, essentially to make sure he is held accountable should he ever transgress."

Perfect. "Seems fair, thank you so much."

"I'll send over my mark-ups this afternoon."

"Thank you."

"Love you."

"Love you too."

It had been a full week since Nate had given me the prenup. I hadn't brought it up again and he hadn't either. I dreaded the idea of confronting him about the infidelity clause, but I knew I had to do it eventually. I texted Nate, "Dinner tonight? Need to talk."

"Sure. Where?"

"Foglia D'alloro's?"

"I'm tired of Italian. Marigold. 7."

"Okay."

It was early so I walked to Greenwich Village. I wasn't exactly sure what I was looking for, but had that lucky feeling. I rifled through the racks at a couple of thrift shops and then meandered back to the East Village. On the way, I popped into a secondhand book store and made my way to the back where there were a number of large, water stained cardboard banker's boxes marked "Vogue". I was surprised to find most of the 80s shoved haphazardly into three or four boxes, in no particular order. After about an hour, I made off with May and June of '82, and June and July of '83 for a total of ten bucks.

I stopped at a small wine shop and paid thirty-five dollars for a nice bottle of Cabernet Sauvignon that the guy at the counter recommended. Marigold was one of the few BYOs left in the neighborhood and I didn't want to show up empty-handed.

Back in my little room at the apartment, I spent the afternoon sprawled out on my bed studying the dresses, flower arrangements, and cake designs in the vintage magazines. It was a guilty pleasure that I didn't want anyone to see, even my roommates.

I got to Marigold a little before seven and wasn't surprised when the hostess confirmed that Nate had called ahead for a table. The restaurant was small and there was no bar, so the hostess seated me alone. I pulled the bottle of wine out of my purse and set it on the table.

"Freddie?" I turned in my seat. Adam was standing to my left.

"Hey! I told you not to call me that anymore." My look implored him: *Please!*

As I stood up I noticed a woman close behind him and stopped to extend my hand. She was classically beautiful, her ash blonde hair was long, with platinum highlights. She had bright blue eyes and perfectly tanned skin. *Wow! She looks exactly like all those women Nate used to date.*

Adam stepped aside. "This is Julia. Julia, this is Fred…"

I cut in, "Wyn! Adam still likes to call me by my childhood nickname, but I really wish he wouldn't. Please call me Wyn."

"Nice to meet you, Wyn," she said.

She was quite a bit taller than me and very thin. The kind of thin that looks a bit painful but is difficult not to admire.

"I'll never call you that," Adam muttered to me.

"Please," I begged.

Nate spotted us across the restaurant and walked over with the hostess in tow.

"Who's this?" he asked as Julia turned toward him.

"Julia," she said before I could introduce her. She offered her hand confidently to Nate and he held it gently in his.

"Julia, this is my fiancé, Nate," I said, relieved to not have to use the word "boyfriend". There was something so childish about that word; I'd always hated it.

Their eyes locked and they smiled.

"Are you just arriving too?" Nate asked.

"We are," she said.

"Why don't you join us?" Nate said.

I looked at Adam. He smiled approvingly.

Julia turned to the hostess. "You don't mind, do you?"

"Of course not," she mumbled.

There weren't two open tables near each other, but she enlisted a waitress and they rearranged a few things until we had a table for four. Julia and Adam sat on one side, while Nate pulled out the chair across from Adam for me.

Julia motioned toward my left hand and admired my engagement ring.

"How did you two meet?"

"Online," I said.

She smiled and nodded approvingly.

"So many people do these days," she said politely, but I sensed an underlying condescension.

"How long have you been engaged?" she asked.

"Oh just a couple of weeks," I said. "You and Adam must have met after that, because I don't remember meeting you the night Nate proposed."

"Ah, it was a few months ago, wasn't it?" She turned to Adam and he nodded.

"Oh." I was genuinely surprised and turned to Adam. "Why didn't you bring her to our engagement? Surely, Nate told you it was plus one."

He rolled his eyes subtly and turned to her. "You were busy that night. Out for a bachelorette party I think, right Sweetie?" Adam's mom and dad had always used pet names for each other. I knew it made his skin crawl, and he knew that I admired it, having grown up with a single mom who never dated and was not overly affectionate.

"Oh yeah, must have been Ashley's bachelorette," she said.

Adam nodded.

"Where did you two meet?" I asked.

"At the gym," she replied. I tried to imagine her thin frame doing anything at the gym.

Adam directed his comment to Nate, "I couldn't take my eyes off her and eventually she noticed."

Barf!

We had three courses and shared three bottles of wine.

"So, what do you do, Julia?" Nate asked. It annoyed me that he used her name. I had observed over the past year that his penchant for remembering names seemed to be directly related to how important he thought someone was, or might become to him in the future. He remembered names adeptly in business settings, while failing repeatedly to remember the names of my friends or my colleagues whom he'd met more than once. *I knew she was his type!*

"I blog about fashion, interior design, and style in general. And cover fashion shows when I can, of course, and all the important social events in the City."

"You're a blogger?" I asked.

She turned to me and smiled. "And a vlogger."

"Oh, I didn't realize that was a career." *God, I sound like my mother.*

"Really? It totally is these days. You're a bit behind if you've never heard of lifestyle blogging or influencers," she said. "Some people make really good money at it."

"Yeah, of course," I said.

"Julia started doing freelance photography for events, covering the high-brow social scene for a suburban glossy magazine. Isn't that right, Sweets? Then she realized that she could cover the events herself on her blog." Adam admired her as he spoke.

"I always thought I'd be an entrepreneur," she said. "I just didn't realize that I would be so successful in my twenties. It usually takes years to build a business, but of course the Internet has changed that."

"So true," Nate said.

Julia reached into her purse and pulled out two glossy, pink business cards that said simply "Julia Weber" in a white script on the front and on the back "JuliaWeber.com".

I looked over at Nate, who was staring at her approvingly. *Ugh!* When the last drop of wine was finally gone I leapt out of my chair.

"Guess we should get going," I said.

Nate followed my lead and thanked them for joining us for dinner.

When we got out into the street he grabbed my hand. "Where're you running off to so fast?"

I turned toward him. "Nowhere, just needed some fresh air."

"Are you okay?"

"Yeah, I'm fine."

"You're upset. I'm sorry for inviting them to eat with us. Sort of crashed our date, didn't they? And you said you needed to talk tonight, didn't you?"

I rolled my eyes. "Yeah, I did. I finished reviewing the agreement you gave me and I have a few exceptions." I reached into my purse and grabbed the copy with Vi's edits.

"I still can't believe you think you need this, but since you do, here are my edits." I handed him the pages. "I assume you will want to talk through them with your lawyer."

He took my hand and pulled me toward him. "Hey, I didn't mean to offend you with this. I love you."

That's three times! "Nate, I understand that when we get married we will be entering into a legal arrangement from different economic positions, and I understand that not all relationships last, but I can't be held to a higher standard than you just because you're rich."

He looked perplexed, as if he had no idea what I was talking about.

"Just talk through my revisions with your lawyer and let me know what you think," I said.

His tone shifted. "And then what? We'll negotiate the terms of our future? Should I have my lawyer call yours?"

"I guess so. You're the one who put legal terms around our future. You're the one who commissioned a legal document to give yourself a get out of jail free card. Marriage is a risk for everyone who commits themselves to it. It isn't easy, but it is God's will. If you get an adultery clause then why bother at all? If you're so sure you'll fail, why even try?"

"It's just that I've seen things fall apart. With my parents. It's not that I don't trust you…" he paused. "I don't know. Maybe, I don't trust myself. Maybe that is my problem."

I shrugged. *He has to want to marry me. I don't win unless he does.* "Nate, this is hard for me too. I've been let down before too, but marriage is about standing by your partner when things get tough. It's about believing in them and supporting them no matter what. It's about making sacrifices for the relationship and growing together. Becoming better through each other's support and faith in God."

"That's why I love you," he said, and kissed my lips.

As we walked the three blocks back to our condo, I had a hard time keeping my exhilaration in check. *This is going to work! He does want to marry me!*

We greeted the doorman and took the elevator up to the penthouse. Nate grabbed his laptop, clearly not in the mood to talk, so I grabbed mine too. I opened a browser and typed www.JuliaWeber. com into the address bar. Across the banner, in the same script that was on her business card, it read, "Julia Weber, fashion + style". On the left side was a table of contents that listed the titles of her newest blog posts: "Best Boho Bargains", "A Fortnight of Fashion", and "Style for Sarcoma". To the right was a professional photo obviously staged to look natural, unplanned, but her hair and make-up were perfect. She had on a black sequin dress, low-cut to show a bit of cleavage. A beautiful diamond necklace sparkled just above her cleavage. All the marks of a formal party were clear in the backdrop: a glass chandelier, an immaculate curving staircase, but they were far enough away from their subject to be unidentifiable. *She certainly is beautiful.*

I scrolled through the dates associated with the older posts until I found the earliest, and then skimmed through the posts one by one. She'd started blogging on a summer abroad program between her junior and senior years of college, while studying at the Fashion Institute in Milan. Her blog seemingly began as a chronicle of her time abroad, primarily as a wannabe fashion critic and designer where she wrote about new trends and posted her own amateur sketches. There were also photos of her in beautiful clothing, with immaculate, famous backdrops. A blood red vintage Armani gown rippling in a light wind on a sunny day on the Spanish Steps, surrounded by young underdressed American tourists. It looked as if, in the beginning the blog was simply a way for her family and friends to stay up-to-date on her adventures, but over the course of the summer, her followers had multiplied, evidenced by the number of likes and comments on her first handful of posts compared to later posts: 50, 200, to 500, and then more than 5,000. All reasonable for a college student who likely already had thousands of friends on Facebook and perhaps more followers on Instagram. I skimmed the more recent posts, some of which had garnered more than 100,000 likes, and thousands of comments, or shares. In the most recent, she posed with three members of the New York Yankees, decked out in uniform with glasses of champagne. The subtitle read, "Batting .500 with the Yankees to raise money for Making the Match", a local charity for sick children. One of the more famous players had even 'liked' the photo and commented; "Always great to see you out for a good cause!"

She was apparently something of a B-List celebrity, in New York at least. *She looks perfect.* I reminded myself: *no one is perfect.*

Over time, Julia seemed to have realized the potential of the blog as a tool to market herself and appeared to enjoy the attention. Her posts revealed that by the time she graduated she had earned enough money in sponsorships and product placements to forgo a serious job search and instead spend the summer in Paris and Saint Tropez. The subjects of her posts expanded to feature the adorable Pomeranian she met while taking her morning coffee, and the attractive young man she spent an evening smoking with on the left bank of the Seine. From there, her following had grown and she began to diversify into makeup and fitness clothing. *How is this a job?*

I heard my phone pop. A Facebook icon appeared at the top of the screen. I clicked on it. "Friend Request: Julia Weber". *That was quick.*

"Have you ever had a threesome?" Nate asked as we were getting ready for bed.

What?!? "No. Why? Have you?"

"Yeah, I have."

"Oh, really?"

"Yeah, it was unforgettable."

"Hmmm."

"I was just wondering whether you'd ever be open to something like that." He watched me carefully, waiting for my reaction.

Jesus, how far is he going to go to make me prove my devotion to him? Two can play at that game!

"Maybe. Let me think about it," I said.

He smiled.

"Oh, I booked a few showings for us next weekend to look at houses in Greenwich," I lied. "Are you free?"

"Next weekend?"

"Yeah, Saturday, but I can change them to Sunday if that's better."

"No, Saturday should work."
"Great."

I went back to my apartment on Sunday to do laundry and get organized for the week. It seemed silly to keep my room in the apartment now that we were engaged and I spent most of my time at our condo, but I liked knowing that I still had my own space.

Back in my room I called a trendy real estate office and asked to be set up with an agent for some showings in the Greenwich area the next weekend. I specified that my husband and I were looking for a large house on the water for our soon to be growing family, and that price was no object. Then I grabbed all of the bridal magazines and laid them out across my bed. From a number of different dresses, I borrowed elements and sketched my dream wedding dress on the back of an envelope. I practiced a few more times on scratch paper and then pulled some scraps of velum out of a college notebook. Once I was satisfied I called and made an appointment at Matilda's. Matilda was known for two things: the A-List stars who swore by her work, and her exorbitant prices, which was more than enough to convince me that she was the only dressmaker in the city I could trust with the job.

THE PLAY

Saturday, October 1, 2016

Chelsea

It had been nearly a week since I'd given Nate the edits to the prenup. I kept telling myself that perhaps his lawyer was just really busy, but I couldn't shake a nagging feeling that maybe he was getting cold feet. I decided to keep my mouth shut, knowing how he would react to being pressured. *Best to be patient and wait for the right opportunity.*

Nate and I met our real estate agent at her office in Midtown. She handed us a few print-outs and loaded us into her expensive sedan. We made awkward small talk on the drive out to Greenwich. The first house we visited had been fancy once, you could tell by the grand entrance and the oversized master bedroom, but it needed significant upgrades and what may have originally been a prime location had been encroached by sprawling additions to neighboring homes.

I could tell Nate was quickly losing interest as we drove up to a large, greyish-blue Cape Cod, surrounded by a well-appointed lawn and garden. Its many gabled roofs peaked haphazardly and its cottage-style windows were framed by traditional black shutters.

The foyer opened into a formal dining room. A long hallway on the left went back to the kitchen and den. Without furnishings or décor, our footsteps on the old hardwood reverberated throughout the house, revealing its grandeur.

At the end of a long hallway was a large room, with floor-to-ceiling glass windows spanning the entire back end of the house. Two sets of glass French doors opened onto a slate patio that wrapped around the back of the house. About a hundred feet beyond the patio Long Island Sound stretched into the distance. The view was awe-inspiring; a million small waves disappearing into the horizon.

"This is amazing," I said.

"It's nice," Nate agreed.

"Just nice?" I teased.

We looked at a few other houses, but the grey Cape Cod stuck in my mind. *It's perfect and it's in Connecticut. How will I convince Nate that it's necessary now?*

"Let's go out tonight," Nate said as we rode the elevator up to the penthouse.

"Yeah, sure."

"I have to go to the office for a bit this evening, but I'll meet you at Detox."

"What time?"

"I don't know. Nine?"

"Sure."

"Oh, and don't bring any of those friends of yours. I want it to be just us tonight."

"Okay." *What does he have in mind?*

Detox was a swanky dance club that Nate liked in Midtown. It wasn't my type, but I needed to keep him happy.

I got to Detox just after nine and headed straight to the bar. It was early, but there was already a decent crowd. I could feel a handful of people in the club watching me as I ordered a drink. I sipped my drink and scanned the club discreetly. Nate was at the other end of the long bar talking to a woman. A tall, thin, blonde. She was leaning back against the bar with her elbows resting on the edge, facing him. Given the size of her breasts and her waist I decided there was no way they weren't fake. Nate was smiling, basking in her attention. I directed the bartender to charge my drink to Nate's tab, and headed toward him. I was intercepted mid-way by a guy who made eye contact and he smiled.

"I was going to ask if I could buy you a drink but I see you've taken care of that." His intonation was the type used among good friends or lovers. He was good looking, maybe late thirties.

"Buy the next one," I said and took a long swig of my drink which was mostly ice anyhow.

"Are you here with anyone?"

I looked toward Nate and motioned. "Yep."

"Oh." He surveyed the other end of the bar, but all of the men nearby were flanked by beautiful women. He turned back to me confidently. "So, what's your name?"

"Jeannie," I lied.

"Hi, Jeannie. I'm Todd. Nice to meet you."

We touched glasses. I watched Nate and the woman with the big boobs. *Nate is clearly interested in her. He said he wanted to have a threesome with me. Maybe I can use this to get him to commit to making the changes I want to the prenup.*

Todd continued to make small talk and I waited patiently until Nate's new friend finally disappeared toward the bathroom.

"Excuse me, sorry," I said and followed her.

I fixed my hair in the mirror above the sinks until she came out and began washing her hands. She looked up, and I smiled at her in the mirror.

"I love your dress. Where did you get it?" I said.

"Oh, this thing? I don't know."

"Well, it looks great on you."

"Thanks."

She pulled lipstick out of her small purse.

"I think he really likes you," I said.

"Sorry, what?"

"Oh, Nate. The guy at the bar."

"Oh, sorry. You know him?"

"I do." I watched her adjust her boobs to maximize her cleavage. "He's pretty hot," I said. "Phenomenal in bed too."

She looked up at me in the mirror. "You're his girlfriend?"

"Well, sort of, but we actually have a different kind of relationship."

"What?"

"Open. We're open."

She smiled, a small, subtle smile.

"You should join us," I said.

"Really?"

"Yeah. He gets really turned on by girl on girl, and I can tell he really likes you." *I can't believe I'm doing this, but whatever it takes.*

She smiled politely, turned, and walked out of the bathroom.

I applied a little more lipstick and followed her back out to the bar. There were more people dancing now, and the club was nearly full.

Nate was standing close to her, whispering something in her ear. I walked over and squeezed in between them.

"Who's your new friend?" I asked.

"Hey," Nate said. "This is Naomi."

She held out her hand.

"Wyn."

She began dancing in place to the thumping bass.

"Let's dance," she said and grabbed my hand. She pulled me toward the dance floor knowing Nate would follow. *It worked.* The lights had been turned down and the D.J. started spinning more aggressive tracks.

After a few songs I returned to the bar for another drink. I leaned back against the bar, sipping slowly and watching them grind against each other. *This is insane. I have no idea who she is or where she's been. What am I thinking?*

Todd slid in next to me, closer than I'd have liked.

"What's your deal?" he said, looking in Nate's direction.

"It's complicated."

"Clearly."

We both watched as she rubbed herself against Nate.

"Sorry, is that your boyfriend?" he yelled in my ear.

"Practically my fiancé."

He shook his head and walked away to begin trawling again.

By eleven I was more than tipsy and the three of us were taking turns dancing together, moving to the beat in unison. Just as I was finishing another drink Nate yelled into my ear, "Meet me by the bar. Need a word."

I followed him to the corner of the bar, as far from the speakers as possible, but he still had to yell. "Talked to my lawyer today. You're asking a lot."

I turned my head, wanting to see his expression, to see if he was mad, but he looked calm, even confident.

"Am I?" I yelled back.

"Yes," he said.

I turned toward the dance floor and watched Naomi dancing alone as men in the crowd began to notice and move in.

"What now? What do you want to do?" I asked.

"There is one thing I've always wanted to do with you, at least once."

I waited and stared straight ahead, watching her dance confidently, adeptly avoiding the other advances.

"I wanna have a threesome with you." He paused and then yelled a little louder, "I have to have a threesome with you."

I knew it!

I turned toward him and yelled into his ear. "How do you know she'll even want to do it with us?"

"She'll want to. No one says no to me." *There it is. His Achilles heel.* A big smile crossed his face.

"Okay," I yelled back, "I'll do it, but only if you sign the prenup with *all* my changes."

He watched her jealously as she danced with other men.

"And we buy the grey Cape Cod in Old Greenwich."

He made me wait, painfully aware of the passing seconds meted out by the thumping of the bass. Eventually he turned to look at me. "Deal," he yelled.

I nodded. *So predictable.*

He headed back to the dance floor. Todd tried to move back in but I shook my head, *no.*

I watched Nate and Naomi from the bar, sipping my drink.

I knew other women, respectable women in college who had experimented. I knew some gorgeous women, and could definitely recognize a beautiful woman when I saw one, but I'd never been curious. There was only one question now: *how badly do I want to be married to Nate, on my terms?*

He bought her another drink and I took a shot for good measure. This wasn't the kind of thing I was going to make it through if my buzz wore off.

Eventually Nate ordered an Uber Black and the three of us hopped in. He sat in the middle seat between us and put one hand on my upper thigh and the other hand on hers. As the driver weaved through traffic, Nate began to feel us both up and down. Then he began to rub my clit over my lacy thong with his fingers. I put my head back and tried to relax. *What am I doing? How has it come to this?*

He massaged both of us in the same way as we pulled up to his condo.

Once inside our condo, I was struck by the awkward self-consciousness that consumes you when you have agreed to something completely out of your comfort zone. I was relieved when Nate popped opened a bottle of champagne and poured three glasses. We each took a glass, raised them in the air, and clumsily tapped them together. I tipped my head back and enjoyed the sweetness of the bubbly wine. *This is it. I'm doing this. I have to seal this deal. Without those edits and the house in Connecticut, it's all been for nothing. I have no choice now. I can't walk away after everything. Besides, normal people do this kind of thing. Whatever it takes. I have to be married to Nate on my terms.*

I followed them to the bedroom, our bedroom. It was odd being with another woman in a place where Nate and I had been intimate. Just as I expected to be left out, a spectator in this bizarre experience, she turned toward me and leaned in. I intuitively knew what was coming, but the sight of her face coming at mine was unnerving. I stepped back. She wasn't deterred and continued toward me, her lips met mine. At first her mouth was closed, but once she was sure I would stay put she leaned in and opened her mouth. Her tongue was small, smoother than Nate's and she was more patient. Nate conquered my mouth when we kissed. He wasn't a bad kisser but his motions were rushed, impatient, dominant. Hers were slower, gentle, she explored a little and waited for my reaction. If I responded in kind, she became more confident. If I hesitated or withdrew at all, she changed course. The result was a mutual exploration. Her motions were tender and soft and pleasurable. I closed my eyes, tried to relax, and began to reciprocate, employing the same technique: first exploring what she liked, then responding to her reaction with small modifications, advances even. As I did, I realized that it was actually turning me on.

She pulled away and Nate, who had been watching us, joined in. She worked him over in the same way for a minute and then pulled her shirt off. I followed her lead. She pulled at Nate's shirt and he lifted his arms in the air. Then she fingered the button on his jeans. I watched her and felt surprisingly jealous. She pushed his jeans back and pulled them forward over his erection. He stood in front of us, completely naked. Then, as if she knew the script, she gently pushed me onto Nate's bed, on my back. She climbed on top of me on all fours and motioned for me to scoot back and I did. She bent forward. Her face was between my legs. *Who is this woman?* She went to work with her tongue in much the same way as she had inside my mouth. Nate entered her from behind. His thrusting into her pushed her tongue forward and backwards rhythmically. My body began to convulse. She pushed her hand all the way inside me and worked in circles. The waves of pleasure that followed were so intense that I was conscious of the effort required not to scream. Just as the pleasure began to subside she began to moan and threw her head back. Nate was moving in slower, more controlled motions and his eyes belied intense pleasure. I watched them finish together. *Have they done this before? Did Nate set this up? Was I his pawn tonight?*

They collapsed onto the bed and I got up and tiptoed to the bathroom. I turned on the shower and let the steaming hot water flow over me. I sat against the wall with my head in my hands and shuddered, disgusted that I'd let myself enjoy anything about that experience. *I've gone too far, let things get out of hand. I let him have control.* I hated myself. I worked soap into a lather and covered myself. Over and over again, I washed and rinsed. When I finally turned the water off the room was thick with steam.

When I tipped toed out of the bathroom, she was gone and Nate had fallen asleep. *He'll think something's wrong if I leave now.* As softly as possible, I climbed back into the bed, hugging the edge. I curled up and tried to sleep.

When I woke up the sun was just beginning to peek through the cracks in the blinds. I laid in bed for a minute. *Was it worth it? Did I seal the deal or will he renege on his promise? What if he backs out and doesn't uphold his end of the bargain? What would I do then? I'm out of leverage.* I had come so far already. Done things I hadn't planned on having to do, wasn't comfortable with, and what did I have to show for it?

I got up. A light was on in the master bath. I tried the handle and it was unlocked, so I walked in. He was standing in front of the sink brushing his teeth. He saw me watching him and I smiled. He swung around, pulled me toward him, and lifted me onto the empty stretch of the long bathroom counter.

"That was so hot," he said as he forced my legs apart. "I really owe you one."

Ugh, not again.

He pulled me toward the edge of the counter and grabbed my ankles. He held my legs apart and shoved himself inside me. I wasn't wet but he worked back and forth anyhow. I tried to relax and felt him begin to move with ease. I looked up to find him watching me with a look of pure adoration.

"Tell me you love me," I demanded.

"I love you," he said.

"Do you love me more than her?"

He laughed and threw his head back, but said nothing.

"Do you?" I repeated.

"Are you kidding? Of course."

"How can I be sure?"

He pushed himself deeper inside me until it was almost painful. I took a deep breath and tried to relax, and began to feel a little pleasure amidst the pain.

"The agreement is on the counter in the kitchen with all of your changes," he said. "Exactly what you asked for. You win."

That was it. I was finally relaxed. Pain turned to pleasure and the contractions of my muscles were too much for him to resist. His release hit me deep inside and I came with him.

Nate got in the shower. I went to the kitchen and thumbed through the agreement. I pulled up Vi's marked up PDF on my phone and looked through to make sure all of her changes had been made. *Finally!* I looked for any text that looked new but didn't see anything suspect.

Nate came out of the bathroom with a small towel around his waist. "We need to sign that in the presence of a notary. We can do it at my office on Monday. Stop by around lunch."

"Sure," I said and put the agreement in my purse. "What about the house?"

"I'll call and make an offer today." He took a few steps toward me, leaned down, and kissed my forehead. "Thank you for last night."

"Thank you for everything."

He smiled.

"I have some errands to run. I'll make dinner tonight," I said.

THE PLAY

Sunday, October 2, 2016

Chelsea

I walked out into the fresh autumn air, overwhelmed by emotions: disgust, guilt, shame, hatred. *I need a distraction.* One of my favorite things about New York City was finding the unexpected but delightful where you least expected it. I stopped at a charity shop a few blocks from my apartment. It was the kind of cluttered store where rich women disposed of last year's gently worn designer clothes to feel good about themselves and get a small tax write-off on the things they wouldn't be caught dead in again anyhow. Something about the potential of finding a diamond in the rough always made me happy and was all the motivation I needed to dig through the stuffed racks. Over time and with persistence, I had scooped up a designer black wool winter coat, a few silk blouses, and a designer clutch that needed some TLC but wasn't beyond repair. I had stumbled upon a cheap but phenomenal tailor in the next block that could make a secondhand dress look amazing. It had allowed me to build up a respectable wardrobe on my meager marketing salary. I got a little lost searching through the old fedoras, sweaters, and jeans. I struck out, but by the time I emerged I'd mostly forgotten about the night before. It felt good to forget. I would just forget it ever happened. *I don't know her, I'll never see her again. Nate had his fun. It was necessary, and I had no choice.*

As I walked the streets of New York City trying to forget, I thought about the beginning, the middle, and the end of my story. *I owe my therapist a visit.* Back at my rented room, I reread what I'd written, removing Nate's name and all of the italicized musings about revenge, and then sent the edited version to my therapist.

A few days later I was sitting in the familiar chair in my therapist's office.

"Wyn, thank you for sharing your story with me," she said. "I'm so sorry you were raped." The words were at once comforting and painful to hear.

"Thank you," I whispered.

"Did you press charges?"

"No."

"What happened to him? Was he ever held accountable?"

I shook my head. "No. He's here. In New York."

"Have you seen him?"

I nodded.

"Wyn, do you still know him? Have you had any contact with him since the rape?"

"He's my fiancée," I said through tears.

"You're in a relationship with him?"

"Yes."

"Wyn, are you living with him now?"

"Yes."

"How long have you been with him?"

"Since a few months after the rape," I lied.

"Have you ever thought about leaving?"

"I don't know. I don't know what I'd do without him," I lied.

"Are you happy with him?" she asked.

"Yes."

"But?"

"I have to do things for him. Things that I don't want to do."

"I think it would be best for you to leave him."

"I don't know how to leave him," I lied.

"You have a job, don't you?"

"Yes."

"Do you have your own bank account?"

"No."

"Are you worried about money if you leave?"

"I don't know. I'm worried about what I would do without him. How I would cope? I've never been on my own before. He takes care of everything."

"You mean financially?"

"I mean everything."

"Do you feel like your life depends on him?"

"I do," I said. "It does." *It does now. I've come too far, invested too much in this con to turn around now.*

"Could you start to put some money away in your own savings account?"

"I don't know. Maybe."

"Why don't you try diverting some of your own income into a separate bank account, and begin saving for your future? Think of it as a contingency plan, if you are ever ready to leave him."

"Yeah, it's a good idea I guess." *But it won't matter when I take everything he's got.*

I woke up alone in our condo on Saturday morning. I'd finally given up my little room in the apartment in Hell's Kitchen and had Nate help me move the rest of my stuff over to the condo. I didn't want Nate to have any reason to question my commitment.

I had an appointment to select wedding flowers at a shop across town in SoHo. The owner said they were so busy that the only way she could guarantee anything, including my appointment, was if I paid the entire bill up front. It seemed a bit ridiculous, but this was New York, and I was apparently already late to the wedding planning game. Everywhere I went I was told that accommodating my request within a year was nearly impossible, and it was only after a lot of begging, a premium added, and an upfront payment near the full amount that I got commitments. After each major charge to the AmEx Nate had given me, I waited for him to say something, but he never did. I figured that either he had even more money than he let on or he was too proud to question me. Either way, I didn't care.

It was the perfect fall day. I threw on some jeans and a light sweater and grabbed a coffee down the street. Just as I walked out of the coffee shop, sipping tentatively from the hot plastic lid, Adam and Julia crossed the street. They walked toward me, holding hands. There was no way to avoid them.

"Hey, Wyn!" Julia shouted and waved with her free hand.

I waved back.

"How are you?" I asked as they got closer.

"Great! You?" she said.

"Good."

"We have exciting news!" She pulled her left hand out of his and held it out. "Look!"

There it was. A large princess cut diamond. Nothing particularly unique, just large, surrounded by smaller diamonds. It sparkled so intensely that it almost looked fake, but of course it wasn't.

"Congratulations!" I managed.

"Thank you so much!" Her arms were around my neck as if we were best friends. I peered up from her embrace and saw Adam watching me. I tried my best to smile. He held my gaze, expressionless.

She let go and turned back toward him, smiling.

"We're getting married in August. Won't that be like a month after yours?" she said.

"Yeah. Wow, that's quick. How will you get a wedding organized in less than a year in New York?"

"Oh, it shouldn't be too difficult. We do have ten months, and I know pretty much everyone worth knowing from product placement and promos I've done over the years. When I announced our engagement on Instagram I got replies from every corner of New York offering us free products and services, it's a great opportunity for their brands."

"Makes sense," I said.

Adam looked down the street avoiding eye contact.

I pulled him toward me for a congratulatory hug. "You've only known her for a few months," I whispered in his ear.

He shrugged and said nothing.

"Well, congratulations!" I said, letting him go.

He turned, took her hand in his and pulled her away. "We really have to go."

"Great to see you," she yelled toward me from the middle of the street. "Watch for our save the date!"

I didn't move, but watched them until they turned the corner at the other end of the block. *Does he really love her or was he just desperate to be with someone because I'm getting married? He wouldn't get married out of jealousy, would he?*

Nate ordered take-out from Hugo's for dinner, making a big deal of plating the meals and pouring champagne.

"What's all this about?" I asked.

"We got the house! I thought we should celebrate."

"Oh Nate, that's amazing. Thank you!"

"I'm just glad you're happy."

We touched glasses in celebration.

"I know we were only there once, but what do you think about having the reception behind the house, overlooking the Sound?" I said.

"You want to have the wedding in Connecticut? At the new house?" he said.

"Well, I've been looking for a venue in New York for almost a month now and haven't found anything in the city that will work for us. Everything is either completely booked more than a year out or is too small."

"Hmmm, yeah, I suppose things book up quickly around here."

"They do, so I was thinking, why not have it at the house? That way we can pick the date we want and not worry about finding a venue," I said. "Plus, it's so beautiful there. It will be unforgettable."

"Hmmmm. Why not do the entire thing at the house then. I was thinking it might be nice to have someone close to us officiate anyhow, since we haven't found a church and a minister we both like yet."

Whatever it takes to have the ceremony in Connecticut. "You don't want to get married in a church?" I asked.

I'd always imagined getting married in a church. When I was young, I used to sneak off to the old Catholic church down the street when I wanted to be alone. I'd sit quietly in the nave on hot summer afternoons as light poured in and the organist practiced. I imagined walking down the aisle in a big white dress to the thundering of Pachelbel's Canon, even though Vi didn't approve of the Catholic Church, or any church for that matter. *But then, this isn't a real wedding. At least, not my real wedding. Perhaps someday, with the right person, I will get my fairytale wedding.*

"I'm just thinking, maybe we bring the Church to the wedding. My cousin Jack will be ordained by the end of the year. I'm sure he would do it at the house for us if we asked."

"Oh, of course." Nate had mentioned his cousin before, but I had never met the guy. "Why not?" *As long as Nate's happy and we're married in Connecticut, then I'm happy.*

"Oooooh, speaking of the wedding there's something I want to show you," I said, and grabbed the vintage bridal magazines, laying June out on the coffee table in front of Nate.

"What do you think?" I asked as I stepped back and watched his reaction.

"Isn't there some rule about me not seeing what you're wearing before the wedding?"

"Well, this isn't the actual dress, more like an approximation. That dress is from 1982. I can't buy it anymore. It would have to be made, from scratch."

"Oh."

"It won't be cheap, but I want to be the most stunning bride ever. I want to be so beautiful that you'll never forget how incredible I looked on our wedding night." I was testing him to see if he would flinch. *How much money does he really have?*

He looked up at me and I put my hands on my hips, posing playfully.

"Of course," he said. "Whatever you want."

Smiling, I sat down next to him on the couch and thumbed through the magazine, while he picked up his laptop and began to work.

PART 2: THE TALE & THE CONVINCER

May 2017 to January 2018

THE TALE

Friday, May 12, 2017
Hell's Kitchen

The winter flew by, for which I was grateful. Vi and Ali insisted on coming to New York to meet Nate before the wedding. They got in late on a Friday evening and I met them at their hotel with snacks and a bottle of my favorite red blend.

"How are you?" I asked Ali, as I poured three glasses of wine. "Working too much as usual?"

"Eh, you know. Fine. A little stressed out lately," she said.

"Yeah, you look like shit," I teased. It wasn't true. She was as beautiful as ever despite her refusal to wear make-up outside of work, save weddings and other formal events. Her first few strands of grey hair stood out against her dark brown hair. She was going to have that same gorgeous silver-grey hair that Vi did, and she would let it go grey early like Vi, without the slightest concern what other people might think. On the other hand, I would probably be dying mine for the rest of my life.

Ali eyed my left hand. "Oh my god, your ring is obscene!"

"You don't like it?"

"It's just so large. It almost looks fake."

"Thanks."

She shook her head slightly and sighed. "So, what's he like?"

"He's an entrepreneur. He was a rower at Penn. Graduated with honors. Started his first business while he was still in college." *Why do I feel like I'm lying to her? That's all completely true.*

"What kind of business?" Ali said.

"He started a company that initially sold supplements and now he's diversified into beauty products."

"Supplements?"

"Yeah."

"What kind of supplements?"

"Um, I don't know."

"You don't know?"

"I mean, it's a little embarrassing."

"Oh come on!"

"Male enhancement."

"Oh my God!" Ali laughed out loud. "That's hilarious!"

"Like I said, he has diversified since then."

"Hopefully his business interests were not driven by personal shortcomings!" She laughed even harder.

"Nice."

"Where's he from?" Vi interjected.

"He grew up mostly in Westport, Connecticut. He has one sister." She nodded, "Have you met her?"

"Not yet. She lives in a small town in South Carolina and only comes up to New York occasionally."

"Oh, that's too bad."

I nodded.

As we talked I began to notice just how alike Vi and Ali were now. They made the same gestures with their hands when they talked. They both said "No?" instead of "Yes?" to confirm that I understood what they meant. They had always been really close. Initially, I thought that it had to do with the fact that Ali was first born and so Vi did everything with her first. It was true that by the time it was my turn they were seasoned, practiced, and the excitement had worn off, but it was more than that. It was something deeper, something within each of us. Whatever it was, Ali and Vi were simpatico. I knew it from a young age and I think they knew it even before I did. *I'm just different.*

"How's Soren?" I asked.

"He's great," Ali said.

"You two have been dating forever!"

"Six years."

"Wow. Isn't that long enough? What are you waiting for?"

"What do you mean?"

"Why don't you just get married? You must love him to be with him for six years."

"Of course I love him, but I'm not sure we'll ever get married. I don't really feel any need to get married. We know we love each other. What more do we need? Besides, we are young, we have a lot of time to do that, if and when we want to."

"Wouldn't it be nice to have some security?"

"How do you mean? It's not like I'm worried about him running off with someone else. I guess if he wanted to do that I'd rather he just leave anyhow. If marriage kept him tied to me, even if he didn't want to be with me, that would be wrong. Plus I make more money than he does, so what security can marriage bring that I don't already have?"

"Oh. Alight." *I used to think that marriage kept people together and that it would be nice to be taken care of, probably because I thought that Vi was on her own precisely because she was never married. I don't know what I believe now. Not all marriages are what they seem.*

"Do you really believe that married people are less likely to cheat on each other? Or are less likely to be unhappy? I don't buy it."

"What about once people have kids. Don't you think it's important for kids to grow up in a house where the parents are together?"

Ali shot Vi a look: *are you going to let her insult you like that?* Vi looked at me, as though she might actually play arbiter this time, but then stayed silent instead.

"Was it so awful growing up in a house with just a mom?" Ali continued.

"No, of course not. Vi was wonderful. I just think that if two people are together and have kids, they should try to stay together for their kids' sake."

"Even if they hate each other and the example they set is of a couple that is miserable?"

"You always make everything so extreme."

"And as usual, you have no defense for the status quo to which you blindly subscribe."

"Whatever."

"Enough," Vi finally interjected. When we were growing up, Vi let us fight until *we* grew tired (I suspect she saw it as the perfect training for a budding lawyer), but these days *she* seemed to grow tired first.

I thought about my father, who I assumed I would never meet and wondered how he and Vi met. *Were they in love? Was he a good guy? Did he want to be a father? Would he love me if he knew me now?*

"What's the plan for tomorrow?" Vi asked.

"I was thinking Brunch at Simone's, and then maybe we could go for a long walk through the city to Central Park. We could get a drink in the afternoon at one of the rooftop bars on our way to the tailor. I need to try my dress on one last time in case I've gained or lost any weight since it was finished. I thought we could go together so that I can try it on and you two can see it. Nate has something planned for dinner but he wouldn't tell me what. Is there anything you want to do tomorrow?"

"Nope. That sounds great," Vi said.

"Ali?"

"Nope, fine."

I met them around ten the next morning for brunch and then we walked. We stopped for cocktails just after noon, taking in a spectacular view of the park and the thin slice of blue water that glimmered between the skyscrapers of Lower Manhattan. It had been a relatively uneventful morning with Ali, for which I was grateful. We got to Matilda's at three-thirty.

I went back to the dressing room and stripped down to my underwear. Matilda and her two assistants barged in without knocking and held the dress open for me, while Matilda unhooked my bra.

"Don't be so shy Darling, we're all women here, and you can't wear that bra with this dress," she said, as she tossed my bra onto a nearby bench and turned me around to zip up the back.

"Breathe out," she ordered.

Once they had pulled and prodded and pinned to adjust the dress to perfection I turned toward the mirror. I was surprised by how beautiful the dress was. *I shouldn't be marrying him in this gorgeous dress. He doesn't deserve this.* My eyes began to well up with tears.

"Oh, Honey, you look so beautiful!" Matilda crooned.

I nodded, wiped my cheeks, took a deep breath, and tried my best to smile.

Matilda opened the door and then followed me out, gathering the back of the dress in her arms as I walked.

Ali and Vi were sitting in two vintage, sling back leather arm chairs in the large styling room, which had floor-to-ceiling mirrors on three of the four walls. Everything but the mirrors was dark grey, which made the white dress pop.

"Oh, I love it!" Vi said with a big smile on her face.

Ali smiled, but looked a little disappointed.

"What's wrong?" I demanded.

"It's a bit old fashioned," she said.

"Well, I wanted something different."

"So you cobbled together all of the '80s?"

"Oh, shut up. Why can't you just be nice?"

"I just thought you were more creative than that."

"Enough," Vi commanded.

Back in the dressing room, Matilda and her assistants helped me climb carefully out of the dress, and put it back in its bag. I met Matilda at the counter, and fumbled in my purse for Nate's AmEx. As I searched, I noticed Vi standing next to me, holding her credit card out. Matilda watched me.

"Thanks, but it's okay." I said to Vi as I handed Nate's credit card to Matilda.

"You can't afford this. Let me help you, please," Vi said.

"Really, it's fine."

Vi stared at the black credit card and watched as Matilda ran it.

We walked out into the acerbic New York air. I took a deep breath, happy to be out of the confines of the shop.

"What time is dinner?" Vi asked.

"Seven."

"Should we walk back to the hotel or take a cab?" Vi asked Ali.

"I'm pretty tired," Ali said.

"Let's take a cab."

We flagged a taxi, which would drop me at the condo before continuing on to the hotel. I stared out the window and watched the blur of a busy Saturday in New York City pass by: colored lights flashing, frenetic movement, tourists gazing up at the towering buildings, and a beautifully outfitted wedding party posing for photos on the steps of St. Patrick's Cathedral.

"Freddie, have you given any thought to whether you want to be walked down the aisle?" Vi asked.

"I hadn't really thought about it," I said. "Do you want to do it?"

"Oh Freddie, of course!" Vi exclaimed. "Why don't we all do it?"

"I was thinking Ali could be the maid of honor," I said.

Ali was visibly annoyed by the suggestion.

"Oh, come on, Ali, you have to," Vi insisted.

"You are my only sister," I added.

"Whatever you want."

"You ordered your dress already right?" I asked.

"Yeah, I got fitted last month," Ali said.

"Oh, good."

"I hate it. It's ridiculous and makes my hips look gigantic."

"I'm sure it doesn't," I said. "Oh, also, I've been asking everyone to call me 'Wyn' now. I know you two will never stop calling me 'Freddie', and that's fine when it's just us, but Nate doesn't know about that nickname and I'd rather not give him something to tease me about. Will you two please call me 'Wyn' in front of him? It's really important to me."

"So grown up these days!" Vi observed.

"Please," I begged.

"Sure."

"Ali?"

"Whatever."

"Seriously. Please."

"Fine."

"Thank you."

I texted Nate, "Be on your best tonight. Ali's not in a good mood."

"Got it. See you at The Foundry at 7."

Back at the penthouse condo that Nate had bought us, I opened a card that had come in the mail. It was a save the date for Julia's wedding shower complete with a website address. I opened the website on my phone's browser to find more details than anyone needed: where to stay, what to wear, what gifts to buy. If it was any indication of how their wedding would be, I was in for a bit of a shock. I checked the online guest list. There was no one else that I knew personally, but a handful of names stood out. They were names I had heard whispered at parties, names that I recognized from newspaper columns and gossip magazines.

The Foundry had opened about six months earlier in an old garment factory in the Meat Packing District. The hostess showed us to our table. Nate was sitting in the corner of the big leather booth with a glass of scotch on the rocks. He stood up.

"Nice to meet you, Vivienne," he said and took my mom's hand gently in his.

"Please call me Vi," she said.

"Ali. My pleasure," he said as he shook her hand.

We piled into the booth around Nate. The table was in the corner of the restaurant with a great view of the cavernous room. The walls of the old garment factory were exposed common brick, and old large metal objects remained around the space: a large winch, the remnants of an old pulley system hung from the ceiling, a big metal gear sat propped up against a wall near the bathrooms.

We ordered a bottle of wine and Vi began her line of questioning with the standards: where was he from, were his parents still together, did he have any siblings? I could see her discomfort when he talked about his parents' divorce. Ali was silent but watched him intently, studying his mannerisms, his every look and movement.

"Is your sister married?" Vi asked.

"She is."

The food was taking longer than expected and the wine was beginning to do its job. After a little more small talk, Ali took advantage of a momentary silence. "Do you believe in God?" she asked Nate.

I watched the look on Nate's face go quickly from amenable to annoyed. "Yes, I do."

"Do you believe in a woman's right to choose?"

"Choose what?" Nate shot back.

"What is best for her."

"Sure."

Vi asked about his work. Nate explained the new product line his team was working on.

"I hear you got your start in dick enlargement," Ali said. "Any particular reason?"

"Ali!" I pleaded.

"I'm well endowed," he shot back and laughed.

"None of that stuff works," she said.

"Probably not."

"So you're a scam artist, and you're proud?"

"I'm a successful businessman, and yes."

Ali rolled her eyes. I finished off my wine and poured myself another glass. *I should have known Ali would be a liability.*

"Did I hear that you two bought a house?" Vi asked.

"Well, actually, I bought a house for us last fall. We've been going there on the weekends when we have time, to get a break from the city. It's in Old Greenwich," Nate said.

"Isn't that in the suburbs?" Ali asked.

"It is. It's quite beautiful."

"I'm sure," Ali said.

"That's where we'll have the wedding," I said.

"Yeah, my cousin has agreed to officiate," Nate said.

"Oh, interesting. Is he a minister?" Ali asked.

"He is just finishing seminary now," Nate said.

"I want you two to know that I would be happy to help with the wedding," Vi interrupted. "I mean financially. Of course Ali and I will help with preparations and whatever else you need done too."

Ali looked out across the large dining room, which had filled up since we arrived.

"Well, thank you, Vi, that is very generous of you, but I'll take care of everything."

"Of course," I heard Ali mumble under her breath.

Vi ordered another bottle of wine.

"So, Vi, I hear that you're a big deal lawyer in Chicago."

"Well, I don't know about that," she smiled coyly. "I've had a nice career. I've started teaching at the university as an adjunct, which I'm really enjoying. I don't think I'll ever retire completely. I wouldn't know what to do with myself."

"I know what you mean," he said.

As dinner wound down and we finished off the second bottle of wine, I grew anxious, anticipating the fight I knew was inevitable.

Eventually, the waitress brought one check for the table in a black leather bi-fold and placed it presumptuously in front of Nate. Vi reached awkwardly across the table and snatched it away before he reacted.

He held out his credit card. "Please Vi. This is my treat," he said.

"Not a chance. We are all adults."

"You are our guests here this weekend," he protested.

"Nathan, I work hard. If you want to pay for your wedding that's your prerogative, but I will buy my own dinner when I please," Vi said.

Nate leaned forward to reach for the bill.

"Nate, please!" I practically yelled, and extended my arm in a futile attempt to stop him. His strength was no match and my arm became pinched between his stomach and the table.

"Ouch!" I screeched in pain.

"Freddie!" Vi exclaimed out of concern.

I shot her a look of reproach. *Don't call me that!*

She looked confused and worried.

The strangers at the three tables nearest ours stared in my direction. Nate sat back against the booth, pulled me into his arms, and inspected my forearm tenderly. I winced in pain as he kissed the red marks. I looked up to see Ali rolling her eyes. Nate smiled at the onlookers reassuringly. I smiled too, in an attempt to convince everyone that I was okay. *Did he hear Vi call me Freddie?*

Nate flagged a cab for Ali and Vi, and he and I got a car home.

"Why did your mom call you 'Freddie'?" he asked as the car pulled away.

"Oh, yeah, she used to call me that when I was little, along with a bunch of other embarrassing nicknames, like Wynnie. It still slips out sometimes when she's worried about me, even though she hasn't called me that in years. I hate all of them, so don't get any ideas."

He nodded, and seemed to buy it. *Thank God.*

THE TALE

Thursday, June 29, 2017
Manhattan

Our rehearsal dinner was in a big room at a fancy club downtown where Nate was a member. The last of our guests were just trickling in. It was a perfect summer evening, pleasantly warm.

I grabbed Nate and we made the rounds together, introducing each other to people who represented other times in our lives, and had made the trip for the weekend. *I can't believe this is really happening! They are all here to witness and celebrate a complete sham of a wedding and marriage. I've done it!*

Dinner was served at precisely seven-thirty around one large, long table. Nate and I sat at the head of the table and watched as our friends and family interacted, a bit timidly at first, but as the champagne flowed their interactions shifted from formal and a bit guarded, to friendly and boisterous. The silver, china, and crystal chattered above their voices, with a few wild laughs punctuating the customary sounds of celebration. Once everyone had been served the first course and the clatter began to die down, Nate stood to offer a toast.

"Wyn and I would like to thank all of you for being here tonight. You are each special to us in your own way, and we are honored to share this very special weekend with you. We would like to thank our parents, John, Maggie, and Vivienne, and our sisters, Ali and Hannah, for all of their help making this evening and tomorrow possible, and to everyone who has supported us in our journey."

He raised his glass in the air. "May love conquer all."

The guests clapped and cheered.

He turned toward me and compelled me to stand.

"We are not perfect, but we are perfectly in love," he said.

He looked me directly in the eyes.

"Wyn Laurent, I have never met another woman like you. I am truly blessed to call you my partner, my best friend, and soon my wife."

The room erupted, glasses clinked, and Nate leaned down and kissed me. We raised our glasses and tapped them together gently.

It was my turn. I had never been very comfortable speaking in front of people and hadn't planned to say anything, but beckoned by the guests and Nate's intense gaze, I stood up and raised my glass.

"As Nate said, thank you all so very much for being here with us this weekend. We are eternally grateful to have you in our lives and to call you friends! Nate and I do not have a romantic 'how we met' story. As many of you know, we met online, as many people do these days. We don't get to choose how we meet the person we will spend our life with, but we do get to define our relationship together. That first encounter that binds us, that moment when we realize that we will never be the same because of this person, and that we must honor that moment and follow it where it leads us...that is what today and tomorrow are all about and I," I paused to correct myself, "we, are ever so thankful that you are here to share it with us!" *Today and tomorrow are all about that encounter five years ago that bound me to this man against my will. That moment continues to define everything, and will do so until I have my revenge.*

I raised my glass a little higher and smiled. Applause and cheers filled the room. I tipped my head back and finished my glass of champagne.

Nate and I wandered around the room catching up with those we had missed earlier, and with those who deserved a little more time. As my mom's friends began to excuse themselves for the evening I heard my name and turned to see Julia walking toward me. Adam was behind her talking to a mutual friend of ours from high school.

"Wyn, darling, you look so beautiful!" she exclaimed and gave me a hug. "We are so excited for tomorrow! Can we help in any way?"

I assured her there was nothing she could do besides show up looking her best, which I immediately regretted, because if anyone would outshine a bride at her wedding, it was Julia.

I moved past her toward Adam.

"Hey, you," he said.

"Hey!"

"How're you feeling? Excited?"

"I'm a little tired I guess, but tomorrow should be worth the lost sleep."

"Yeah, I'm sure."

"You'll be there, right?"

"Of course. Wouldn't miss it!" He was surprisingly upbeat about my wedding. I wrapped my arms around his waist and pulled him toward me. He held me tight.

"All right, break it up you two!" Nate bellowed from across the room. "I need a beautifully rested bride tomorrow. Time for bed, Lady of the Hour."

As the party wound down, Vi, Ali, and Hannah helped us load wedding gifts into Nate's car, and then Vi, Ali, and I walked the three blocks to our hotel. Vi had booked a suite for the three of us, after insisting that I not sleep with my husband-to-be the night before our wedding. Our suite had two rooms and they had beat me there earlier in the day and decorated the larger room with white balloons, paper streamers, and white and light pink roses.

Exhausted from entertaining, I fell asleep as soon as my head hit the soft down pillow.

I woke up early and laid in bed for a while trying to get a little more sleep, but my mind raced. *I can't believe that by the end of the day I'll be married to my rapist.* My stomach churned with excitement and nerves.

My thoughts turned to logistics. Stella, our wedding coordinator would manage the event, but there were things that I just couldn't trust to anyone else, like making sure that my sister had her hair and make-up done so that she didn't show up to my wedding with the messy bun she wore almost every day and just a touch of mascara. I had hired a hair and make-up duo just for Vi and Ali that would meet us at the Greenwich house along with my hair and make-up artists.

I slipped on my running shoes and headed for the hotel gym to sweat out the few drinks I'd had the night before. Vi was sitting in the living room reading a newspaper and sipping coffee from a paper cup.

"Be back in half an hour," I said.

"Morning," she replied without looking up.

Around noon we headed out to the Old Greenwich house.

The hairdresser was finishing my up-do and a highly lauded make-up artist was waiting her turn, as I watched from the master bath window as the first few wedding guests began to arrive.

Ali sat in the corner of the bathroom. She was already dressed in her bridesmaid's dress, which was gold and looked lovely with her dark hair and olive skin. She was fidgeting with a bobby pin like a little kid dressed up for Sunday school. I watched her pick at her painted eyelashes in a small mirror.

"Stop it. You're going to ruin your makeup," I said. She paid no attention and continued picking.

Vi was painting her toenails on the edge of the bathtub.

"There's Max and it looks like he's alone. Ali, why don't you go get a glass of wine and welcome the guests," I said.

Max was Ali's high school boyfriend. He was a bit of an oddball back then but had become a celebrated artist in his early twenties. Now I imagined him living in a loft in Greenwich Village with a woman named Camille who makes second hand throwaways look cool. He and Ali had always been close, even after they broke up.

"Anything else, Bridezilla?"

"Don't start down the aisle until Stella tells you to," I warned, but she was already out the door.

By five o'clock the chatter of the guests was audible upstairs, and by five thirty it was clear that they were being well-attended by the catering staff because they grew louder by the minute. Then just before six, right on time, the voices grew faint, as they had all been shepherded out to the water's edge.

The sun was just beginning to descend in the sky, casting a rosy glow over the dark blue water. It was perfect, warm but not hot, and there was a subtle breeze off the Sound. Just enough to make it comfortable, but not enough to mess up my hair. The house and yard looked perfect. Nate had gone all out, hiring a crew to do the landscaping to ensure that everything was in bloom at just the right time.

Vi helped me into my dress and I put on the few remaining finishing touches, like the modest but beautiful diamond necklace and earrings Nate had bought me for my birthday. Despite all of the commotion in the house as the staff began to prepare dinner and the crowd assembled by the water, I felt a deep sense of calm as I descended the staircase and spotted Stella fluttering around, working to get the wedding party organized for the procession.

I waited at the bottom of the stairs and watched the last few guests scurry toward the water while the catering staff hurried to collect the empty wine glasses left around the house on shelves, tables, and any other flat surface.

As I waited and watched the wedding unfold, I felt more and more like I was playing the lead role in someone else's melodrama. This moment that I'd been waiting for, planning for, and working so hard for, that was years in the making, had finally arrived. Everything was exactly as it should be, as it had to be. It was really just another beginning in a long saga, but it would be the biggest test so far of my ability to deceive. Up to now, I'd primarily had an audience of one, and while he was the most important witness to the scheme, he'd provided the material and been a willing, if unwitting player. Now I needed to convince hundreds that I was the loving wife that Nate believed me to be, but I had one key advantage: we often see exactly what we want and expect to see. We see what we're prepared to see, whether it's there or not.

"Ready?" Stella asked as she burst through the French doors and hurried toward me.

Ready as I'll ever be.

Vi was waiting just beyond the doors watching the crowd at the end of the lawn. She turned to look at me and a wide smiled crossed her face.

"Belle!" She exclaimed as I walked toward her.

I took her arm and we set out down the runner of gold muslin that led from the house to the water's edge. A string quartet played La Régente near the end of the carpet. Everyone watched as we moved slowly toward the water where Nate stood flanked by his three best friends. My bridesmaids were assembled to the other side, including Ali who was wearing a wreath of flowers atop her fancy up-do.

Adam caught my eye as we passed. His lips were pursed, the corners of his mouth turned slightly down. I knew that look, the same one he used to have when we stopped at McDonald's instead of A&W on long road trips through Wisconsin as kids, not happy but resigned to make the best of things. I smiled.

As we got to the end of the aisle, Vi released my arm and turned toward me. She took my face gently in her hands and planted a kiss on my forehead.

"I want the best for you, always," she said. "I love you."

"Love you too."

I turned to Nate.

Nate took my hand and together we took a few steps toward Jack, who was waiting with his back to the water. He wore a black business suit with a white pocket square.

He began, "Friends and family, beloved Lord," and proceeded to mix our favorite verses eloquently with the highlights of our story.

We read our vows and then Jack pronounced us wed. Nate pulled me toward him and kissed me unequivocally. Goosebumps covered my entire body. *That's it! I've got him exactly where I want him.*

Guests threw flower petals into the air that fluttered above us in the gentle breeze and danced slowly toward the emerald grass below our feet. Nate caught me by surprise when he scooped me up and carried me back toward the house.

"What a lucky guy I am!" he said as we got near the house and he put me down on the terrace steps.

Family and friends filed past us, pausing to offer congratulations and best wishes before going into the large white tent that filled the rest of the back yard.

Adam and Julia were holding hands when they finally came by. "We are just so freaking happy for you! You are such a wonderful couple," she said.

Adam shook Nate's hand firmly. "Congrats, man," he said and then turned to Julia. "What would you like to drink, Sweetie?"

"Champagne of course!" Julia replied as they wandered into the tent. "There's no better way to celebrate!"

The guests continued to flow past. Jack was last and had a black leather portfolio in his hand. "I'm going to need your autographs to make this official," he said.

He put the folder down on the stone wall at the edge of the terrace. Nate stepped forward and signed his name on the first of four lines. I took my turn and signed on the next line. Jack looked up and spotted Nate's sister, Hannah at the back of the terrace coming out of the house.

"Hannah," he called. "Will you please do us a favor and sign as our witness?"

"Sure thing!" she said. She signed on the third line and then Jack took a stamp from his pocket and stamped just below the last line. He signed and dated in the appropriate places within the stamped area.

"I'll send you a copy tomorrow and then this gets filed with the State of Connecticut," Jack said. "Congratulations, you two!"

"Shall we?" Nate asked, holding out his hand to me.

"Give me a sec. Just need to check my make-up."

"It looks fine," he said, as I turned and went into the house.

A waitress passed me in the front hall with a tray full of perfectly golden bubbly on her way to service the guests. I grabbed two glasses and smiled. She continued on and I threw my head back and finished both.

I checked my make-up in the front hall mirror.

Nate was waiting on the patio, alone. I took his hand and we walked into the tent, where we were introduced to a raucous applause. We danced, we drank, we entertained. The illuminating bursts of the flash bulb left me blinded. When the last of the guests waved goodbye, my head was spinning. I grabbed a bottle of water.

"I will be carrying you up these stairs, Wife!" Nate said as he came around the corner. "You ready?"

Never ready.

The clatter of dishes emanated from the kitchen. Stella opened the door.

"Congratulations, again!" she said. "I will take care of everything, don't worry. Get some rest!"

Nate handed her a wad of cash.

"Thank you," he said. She demurred but was easily convinced to keep the tip.

"I will coordinate with the photographer to get you photos as soon as possible. Although I know that he will want to do some work to adjust lighting and such."

"Thank you," I said.

"Goodnight."

"Goodnight."

Nate bent forward and lifted me into his arms. He carried me up the main stairs to our bedroom and threw me onto the bed.

"My hair!" I complained as the massive bobby pins hidden in my up-do caught the comforter.

"I'll ruin it soon enough!"

He walked back and closed the door, then over to the dresser, and pulled out two pairs of handcuffs.

"I'm really tired," I said.

"You don't want to consummate our marriage?" he asked.

"Because we haven't before?" I said sarcastically.

"But I have something special planned." He held up the handcuffs and jingled the metal.

"Seriously, can we take a rain check? I would just rather do it when I have more energy," I said. "I'm exhausted from entertaining all weekend."

"You think you'll get off easy now that we're married?"

I didn't respond.

"I hope you didn't think I was the kind of guy who would just all of a sudden take no for an answer."

I shook my head.

He took a few steps toward the bed. "Relax, you might even enjoy yourself."

"Really," I said, "not tonight."

He smiled. "Everyone has sex on their wedding night."

How much longer will I have to keep this up?

He took the last few steps toward the bed silently and grabbed my left arm. I resisted gently. He quickly handcuffed me to the iron post.

"Please stop!" I said.

"Yeah, that's so hot," he said under his breath.

He walked around to the other side of the bed and handcuffed my right wrist to the other bed post. He loosened his tie and grabbed for my right leg. I resisted but I was no match for him.

"Oh, you little tease!" he said. "You know I can't help myself when you fight back!"

He bound my right ankle to the bed post, and picked a luggage strap up off the chair by the dresser. He bound my other ankle and pulled tight. I braced myself.

"Come on. Say it again," he demanded as he took off his vest.

"Please," I begged.

"Please what?" he taunted me playfully.

"Please stop." *Really, stop!*

"Yeah, that's it, so hot!" he said. "You really know how to turn me on."

He took his belt off and let his pants fall to the floor.

"I said 'No!'"

"Oh God, that's it. Look!" He was looking down at his erection.

I guess I should have known that nothing would change. My job will still be to give him whatever he wants until it's over and I make him pay.

He stepped onto the mattress and kneeled down in between my legs. "I'm going to fuck you hard," he said and forced his way inside me.

No.

He began to thrust back and forth aggressively.

This isn't worth it. Fuck. I'm right back where I was in that frat house five years ago. I began to panic; my heart beat rapidly and I felt dizzy. With each thrust my body was thrown back further until my head was pushed painfully against the headboard. I did the only I thing I knew would bring an end to it quickly and clenched every muscle in my body as tightly as possible. I saw his lower abdomen begin to clench and release against his will. *Oh, thank God!*

"Such a naughty wife!" he mumbled as he began to cum inside me.

When he was done I could feel his dick go limp as he pulled out. He laid down on the bed next to me.

I have to get out of here. I'm going to lose it. "Cuffs? Can you take them off please?"

He sighed deeply, clearly annoyed, and got up to get the keys.

"Thank you," I said as he unlocked both hands.

I ran to the bathroom, fell apart, and sobbed inconsolably on the bathroom floor. *I can't do this anymore. I have to get away. How much longer can I stand letting him do whatever he wants to me? Is getting revenge worth letting him rape me again and again?*

Eventually I regained my composure. When I finally opened the bedroom door I saw him sleeping soundly in our bed. I forced myself to get into bed next to him. He rolled away from me without waking up. I laid down, let out a faint sigh, and tried to relax.

When I woke up the sun was already above the horizon casting a warm yellow glow on the dove white ceiling of the bedroom. I rolled over expecting to see Nate sleeping next to me, but he was propped up against the headboard with his phone.

"Morning," he said.

"Morning," I grumbled.

"What's wrong with you this morning?"

"Nothing." *Everything. Last night. You!*

He continued reading and then abruptly stopped and sat up a little straighter. "Hey, you're not going to believe what happened last night."

"Really?" *I'm not?*

"Yeah, you'll never guess what your sister said to me."

"Ali?"

"She is your only sister, isn't she?"

"Yeah," I said. "What'd she say?"

"She threatened me. Told me that she knew my type and that my type is never faithful. She said that she personally looks forward to destroying me if I ever hurt you."

Awww, she does love me. "Oh come on. She was just kidding, I'm sure." *I'm counting on you being your type and cheating soon. I just have to figure out a way to catch you at it so I have some proof.*

"I don't think she was."

"She's just trying to protect me then. That's what older siblings do."

"Nice way to be welcomed to the family."

"She can be melodramatic sometimes. I wouldn't let it bother you," I said.

He went back to reading.

"Is she right about you?" I asked.

"Of course not. I'd always invite you to join me if I were going to look for pleasure outside our relationship," he said.

"Great," I said. "You do know the definition of adultery, right?"

"Oh, come on. I'm just kidding."

Hopefully you're not. Everything depends on you living up to your reputation.

"Yeah, of course," I said.

THE ROPE

Saturday, July 15, 2017
Evanston, Illinois

I promised Vi that I would come home to go through my old
things that were still in boxes in her attic, since her house was already
on the market. She wanted me to decide for myself what memories to
keep and what to toss.

While I waited for my flight to take-off, I opened Instagram. At
the top of my feed was a post by Julia. The headline read, "Just found
the most fab wedding dress ever thanks to @Serafina Can't wait
for the big walk! No peaking yet! #ad" In the accompanying photo,
she posed in a white slip in front of a room full of wedding dresses.
Every delicate ripple of her silky slip was in focus, while the dresses
behind her faded into a creamy patchwork. The post already had a
little over 10,000 likes and a bunch of comments, which probably
all went something like, "Can't wait!" or "Wow, you look amazing!" I
didn't need to look. Instead I couldn't help myself and clicked on an
article next to the post titled, "10 signs he may be cheating." I got to
number three, put my phone down, and closed my eyes.

I took a car from the airport to Vi's house, feeling a bit nostalgic
as the driver turned off the highway in Evanston and took Sheridan
Road which followed the curve of the lakefront and offered the
best views of the stately homes that lined the North Shore of
Lake Michigan. It was an exhibition of 19th and early 20th century
architecture: Italianate, Colonial Revival, Federal, Tudor Revival, a
number of Chateauesque monstrosities, and even a Greek Revival.

It had been twenty years since Vi had bought the gorgeous,
late 19th century Painted Lady on a little street tucked away near

the beach, and she had tended to it meticulously. She oiled the oak banister every year, not with products from the local hardware store, but with olive oil that she bought in bulk at the discount grocery. We teased her about her old world ways, but appreciated the traditional cooking skills that she had begrudgingly picked up from her mother. It was always an unexpected treat to walk into the foyer after she had been at work on one of her projects. The warm peppery aroma of olive oil would permeate the spring or fall air despite the open windows.

My driver pulled up to the house and I saw Ali's car parked out front. I let myself in through the side door. Ali was sitting at the kitchen island cutting up an apple. I walked in and set my purse on the kitchen table.

"Hey," she looked up and smiled.

"Hey, where's Vi?" I asked.

"She ran to the hardware store to get some dust masks. When we pulled open the attic door it rained dust on us. I'm sure she hasn't been up there in ten years."

"Ooooh, maybe we'll find some interesting things then."

"Maybe."

"What if there's an old sketch by Max in one of your high school notebooks and we can sell it and all stop working!" I didn't know exactly how much Max's painting sold for these days, but Ali had said he was doing extremely well in New York.

"Only you would want to stop working!" she replied. "Mom loves her work. She has enough money, you know that. She could probably retire now if she wanted to, but she doesn't because her career gives her purpose. I wouldn't expect you to understand that."

"You say purpose, I say an excuse to be alone."

"She didn't want to marry. Leave her alone. She's a grown woman."

We sat silently and I watched as she fidgeted with the label on a glass jar, wedging her thumb nail under the corner and slowly peeling it back.

"Anyhow, what are you guys up to tonight?" I asked.

"Well, it's Soren's birthday, so I made dinner reservations for seven at La Fattoria. I have to hit the road around four-thirty to make sure I'm back by then and have time to get cleaned up."

"And then a romantic evening at home?" I teased.

"I have my period, so probably not!"

"Eh, that's okay, you can make it up to him."

"Make it up to him? Like I did something wrong?" Her disgust was palpable.

"Well, not wrong, but you know. When you can't have sex."

"I am a hundred percent against it when I have my period. Won't do it. Never. Not even on his birthday."

"You can't be serious? Don't you worry that someday, he'll go looking for it somewhere else?"

"If he can't wait one week, then he's already looking."

"Hmmmmm." *Fair point.*

Vi walked into the kitchen and over to the island to give me a hug.

"What are you two girls talking about?" she asked.

"Blow jobs," Ali said.

"You two are so lucky to have each other!" Vi said and turned to me. "How are you, Freddie? How was your flight?"

"Fine. It was fine. How are you?"

"Oh, I'm good. I am gonna miss this old lady when I move, but it's time. It's too big for me now that you two are gone. Should we go up and get started?"

"Yep."

We followed her up the wide front stair case of the old Queen Anne, and I couldn't help thinking about all the times Ali and I slid down the ornate banister when Vi wasn't around.

"So, when do you close on your new place? And where is it?"

"Last week."

"Oh, it's final already?"

"Yeah, but I don't think I'll move until I have an offer on this place. My agent says it's easier to sell a furnished house."

"Where's the condo?"

"It's in Streeterville, downtown, near the lake."

"I can't believe you're selling after all these years. You love this house."

"I know. You were so young when we moved in," she said and squeezed my shoulder.

Vi and Ali had set-up shop on the second floor landing, which meant the old speckled canvas tarp was spread across the landing, the wooden ladder to the attic was down, and two mugs of cold coffee sat on the lowest rung.

"Here's a mask." She handed Ali and me each a drywall mask.

Vi put her mask on and led the way up.

"Watch your step," she yelled down as she gracefully maneuvered up the final step and into the attic.

There was one small round window in the attic that faced west and was little help at this hour. A single lightbulb hung on a cord in the center of the attic. Vi had always talked about turning this into a useable space, but now that I was finally in it, I realized why that impractical idea, among many others over the years, had never come to fruition. It was dark and smelled a bit like sweaty socks, and each step kicked up enough dust to cause a sneezing fit. Vi pointed to two boxes in the far corner, one of which had "Ali" and the other "Freddie" scrawled across the sides in her elegant script.

"Start there. I consolidated your things when you left for college into just a few boxes each. Anything you don't want to haul home goes in here," she said as she pulled a garbage bag out of her pants pocket.

Ali and I pulled our boxes into the middle of the room and began to dig through an assortment of memories, filled with people we hadn't seen in ages and fashion that hadn't been popular in over a decade. Sifting through time was more difficult than I had imagined it would be. Things that should have been thrown away years ago were mixed in with welcome memories that had been all but forgotten. Looking through stacks of photos of the young, naïve girl that I was before that night in the frat house made me immeasurably sad. The happiness and optimism in the kind eyes staring back at me didn't exist anymore.

"Really Mom!" Ali said, holding up an array of beautifully colored swimming ribbons: ninth place, sixth place, eighth place. Ribbons weren't supposed to be pink, purple, yellow, and green, but neither of us had been particularly athletic.

"But you were so cute in your little swimsuits," Vi replied.

"Garbage," she said as she threw them across the attic. Only a few landed in the plastic bag.

"You'll regret that someday. I promise," Vi said.

"Yeah, your kids won't know what a swimming star their mom really was," I teased.

"What kids?" She said.

"Oh, Ali. Never say never," Vi said tenderly.

A comfortable silence permeated the musty attic while we sorted through our childhoods.

An hour later, we were still wading through yearbooks and prom photos.

"Garbage is full," Ali declared.

"Great, that means you're making some progress!" Vi said.

"Well, *I* am." Ali said, looking in my direction.

"I don't see why I should throw any of it out. I have space at the house to store it," I said, as I paged through a high school yearbook.

My eye caught the note next to a photo of me and my chemistry lab partner, the most handsome boy in our graduating class. "Thanks <u>A</u> bunch," it read, referring of course to the A we both got in the class, thanks to my hard work. It wasn't that I was particularly good at chemistry, but rather that Vi ran a tight ship and studying came before sports or clubs or any other activity for that matter.

"You live in New York. How do you think you're going to get all that stuff back there?"

"I don't know. Ship it I guess."

"Not worth the money," Ali snickered.

Ali finished going through the last of the boxes that had her name on it and ventured toward the stack of boxes that Vi had been slowly working through. She picked up a small box marked "Letters".

"I'll go through that one," Vi said. Her tone made it clear that the contents of the box were private.

Vi got up and pulled the garbage bag loose from its perch.

"Anyone want anything to drink while I'm downstairs?" She asked.

"Iced tea," I said.

"I'll have one too," Ali said.

"Let me help you with that," I said and began to get up.

"Got it, thanks!" She looped the garbage bag handles around her wrist and slid gracefully back down the ladder.

I picked up a medium sized box with no markings.

Ali looked up at me. "I still don't understand why you would do that, it's so degrading."

I knew her so well, that I immediately realized that we had jumped right back into the midst of the blow job debate that Vi had interrupted hours earlier.

"Sometimes you surprise even me," I said. "You sure you like men after all?"

"Funny. When was the last time he did that for you?"

I deflected. "He hasn't lately because I'm off birth control," I lied.

"What?" She looked confused.

"Yeah, well, you know."

"No, I obviously don't. You aren't trying to get pregnant already are you?"

Oh, this will be fun! "Of course we are. We're married and I'm not getting any younger." *I do want to have kids someday and I don't want to be an old mother, but not with Nate of course.* It was always fun to rile Ali up a bit.

"But you are so young," she said. "What about your career?"

"You mean my job?"

"I mean your career. The thing that gives you freedom," she said. "Security. Makes you someone. Someone who has done something."

"I don't need a career to be someone who has done something. I can be a wife and a mother. You know, having kids is sort of important too. Contributes to the survival of our species and all. Isn't that the most important thing we can do?"

"You can't really count having kids as an accomplishment. Literally anyone healthy can do that, it's the default option in life. The definition of mediocrity if you will," she said. "Is that what you want in life now, to be mediocre? What happened to your dreams? You used to say you wanted to be famous. Remember? You used to want to be a dancer, or an actress, or something."

"I wanted to be on the Real World, and I was sixteen."

"Oh, yeah, that's right!" she laughed. "You wanted to be a reality t.v. star."

"Yeah well, Vi said she wouldn't pay for college if I studied acting or art or whatever."

"Good thing too! I mean, come on, you don't need a college degree to be a reality t.v. star. That's a joke."

"No, you don't, but you do need connections. Something to set you apart. An education doesn't hurt."

"So what happened?"

"It just didn't work out exactly like I planned."

"It usually doesn't."

If only you knew. If only I could tell you what he did to me. How he changed the course of my life.

I opened the box in front of me. Old family photo albums were stacked on top. Vi's father, Theo had been a prolific documenter of his young family's life. The result was piles of photos, yellowing around their wavy edges, many of which looked identical to the untrained eye. Vi in a cowboy hat, boots, plaid shirt, and denim skirt. Vi in her high school band uniform, dark brown hair curled at the ends. I pulled out the albums and loose photos and piled them in front of me, worried that Vi wanted us to do the culling. A weathered black leather bound book sat at the bottom of the box. I pulled it out and was pleased by the smell of aged paper and ink as I thumbed through the thick pages. The pages were filled with dates, followed by diary entries in a tidy cursive hand that could only have belonged to my mother, when she was young.

I didn't know a lot about Vi's childhood or family. She had always been very secretive. I did, however, know that her parents were both second generation Americans. Their families were both of French origin and had lived in New Orleans. I knew that her dad had been a mechanic in the Airforce, stationed somewhere near Shreveport, after marrying Vi's mother, Ana. I knew that Vi was an only child and that her father died quite young. She kept a faded, black and white picture of her parents in a simple silver frame on the fireplace mantel while I was growing up. It was one of the fixtures of my childhood.

I knew Vi went to college far from home after her father died, and that she had been more or less estranged from her mother after that. I understood that they had a fraught relationship based on the few comments Vi had made when I was younger, and I sensed that things had only gotten worse after her dad died. Vi took us to her mother's funeral when we were young, but I didn't remember ever meeting her before she died. What I did remember was Vi making a strange comment at the funeral, about how I reminded her of her mother. I knew, from a few other off hand comments Vi had made over the years, that her mother was very traditional and quite conservative.

I flipped back to the first page of the diary.

July 14, 1984

Shreveport, Louisiana. *Mom didn't talk to me all afternoon while she made Beef Bourguignon. This morning she asked me to go shopping with her, but who wants to spend Saturday being hurried from store to store downtown, especially on a glorious day like today. It was a perfect summer day to be out on the river, not too humid. Dad and I went out early and caught four fish. Mine was the biggest! He did have to help me reel it in a bit at the end, but I think he was proud. When we got back to the riverbank, he set up his new Kodak camera on a picnic table, set the timer, and took a photo of us together, holding the fish together with the boat and the river behind us. He said that when he was young cameras didn't have self-timers. He's so old! When we got back to the house we fixed the old lawnmower together. Dad says I'm really smart and should be an engineer or a lawyer someday. He says that I'm good at arguing like my mother which would make me a great lawyer. After Mom got home she hardly said a word for hours so I made her favorite cheese Galette to cheer her up. By dinner she seemed to have forgotten that she was upset and even brought us fresh squeezed lemonade while we sat on the back porch, watching the sun set.*

I flipped ahead through the yellowed pages. The handwriting took on more of a forward slant and became decidedly more mature looking with narrower curves and tidier arcs.

December 20, 1986

Shreveport, Louisiana. *Mom demanded that I go to town with her to get the last few things for Christmas. We took the streetcar, had lunch at Antonio's and then went to the department store. They had Converse All-Stars and I've been saving my allowance for months to buy them, but Mom said they're boys' shoes and I should get a pair of girls' shoes instead. I told her no. Dad says I*

*can buy whatever I want with my allowance. She raised her voice
and told me to do whatever I wanted but no wonder none of the
boys in the neighborhood ever came by the house asking about me.
She told me that when she was young all of the best looking boys
in her neighborhood would stop by asking about her. It's 1986! No
boys would come stand outside my window! How old fashioned! I
bought the shoes despite her protests. I don't care what she thinks!
What does she know anyhow? All the boys in our neighborhood and
at school are dumb. I wouldn't want them to like me! Well, there is
this one older guy who hangs around downtown sometimes in the
afternoon. I've seen him a few times on my way home from school. I
think he graduated last spring. He's so hot! He rides a motorcycle,
and not the lame kind that dads ride, it's a cool, fast motorcycle.
Mom would die if I ever got on a motorcycle!*

"A little help" was more of a command than a request. A round
silver tray with three glasses of homemade rosehip iced tea, the kind
Vi had been making since we were little kids, popped up through the
opening in the attic floor. I quickly hid the leather diary inside the box
with my yearbooks. Ali jumped up, grabbed the tray, and set it down
in the middle of the room. She held out her hand and lifted Vi's petite
frame up over the opening.

Vi placed the tray on a box and handed us each a glass.

"Freddie is trying to get pregnant," she announced almost as
nonchalantly as if she was talking about the weather. *Ugh, I probably
should have known that Ali would say something.*

"Ali!" I said.

"You think you're ready for that?" Vi asked.

"Why do I tell her anything?" I mumbled under my breath. "It's
not always easy, you know. Not everyone gets pregnant right away
naturally. It can take months or even years."

"Do you have any reason to think that you'll have trouble?" Vi
asked.

"Not particularly."

"Sounds like an excuse to me," Ali said. "A great reason to quit
working."

"Yep. That's right. I'm just looking for a reason to quit my job and be a stay-at-home mom as soon as possible," I said with a hint of sarcasm.

"You would be an idiot to quit your job," Ali said.

"Well, you should at least think long and hard about it before you do," Vi added.

"It's Nate isn't it?" Ali asked. "He wants you to quit your job, doesn't he?"

"He's supportive, that's all."

"I knew it!"

"It's just that I've been under a lot of stress at work lately."

"It's called being an adult," Ali said.

"Freddie, you know how I feel about it. I won't tell you what to do, but I think you should give it some time. Don't rush into a decision like that," Vi said.

"You had Ali when you were eighteen. I'm twenty-four. I think I'm old enough."

"You are older than I was, but you're still so young. You have plenty of time to have kids. I'm just saying…"

"You're just saying having kids was a big mistake?" I said.

"No, I'm not saying that. Neither of you were exactly planned, I've never been dishonest about that, but even if I could go back I would never change having both of you. Having a young child when I was young and just starting my career made things much more difficult than they had to be," she paused and it seemed as if she was reliving the pain of the difficult moments as she spoke. "In hindsight, when I got pregnant the second time I thought I was so mature, but I wasn't. I was still a kid myself. I'm just saying wait. Take your time. What's the hurry?"

"I don't know. I don't love my job like you do," I said.

"You mean your career?" Ali said.

"I guess so, but I don't think of it that way. For me it's just a job."

"No, it's the thing that gives you freedom and security. I thought you wanted that and more."

"That's what you both want and you expect the same from me without stopping to ask me what I want."

"You're probably right," Vi said, with a rare contribution to one of our arguments. "We've probably put our expectations on you more than we should have over the years, but we just want what's best for you."

"Maybe what's best for you isn't what's best for me," I said.

"How can having financial independence and security not be best for you?" Ali asked.

"I'm not saying that it isn't important, I just think that there are other important things in life that I want, like a family of my own, so I don't end up miserable and alone."

"I still don't see why you can't have both, a career and a family," Ali said.

"Enough," Vi sounded tired. "I think it might be helpful if you talk to a professional about all of this. That has helped me through making some big decisions in my life."

"Sure," I said.

"What do you want us to do with all of these?" I changed the subject, holding up a handful of loose photos.

"Oh, Theo's photos!" Vi said.

"There are a lot of duplicates."

"Yeah, I need to go through those. Leave that box by the hatch please."

I placed the photos back in the box and folded each of the four leafs of the box top, one at a time so that they locked together. I slid the box across the floor to the side of the hatch and pulled another box down from the stack. I began sifting through our old baby clothes and childhood Halloween costumes.

By three o'clock my mouth was dry from the layer of grey dust that had transferred from the collection of memories to coat everything that was exposed. I packed up one small box of my things, put Vi's diary in my oversized purse, and the pestered Vi until she agreed to ship my box across the country to me.

Vi caught me alone after dinner. "Wyn, how are you? How are things going with Nate? How is work?" she asked.

"Things are good." *Well, on track at least.* "Work is fine."

"Just fine?"

"Yeah, like I said, I don't love it like you do."

"Is quitting work your idea or his?"

"Mine." *If I'm not working and I tell a judge that I'm pregnant I might get more alimony in the divorce!*

"And Nate thinks it's a good idea."

"He does."

"Of course," she mumbled.

"Excuse me?"

She practically whispered, "I'm just not sure he has your best interest in mind."

He doesn't, but who does? Who can I trust anymore?

"He's my husband," I said, tired of defending a life that I'd wanted so badly but which had been born out of a nightmare.

"Yes, he is, but that doesn't mean that he knows what is best for you all the time."

"And who does? You?" *You have no idea what I've been through. How can you know what's best for me?*

"I think I know as much as he does about you and what you need," Vi said.

"Maybe you just want me to need what you've needed," I said.

"Maybe he just wants to control you."

Maybe I'm in control. "It's always about that, huh? Men controlling women?" I said.

"In my experience, it usually is."

"Yep." I began to get up.

"Wynafreda!" she said sternly, "do not quit your job. I know you will regret it."

THE TALE

Saturday, July 22, 2017
Manhattan

I was fashionably late on Saturday for Julia's wedding shower, which was held in the party room of a fancy restaurant in Midtown. I grabbed a glass of wine immediately and tried to blend in with the crowd of mostly women, although there were a few well-dressed men sprinkled throughout.

I made small talk with another young woman named Kassie who also looked out of place. She said she had worked with Julia at a women's clothing shop in college, and she didn't seem to know the other women who were catching up loudly about their sorority days.

A woman in the center of the room tapped a fork against her glass and everyone joined in. Julia entered from the back side of the room wearing a bright pink dress. Her long platinum hair fell in loose rings below her shoulders. She looked even thinner than when we'd first met.

She motioned for everyone to sit at the long table. My new friend, Kassie and I sat at one end surrounded by Julia's college friends.

"Did you hear who is getting divorced?" a petite woman with blonde hair and freckles asked.

A few of the other women responded, "Who?"

"Aubrey!" she exclaimed.

"Oh, that's not too surprising," another woman replied, without trying to hide her disappointment.

"I told you she was settling when she married him," another added.

"How many kids does she have now?"

"Three. The last two are IVF twins."

"Mmm hmmm."

They all nodded as if IVF was as commonplace as birth control. I looked around the table and realized that not one of them was bigger than a size four.

"Caroline, did you have IVF with your last one?" one woman asked

"I did. What a pain in the ass, but totally worth it of course," Caroline said and immediately pulled up photos on her phone.

"Oh, he's just the cutest thing in the world, isn't he?"

"Oh, thanks, Jenny," she said. "You know, you've never looked better. I can't believe you gave birth just last week. How is your little one doing?"

Jenny grabbed her phone and showed off pictures of her one week old girl swaddled in a magenta blanket.

"Oh my gosh, how sweet!" they all crooned.

Must be nice to have things work out just like you always hoped.

Various plates with small bites were delivered to the table and side conversations picked up.

"Doesn't Julia look fabulous?" Jenny asked.

"Incredible," they all agreed.

"I don't know how she does it," Caroline said.

"Right!" Jenny added. "Have you seen that woman eat? I can't believe how thin she is. I wish I knew her secret!"

"I know. I'm so jealous," one of the others added.

I laughed to myself thinking about how disgusted Ali would be by their conversation.

The women at the other end of the table began cheering. I looked toward them and saw Adam enter behind Julia. He pulled her around, they kissed, and the cheering grew louder. I clapped and watched as he followed Julia's lead and every move. Martina, Julia's personal assistant and photographer, got into position about fifteen feet in front of them and took a few photos.

When Adam was finally relieved of his ceremonial duties, my eye caught his, and he smiled convincingly. I looked away. Julia commanded all of her guests to crowd around her. She tousled the top part of her long blonde hair a few times and then pulled it forward over her left shoulder. She tucked herself in front of Adam and then compelled us to lift our glasses into the air. Martina took a few shots of the group and then a close-up of Julia and Adam.

Julia opened presents after we were forced to play a silly game about the couple's history together and unique habits.

When the party finally started winding down I made sure to congratulate them before heading home.

Nate was out when I got home, so I settled in with Vi's diary to pass some time.

September 23, 1988

Shreveport, Louisiana. Mom and Dad had a big fight again tonight. It started when Dad overcooked the meat on the grill and Mom said it was because he was drunk. He might have been a little tipsy but he wasn't drunk. I've definitely seen him worse, but he did overcook the meat. It was burnt and chewy. He stormed out and I haven't heard him come back in yet. Sometimes he doesn't come home by bedtime and I wonder whether he comes home all night. I asked Mom once and she wouldn't even acknowledge me. She said he always comes home, but sometimes much later than he should. I wonder if she lies to me because she thinks I can't handle it, or shouldn't know the truth, or maybe she really believes her own lies. She's so weird, but it makes me sad too. I want Dad to be good but I also want her to be honest and stand up for herself sometimes.

September 28, 1988

Shreveport, Louisiana. I was walking home from school today and crossed the street out of my way to walk past him. He looked up and said Hi!!! He has really beautiful eyes! He was smoking a cigarette and he took it out of his mouth to smile at me. I smiled back and said Hi too. I could feel him watching me as I walked away. I had my new All-stars on!

October 11, 1988

*Shreveport, Louisiana. It was hot out for early October and as
I walked home and passed by him, he asked if he could buy me an
ice cream at the drug store. I said yes! As we walked the few blocks
together to the drug store he held my hand! I got a scoop of chocolate
in a cone and we sat on a bench behind the shop. He watched me
with a funny look in his eyes as I licked the ice cream. When I was
done he turned to face me. He said he thought I was really pretty and
then he leaned forward and kissed me. NOT ON THE CHEEK!!!
He pushed his lips against mine gently at first. Then he gave me a
French kiss! His tongue was in my mouth!! It was amazing!!! He
tasted like chocolate ice cream! He is such a good kisser! I know he is,
even though I don't have anything to compare it to except the kisses
I've seen in the movies.*

I had to laugh. I had always figured Vi was a bit of a prude, and it
was funny to read about her reaction to her first kiss.

I heard Nate at the door.
"Hey!" I called.
"Hey!" he called back. He opened and closed kitchen cabinets as he
made himself a snack.
"Whatcha up to?" he asked.
"Just reading," I said.
"Whatcha reading?"
"Oh nothing. Just an old diary I found at my mom's house when
we were packing up her attic."
"Does she know you're reading it?"
"No."
"And you don't think she'll mind?"
"Not if she doesn't find out."
He nodded and looked away.

"Hey, did Jack send you a copy of our marriage certificate yet?"
"No."

"Oh, can you ask him for it please? I need to get a new ID and change my social security card soon."

"I thought you weren't changing your last name?"

"Why would you think that?"

"I don't know. Maybe because your mom never did."

"Oh, I guess I hadn't thought of that." *Total lie. Under normal circumstances I wouldn't hesitate to take my husband's last name, but in this case it's just another means to an end.*

"Just doesn't seem like the kind of thing women in your family do," he said.

It's not, but I need proof. I need to see it with my own eyes. I have to know that we're legally married in Connecticut.

"I'm not like the other women in my family," I said. "I always thought I would change my name when I got married." *I have to see that marriage certificate. I have to know that it's official. We have to be married for this con to work.*

I continued, "I think I'd like to be Mrs. Ellis, that's all." *If I have to change my name to see the certificate, then so be it.*

"I don't get it. You already have a career. Everyone knows you as Wyn Laurent. Don't you like your name?"

"Yeah, I guess I do, but then again, we're married now, and I like the idea of being Wyn Ellis," I lied. "Will you please ask Jack?"

"I don't think you should change your name, but sure, I'll call him today."

"Thank you."

THE TALE

Saturday, August 5, 2017
Manhattan

Adam and Julia's wedding was on the Saturday of our one month anniversary. Vi had flown in the night before and was staying in our guest bedroom. Adam's mom, Adrienne, had invited Vi to the wedding. The invitation read:

Adam + Julia
Saturday, August 5
At 3pm eastern please call 585-420-2326
Rye, NY

I began to get ready around two o'clock. I blew out my hair and got out my best make-up. I went all out: smoky eyes that faded to a lighter charcoal grey; fake lashes that I glued on one by one with a pair of tweezers; and a dark pink lip stain.

Just after three, I picked up my cell phone and dialed the number on the invitation. A pre-recorded message provided the following details: "Your prompt arrival at 330 New England Road is requested at five o'clock. This information is confidential. Do not share it with anyone who was not a direct recipient of an invitation to the event." *Jeez, who does she think she is!*

I yelled to Nate, "Leaving in twenty!"

Twenty minutes later I was ready and on my way downstairs just as he went up to throw on pants and a dress shirt.

"Don't forget your dinner jacket!" I yelled after him.

Vi was waiting in the living room. We piled into Nate's car.

We pulled up to the end of a long line of cars at the end of a long driveway. A sign on the side of the road read, "Highclere Castle". *Figures, not to be outdone, she's rented out a country estate that is a replica of a castle!*

Nate handed the keys to the valet and we followed the other guests down a long brick walkway protected by a trellis covered in baby pink roses. I walked slowly, careful to avoid losing a heel between the bricks. At the end of the walkway, the path gave way to a large lawn, bordered by mature trees. A large white tent sat at the back of the lawn, and wooden flooring had been laid between the tent and the back of the Jacobethan style mansion; its smooth terra cotta brick looked soft against the embellished stone carvings, Tudor arches, and steep roof gables. *It is beautiful.*

A small ensemble played jazz in the back corner of the tent, as waitresses offered champagne and hors d'oeuvre. I spotted Kassie, the friend I had made at Julia's bachelorette party, and made my way over to say hello. She introduced me to her husband, and Nate offered his hand distractedly to each of them. The four of us stood together and made small talk about the weather and the wedding party. Just as I was beginning to feel the warm flush of the champagne cloud my senses, a voice overpowered the band and instructed us all to proceed inside.

We followed Kassie and her husband into the castle. Candles flickered high within the vaulted ceilings. I wondered how they had been meticulously placed so far above the floor. The mood was similar to the moment of illumination that occurs just as the sun dips below the horizon. An organ bellowed the first notes of an indiscernible ancient hymn. The procession began. A young girl about four years old was prodded by her mother at the far end and goaded toward the altar by her father. She threw bunches of rose petals as she wandered down the aisle.

A series of couples wearing the same black tie arrangements and long pink dresses made their way down the aisle. The transition to the first few notes of Pachelbel's Canon were seamless, reverberating throughout the immense space. All eyes locked on Julia as she appeared at the end of the large hall. She looked tiny within the cavernous space. She was alone, except for the women who endeavored to fan the train of her dress to perfection behind her. She began to walk slowly toward us.

As she passed I could see the large smile plastered on her face

Maren Foster

as she fought back tears underneath a billowing white veil. *Does she really love him or is she just putting on a show?* We sat through nearly a full mass. The bride and groom said very little but went through all the appropriate motions. Just as I was becoming bored they kissed and made their way back down the aisle to boisterous cheers.

We were directed back out to the lawn where the champagne continued to flow while we waited for the wedding party. I walked around the tent inspecting the names on the tables, ostensibly looking for ours, but really getting a sneak peek at the guest list. Senator and Mrs. Cameron Hughes, the fashion designer Jean Dubois, famed local restaurant critic Margarite Bordeaux. The list went on and included B-List actors and members of the intelligentsia, whose art or commentary often appeared in well-read publications or must see shows around New York. Some of the storied surnames were a stark reminder of the Ellis' humble beginnings.

Dinner was exquisite. The cake was decadent. Everything was over the top. Champagne glasses were refilled for the toast. Julia talked about the first time they met, the different childhoods that had preceded their relationship, and their hopes for the future. Adam described Julia in detail, from her success as an influencer, to her artistic talent and her penchant for making new friends, to her ability to eat whatever she wanted and still maintain a flawless figure. He lauded her many accomplishments and showered her with praise. I couldn't tell if the single tear that ran down my cheek was a result of joy or sorrow.

They danced to "Can't Help Falling in Love", which seemed a little cliché but the older crowd loved it, and eventually we all joined in as the band began to play well-known favorites. Nate and I danced to a few of the slower songs. He held me tight against his chest and I made sure to get a kiss at the end of each song. Once the sun set, the band packed up and a d.j. took over. We called a car for Vi and sent her back to our house alone.

Toward the end of the evening, we were finally able to congratulate the newlyweds.

I gave Julia a quick hug. "Congrats!"

"Oh my God, thank you. Guess what!" she yelled back.

I shook my head. "What?"

"We bought a house."

"Oh, congratulations."

"It's the one right next to yours," she said. "We're going to be your neighbors." She jumped up and down excitedly.

"Wow!" I said.

"Isn't it great?" Adam stepped in.

"Yeah, congratulations," I said. *It will be nice to have a friend close by, but next door? A little odd? Does he think I need protecting?*

Nate and I left just after one in the morning and passed out as soon as we got home.

I woke up early as the morning sun threw shadows across our bedroom walls. I went to the bathroom and pulled off the last of the stubborn fake eyelashes. Downstairs in the sun room off the back of the house, I picked up yesterday's newspaper.

Vi was up too, reading a book. She looked up as I settled in across from her with a cup of tea in my hand.

"Morning."

"Morning," I mumbled.

"How're you feeling?" she asked.

"Fine."

She chuckled.

"I'm fine," I insisted.

"Are you?"

"Yes! Ugh, stop asking."

"Sure. How was the rest of the party?"

"Nothing special. We left before the DJ stopped playing."

She went back to reading for a few minutes and then broke the silence. "I really thought you would end up with him someday."

"Awkward. He was my best friend," I said.

"Sometimes friendships grow into more."

"Yeah, well, it hasn't."

"Adrienne and I always hoped we'd be able to raise a grandchild together."

"Well, sorry to ruin your plans."

Our phones both sounded simultaneously. Vi didn't move. I swiped my screen.

"FYI" read a message from Ali with a photo of her left hand wrapped around Soren's, a thin gold band encircling her left ring finger.

"OMG! You got married?" I replied. "CONGRATS!"

Her reply came a few minutes later, "No, just engaged."

"Wow, great! When's the wedding?" I replied.

"Who knows! Still getting used to the idea of being engaged."

"So happy for you!"

"Ali's engaged!" I said. Vi picked up her phone. Ali answered and Vi put her on speakerphone.

"Congratulations!" Vi said.

"Thank you," Ali said. "I think it's a good thing."

"Why on Earth wouldn't it be?" I asked.

"I don't know. It's a big commitment. I just never imagined myself married, you know? Someone's wife," she said.

I shook my head.

"You'll figure it out," Vi said.

"How did he ask you?"

"He wrote a critique of an article in The Atlantic magazine and it was included in 'The Conversation' in the print version this month. He knows I read every word of that publication. At the end of his critique he wrote "A.L., will you marry me? S.S."

"How thoughtful," Vi said.

How nerdy!

"So, what's up with you two?" Ali asked. "How was the wedding?"

"Good. It was lovely," Vi said.

"What are you up to today?"

"Oh, we're just hanging out at Freddie's right now," she said. "I fly out tonight."

"Okay, sounds good. Have a good flight."

"Yep, thanks, love you."

"Love you too."

Nate appeared around ten with the Sunday paper and Vi went upstairs to take a shower.

"Morning," I said. "Did you hear Adam and Julia's news last night?"

"No."

"They bought that house next door."

Nate nodded and grumbled something unintelligible.

"I can't believe they're going to be our neighbors."

170

"Shouldn't you be happy? Just last week you were complaining that this neighborhood is too quiet," he said. "You've been complaining since we moved here about how hard it is to make friends when you don't have kids."

"Yeah, I am happy. I mean, she's not my favorite, but it will be nice to have them next door."

"Yep."

"Their wedding was really nice, wasn't it?" I said.

"It was," he said. "You looked really beautiful."

"Awww, thank you. You looked great too. I love dancing with you like that."

"Oh yeah?"

He stopped as he passed by me on his way to the back deck with the morning paper and his coffee.

"Yeah, it was sweet," I said.

"It was," he said and leaned over and kissed me on the forehead. I looked up and kissed him on the lips.

"You're not a bad date," he said.

"Right back at ya," I said, smiling. *Barf! I can't do this much longer.*

With Nate outside I tried to read my paper in the den, but I couldn't concentrate. I kept looking at the empty house next door, imagining them moving in, stopping by unannounced to borrow eggs. I opened the style section of the paper. The front page was covered in photos of Julia and Adam, looking utterly blissful. The headline read, "A country wedding celebrates the classics." I couldn't bring myself to read it.

THE TALE

Saturday, August 19, 2017

Old Greenwich

The moving truck was already in the driveway when I woke up on Saturday two weeks later. I made a latte and curled up on a loveseat in the living room to watch the commotion. Julia seemed to be in charge, walking back and forth and pointing at boxes and furniture, and then the house. There were four young guys taking orders. Adam floated in and out of the frame, seemingly to little effect. She directed and he nodded.

Once the truck pulled out of the driveway I got up and went to the kitchen, grabbed a tin of chocolate chip cookies, and walked next door. I knocked on the front door and Julia answered.

"Hey neighbor!" I said.

"Oh, hi Wyn. How are you?"

"I'm fine, thanks. Just thought I'd come over to welcome you to the neighborhood." I smiled and handed her the cookies.

"Thanks!" she said peeking inside. "Oooh, these look good!"

As if you'll even try one! "How was your honeymoon?" I asked.

"Oh, it was amazing! The scenery and the wildlife were incredible. Seeing lions in the wild is so much different than seeing them at the zoo. You just have to go on safari!"

"You'll have to show us photos."

"Oh, they're all on Instagram already."

"Great. I'll check them out," I lied.

"Yeah. So, how do you like it?"

"Like what?"

"The neighborhood."

"Oh, it's nice, quiet. We haven't met many people yet," I said.

"Hmmm, we know a few people already. We'll have to introduce you."

"Yeah, great. Look, I should go so that you can get back to what you were doing. Tell Adam I say 'hi'."

"Will do. Thanks again for the cookies."

"Yep. Welcome to the neighborhood."

I had an appointment with my therapist in the afternoon.

"Wyn, how are you?"

"Okay, thanks."

"Have you been able to start putting some money away for yourself like we talked about?"

"I tried but he noticed and told me to stop," I lied.

"What did he say?"

"He threatened me," I lied again.

"What happened?"

"He accused me of not trusting him. He said that if I didn't trust him enough to have a shared bank account then maybe we shouldn't be married."

"Wyn, did you marry him?"

I nodded.

She shook her head subtly and then changed the subject.

"How have things been with him, in general? Has he hurt you recently?"

"Um, okay. He did get a little aggressive one night recently." *Our wedding night.*

"What happened?"

"Nate was being silly at first and kind of sweet. He carried me upstairs and put me on the bed."

She nodded.

"Then he pulled out handcuffs and I told him no."

"And then what?"

"He said that it was turning him on, that I was saying no. I guess he thought I was just playing a game. He thought I wanted to have sex and was just saying no to turn him on."

"Do you really believe that?"

I nodded.

"Did you have sex?"

"Yes."

"Wyn, you said no and he forced you to have sex. That's rape."

I shook my head.

"It is," she said.

"I'm such a failure. I should have just kept my mouth shut. He's better when I don't protest."

"Wyn, it's not okay for a man to force a woman to have sex with him regardless of the situation or relationship. You said no and he didn't listen. It doesn't matter if you're married. That's rape."

I shook my head. "I'm just worried that he will leave me if he isn't satisfied."

"Wyn, you said 'he's better when I don't resist' or something like that. He is responsible for his behavior. Him being better shouldn't be reliant on you or your behavior."

"I just can't lose him," I muttered.

"Even in a normal relationship there is a fine line between knowing when to compromise to make your partner happy and knowing when you have crossed a line and are doing something you don't want to do and aren't comfortable with, to please your partner. I don't believe that this is a normal relationship, and I believe that you crossed that line a long time ago."

"I know." *God, do I know.*

"Wyn, I want you to write down anything he says to you that is critical. Like if he criticizes you or tells you that you are doing something wrong, or that you are not successful or capable. I want you to bring that list with you next time so that we can look at it together. I also think we should meet more often. I would like to see you again next week."

I nodded.

"I think the Prozac is really helping," I said. "But I think I might benefit from a higher dose."

"Wyn, I'm worried that the medication is allowing you to remain in a very toxic and unhealthy situation by reducing your anxiety levels."

"I think I need more if I'm ever going to get up the confidence to leave him." *I need more to get through the next few months so that I can finally fix this for good.*

"When is your next appointment with your psychiatrist?"

"Next week I think."

"Ask her about increasing your dose at your appointment. I'll make a note that we talked about it too."

"I will. Thank you."

"Wyn, I'm worried about you. I'm worried that your situation is deteriorating and you aren't taking him seriously enough. I think he could be dangerous."

I nodded. *I can't stop now.*

"Please begin to think about a plan. How you could leave. What you would need to take with you. Where and how you would live. There are safe options." She handed me a brochure.

"Okay. I will." *She doesn't understand. I'll never be safe.*

Everything moved slower in the suburbs and took more time. I had to get up earlier than before to commute in to my office in the city. Every morning I took the new car that Nate had bought me to downtown Greenwich, which was a hodgepodge of old and new-meant-to-look-old. I parked near the train station, boarded the 7:01, and slowly sipped my coffee as I watched the leafy green suburbs pass by. Out the windows, the tree-lined streets eventually gave way to low-rise grey office buildings, parking lots, and suburban shopping malls. Another ten minutes and the office buildings transformed to one and two-story industrial buildings with loading docks surrounded by concrete and the tangled metal of intersecting train tracks. Finally, as we crossed the river, high rises came into view, rising above the water to towering heights, blocking the sun and reminding me that a small cubicle on a large open floor awaited me at the end of my trip. The reverse trip at the end of the day was always more pleasant, as the concrete faded back to verdant green. I enjoyed watching the gritty, industrial landscape transition to lush parkways and large secluded houses surrounded by mature trees. The changing scenery was like a kaleidoscope spinning to reveal a new pattern with each click.

By the end of the week I was exhausted and ready for an evening in. I got home from work a little early. Nate wasn't home. I poured myself a glass of red wine and began to chop an onion and a few cloves of garlic. I browned some meat, added vegetables and left it to simmer.

An hour later, as I checked the stew, I texted Nate. "What time will you be home?"

Nearly half an hour passed before his reply came, "Sorry, it's gonna be a late one tonight. Eat without me. Home ASAP."

I put a lid on the large pot and turned the burner down as low as possible.

My phone lit up as I poured a small serving of stew into a ceramic bowl. *Maybe Nate changed his mind.*

The message was from Adam instead, "How's it goin?"

I responded immediately, "Good. You?"

His reply came almost instantaneously, "Good. Coming over to borrow some milk."

"Sure"

A few minutes later he was at the kitchen door.

"Here you go," I said, handing him a big bowl of stew.

"But I need milk."

"Cereal again?"

"Mac and cheese from a box."

"Julia out again?"

"Yeah, some big event downtown."

"You didn't go with her?"

"She said it wasn't really a couple's thing. Plus I went to one last week and the week before. I can only handle so many of those parties."

"Nate's out late tonight too," I said. "Why don't you stay?"

He nodded.

I set the table and poured another glass of wine. We sat down across from each other.

"So, how's work?" I asked.

"It's been good lately. I really like my new role. How're things for you?"

"I don't know. I should be up for a promotion this year. I'm overdue."

"Well, I hope you get it," he said raising his wine glass.

"Thanks." I tapped my glass against his and took a sip of wine.

"So where's Nate?" he asked.

"Not sure. He said he needed to work late tonight. Said he wouldn't be home for dinner."

"He works late a lot, doesn't he?"

"Yeah, bit of a workaholic I guess."

"I'm sorry."

"Nah, it is what it is," I said.

We finished dinner and he kept me company while I did the dishes.

I woke up early the next morning. Nate was sprawled out on his side of the bed, snoring lightly. I slowly swung my legs around and climbed off the bed as quietly as possible. I tiptoed over to the dresser and slowly slid open two drawers to find my sports bra and yoga pants. As I pulled my bra on over my head, my eyes caught the mirror above the dresser and I saw Nate propped up against the headboard watching me.

"Morning," I said.

"Morning," he muttered back. I continued to pull on my thong and yoga pants.

"What time did you get home?"

"Late. Sorry, you were already asleep."

I nodded.

"Have you stopped going to yoga?" he asked. This was of course his way of pointing out that I had gained a few pounds since our wedding.

"I haven't had time to go for a few weeks. I told you things at work have been pretty busy lately."

"Why don't you quit then?"

"I don't know. Don't you think it's a little early for me to quit."

"What do you mean early?"

"I mean I'm not even pregnant yet."

"Yeah, but didn't your doctor say that the pressure you are under at work may be making it harder to get pregnant?"

"He did." *Totally didn't but Nate had bought that story without question.* "But what if I don't like it? What if I get bored?"

"Bored with what? Doing whatever you want?"

"Yeah."

"Ugh, I'm so tired of this. It's exhausting. Can't you just make up your mind already?" he said.

"Sorry. I just don't know what to do."

"Haven't you been going to therapy? Isn't that supposed to help you decide?"

"I have, but it's not that easy."

"Seems like you're starting to lose it. You always seemed so sure of what you wanted before. This indecisiveness isn't like you. I don't know what's going on, but please figure it out. I don't want to be married to one of those crazy women."

I nodded. *Crazy like marrying your rapist for revenge?*

"Oh, did you ask Jack about our marriage certificate?" I asked.

"No, sorry, I forgot."

"Could you give me his phone number so I can call him?"

"I'll call him today. I promise," he said.

"I really need it to get things sorted out."

"Sure."

Liar! What are you hiding? What games are you playing?

After yoga I had brunch with Jenna, another young woman who was a regular and had been unusually friendly after the first couple of classes I attended. She and her husband had moved to the area about a year before after she had her second child. According to her LinkedIn profile she was "President of Domestic Affairs at The Holloway Residence".

We ate at a small café near the yoga studio. She spent the majority of the time talking about her baby, but did ask me a few questions about how I was settling in and how I liked the area.

"It's fine," I told her. "My commute is much longer than it was before though."

"Oh, yeah, I'm lucky that I don't have to deal with that."

"Yeah, my husband thinks I should quit my job."

"Why wouldn't you?" she asked.

To have some security and independence…then again, alimony is usually easier to get if you're not working, especially in a state like Connecticut that still considers fault during divorce proceedings. "I'm not sure. My mom and my sister don't think I should quit," I said.

"Why not?"

"They think I should be financially independent, just in case."

"Just in case, what?"

"You know, I end up alone for any reason."

"Why would you end up alone? Your husband has life insurance, right?"

"Yeah, of course. I think they are just really cautious, that's all."

"You can always go back to work if you have to."

"Yeah, I guess so."

"And you want to have a family, right?"

"Yeah."

"I'll probably be pregnant again in the next six months. It would be so fun to be pregnant together!"

"It would!" I tried to match her enthusiasm.

Nate was gone when I got home. I grabbed my laptop and began to do some research. Nate's hesitation to get our marriage certificate from Jack was starting to worry me. It hadn't occurred to me before the wedding that he might stage the whole marriage, but I was starting to wonder. Hadn't I read about some famous British rock star who had done just that to his wife? They'd had a big wedding, were married by someone he recommended and then he conspired to have the required steps avoided so that they weren't really married? *Would Nate really try to pull something like that? I guess he is a bit of a commitment-phobe, but that seems pretty extreme, even for him. Still, I need to cover all my bases if this thing is going to work.*

I searched the web for marriage law in Connecticut. I found a few helpful summaries with hyperlinks to various case law. I began clicking the links and skimming: Dennis v. Dennis, 68 Conn. 186 (1896); Catalano v. Catalano, 148 Conn. 288 - Conn: Supreme Court 1961; Carabetta v. Carabetta, 182 Conn. 344 - Conn: Supreme Court 1980. They all dealt with marriage but weren't exactly what I was looking for. After more digging, I stumbled upon Perlstein v. Perlstein, 152 Conn. 152, decided by the Connecticut Supreme Court in 1964, which said, "A marriage ceremony, especially if apparently legally performed, gives rise to a presumptively valid status of marriage which persists unless and until it is overthrown by evidence in an appropriate judicial proceeding." *Hmmm, what does "a presumptively valid status of marriage" mean? And what does an appropriate judicial proceeding mean?*

I clicked a link within the case law brief: Hames v. Hames, 163 Conn. 588, decided by the Connecticut Supreme Court in 1972. I skimmed the summary: "The policy of the law is strongly opposed to regarding an attempted marriage...entered into in good faith, believed by one or both of the parties to be legal, and followed by cohabitation, to be void." *Bingo! So we are married in the eyes of the law! Hah! He thinks he's so smart, but for my purposes, it doesn't matter whether he or Jack ever sent in the paperwork! No need to worry about getting the certificate or changing my surname after all!*

THE BREAKDOWN
Friday, September 28, 2017
Manhattan

Friday morning I got to work early. I hadn't checked my email since I'd left the night before, so there were a bunch of unread messages in my inbox. I quickly deleted about seven system-generated emails notifying me of new workflows. I responded to a couple of the easiest messages and ignored a couple more that I knew would be trouble.

At a quarter to nine, I heard the familiar sound of a key in the lock of my boss Ethan's office door. "Wyn, coffee!" came at the usual time.

At first it had been small requests, like 'Hey, Wyn. Could you grab that document off the printer for me?' when I was already going in that direction. They were reasonable asks, the kind of thing a good employee does without hesitation, but the next thing I knew, it was coffee first thing every morning, scheduling meetings that I wasn't asked to attend, maintaining the staff contact list. I knew I was young, relatively early in my career, but I also felt like a caricature of an overqualified, underappreciated secretary, and that wasn't even my job description. In the past, every time I'd had that thought I cringed, worrying that I was turning into Vi or Ali. At first, I actively resisted what I thought was just an ingrained cranky Feminist view of the world that Vi had instilled in me, but with every act of humble subservience I became more irritated, and overtime my resentment built.

I spent the hour before lunch prepping for a one o'clock meeting of the senior leadership team. I'd been asked to set-up and take notes. I settled in with my laptop at the end of the long table, out of the way but close enough to hear the discussion. The VPs and Senior VPs began to file in and make small talk about the weather, sports, and other mundane topics. Just a moment before the meeting started, Ethan and his boss, Alan, came in discussing the timing of a new product launch. As they sat down, I sat up a little straighter in my chair and rested my fingers lightly on the home keys.

The Chief Operating Officer commenced the meeting. "Thanks everyone for joining us today."

As they were still settling in I heard Alan say, "Cup of coffee."

I looked up. He was looking directly at me, expecting me to fetch his beverage of choice. The coffee station was in the corner across the room.

"Alan?" the C.O.O. said.

"I would like a cup of coffee, please," Alan said, still looking at me.

"It's in the corner as always," I said, meeting his gaze.

"May I please have a cup? Two sugars, no cream," he instructed.

"You may," I said and didn't move a finger.

He didn't look away.

The silence in the room was deafening.

"Oh, for God's sake," an older woman mumbled as she got up to get Alan his coffee. Nancy was the only woman on the senior leadership team, head of Human Resources. As she fetched his coffee I wondered how many calls she'd had about him over the years, and if perhaps, despite her best efforts she knew he would never change. He did at least mumble "Thank you" when she handed him the cup, but it was hardly consolation. He'd had his way.

I took extremely detailed, diligent notes, almost word for word to distract myself. As the meeting began to wind down and the conversation devolved to tangential topics, I made sure to save my notes and then opened my email to see if anything important had come in. There was an email chain with initial thoughts about a marketing campaign that I'd been keen to get involved in. I was so absorbed catching up on the emails that I hadn't noticed that most of the meeting attendees had packed up and either left or were nearly out the door.

"I'd like to see you in my office," Alan said.

Am I going to be fired over the coffee thing?

I was startled by the heaviness of his hand on my shoulder. I looked around the room. *Why is he touching me? We are alone.* His hand lingered longer than it should have. He wasn't actively massaging my shoulder, but he squeezed it in a way that was more than paternal. My skin began to crawl under his hand. Then, as I searched for the appropriate response, he turned and left the room.

The feeling that I'd just been a party to something wrong, something dishonest, swept over me. All of the things I could have said, should have said, played in my head. *Get your hands off me. Don't touch me. Do you know what sexual harassment is?* They all seemed so extreme for what, I reminded myself, he might have thought was a harmless gesture.

I got back to my desk and tried to work but my mind wandered. *Did he think it was okay because I hadn't said anything? Does he know how uncomfortable that made me? If I tell H.R. what will he say? Will he just deny it or say that he didn't mean anything by it? Maybe he'd say that it was just a harmless gesture from an old man? That when he was coming up at the company that kind of thing was completely normal, and he just couldn't understand why Millennials were so sensitive?*

Regardless, I couldn't focus and there was no way I was willingly submitting to a one-on-one in Alan's office, so I told my direct boss, Ethan, that I had a headache and went home early.

I walked into the house and found Nate sitting on a bar stool at the oversized kitchen island. He was leaning slightly forward, his tanned forearms resting on the counter in front of him. A glass of scotch on the rocks in his favorite Waterford crystal glass sat inches in front of his right hand. Across the island, Julia was leaning against the counter in a low-cut t-shirt with a glass of white wine.

"What're you doing home so early?" I said.

"We were having a business meeting of sorts. I asked Julia to come over to discuss whether or not she would be willing to promote our new line of women's skin care products that I told you about."

There was a small bag with Nate's company logo sitting on the counter in front of Julia.

"I'm just picking pick up some samples to see if the products are up to my standards for promotion," she said.

"Oh, how do you select what you'll sponsor or promote?" I asked.

"Well, it's all about the product," she said. "Whether I like the scent, the design of the packaging, the way the products make me feel when I use them."

"So, not whether or not they actually work?"

"Well, of course that should be important, but sometimes it's hard to tell. You know?"

I nodded.

"If I think other women will like a product, then I promote it," she said.

"You're home early," Nate said.

"Yeah, I had a bad day at work," I said.

"Did you quit?"

"No, but maybe I should have." I circled around the island behind Nate, putting my hands on his muscular shoulders, like an adolescent laying stake publicly to a new crush.

He turned his head and gave me an obligatory peck on the cheek.

"Anyhow, I'll let you get back to your meeting," I said.

I headed up to my office and settled into the large brown leather armchair in the corner, which gave me a lovely view of a few treetops and, in the distance, a glimpse of the horizon where the dark water of the Sound met the stone grey sky.

My mind began to wander. *Is he in love with her? Are they having an affair? Does Adam know?*

I spotted Vi's diary on the side table and picked it up, needing a distraction.

October 11, 1988

Shreveport, Louisiana. *He almost blew it! I was downtown with Mom running some errands and he smiled at me across the Brookshire's parking lot. She looked at me sternly and asked me how I knew him. I said that I didn't and maybe he was just being friendly. She said that he is white trash and I shouldn't be nice to him. I knew that dating him would upset her, but I didn't realize how much!*

October 21, 1988

Shreveport, Louisiana. We met up after school as usual and he handed me his helmet. I've been on the motorcycle once or twice before but not for long rides, mostly just around the block. I get a little scared when I'm on it because Dad said that his best friend from school died in a motorcycle crash, but it's thrilling too! I understand now why people like to ride them so much. We drove to a little park out of town. It has a babbling brook running through it and he put his leather jacket on the ground for me to lay down. He laid next to me in the shade of a big willow tree. It started to get cold as the sun went down. He wrapped his arms around me to keep me warm. We talked about life and we kissed. He slipped his hand up under my bra and felt my boobs. I was worried that he would think they are too small but he didn't seem to care. I think he really likes me! I told Ruth and Elizabeth and they said that he probably wants to have sex. They said that sex before marriage is a sin. That's exactly what Mom would say. I think it sounds exciting!

Jeez, this is getting interesting! I felt a little guilty reading about my mom's first real crush, but couldn't help myself.

November 10, 1988

Shreveport, Louisiana. I can't believe Dad's gone. He was here yesterday, sitting in that big worn armchair of his, and now he's gone, just like that. And he was only fifty-one. Mom says that God works in mysterious ways and that even this tragedy will teach us something, but I hate it when she says things like that. It's so unfair! If there's a God, why do bad things happened? Why would good people die? He was the best dad ever! They were fighting more and more lately. Maybe she killed him! I don't mean that. I mean, maybe all their fighting killed him. He loved her so much. Maybe the fighting broke his heart. Maybe he died of a broken heart. The doctor who came to the house said it was probably a heart attack.

The wake was today. The funeral will be on Saturday. I've already cried so much, I don't think I can cry anymore. I would do anything to stop the pain, the aching inside. What will I do without him? Who will take me fishing? Mom and I are so different. She's only interested in cooking and shopping.

It went on but I couldn't read it. It made me sad to think about the grandfather I never met, leaving a middle-aged wife and a young daughter alone. *Maybe that's why Vi never married. Maybe she was scared of being left alone again. I guess I knew that her dad had died relatively young and I knew they'd been close, but his death must have been so hard for her.*

I skipped ahead.

November 18, 1988

Shreveport, Louisiana. *We did it! He picked me up on the motorcycle after school and we drove to the creek. It was a little chilly out but he had a blanket and he wrapped it over us. The sun was out, so I wasn't too cold. He started kissing me and put his hands on me. He felt me up and then he pulled up my skirt and unbuttoned his pants. He held himself over me and then he did it. I have to admit that it hurt more than I thought it would and I wouldn't say that it felt good, but I smiled and pretended that I was enjoying it because he seemed to be. I guess he enjoyed it a lot because he began to shake and moan and then he collapsed onto me. He was sweating too. It definitely wasn't as exciting as I was hoping. I don't really get what everyone is so worked up about. I'm not sure what I'll do if he wants to do it again. I don't think I regretted it, I wanted to try it, but it did hurt. I'm not sure I want to do it again.*

So Vi wasn't the prude I've always thought she was! I guess that's why she didn't want us to date when we were in high school. It's hard to understand why she thought we would get pregnant so young like she did. It was such a different time. She could have just told us about birth control!

THE TALE

Saturday, October 14, 2017
Old Greenwich

The weeks passed slowly. I relished in the weekends when I didn't have to commute into the city. My phone lit up on the arm of the chair next to me. I swiped a familiar pattern on the screen and read a new message from Kassie.

"Bunch of us are going to Simon's tonight ~9pm. You in?"

"Is Julia going?" I replied.

"Probably. Candace texted me about it," Kassie replied.

I actually was in the mood to go out and Nate had plans with some old high school friends, all guys. Other than Nate, they all had kids now and made a point to escape one Saturday a month for what they called "poker night". I didn't ask any questions and didn't really want to know what they did, but was just glad that none of their activities ended up in my Facebook feed.

"Okay, we'll see. Might make it if I get a nap first," I replied.

"Let me know if you need a ride," she replied.

I texted Jenna, "Ladies night out tonight if you want a break from the kids. Simon's. 9ish."

I fixed up a quick dinner for myself and pulled a frozen meatloaf from the freezer, so that Nate would have something to eat when he got home, which I assumed would be in the early hours of the morning. Then I curled up on the couch in front of the TV and fell asleep.

I was woken by a soft kiss on my forehead. "Hope you have some more exciting plans for the evening," Nate said.

Maren Foster

"Yeah, going out with Kassie," I said, groggy from my nap. I looked at my watch: 8 p.m.

"Shoot, that nap was longer than it should have been. I need to get ready."

"No time for a quickie," Nate said and moved forward to give me a kiss. His lips landed softly on my mouth but I kept mine closed tightly.

"Got it, no time for that, as usual. See you later," he said.

I showered and put on my best black skinny jeans and was ready by nine-thirty when Kassie pulled up to the house.

She turned the radio down as I climbed up into the passenger seat. We parked less than a block from Simon's, which was the kind of bar that you snuck into in college before you turned 21. It was firmly rooted in as many generic bar themes as they could get away with: Irish, pool house, honky-tonk. It reminded me of our go-to place in high school. It was safe, frequented by the random dads who had snuck out for the evening, but not entirely uncool.

It was still pretty early. There were a handful of guys at the bar watching a game on t.v. and a few more playing pool in the back corner. A group of five women, including Candace, was sitting around a table with drinks in hand. Sure enough, Julia was seated in the middle of the table and all eyes were on her. She was smiling, basking in the attention. I recognized the other women vaguely but couldn't place them. I figured they had probably been at her bridal shower and the wedding.

Kassie and I went to the bar and ordered drinks. We pulled another table and a few more chairs over. One woman was talking about a vacation she'd recently taken. Another was talking about her recent boob job.

"What does your husband think?" one of the women asked about the boob job.

"The better question is; what does your boss think?" another offered sarcastically.

"Well, he can't keep his eyes off my chest," she replied.

"Which one?" the first woman asked.

"Both!" she exclaimed. "And their hands too."

The women around the table were equally amused and horrified, mostly because it was unclear whether she was serious or joking.

"I've been thinking of getting some myself," Julia said.

"Are you kidding?" the second woman challenged. "You have the perfect body. You don't need a boob job!"

"Hey! What am I?" The boob job lady tried to hide her wounded ego with sarcasm.

Julia filled the awkward silence that followed; "But I was thinking that I might wait until things get stagnant with Adam. At least I've heard that happens eventually. I was thinking I'd keep that one in my back pocket in case I need it someday."

"Awww, newlywed sex," one of the women crooned.

"Well, our sex is pretty fantastic, but it's not like we waited until we were married, so it hasn't changed that much lately."

They all nodded.

"Well, that's not exactly true," she continued. "There's something about married sex that is inherently a bit boring, isn't there?"

She paused to make sure everyone was listening. "It's like, it was hot and unpredictable, and then he put a ring on it and it changed overnight. It's bizarre actually. I didn't think that would happen to us."

"Yeah, isn't it crazy how married sex can be pleasurable, satisfying, and yet . . . boring," a friend of Julia's added.

Candace chimed in, "Speaking of sex and shocking, have you seen the news about that Hollywood mogul?"

Julia shrugged. "Yeah, who is he?"

"I read that he's one of the most powerful producers in Hollywood."

"Did you see who accused him of rape?"

"I know. Rose McGowan. Can you believe it?"

"Oh my God, I loved her in Charmed when I was in high school!"

"I mean, yeah, he seems like a total creep, doesn't he?" I said.

"Really?" Candace said. "Can't you see that it's all about the money? As far as I've seen, none of them have any proof that he did anything wrong."

"Yeah, I don't get it," Julia said. "A bunch of beautiful women say they were called to his hotel room or house and he was acting inappropriately. Why didn't they just turn around and leave? It's not like he tied them up or something, did he? They could have just left."

"Exactly!" Candace said.

Maybe by the time they realized what was going on it was too late. "Do you not understand the idea of 'abuse of power'?" I said.

"I just don't buy it," she said. "He obviously had something they wanted, and it wasn't looks, and they did what they had to do to get it."

"But isn't that the point. They shouldn't have had to do that to get a job."

"Are you really that naïve?" Julia asked.

"So, it's naïve to expect that a woman can go to work and not be raped or sexually harassed?" *Oh my God, do I sound just like Vi and Ali?*

"You don't even know that they're telling the truth. What if they're just mad that they didn't get the job?"

"All of them?"

"Who knows?"

I looked down at my drink and shook my head.

Julia continued to drink and play hostess. I sipped a Margarita and watched as she got louder and louder. Eventually she and her friends headed for the dance floor. Kassi and I watched from the table as a group of young guys moved in. She didn't seem to put up any obstacles and pretty soon she was grinding with the best looking guy in the bar. I watched and wondered why she had married Adam at all. She certainly didn't seem to need his money. He wasn't unattractive, but he just didn't seem like her type either. He was a little too decent and she was a little too self-absorbed. She probably could have married just about anyone she wanted. *Maybe it's the way he adores her. Maybe after I rejected him, he was determined not to lose the next one.*

"You ready to go or you want to stay and watch this train wreck until the bitter end?" Kassie said handing me a glass of water.

"Yeah, just a minute," I said. "Need to go close my tab."

I picked up my phone and headed to the bar. As I waited for the bartender to close my tab I held my phone up as if I was reading something, but hit record and zoomed in as much as possible. After a minute of Julia on camera, grinding and fondling with the young guy, I figured I had enough. I signed the receipt and Kassie and I headed out.

Nate was sitting in the big armchair in the living room when I got home. He had a nearly empty glass of whiskey in his hand.

"Hey you," he said as I walked into the kitchen.

"Hi."

"How was your night?"

"Fine, I didn't think you'd beat me home."

"Guys all had stuff to do early tomorrow."

I nodded.

"Hey, come over here," he said slyly. "I have something for you."

"I'm not really in the mood," I said. *I know I'm supposed to do whatever it takes, but I'm tired.*

"You never are anymore are you?"

I shrugged.

"You're not getting it somewhere else are you?"

I was surprised that he would actually ask me that question.

"I can't imagine it's better than with me, but if you are, you should just tell me," he said. "Maybe we can open things up."

"No, nothing like that, I just haven't been turned on lately, sorry."

"Come here," he demanded.

I knew he wouldn't give up and I knew I needed to keep him happy until I had proof, so I gave in. He put his drink on the side table next to the chair and pulled an old sweatshirt off his lap which I hadn't seen from the kitchen. He was naked and already aroused. He slid toward the edge of the chair.

"Why don't you catch up on all those squats you've been missing out on at the gym," he said. It was more of an order than a question. Anger coursed through me. I suddenly noticed how silent it was in the house.

"I'll make it worth your while," he added.

All of this living hell will be worth my while someday, if I stay committed and see it through to the end. I wiggled out of my skinny jeans and took off my thong. *At least I'm still tipsy.*

"Don't you come over here with that sweater on," he said.

I pulled my sweater off over my head, crossed the living room and stopped in front of his chair. I turned around and began to lower myself onto his lap.

"I don't even get a kiss," he said.

I stood up and then kneeled down on the edge of the chair, hovering above him. I bent forward, sucking in my stomach, and he kissed me aggressively, biting my lower lip. I kissed him just enough to get turned on, and then turned my back to him again and sat down. I began my work out for his viewing pleasure, raising myself up and then back down again. Eventually, he came and I went upstairs to bed.

I woke up just after three in the morning. I tossed and turned for a while and then admitted defeat. I tapped the Facebook icon on my home screen and began scrolling through the images and posts. The typical assortment of posts filled the screen: pictures of groups of people out partying, photos from weddings, scenic panoramas from once in a lifetime adventures, but one particular photo caught my attention. It was a photo of a children's chalkboard easel with a handwritten message in curly cursive: "Baby Jensen. Coming 2018." My sinuses burned and a tear ran down my cheek. *Why do other people get to have babies and move forward easily to the next chapter of life while I'm stuck here grappling with the past? Why does it look so easy for them? Is it really that easy or is it all fake? Why have things been so different for me? Why did he have to ruin my life?*

This is why I hate Facebook. I should just delete my profile. I had done that before but always restored it within a couple of weeks. The pull was too strong, too irresistible. Despite knowing how damaging the deceitful barrage of self-promotion and celebratory posts were, I couldn't help it, because for each of those there was one that confirmed that someone else was suffering too. That I wasn't alone. Those details weren't paraded around but they were there if you knew where to look. The soulful selfie in the park or the photos of decadent meals enjoyed alone. Then there were the truly difficult to read posts. The touching tributes to a loved one lost. The frank portrayals of struggles with disease and sickness. These too were some sort of perverse consolation. A reminder that, in some ways, it could always be worse.

Eventually I dozed off and was awoken by the clatter of pots and pans in the kitchen downstairs, which gave way to the heavenly smell of bacon.

I found Nate in the kitchen. He piled scrambled eggs on two plates and topped them off with a few slices of fresh avocado.

I sat down across from him at the table and picked at the food.

"You were up really late, weren't you?" he said.
"I couldn't sleep."
"Something bothering you?"
"I don't know," I lied. *How to set the next phase of the con in motion*

and how much longer can I stand this life? That's what's bothering me. "Not particularly."

He got up and started to clean up the mess he'd made in the kitchen.

"Guess who's pregnant," I said.

"Julia?" he asked.

I paused, a little surprised that she would be the first person to come to his mind.

"No, Jordan Jensen," I said.

"Who is that?"

"My sorority sister and roommate in New York. You met her a few times at my apartment after we first met, and she was at our wedding. She's married to that gastroenterologist."

He shrugged.

"She was one year ahead of me in school."

"So?"

"So, it's hard to see other women get pregnant so easily," I said. "So young."

"How do you know it was easy for her?"

"I guess I don't, but you know what I mean."

"No."

"She just looked so happy in the pictures."

"Oh, you saw it on social media, didn't you?"

"Yeah."

"You know that stuff is complete bullshit," he said. "I told you to get off it a long time ago."

"But you're still on it."

"Yeah, but I don't obsess about it like you do."

"I wouldn't say that I obsess about it."

"I would."

I shook my head.

"You know how I feel about it. If you want to start trying to get pregnant, quit your job."

"I can't just quit my job."

"Why not? You're clearly unhappy and stressed out. You know that stress can impact fertility and clearly you want to be pregnant. So quit already."

I was silent. *There's no way in hell I'm having your child. I just need a little more time.*

He continued, "It's pretty clear that you can't handle working and everything else. How do you expect to be able to handle having kids and working if you can't even manage to work and take care of things around here right now?"

"I didn't think I was doing that badly." *You son of a bitch!*

He ignored me. "Plus, you can always go back to work if you don't like staying home. Or do something else."

"I don't know."

"I don't get it. When we met you said you wanted to stay home, have kids, just be a mom," he said. "What changed?"

"I don't know. People change their minds."

"Or are brainwashed by their families."

"What?"

"You know what I mean," he said. "You're worried what Vi and Ali will think, aren't you?"

"I don't think they would be very supportive of me quitting my job right now."

"They don't know you as well as I do."

Really? My mom and sister don't know me as well as you do? I shrugged.

He continued, "I'm serious. When was the last time you talked to either of them about how you are feeling about all of this?"

God, he knows how to push the right buttons.

I didn't answer.

"What do you have to lose anyway?" he asked.

"I don't know. Vi and Ali think I will regret not having my own career."

"But you don't even like your job."

"Yeah, but they think I should have my own income."

"You have more than any woman could want," he said. "What do you need? You can have it."

"That's not the point."

"I don't get it," he said. "You want to have children more than anything. You didn't have a problem with the idea of staying home before."

"I know, I just think that maybe Vi and Ali have a point. Just because you can buy me things doesn't mean I have security. It means I have you," I said. "What if someday I don't?"

"Oh, come on, Wyn. We've talked about this before. I have a phenomenal life insurance policy, of which you are the sole benefactor. You have nothing to worry about."

"What if I quit and then I get bored and want to do something else? You know, be my own boss." *What I really mean is, what if I quit and then the con doesn't pay? Then what?*

"Won't you be your own boss the minute you quit?"

"Funny. If that's the case, then I'm already my own boss. The boss of the laundry, grocery shopping, cooking dinner…"

"You know what I mean. You can do anything. Why do you want to be a boss?"

"I'm not saying I do, but what if I might?"

"Really, you?"

"Sure. Why not me?"

"I just didn't think of you as that type."

"What type is that?"

He didn't say anything.

"You don't think I'm smart enough, do you? Or is it about motivation?" I said. "You think Julia is so smart, don't you? With her little blog and her Instagram followers."

"I didn't say that. It's hard work being a boss. I just don't think that's who you are."

"What if I want to start my own business?"

"What would you do?"

"I don't know. It's just a hypothetical."

"Fine. Sure," he said. "What do you want me to say?"

"That I could start a business, whatever the cost, with some of our money."

"Well, I don't know about whatever the cost," he said. "You'd have to develop a business plan and justify whatever investment you need."

"Oh, so Shark Tank Home Edition?"

"Come on, you know what I mean."

"Really? Do I? Did Julia have a business plan when she started her blog?"

"She did that while she was still in school, I think. Besides, what does Julia's blog have to do with anything?" he asked. "If you want to start a blog, go ahead. You can do that right now if you want, for the cost of a night out with the girls."

"Yeah, sure."

"Are you going to quit your job or not?"

"I don't know. I'll think about it."

"Ugh, you're exhausting."

THE TALE

Wednesday, October 18, 2017

Greenwich

When I got out of my car at the train station on Wednesday morning, I was surprised to see Julia. She was facing the end of the platform, watching for the train to the city. I waited on a bench near the station house, sipping tea from a to-go cup. When the train pulled up I watched her get on the first car, followed by about five or six businessmen. I followed. She took a seat about halfway down the car. I walked toward her and we made eye contact as I approached.

"Julia!" I said, perhaps a little too enthusiastically for a weekday morning.

"Wyn, hi," she said. I stopped in the aisle. The train car wasn't entirely full yet but there weren't many completely empty benches left either.

"Mind if I join you?" I asked.

"Of course not," she said and reached over to move her large purse off the seat next to her.

"How are you?" I asked as I sat down.

She nodded, but didn't look up from her phone.

"You're going downtown early today," I said.

"Yeah, I have a fitting for an event."

"Oh, nice. Which designer?"

"Port Azalea."

I nodded.

"How was the rest of your night at Simon's?"

"When, Saturday?" She acted as if she'd already forgotten.

"Yeah, did anything exciting happen after I left?"

"Not sure when you left, but no, why?" she asked without looking up at me. I could sense irritation in her voice.

"I mean, I was just wondering," I said. "You know, I was wondering whether Adam knows."

She looked up and stared directly at me, so intensely that I wanted to look away.

"Look," she said. "Adam and I have an understanding. He never expected me to be the kind of wife who sits around at home all the time, waiting for him, and so I'm not."

"Sure," I said. "Got it.'

We sat next to each other pretending to have more important things to do for the rest of the nearly hour-long ride into Grand Central Station. I pulled Vi's diary out of my purse.

February 17, 1989

Shreveport, Louisiana. It's been more than three months since my last period. I went to the library and read everything I could find about what to do when you're pregnant. I didn't dare check out any of the maternity books because then the librarian would know and God knows who she might tell. First, she would tell a friend, not because she meant any harm, but because she was bored, and then it would spread like wildfire in this small town. Then Mom would know. Well, she'll know eventually I guess. There was one book tucked away behind the others in the small maternity section that didn't have a barcode or the library stamp on it. The book said my stomach is going to start getting bigger soon. It's already starting to get harder to suck my stomach in. It won't be long before I'll have to start wearing my frumpiest dress around everywhere to hide it. It also said that there is a way to not be pregnant anymore. It's called an abortion.

February 24, 1989

Shreveport, Louisiana. I told her. I'm pretty sure she already knew even though I'm just barely starting to show, but she nearly killed me all the same. I've never heard her utter a swear before and

tonight she produced some of the ugliest I've ever heard in my life!
And then some. In some weird, backwards way, I think I thought it
might make her happy since Dad is gone. I thought maybe she would
be happy to have more family. She wasn't. She just regurgitated
everything I've ever heard in Church: sex before marriage is a sin;
an unwed mother is a shame…a whore. "You'll go to hell!" She
said that! She knew immediately who the father is and that made it
even worse. She called him awful things like Cracker, White Trash,
Scumbag, and Son of a Bitch. And then she said the most outrageous
thing…she said that we should be married before the baby comes.
I told her that's the last thing I want right now. She said I might
as well be a prostitute then because it's the only way I'll be able to
provide for the little bastard, and slammed the door in my face. She
can go to hell. I hate her anyhow. I can't wait to get out of here.

I did the quick math in my head. Ali was born on August 25, 1989.
It's Ali! So that's how Ali was conceived. I wonder if my origin story is in
here somewhere.

The train rolled slowly into the station. We gathered our things
and joined the crowd queuing to disembark. I turned back toward
Julia.

"Look," I said. "I didn't mean to be nosy. I won't say anything to
Adam."

She didn't respond but I noticed her nod her head almost
imperceptibly. Just as we stepped off the train, about to go our
separate ways she said, "Have a nice day."

"You too," I stuttered back, caught off guard by the pleasantry.

My direct boss, Ethan, had put a meeting called "Annual Review"
on my calendar at ten-thirty. I went to the office kitchen to get some
more caffeine. I selected the least offensive flavor from the assortment
of little plastic coffee pods, just as two of the newest additions to our
marketing team walked in.

"Congrats on your promotion," the young woman said.

"I only got ten percent," the young guy, who had been assigned to
the sexy new marketing campaign, said.

"I heard that only two people got promoted this year."

"Jeez, that sucks," he said. "But I could be making way more somewhere else."

"Yeah."

"Who's the other promotion?" he asked.

"Not sure. You were the first to meet with Ethan, right?"

"I guess so."

Could it be me? Mike joined the company after me. If he got promoted, I must be the other promotion.

I walked to Ethan's office, clutching my coffee mug, and full of anticipation.

"Hey, Wyn. Please sit."

I complied.

"So, Wyn, you were up for a promotion this year, along with quite a few other Senior Media Planners. Your case was very strong, but there was a lot of competition. In the end only two staff at this level were promoted because our earnings as a group were a little below plan."

I nodded.

"Unfortunately, your case was not the strongest. You were not promoted this round, but I expect that next year yours *will* be the strongest."

"Thank you." I said. *Why am I thanking him for not promoting me?* "What were the differentiators that separated me from those who did get promoted?"

"Well," he paused, as if thinking about it for the first time. "You have only been here for two years. Most people don't get promoted in their first two years."

"Mike joined after me and he just got promoted."

"True, but he came in last week with an offer from a competitor and he is assigned to our most important client, so we couldn't afford to lose him."

"Speaking of client assignments, why was he assigned to that client over me?"

"He expressed interest."

"You assigned him to that client, right?"

"I did."

"How were my sales numbers compared to the other Senior Media Planners?" *I already knew the answer.*

He studied the sheet of paper in front of him that had our team's performance measures and my numbers.

"Above average."

"So, I've been part of the teams that brought in the most new business this year, but I'm not getting promoted?"

"Look Wyn, you are one of our best young employees, but it was very competitive this year and many deserving Senior Media Planners who joined before you didn't get promoted either."

"So that's it. I have to wait another year?"

"I'm sorry. The decision has been made," he said.

"Great, thanks. So has mine." I stood.

He looked up at me.

"I quit!" I said.

"Excuse me?"

"I quit. I've wasted enough time here already. I'm not going to sit around for another year, fetching Alan's coffee, just to be disappointed again."

"Wyn, success in a large company takes time. You need to have patience."

"Mike didn't need patience. It doesn't matter. I don't need this. I quit." I left before he could say anything else.

My head was spinning. *Did I just make a huge mistake? Did I let my ego and emotions get the better of me? Doesn't matter. I can't go back in there and ask for my job back. It is what it is. I will just have to get Nate to pay up. That will give me some time to figure out what I really want to do in life.*

I deleted all the passwords, cookies, and history in my web browser along with the one folder on my hard drive where I had kept personal documents. I shut down. I threw the few personal items on my desk into my purse, and took a deep breath. *What else? Don't forget anything when you leave this place. You don't want to have to come back, even momentarily.* I grabbed an old Tupperware from the kitchen that had my initials on the bottom in faded permanent marker. *That's it. Done,* I thought as I pushed open the heavy glass door that led out to the elevators.

As I waited for an elevator, I heard Noreen call behind me, "Hey! What the hell?"

I turned around. She was walking toward me quickly with a big smile on her face.

"I can't believe you're leaving, but good for you!"

She gave me a hug.

"Thank you!"

"And don't come back!" she yelled dramatically, smiling. "Call me next week. I want to hear all about how fabulous freedom is!"

As I walked to the train doubts turned to relief. *No regrets. I hated that place! Plus, this could help when I finally divorce Nate.*

I usually timed my arrival at the train station perfectly, but leaving in such a hurry I hadn't considered that the next mid-day train was almost an hour from scheduled departure. I considered going back out to a tavern across the street from the station to kill some time and celebrate with a mimosa, but suddenly felt exhausted and just wanted to get home. I sat on a bench near the platform and tried to relax. Staring blankly at the tracks, I could hear the low rumbling and feel the vibrations caused by engines starting up. The station was relatively empty, but a few people still scurried up and down the platforms to board other trains.

At home I texted Nate, "ETA tonight?"

His answer came immediately, "Late."

"How late?"

A few minutes later my phone vibrated, "Really late, sorry".

Hopefully you're late because you're having an affair with Julia! But how am I going to catch you in action? I need proof!

I tried to watch t.v. but could barely sit still. I had just quit my job in the most dramatic way I could have imagined, I wanted to celebrate but instead I was alone.

I texted Adam, "What's up?"

"Nothing. You?"

"Home. Alone. Nate's working late tonight."

Adam didn't respond. I went for a run and then got in the shower. I stood under the showerhead and closed my eyes. The water was so hot that it gave me goosebumps. When I opened my eyes, Adam was standing on the other side of the glass, naked. I practically jumped.

He opened the door and stepped in. He was thinner than Nate, but fit. He stepped toward me, pressing his warm body against mine. *This shouldn't be happening. Not like this. There have been so many opportunities over the years that were so much more romantic than this.* There had been so many moments when we were younger when I'd wanted him to kiss me, to undress me, to make love to me, but I'd stopped him. I was scared of what it would mean, and I was scared of losing what we had, but now I wasn't sure. We weren't as close as we'd been before. *No, things are too complicated right now! To get Nate to pay up in a fault divorce I have to be the virtuous one. I can't risk getting caught cheating right now. That could ruin everything.*

Adam put his hands on me and pulled himself closer. *But Nate is working late tonight. What do I really have to lose? What are the odds he'll come home now?* I didn't resist. He kissed me and it sent a wave of electricity coursing through my body. His kiss was wet, sloppy, and energetic in a way that Nate's never was. I wanted more but all I could think about was how much I'd invested in conning Nate. If I slipped-up now and Nate found out, the last two years would be for nothing. *I've sacrificed too much to throw it all away now.*

"We can't," I said and pulled away.

He looked at me with a sadness in his eyes that I had only seen once before, when I'd rejected him on prom night.

"I'm sorry," I said. "We can't. Not now."

He stepped out of the shower and quickly began getting dressed. I followed him and grabbed my towel.

"Hey!" I said. "I'm really sorry."

"Whatever, not like it's the first time."

I grabbed his hand and tried to pull him toward me but he pushed me away.

"Why are you even married to him? Do you actually love him?"

"It's complicated."

"It always is with you."

"Look, he isn't right for me. I know that."

"Then why did you marry him?"

God, I want to tell you so bad, but I can't. Not yet.

"You were wrong about him. He isn't the guy you think he is," he said.

And Julia isn't who you think she is either! "What do you mean, he isn't who I think he is? Who is he?"

He shook his head. "Too late now, never mind."

Do you know that Nate's a rapist? How long have you known?

"Oh, come on," I begged. *If you do know, then you didn't bother to warn me before I married the guy. Can I even trust you anymore?*

"No," he said, and turned to leave.

"I could say the same thing about Julia," I yelled after him.

I got dressed and poured myself a glass of wine. *I can't believe that just happened. He does still want me after all these years!* I turned on some terrible '90s chick flick that I'd seen a million times.

Lying in bed alone, I tried to fall asleep but my mind wandered to Adam. I had always been a romantic, and I knew that for all of his pretending otherwise, so was Adam. It was the way he looked at me, watched me, and the way he had always held my hand. I thought back to the shower. I couldn't forget the look in his eyes when I said no. *Does he really love me?* Then I began to wonder about the kind of relationship he and Julia had. *Am I wrong about him? Are there others? Am I simply another fleeting pleasure amongst the spoils of their bizarre arrangement?*

Is Nate somehow involved? The evenings I spend alone with Adam are only possible because Nate and Julia are both gone. They must be having an affair. Does Adam know?

The sound of the deadbolt woke me up.

"You're late. What time is it?" I said when Nate tiptoed into the bedroom.

"Yeah, sorry. Almost midnight."

"It's Wednesday night."

"I know. We're launching a new product on Friday, so we're down to the wire on the last few details for the launch."

Nice excuse. I pictured Nate and Julia having sex. *Where are they doing it? Now that I'm not working I'll have time to follow them and get proof!*

"I quit my job today," I said.

"Oh, great! Good for you."

"Yep, that asshole didn't promote me after all the bullshit I've put up with, so I told him to fuck off!"

"That's my girl! Congratulations. I'm sorry I wasn't home earlier to celebrate with you."

"Thanks."

He walked over to the bed, leaned down and kissed me. I could smell his favorite whiskey on his breath.

"Does that mean you want to start trying? You'll have time to take care of a baby now," he said.

"Yeah." *Of course I do, but not with you.*

"Thank you for being supportive," I said.

"Yeah, of course. I told you from the beginning that you can depend on me. I'll take care of you."

"Love you," I said, testing him to see if he was still invested in us despite whatever he was doing when he stayed out late.

"Love you too," he said.

Yes, I've still got him!

THE CONVINCER

Thursday, January 18, 2018
Old Greenwich

When I woke up the sun was just beginning to peak above the window sill, filling the room with the low grey light of a mid-January morning. I rolled over. Nate was already gone and it was eerily silent. *It's been three months since I quit my job and I'm no closer to my end goal now than I was when I quit. Three months of casual snooping, watching, and waiting and I have zero evidence that Nate is actually cheating. What if he isn't? Or what if he is and he's just too good to get caught? I need proof or I'll never get my revenge. I need hard evidence that he's cheating or he'll never have to pay for what he did.*

For my sanity I needed to get out of the house, so I went to yoga. Jenna and Candace were there too. After class, Candace suggested that the three of us get lunch.

We sipped mimosas and they gossiped about couples they both knew. When they finally ran out of gossip Jenna excused herself, and Candace and I sat a little longer sipping our drinks.

"You know. I think you and Nate might enjoy one of our parties," Candace said.

It was an odd statement; *what kind of party wouldn't we enjoy?* "We usually like a good party," I said.

"Well, these aren't just good parties," she said.

"No?"

"Only couples are invited," she said.

Hmmmm. "Okay. I'll be sure to bring Nate, then."

She continued, "...because there has to be an even number of people. Well, actually we've done it with an odd number before, but that really only works if the stag is a woman."

The stag? Is this what I think it is? How risqué! I feigned innocence, "Why? Is it a game night or something?"

"Not exactly," she said. "I mean, it could be. That could be fun actually, to mix things up a bit." She seemed to be lost in thought for a minute, perhaps dreaming up some kind of entertainment.

Candace took a long sip of her mimosa and then continued, "We swap," she said. I furrowed my brow and kept silent and she immediately followed up with, "partners."

She hosts swinger parties! How did I not know this? It's perfect. "What do you mean?" I asked.

She let out a howl so loud it felt like all of the eyes in the restaurant were immediately on us. When she stopped laughing she said under her breath, "Sex partners, duh".

Duh!

She continued, "We are very discreet. It's a bit of a private club. I'm only telling you because I know that you'll be discreet about it too. If you're not interested, that's fine, but please don't mention it to anyone."

"Why don't you think I'd be interested?"

"I mean, I'm telling you because I thought you and Nate might be interested."

"You mean you thought Nate would be interested."

"Well, yeah. Like I said, if you don't think you want to try it, no big deal, just don't go telling everyone that you were invited, please."

"Okay."

"I mean, not everyone gets asked, so some people will talk shit about it because they're jealous."

I nodded. "Thanks for the invitation. I'll let you know," I said.

We paid the bill and I drove straight home.

I heard my phone vibrate on the counter. It was a text from Jenna, "Did she ask you?"

I replied, "What?"

"Did she invite you to one of her parties?"

"No," I lied.

"Good. She's just some slutty whore who throws parties so that she can sleep around with other people's husbands. It's sad really... she must hate her own."

"Oh, I had no idea," I replied.

When I woke up the next morning, Nate was still asleep. The first rays of sunlight were just beginning to bounce off the dark bluish-grey waves of the Sound and reflect onto the ceiling of our bedroom. I laid in bed and scrolled through my Facebook feed, catching up on all of the posts I'd missed over the past twenty-four hours.

There was a picture of my pregnant friend, Jordan, with only a black sarong wrapped around her less public parts, with the caption, "Can't believe it's only 12 weeks til baby Jensen arrives! #24weekspregnant"

As usual my feed was filled with photos of Julia. As I scrolled down there was a photo from a recent weeknight. She was at a black tie awards event, dressed in a floor length black gown with a revealing low V neckline. She was posing alone in front of a large marble sculpture of a warrior. The caption read, "The competition is fierce at the Annual Influencer Awards".

There was another picture of her amongst a crowd of well-dressed party-goers. It caught my eye by chance, but at the same time, it couldn't be missed. It was only the back of his hand resting casually at her waist, but I knew immediately that it was his because of the wrist watch. That gorgeous piece of machinery was unmistakable. *Nate and Julia are hooking up! It's confirmation, which is good, but it's not enough proof.*

I couldn't help but study the picture. There was no question she was beautiful and successful in her own way, and more than anyone else, I knew what a monster he was, but for some logic defying reason I felt a pang of jealousy. *Is he in love with her or just bored? Stop it. Who cares? This is exactly what I need. I just have to keep him interested long enough to get conclusive proof.*

Nate rolled over and began to stretch out next to me.

"Do you know what was amazing?" he asked.

"What?"

"That threesome we had. Remember that?"

"Yeah, of course." *No matter how hard I tried to forget.*

"Would you ever want to do something like that again?" he said.

Hmmm, Candace's party?

"Because just thinking about that makes me so horny." He was visibly aroused.

I let the tension between us build. He sat up against the headboard.

"Do you remember Candace Walters?" I asked. "Julia's best

friend?"

"Sure." It was clear he didn't, but it didn't matter.

"Apparently, she hosts swinger parties."

"Really?" he turned to look at me.

"Yeah, and she invited us."

"Do you want to go?" he asked.

"I don't know, do you?"

He didn't hide his curiosity. "Why not?"

"Yeah, sure," I said. *We have to go! It's the perfect opportunity! It just can't seem like I'm enthusiastic.* "I guess we could try it once."

"When is it?" he asked.

"I don't know. I didn't say yes. I said I'd ask you first."

"Oh. Well, sure. I say yes, so ask her when and put it on the calendar."

Of course you say yes. I nodded. "Okay."

He got out of bed.

I texted Candace a little while later; "We'd like to come to your next party. When is it?"

She replied almost immediately. "Great! Next Saturday 1/27, 8pm. I'll put you on the list.

The days moved slowly as I waited and anticipated the big night. I was nervous, so I picked up Vi's diary to pass the time and keep my mind occupied.

February 26, 1989

Shreveport, Louisiana. He's in jail. They arrested him last night. I found out in church this morning. Everyone was talking about it. The place was buzzing like it was full of bees and they were all watching me. Their looks were full of pure scorn and contempt. I ran out of the church before the sermon had even started. I could feel the weight of their eyes on me and I couldn't stand it any longer. I cried all the way to the police station. When I got there and asked to see him they said it wasn't appropriate for a pregnant girl to be in the station and that I couldn't see him because I'm not his wife. I began crying and told them that I wasn't leaving until I got to talk to him. Finally they took me back and he held my hand through the metal bars of his cell. He said that he was accused of statutory rape which is a felony. He said that the punishment is something crazy like 10 years in jail and a $5,000 fine. He asked me who I'd told that I was pregnant. He said that he hadn't been with anyone else but me. I told him that I had only told my mom. I hadn't even told my best friends, Ruth and Elizabeth, yet. He said, "Of course." I asked him what he meant and all he said was, "Your mom." It was weird. I'm not sure what he meant. As I turned to leave he said "I love you." He's never said that before. I don't think I love him. I mean he's really handsome, and I enjoy being with him, but I'm not sure that's love. I'm so confused. I left without saying anything. I felt really bad about it as I was walking home. Should I have told him "I love you" back?

When I got home she asked if I feel guilty that he's in jail. I said not really because we both wanted to have sex (which is only sort of true...it was mostly him, but whatever). She said I should feel guilty because it was my sin, just like Eve's, that led to this. She said that I should repent and ask God for forgiveness and then maybe he would show me a way out of this mess.

THE CONVINCER

Saturday, January 20, 2018
Manhattan

My therapist's office is more depressing in winter. Something about the blank, off-white walls, and institutional-grade grey window frames feels as if winter is creeping inside. She welcomed me in and I took my usual place on the couch.

After completing the standard symptom checklists, she asked to see the list of critical things that Nate had said to me since my last visit, which she'd asked me to keep. I took out a page of handwritten notes: a catalog of critical, even cruel things, some of which were true, like the comment Nate made about me gaining weight after our wedding, some of which were fabricated. *She has to believe that he's in control and I'm helpless. Securely attached and entirely dependent on him.*

We sat in silence as she read through the list. Then she read from the page, "Why do you always mess this up, Wyn? It's not that difficult. Really, a 3rd grader could get it right."

I nodded.

"Wyn, how did that make you feel?"

"Bad. I mean, it makes me feel like I'm failing at everything. All the time."

"How did you respond?"

"I don't know. I just want to make him happy. When he's happy, things are so good."

"Did you tell him how this made you feel? That it hurt you?"

"No."

"Do you love him?"

"I guess so. At least in some ways I love him or maybe I just need him."

"What do you mean, you need him?"

"It's messed up, isn't it?"

She waited in silence.

"I don't know," I continued. "It's strange. I hated him at first, of course. I even wanted to kill him for a while, but I knew I could never do that. I began to think that if I just got close to him, figured out what made him tick, maybe I could forgive him, get over, and finally move on, but I got too close. In the beginning, when I was near him, all I could think about was what he was capable of. I began to do things that I didn't want to do, but had to do, in order to keep him happy, because I was scared. I should have walked away but I couldn't. I was in too far. I was so committed, so obsessed with figuring out why he did what he did, that I got lost. The line between who I was before and who I've become began to fade. Living with him became almost normal. I learned that as long as I keep him happy, he's harmless and I can actually relax a bit…I almost enjoy myself. He's even been sweet sometimes. I know that sounds crazy, but he can be incredible."

"Wyn, I think you are showing signs of trauma bonding. Trauma bonding is similar to Stockholm Syndrome, which happens when people held captive come to have feelings of trust or even affection for their abuser. This can be a survival strategy in the case of acute trauma, but it can also occur when a person is in a long-term relationship with their abuser."

Bingo! I'm playing my part perfectly if that's what you think. This will only help my case if Nate tries to turn things around and say that I defrauded him or something because he doesn't want to pay alimony. I shook my head for effect.

"Wyn, I'm really worried about you. I think you need to get out."

I nodded. *Soon enough, but I'm not done yet. I have more to do. I need proof for this to work.*

"Wyn, if you don't get out now, his abuse could escalate. You may not feel unsafe with him right now, but that could change. Sometimes stressful events in life, such as health or financial troubles, can turn someone like Nate back into a dangerous person. And the longer you're with him, the harder it will be to extricate yourself when you need to. This behavior tends to be cyclical. Just because he's being a good partner right now, doesn't mean he won't be dangerous in the future."

It has to be the perfect moment. At the perfect moment, the touch will come off without a hitch.

"Wyn, here's some information about a shelter, in case you need it. I want you to think about going to the police." She handed me a brochure.

"They won't believe me," I said.

"Please consider these options. There are wonderful women at that shelter that can help you. They *will* believe you."

I promised to give it some thought and left.

The next morning on my way home from yoga I saw Julia drive by in her unmistakable red Porsche. She was headed toward town and waved. I waved back, then parked and went straight to Adam's house. The front door was open and he was laying on the couch in the back sunroom with all the sections of the Sunday paper spread out around him and a coffee stained mug in front of him on the table.

"What's up?" I said.

He ignored me.

"Hey!" I said.

He still didn't look up from the paper. *Crap, is he still mad at me about the shower thing?*

I jumped on top of him and started to tickle. "Hey! Don't be rude!" He cracked, began laughing, and playfully tried to fight back.

"Stop!" he begged.

"You know you can't ignore me for long."

"Coffee's in the kitchen if you want some," he said.

I got up. "You want more?" I asked as I walked to the kitchen.

"No thanks!" he yelled.

I poured myself a small cup and settled back onto the couch next to him. He'd picked up the paper and started reading again.

"How're you?" I asked.

"I'm okay. How's work?"

"I quit."

"Oh yeah? Is that good or bad?"

"I don't know. Good for now. It's been nice to be home."

"How are things at home? He's been gone a lot lately, hasn't he?"

"Yeah, but probably not more than she has."

"True."

"We got invited to Candace's for a party next Saturday."

"Really?" He put the newspaper down and looked up.

"Yeah, why?"

"Just didn't think that was your kind of thing."

"Not sure it is," I said. "Have you been to one?"

"Yeah, of course," he said. "She's Julia's friend. Julia said she was curious and wanted to go, just to try it."

"Yeah, how was it?"

"I mean, it's classy as far as that type of thing goes. If you like that kind of thing."

"I take it you don't?"

"I mean, I'm not blind or oblivious, but I don't feel the need to experiment like that either."

"Really?" *So I wasn't just another notch in the belt in the shower that night?*

"Well, yeah. I mean it was okay."

"Who did you hook up with?" I teased.

He looked straight at me and shook his head, 'no'.

"Oh, come on!" I implored.

"No way! Not telling."

"Why? Is it embarrassing?"

"No, not really."

"Oh, come on!"

"Nope. I don't think you know her anyhow."

Holy shit, he did hook up with someone else!

I climbed onto the couch next to him. "Fine, but will you come next weekend?" I nearly begged. "For me."

"I don't know. I think we have other plans. Not sure."

"It's just, I was thinking…about that other night, in the shower." *This might not work if Julia isn't there and she's probably more likely to go if Adam is going, right?*

"Oh yeah?"

"I was thinking that the party might be the right time, you know?"

"Really?"

"Yeah. The thought of doing anything with anyone else makes me sick. And I was thinking that Nate can't be upset if we hook up, since he's the one who wants to go to the party."

Adam nodded.

"So you'll go?"

"I'll talk to Julia, but I don't see why we couldn't go."

I smiled and heard the front door. I practically leapt off the couch, and disappeared quietly out the back door. As I closed the door behind me I heard her yelling to him.

THE CONVINCER

Thursday, January 25, 2018
Old Greenwich

Ali had a business trip to New York mid-week and was going to stop by and stay with us for a night, which I hoped would help get my mind off of Candace's party. I had spent most of an entire day and a half cleaning the house, in part to impress Ali, and in part because I really didn't have anything else to do. She let herself in around four-thirty, just as I had settled in for some light meditation.

"Hey sis!" she exclaimed from down the hall.

"In the kitchen," I called back.

Ali walked in and I stood up to give her a hug. She immediately started in on me. "What the fuck is this?"

She picked up the adult coloring book I had been working on and flung it across the counter. "You quit your career to sit around and color by numbers like a fourth grader?"

"Hey, lay off. My therapist said it might be good for my anxiety," I said, defending one of my guilty pleasures since quitting.

"Is this really the life you want?" she asked, waving her arms around.

"What's wrong with this life?" I asked.

She rolled her eyes. "Never mind."

"Sorry," I said. *I wish it was different but I have no choice.* "Welcome," I continued. "Can I get you a glass of wine or something else? Maybe a Xanax?"

"Sure," she said, "...to the wine."

I poured two glasses of Merlot.

When she had settled in, she asked, "So how's life?"

"Fine."

"Just fine?"

"Yeah. I mean, Nate's not here much. It's a bit lonely, but I'm not complaining. I knew it would be like that when I decided to stay home."

"Yes," she said firmly. "We warned you."

"You did," I said, to placate her. I wasn't in the mood to fight with her for the next few hours.

"So, are you still satisfied with your choice?"

"I am. I just need some time to adjust."

"Well, take your time. Clearly you're rediscovering a real talent for coloring."

"Ali," I warned. "It's just something I've been doing to take my mind off other things."

"What other things?" she asked. "Like where your husband is and who he's doing?"

"Thanks."

"I never liked him."

"I know," I said. "…and Soren is so perfect? He works so much he could have another wife somewhere. Maybe a few kids and a white picket fence across the country?"

"He's not like that."

"How do you know?" I asked. "And why do you assume Soren isn't but Nate is?"

"I just know. It's a feeling."

"Sure," I said.

I was grateful when she changed the subject.

We ate a frozen pizza, sipped Merlot, and played grown-up truth or dare, which primarily entailed secret telling, but occasionally, when we were tipsy enough, ended in immature challenges, one of which years ago had seen Ali call a dial-a-prostitute and me order a lovely basket of penis-shaped bachelorette toys and accoutrements online to be shipped to Vi's house.

It was my turn and I chose 'truth'.

"Do you think Nate's cheating on you?" Ali asked.

"Probably," I conceded. "I saw him in a photo a couple weeks ago on Facebook at some black tie event with another woman," I said. "He told me he was working late that night." *Ugh, if only I could tell her everything, she wouldn't think I was such a sucker.*

"Oh my god! Who?"

"That's not how this works. You get one question. It's my turn."

"Do you think Soren has ever stepped out?" I asked.

"No, honestly I don't," she said. "Who?"

"Julia," I said.

"Adam's wife?"

"My turn," I said. "What would you do if you found out Soren was cheating?"

"Leave. Immediately."

"You sure?"

"My turn," she said. "You're in love with Adam, and your husband is screwing his wife! What's a step above a love triangle? Would that be a love quadrangle or a love rectangle?" She laughed out loud.

I gave her a stern look.

She stopped laughing. "I'm sorry."

"Why did you say I'm in love with Adam?"

"Oh come on! I don't even have to waste a turn on that question to know the truth. That's been obvious since you were in the sixth grade. I always wondered why you two didn't end up together."

"It's complicated."

"Yeah, now it is. You're both married, but living conveniently close to each other. What's that about?"

"I don't know. He and Julia moved in next door after we bought this place."

"Strange coincidence, don't ya think?"

"I don't know."

She looked at me skeptically.

"How's mom?" I asked, changing the subject abruptly.

"You're gonna waste your next question on that?"

"That's not my truth or dare question, I'm just asking."

"She's great."

"Is she seeing anyone?"

"No. Why? Why do you want her to date so badly?" Ali said.

"I'm just worried that she'll be lonely. I can't imagine growing old alone."

"Freddie, she's been alone a long time. Clearly it works for her."

"I don't know," I said. "I feel like she's unhappy alone but something is holding her back."

"Maybe that's her business or maybe you're just projecting."

"I didn't realize you were a psychiatrist now." I thought of Vi's diary but didn't say anything.

"I should get ready for bed. I have an early client meeting tomorrow downtown."

"Sure. Thanks for coming to visit. It's always great to see you. And play some truth or dare."

I turned on the t.v. The news came on and the lead story was about the hashtag that had been gaining momentum in the wake of the Weinstein accusations.

"Have you been following this?" Ali asked, standing up to leave.

"I saw the initial accusations, but I haven't been following it that closely."

"Of course not. Oh my god, it's incredible!" she said. "I mean, it's terrible that they were raped, of course, but that these women are going to bring down one of the most powerful men in Hollywood!"

"Hmmmm."

"We're witnessing the resurgence of Feminism. Isn't it exciting?"

"Sure."

"You suck! You are such a traitor to our sex," she said.

"Guessso."

"Well, goodnight. I might not see you tomorrow if you're not up early. Don't bother on my account either."

"Okay."

"Thanks for letting me stay over," she said as she put her wine glass in the sink. "Oh, and sorry I gave you so much trouble about the coloring book. I just love you and want you to be happy and healthy and I worry that you're not right now."

If you only knew. "Thanks. I'm fine," I lied. "Love you too. Night."

It was still pretty early, so I made a cup of chamomile tea, went up to bed, and flipped open Vi's diary.

March 1, 1989

Shreveport, Louisiana. *Tonight Mom asked me if I had been praying about my situation. I told her it was none of her business. She said that she had been praying about it on my behalf and that He had answered her prayers. She said the answer was that we were already married in God's eyes when we had "intercourse" (her silly word, not mine!) and that we were just "consummating"*

our marriage that day. She said that she had already talked to
Father Connelly and that he had agreed that the intercourse was
the consummation of our marriage in God's eyes. She even had
a marriage certificate with our names on it! Father Connelly had
signed it and it was dated November 12, 1988. She said that the only
way to redeem myself and my honor was to be married. I asked her
how she thought that anyone would believe that we were married
in November without a wedding. In this small town there's no way
someone could get married without other people knowing about
it. She said that she and Father Connelly had a plan. They would
say that we had threatened to elope and so Father Connelly agreed
to marry us the very same day in front of our parents. I ripped the
fraudulent certificate into pieces and she had a fit. She said that she
was trying to save me! If there's one thing I'm sure about, it's that
I don't want to be married right now. What I'm not sure about is
whether I want to have the baby. I'm scared. I asked some of the
older girls at school about an abortion and they said that it's a sin.
I'm not entirely sure what it entails, but it seems like the only way
for a pregnant woman to not have a baby. My belly is getting big. I
wonder if an abortion is even possible at this point.

Just as I was starting to fall asleep, I heard the familiar clicks
and thuds of kitchen drawers and the refrigerator being opened and
closed. *Nate's home.* I put Vi's diary back on the nightstand, rolled
over, and fell asleep.

At some point, early in the morning, I heard the click of the latch
on the front door. I rolled over and went back to sleep.

I woke up to the sound of Nate brushing his teeth and the low
winter sun breaching the horizon.

"Morning," I yelled from the bed.

"Morning," he said as he disappeared into his closet.

I waited until he came out. "Hey, sorry to bug you about it, but did
Jack send you our marriage certificate yet?"

"No!" he said. "Please stop asking me."

Jeez, just figured I'd ask one last time.

"Hey, don't forget that party at Candace's is tomorrow night. Are you still free?"

"Sure," he mumbled.

"I told her we'd be there."

"I'll fucking be there," he yelled.

What the hell happened to him?

"Okay, thanks! Have a good day," I said, as he headed downstairs.

I paced around the house most of the day, and made an appointment to have most of my body waxed, just in case. *Just in case something finally happens with Adam.* It seemed completely inappropriate to show up to a swinger party unkempt. Plus, it was something to do.

I texted Ali, "Thanks for coming to stay. It was great to see you. <3"

I got a pedicure and tried to preoccupy myself with a useless gossip magazine while the woman in the salon worked on my feet.

I checked my phone. *Ali hasn't responded. That's odd. She must be busy with work.*

I couldn't help myself and texted Adam, "Did you talk to Julia about Candace's party?" *I need you to be there!*

Hours later, when I was back at home getting ready to make dinner, Adam replied, "Yeah, she said fine."

"So you'll both be there?"

"Yes."

"Great." *This just might work!*

"Is this really how you want it to be?"

"Not sure what you mean." *Because randomly having sex in my shower is the more romantic option?*

"Never mind."

Ali still hadn't texted back after dinner which wasn't like her. *Maybe she's still on her flight home.* I texted again, "How'd your client meetings go?"

THE CONVINCER

Saturday, January 27, 2018

Old Greenwich

On Saturday I went to yoga. I knew I couldn't sit around all morning in anticipation of the party. After class, Jenna wanted to get lunch. I figured she could be a worthwhile distraction. She tended to do most of the talking and never seemed to run out of things to tell me about her children and various PTA gossip.

"What're you guys doing tonight?" she asked while we waited for our food.

"Not sure. You?"

"Nothing really, but I heard that Candace is having one of her parties."

"Oh, really?"

"You weren't invited?"

"No," I lied. I didn't want to add fuel to what was clearly already a raging fire.

"Oh, I thought I heard that she had invited you guys."

So much for discreet. "I mean, she mentioned that she has parties now and then and that we are welcome, but she didn't say any more and I didn't ask."

"But you knew what kind of parties they were because I told you."

"You did mention that, yeah."

"Do you want to go? Does Nate want to go?"

"I'm not sure." Her grand inquisition was beginning to bother me. *She is never this nosy, why now? Am I just being sensitive? Nah, Candace's parties are probably the most exciting thing to happen in this sleepy suburb in years.*

I was grateful when she finally changed the subject. "Are you going to Julia's birthday party next week?"

"Yeah, I think so. I put it on our calendar." I hadn't wanted to mention it because I wasn't sure she'd been invited. "You'll be there too, then?"

"Yeah, of course," she said.

She continued talking, and I listened as attentively as I could to a story about her son's newfound interest in dinosaurs and her husband's involvement with the men's volunteer committee at church. I finally excused myself, and stopped at the gas station on my way home. I had only smoked a handful of cigarettes in my life, but I figured I might need an excuse to get some fresh air at the party, so I bought a pack and lit one up as I pulled out of the gas station.

There was a pile of mail on the floor behind the front door. I stood in the kitchen, picking through the pile. *Junk. Junk. Junk.* I threw all but one piece at the recycling bin. It was a shiny, magenta, gift-card-sized envelope with embossed gold lettering on the front. I grabbed a small, sharp knife and slit open the top neatly. Gold glitter, so fine that it immediately clung to everything, emanated from the envelope as I opened it. Inside there was a single, thick, magenta card with gold lettering.

"The Exchange" House Rules

He or she who enters is expected to abide by the following, with no exceptions:

— *Everyone is available.*
— *A tap on the shoulder is an invitation. A shake of the head is a rejection of such offer.*
— *No means no. At any point, all activity will be immediately discontinued.*
— *Protection is provided in each room and required at all times.*
— *Discussion or recitation of events to uninvited parties is strictly prohibited.*
— *No video or photography is allowed, at any time.*
— *Check your inhibitions at the door!*

Above all else, please enjoy yourself and have fun!

I locked the door to the master bathroom and got in the shower. I scrubbed my skin clean, working over my body at least three times, first with a loofa and bath gel, then a bar of soap, and finally with shampoo as I washed my hair. I blew out my hair, thinking of Krista as I did.

I put on my sexiest little black dress and admired myself in the mirror. *I have no idea how to dress for this. Am I overdressed? I should have asked Candace.* The dress had a low V-neck that plunged below my breasts. The capped sleeves stopped where my shoulders peaked. I put on a simple necklace with large black beads punctuated at random by semi-precious stones. *I look great. Who cares!*

I sprayed perfume, grabbed a small black leather purse, and threw my wallet, keys, and the pack of cigarettes in.

Wondering where Nate was, I walked through the house. He wasn't home and it was already seven. *Where is he? Maybe he's already been with her today. What if he has and now he doesn't want to go to the party?*

As I got back to the kitchen I heard the latch turn.

"Nate?" I said.

He didn't respond. I walked toward the front door just in time to see him bound up the front stairs. The thud of each powerful step seemed to sync perfectly with my escalating heartbeat.

Am I really nervous? Is it the thought of what could happen with Adam tonight or not getting the proof I need? I imagined Adam's hands finally on me without restraint. I thought about his tongue in my mouth and him inside me. *What will I discover? Will I finally know that we are perfect for each other and meant to be? Or perhaps that we have no chemistry, that I've imagined it all along.* Perhaps it was a fear of the latter that had kept me from going through with it for so many years. *Am I really ready to find out? I have so many other things to worry about right now, like how to catch Nate red handed without being exposed.*

Nate drove to Candace's house. There was a valet service set-up in her driveway. We got out and I handed Nate the magenta card. Without reading it, he threw it into the bushes along the driveway.

The Walters' house was magnificent: a large white Colonial on the water with a long, extravagantly landscaped entrance.

The door opened in front of us and Candace stood a few feet

behind the door, beaming radiantly.

"Welcome!" she said. "I'm thrilled that you came!"

"So are we," I said as she kissed each of my cheeks and moved on to Nate.

"Please help yourself," she said and a server stepped forward with a tray full of champagne glasses.

I took a glass and continued into the large, dimly lit foyer. I passed a room in the hallway. The door was closed and there was a sign made of wood hanging from a metal hook. On it there was an arrow that could be manipulated to indicate that the room was either "Occupied Exclusive", "Occupied Welcoming", or "Free". The dial pointed to "Free".

There were about twenty people, all dressed in sleek cocktail attire, spread around the well-appointed living room. They were talking, laughing, and sipping champagne, as if they were at *any* cocktail party.

I scanned the room and saw two couples I knew. Justin and Maureen Hamell, and John and Ginny O'Hara. I had met Justin and Mo at a house warming not long after we had moved in. Justin looked good. He was about average height with unremarkable, but well-proportioned features and beautiful black hair with just the right amount of silver in it. Mo looked fine for her age, but was pretty clearly already a mom, evidenced by that stubborn padding around her hips and stomach. I knew Ginny from yoga and had been introduced to John in passing after class one day at the juice bar downtown. He was the type that wore spandex at the coffee shop on a busy Saturday with no shame, but he was fit enough to pull it off.

I wondered why they were here and who would tap whom. Adam and Julia were not among the small crowd. *Where are they? They have to be here or this might all be for nothing. Just another time Nate has pulled me in too deep and made a complete fool of me.*

I took another glass of champagne.

A tall guy with loose blonde curls walked toward me. He looked incredibly fit for his age, which I guessed was at least forty. Out of the corner of my eye I watched Nate. He was talking to a busty blonde that reminded me of the women he had dated before me.

"Well, hello. You're new aren't you?" the blonde forty-something said.

"Sure."

"Oh, not friendly I see?"

Julia walked in, champagne glass in hand. She was stunning. Her hair was pulled back artfully. She was wearing a gold sequin dress that looked uncomfortable and difficult to take off. *God, I'm underdressed.* I watched as all of the men in the room turned to admire her, including Nate. *Where is Adam?*

"Who's your date?" The blonde guy was still at my side.

"My husband." I motioned in his direction with my champagne glass. "Isn't that question against some rule or something?"

"Ha, if it's not, it probably should be," he said. "I'm Chase, by the way." He held out his hand. "My pleasure."

"Wyn."

"What do you do, Wyn?"

"I'm a con artist," I said.

"You are not!"

"Sure."

He laughed. "You're funny."

"So, what do *you* do, Chase?"

His eyes lit up. "I'm a trader."

I smiled politely. "Sorry, excuse me for a second," I said and moved past him. I felt his hand caress my ass, and turned toward the offender, but by the time I looked back the moment had passed. He was on to his next prospect and I realized how foolish I would look accusing him of an unwelcome advance given the occasion.

I stood alone and was rescued by a good looking woman with short dark hair and flawless makeup.

"He likes you."

"Really? I couldn't tell," I said sarcastically.

She smiled.

"Do you know him?" I asked.

"Yep," she said. "He's my husband."

"Oh," I stuttered.

"It's fine," she reassured me.

"Of course," I said.

"Really. It's good for him."

"What is?"

"Rejection."

"Really?"

"Perfect actually. We're here because *I* want us to be," she said.

"Really?" I was intrigued.

"Look, before we discovered this," she motioned toward the other couples and lowered her voice, "he was gaining weight, getting lazy, taking me for granted. I tried everything else I could think of first, but nothing worked until we came here."

"Wow."

"This gives him all the motivation he needs," she said. "It's a small price to pay."

I smiled. *Wow, is it though?*

A tap on the shoulder in the corner of the room caught my eye. I didn't know either of them but I watched as they betrayed their intentions publicly. She nodded, smiled, and followed him out of the room. *So that's how it works.*

I watched as Nate tried to maneuver nonchalantly toward Julia. He kissed both of her cheeks and they tapped champagne glasses. They each took a long sip.

From a dark corner I watched them pretend to make small talk for a few minutes, but it was clear from his body language that he was shielding her from other would-be partners and defending his territory. Finally, he reached out and put his hand on her shoulder. It was less of a tap and more of a command. They turned and left the room. I emptied my glass of champagne and made my way toward the door. I followed slowly, trying not to attract attention. As I crossed the room I passed Chase, who again coped a feel. Again, I said nothing but became a little more enraged. *What makes him think that's okay?*

Nate and Julia were out the back, toward the kitchen. I followed cautiously. They turned down a hallway off the kitchen. I peeked around the corner just in time to see them disappear into a room and shut the door. As I approached the closed door I heard the lock click and saw the arrow, which had been turned to "Occupied Exclusive".

I walked back toward the party. As I crossed the foyer I felt a hand on my shoulder. *God, not Chase again!*

I turned and saw Adam, who looked great.

He pulled me gently toward him. "You okay?" he asked.

I shook my head and pulled away. I walked quickly across the foyer and smiled at the valet as I walked out the front door of the house. I pulled the pack of cigarettes out of my purse and paused to light one.

I felt Adam behind me as I took a left and walked along the front of the house toward the east wing.

"You don't smoke," he said.

I kept walking. I'd gone about fifty feet before I was confident that a set of large double-hung windows with a low light on belonged to the right room.

I snuck around the thick hedge that bordered the house until I was pressed against the window. The curtains in the room hung haphazardly but allowed enough of a view. I dropped the cigarette in the dirt and pulled out my cell phone. I held my phone up to the window and hit record. I could feel Adam next to me.

Nate fumbled with the zipper on Julia's dress, eventually pulling the dress off. She unbuttoned his collared shirt and pulled at the buckle on his belt. His pants fell to the ground. He stood naked in front of her. She was dressed in gorgeous black lingerie. He kissed her neck and breasts and then threw her onto the bed. He forced her legs apart, held them open, and went to work with his mouth. She grasped for something to hold onto. Then just before it seemed like she might succumb, he stood up and shoved himself inside her. She pushed her hands against the headboard, clenched the sheets and occasionally looked up at him. The intense pleasure was evident in her contorted features. When they were finished, they laid down next to each other for a minute. Before I could hit stop on my phone he was up again with his head between her legs, her back arched, and her hands again searching for something to grasp. I hit stop.

I turned and saw Adam, watching me in pure shock.

"Oh, come on. You knew, right?" I said.

"What the fuck?"

"You might want to ask your wife that question."

"I mean you," he said, "recording that shit. What the fuck?"

"It's complicated."

"Fuck you," he said. "You'll never open up."

I stared straight at him. The look of betrayal in his eyes burned permanently into my memory.

I inhaled deep and fought back tears.

"Nate raped me," I whispered.

"What?"

"I said Nate raped me. More than once actually."

"Oh my God. When?"

Tears began streaming down my face.

"Wait, what? What do you mean, Nate raped you? When?"

"First in college. Again since I moved to New York. While we have been married."

"I don't get it. You knew him in college?"

"He was visiting a friend and we met at a frat party."

"Oh my God."

I nodded.

"I'm so sorry," he said. "But why did you marry someone who raped you?"

"I was pregnant. I had an abortion that summer, after the rape."

"Holy shit," he said. "Why though? Why did you marry him?"

"It's the only way."

"The only way for what?"

"Justice."

"What? What do you mean?"

"He said he would ruin my life if I told anyone. My own roommate, who was at the party, didn't even believe me."

"That's fucked up," he said.

I didn't say anything or look at him. Instead I looked down at the video on my cell phone.

"That's crazy?" he said.

I shook my head in disbelief at his words. *I was raped and I'm the crazy one?*

"Look at me!" he demanded.

I looked up.

"Jesus Christ."

"He has to pay," I said, trembling.

"Oh my God. This is crazy," he said.

I stared back at him, the pain evident in my eyes.

"I mean, holy shit. Nate's a rapist. Freddie, I'm so sorry. I knew he was a bad guy, but I had no idea."

I nodded.

"That motherfucker," he said and turned to watch his wife

entangled passionately with a monster.

Adam turned back toward me. "I'm so sorry. You aren't crazy. I shouldn't have said that. Come here."

He pulled me into his arms and I didn't resist. I sobbed against his chest.

"What do you need?" He whispered.

I shook my head.

"Anything. You know that, right?" he said.

"Please just stay out of it for now. You weren't supposed to know."

"This is the secret you were keeping all these years?"

"Yes." It felt so good to finally tell him.

He held me, for what felt like a long time, but when I peeked back into the window, Nate and Julia were still lying there admiring each other. *Breathe. I finally got exactly what I needed. This is going to work!*

I turned to Adam. "How's my face?"

He wiped under my eyes with his fingers. "Let's go."

"That bad?"

"Come on. We shouldn't be here."

We got into Adam's car and drove home. He pulled into his driveway.

"Come in," he said.

"I can't."

"After what just happened, I don't think you should be alone."

"Things have to look as normal as possible," I said.

"I don't want you living in the same house as him," he protested.

"I've been doing it for years. It's no different now. I'll be fine."

He didn't say anything but furrowed his brow.

"He only gets aggressive when he wants something he is told he can't have. He knows he can have me now. That bores him. There's no real risk."

He leaned across the console and pulled me toward him. He kissed me passionately. I kissed him back. For a few brief minutes, I let myself get lost in his kiss. Then I pulled away.

"Freddie, will you be okay?"

"Yes," I said.

"I'm so sorry," he said.

"Thank you."

I opened the car door.
"Good night."
"Good night," I said and made my way inside.

I knew I would have trouble sleeping after what had happened, so I made a cup of herbal tea, climbed into bed, and opened Vi's diary.

March 27, 1989

Shreveport, Louisiana. Mom was being difficult again today. She kept nagging me to go to the bank to check on Dad's pension payments and talk to the banker about why the payments are so small. I'm starting to realize how much of their finances Dad took care of and controlled. I'm not sure she's ever really taken care of herself in that way. She never worked. At least not outside the house. There's no question that she's an excellent cook and she always took care of the house, but it's pretty clear that she never knew how much dad's pension would be, or that he wasn't saving any extra money for retirement.

After I went to the bank and ran some other errands for her, she had the nerve to ask me to cook dinner too, because she said she was tired. Then, she just sat on the couch all night watching crap t.v. I am starting to feel like she expects me to do all of the chores now that Dad's gone. It's almost as if her whole motivation and purpose before was to serve him. She needs to finally learn how to take care of herself! I can't wait to go to college! Dad and I always talked about the schools that I would apply to and I already picked up all of the applications. I have to get out of here! Even if I end up all alone and pregnant.

Wow, so that is it! That's why Vi has always been so adamant that we support ourselves. I wish she would have told me. I wonder why she didn't. I think I would have understood if she had told me. Does Ali know? Maybe that's why she always understood Vi so much better than I did. But how would she have known?

March 30, 1989

Shreveport, Louisiana. *I got into Northwestern!!! It's all the way across the country in Chicago, Illinois. I have no idea what Chicago is like, but I'm excited! I guess it's a really expensive school but they are going to waive my tuition because I got a full academic scholarship. The application for the scholarship was so long and annoying. It included an extra essay. I almost stopped filling it out half way, but I'm glad I didn't! I will probably still have to get a job so that I can afford groceries and the other things that the scholarship won't cover, but I will be on my own and I will prove Mom wrong! I am scared about having the baby on my own but I will finally be free from her! Maybe I will give the baby up for adoption. I think that would be really really really hard, but it will also be hard to raise a kid on my own. I don't know what to do, but at least she won't be there to tell me how to live my life!*

PART 3: THE SEND & THE TOUCH

January 2018 to June 2018

THE BREAKDOWN

Sunday, January 28, 2018

Old Greenwich

I slept as late as I had in years, and woke up to an overcast sky. The daylight barely penetrated the room, although it was already nine. I sat up and realized that I was alone. The unopened New York Times was on the bed next to me.

I got up and took the paper downstairs. Nate was sitting at the kitchen counter on a bar stool reading the Wall Street Journal.

"Were you up early?" I asked.

"Couldn't sleep."

"Oh, I'm sorry. Something wrong?"

"No," he said.

I sat down next to him and opened up the Style section of the paper.

"Did you have a good time last night?"

"Yep." He didn't look up. "Candace said *you* did too."

"I left early. I wasn't feeling very well," I said.

"Oh."

A long silence ensued as he continued to read and I thought about how best to bring up his infidelity.

"I'm glad you enjoyed yourself."

He ignored me.

I continued, "Did you really think I didn't know about you and Julia before last night?"

He mumbled something in response.

"Please look at me," I said. "This is important."

He folded up his newspaper and put it down on the counter.

"What?"

"I can't do this anymore." I stood up. "I can't sit here and be your fool while you fuck the neighbor's wife." *Too melodramatic?*

He rolled his eyes. "Isn't that what you're doing?"

"I have never been unfaithful."

"Yeah right."

I threw my paper on the counter. "I want a divorce!"

The corners of his mouth turned up.

"Are you smiling?" I yelled.

He shook his head slightly and his expression changed.

"You have nothing to say?" I demanded.

"You can't have a divorce," he said calmly.

Let me guess, because you told Jack not to send the forms in to the State. You think you're so smart, but you're not.

I took a deep breath. "Yes, I can," I said calmly. "I'll have a divorce if that's what I want. I have proof of your infidelity now. I'll have no trouble getting a divorce."

"You won't get a divorce," he said flatly.

"I have video of you cheating on me. I have proof," I said.

"It doesn't matter," he mumbled.

"What did you say?"

"It doesn't matter," he said.

"Why?" I asked. I knew his next move and was enjoying patiently goading him into what he thought was his moment of triumph.

He was silent.

"Because of the prenup?" I asked. "It doesn't protect you from yourself."

He shook his head.

"Then what?" I said. *Come on already! Admit what you did.*

His phone vibrated. He checked the incoming notification and then looked up at me. "Because we aren't really married. We never were."

There it is. "What do you mean?" I said, acting surprised.

"You heard me. We aren't legally married. Jack never sent in the forms. We burned them." He smiled. "There's no record of our marriage, anywhere."

You think you're so smart, but I've got you beat. "So that's why you didn't want me to change my name. You didn't want me to know that there was no marriage certificate," I said, playing naïve.

He smiled sheepishly.

"But we had a wedding," I said.

"So what? There's no formal record of our marriage. Anywhere." His cockiness was disgusting, but it would make the next bit even more fun.

"Oh come on. I'm not stupid. You know as well as I do that it doesn't matter."

"Of course it matters. We weren't actually married."

You think I'm just going to believe that and walk away? "Wow, I thought you were smarter than that," I said, and he perked up.

"Smarter than what?"

"We had a wedding ceremony. We exchanged vows, and we were pronounced married by a man of God in front of our family and friends. Right?"

He nodded.

"You had a lawyer prepare a prenup, but you obviously didn't run your little plan by him or he would have told you that in 1972 the Supreme Court of Connecticut ruled that a marriage entered into in good faith, believed to be real by one or both parties, and followed by cohabitation is a legal marriage. Hames versus Hames was the case, I think."

"What are you? A lawyer?" he said.

"No, but I'm also not as dumb or helpless as you think. You haven't always been the most trustworthy partner. I did a little research, out of curiosity."

"You're the one who wanted to get married," he said. "So I gave you what you wanted."

"Yeah, I did, and you obviously didn't," I said. "But why would you fake a marriage after I signed your stupid prenup anyhow?"

"I guess I wasn't totally sure about you," he said.

Does he know? "How come?"

"It just all seemed a little too good to be true. You always say exactly the right thing. You didn't seem to care about my DUIs or about the sexual assault accusations."

"Isn't that what a good partner does? Support her significant other."

"Sure. It just seemed so easy with you. Too easy. And I was worried that you were just after my money."

So he doesn't know who I am. He doesn't know what he did to me. Thank God!

"Let's just make this easy. As painless as possible," I said.

"Make what painless?"

"Our divorce. We're married, so I *can* have a divorce, and I have grounds for one, so I'll have a divorce."

"Sure, whatever. Hire a lawyer and let's get divorced, but you won't get a penny," he said.

"You said you would always take care of me, Nate. You told me to quit my job, and then you cheated on me."

"So?"

"So, you'll give me the support you promised. You'll provide for me like you said you would."

"No, I won't, because I can't," he said.

"What do you mean, you can't?"

"There's no money. I've been bleeding the business dry to pay the mortgage on this place. Our entire lifestyle depended on me. On *my* business. You have no idea what our finances are like."

Is he lying? I should have been more involved in his business, but then, he never would have married me if I'd been nosy and overbearing.

"I made money too. I've contributed."

"Yeah, a drop in the bucket. Do you know how expensive this house is? Your new car?" he said. "Don't you get it? You're nothing without me. There's nothing in the bank. Take me to court. I dare you! They won't find anything. The only thing they'll find is evidence of this beautiful illusion," he said.

I shook my head. *I should have known. Fuck. How did I drop the ball on that?*

"Look, you can do whatever you want. I won't make you stay if you want to leave, but know that if you walk out that door, that's on you. I will fight you in divorce court every inch of the way, and I'll win," he said.

Was it all for nothing then? Did I have sex with my rapist for nothing? Did I live with my rapist all these years for nothing? I stood there unable to move, struggling to breathe.

He continued in my silence, "Or stay. Mind your own business. Be a good wife. Do whatever you want, I won't stop you. Have kids. Don't work. I'll take care of everything. I'll keep paying the mortgage. Your credit card will never decline. But don't you dare play detective, sticking your nose in my business, or make a mistake like this, ever again."

What kind of woman would accept that bargain? Crap, I need time. Time to come up with another plan. I can't walk away now or he's won. I need him to believe I am helpless without him, that I believe that I need him and genuinely want to stay.

I looked up at him and he continued, "Come on. What choice do you really have? You said it, *you* quit your job. And I know for a fact that you don't want to work anyhow. So stay with me." His tone became surprisingly conciliatory.

"Do you love me?" I said. *Are you going to keep fucking Julia?*

"Sure. If it matters to you. We have a life together. The life I thought you wanted."

"I did."

"Look, I don't appreciate being called out for cheating, but I get it. You were hurt and thought you had the upper hand. I'm sure you're sorry. If you apologize and make it up to me, then I'll forget this ever happened," he said.

Our eyes met. I choked back tears. "I'm sorry," I said. *God! What am I doing? I can't live like this, begging my rapist for forgiveness.*

He smiled. "That's right. But why?"

"Nate, I'm sorry I got upset about you and Julia. We went to a swinger party, so obviously I knew what to expect. I guess I just got jealous when I saw you with her," I lied. "I was upset and I overreacted. I just don't want to share you with anyone else, because you mean everything to me." I let a tear roll down my cheek. It was a tear for everything I had sacrificed and for his momentary victory and my setback. *Is he buying this?*

He waited for a few moments, watching me.

"I understand. Apology accepted. Just don't let it happen again. It might be good to talk to your therapist about jealousy. It's a nasty sin, you know."

"Yeah, of course," I said.

He took my face in his hands and kissed me. My stomach churned.

"I think I'm going to go for a walk," I said and left the room.

I got in my car and drove to Hammonasset Beach. It was cold and grey, and the wind whipped around me. I walked for a long time to clear my head. *So that's it. What now?* Waves crashed onto the sandy beach. *I can't walk away from him now, after everything. I've invested too* much. *Given up so much.* A large dog bounded down the beach toward me, its owner just a figure in the distance. *Am I in this predicament because I didn't go through the formal channels? Because I took justice into my own hands? Had I tried to play God? Am I being punished for my hubris?* I shook my head. *How silly! Justice is justice. What kind of God would punish me for trying to make a monster pay for what he did?* I thought about it for a while. *Wanting revenge is wrong, but isn't injustice wrong too? Isn't it wrong to let someone like Nate off with no punishment? An eye for an eye.*

I walked toward the figure in the distance.

I have to keep it together. There has to be another way. How can I use his other weaknesses against him? How can I expose him for who he really is? I just need to figure out Plan B. If there's no money, then all that's left is his reputation and his freedom.

THE BREAKDOWN

Monday, January 29, 2018

Old Greenwich

Nate seemed unusually chipper all week. It was clear that he was pleased with his ruse. I tried my best to be pleasant. It was easier that way.

He needs to think that I've given up and am grateful for a second chance at this life with him. The longer he thinks he has out maneuvered me the better, because the more time I have to come up with a Plan B.

I spent every waking minute analyzing the situation, racking my brain looking for a way forward. *It can't all have been for nothing. There has to be a way to make him pay.* I read accounts of women who had accused their husbands of rape. The odds of winning seemed bleak and the trials had left many of them in ruin.

Rereading Hames v. Hames, a footnote led me to Dennis v. Dennis (1896), whose headnote read: "A divorce sought by the wife upon the ground of her husband's adultery, will be refused, where the act of adultery relied upon was brought about by the connivance of the wife." *An old fashioned honey trap. So not only does Nate say that there's no money, but even if he's lying and I try to divorce him, he could argue that I brought up the idea of going to the swinger party and was conniving to catch him cheating. He was the one who wanted to go to the party, but he'd never admit that and it would be his word against mine. Plus, I was the one who texted Candace about it. Hmmm, that might not work. If a divorce is out of the question, how else can he be held accountable and made to pay for what he's done? How can his own flaws be used against him?*

I remembered an article I had read in an undergraduate intro to law class, that I had taken at Vi's insistence. The article was about the legality and ethics of pre and post-conviction DNA testing. *Nate's DNA should be in the system from the rape kit I had done all those years ago. If Nate is arrested and forced to provide a DNA sample, it should come back as a match to my rape kit!* I Googled and skimmed recent news related to DNA testing laws in Connecticut. It seemed that Connecticut had passed a law, which took effect in 2011, making it legal to collect DNA upon arrest for a serious felony, prior to conviction or even arraignment. It said that, once collected, the DNA would be entered into a state database and then run through a federal system to see if it matched any DNA from unsolved crimes. *Yes! That's it. That's Plan B! If there's no money, maybe there's another way to finally make him face his demons! But he needs to be arrested first. How on Earth can I make sure he gets arrested so that he gets DNA tested? And what is a "serious" felony anyhow?*

Reading further, a "serious felony" included murder, arson, kidnapping, robbery, assault, sexual assault, and home invasion. The law also said that a prior felony conviction was required. *Hmmm, that's not gonna work. There's no way I can frame Nate for one of those things without a complicated effort and without showing my hand. Plus, this has to be believable. Whatever happens, he can't know that I caused him to be arrested. He'll lose it when he finds out it was me who turned him in...he needs to be safely in custody without possibility of release when he finds out. If I can turn him in without having to directly and publicly accuse him of something, then maybe there will be enough time to get justice after all.*

I looked into New Jersey's laws on DNA testing. New Jersey also allowed pre-conviction DNA testing, but also only for various violent offenses including murder, manslaughter, sexual offenses, etc. *It has to be something more mundane. What about New York?*

A quick search revealed that New York only collected DNA samples post-conviction, but it did say, "Since 2012, any defendant convicted of a misdemeanor or felony must give a DNA sample to be added to the New York State DNA Databank....The police use this database to look for matches to DNA collected from crimes." *So to make sure he gets DNA tested in New York, I just have to make sure he gets convicted of a misdemeanor. How difficult could that be?*

I got up and poured myself a glass of Nate's favorite whiskey on the rocks. I held the crystal glass in the palm of my hand, watching the ice begin to crack in the caramel colored liquor. *Wait, maybe that's it! Nate drinks and drives. If I call him in for drunk driving and he gets*

*pulled over in New York state, that has to at least be a misdemeanor. I
searched the web just to be sure…and sure enough, driving while
intoxicated and aggravated driving while intoxicated were both
misdemeanors for a first offense. That's it! I can call the minute he
leaves a bar in New York drunk and alert the cops. So I just have to be out
somewhere with him where he is drinking and I need to outlast him and call
when he leaves by himself. I just can't use my own cell phone to make the call.*

*Julia's birthday is coming up and her party is in Manhattan. But will
he stay late hoping to hook up with her? He'll definitely want to drive. He
always does.*

Nate had made Friday night dinner reservations at our favorite
spot in the city: the little French bistro in Seaport that was off the
beaten path. Presumably as a sign of good will after our fight over his
infidelity. I hurried to get ready and was downstairs at ten to six, just
in time to catch the six-fifteen train to Grand Central and get a taxi
to Seaport.

Wall to wall mirrors ran the length of a long black wall, a
long wooden bar filled the center of the room, and the tables were
uncomfortably close together, but Nate was convinced that they had
the best shellfish in the city.

Nate was waiting at the bar when I arrived, dressed unusually
fancy in a designer business suit. He nodded to the hostess and she
showed us to my favorite table in the house. We sat next to each other
and split a bottle of red wine.

"How's work?" I asked.

"Fine."

"Must be really busy."

"It is."

"What's going on?"

"We're getting ready to launch another new product."

"Oh yeah, what is it this time?" I asked.

"Hair loss prevention and regeneration."

"Have you been making everyone else pull long hours too or just
working like a dog by yourself?"

"There've been a couple of late nights for the whole team," he said.
"At least when I make 'em stay late I buy pizza and beer."

We split a buttery duck liver pate and a bucket of oysters, and I stole a profiterole off his plate. We tipped back the last drops of wine as the bar started to fill up.

After dinner he asked if I'd go for a walk with him. I thought it was a little unusual since it was a blustery winter evening and we had a bit of a drive to get home, but he insisted. He took my hand and led me through City Hall Park to the footpath onto the old Brooklyn Bridge. I walked next to him in my heels for as long as I could, but when the trail transitioned from poured concrete to wooden boardwalk I slowed my gait to avoid losing a stiletto in the cracks.

"Hey, I can't go much further." I said, looking down at my feet.

He turned, smiled, and scooped me up in his arms. He carried me to the first tower and put me down gently where the path bowed out around the massive stone structure. The view looking back toward Manhattan was spectacular. It was a clear night and the nearly full moon lit up the sky and the bridge cables that soared above our heads.

Nate turned and took my hand.

"Look, I'm sorry about what happened at that party. I'm glad you decided to stay."

Good. This is exactly where I want you.

I turned and saw a small box in his hand. It was wrapped in beautiful gold paper and had a small bow on top.

He smiled and held the box out toward me.

"For putting up with me," he said.

I unwrapped the box carefully, took the lid off, and peeled back the tissue paper. A delicate gold lock in the shape of a heart was engraved with:

NPE + WRL
07-01-2017

I held it in my hand, admiring the way the lights of the bridge illuminated the engraving on the face of the lock, against the glittering backdrop of the City in the distance.

"Oh, Nate!" *Pretty impressive actually! He's totally committed to this.*

He kissed me on the mouth, took the lock from my hand, bent down and affixed it to the painted, weathered railing.

"They come by and cut them off all the time now, so we shouldn't leave it here, but I thought you might want some photos," he said.

"Yeah, of course."

He asked the only other couple around to take a few pictures of us next to the lock. Then he took an artistic close up of the lock with the city lights glittering in the background.

"I thought it might make a nice locket," he said as he unlocked it. "I can have the loop removed and a chain put on it if you want."

"Yeah, that would be great," I said.

He carried me almost all the way back to the car.

The next morning I laid in bed pretending to read the newspaper that Nate had left next to me, but instead I thought about my plan. I ran through scenario after scenario and the risks involved. *What if he doesn't get drunk at Julia's party? What if he does get drunk but doesn't get pulled over on his way home? What if he gets pulled over and they don't arrest him? What if he tries to bribe the cops to let him off?* Hadn't I also read that the State of Connecticut collects a DNA sample upon arrest for sexual assault in spousal or cohabiting relationships, which is a felony? *Should I just call the cops and accuse him of sexual assault instead? They'll ask for proof and I'll have none. It'll be his word against mine, and worse still he'll know that I'm up to something. No, the DUI is the best option. It's not guaranteed, but I'm out of options. There's no money and I can't just call the cops in Illinois now and tell them that all of a sudden I know who raped me all those years ago, and guess what, I'm married to him. They'd wonder why I came forward when I did and why I didn't tell them the truth when it happened. No, Nate has to be arrested for something unrelated to the rape and then DNA tested so that the discovery of his connection to my rape seems coincidental, there's no obvious connection back to me, and he's never let out of prison. That's the best way.*

THE BREAKDOWN
Friday, February 16, 2018
Old Greenwich

Julia's birthday was on Friday and she'd planned a Carnival-themed costume party and rented an entire room at Velvet, the swankiest restaurant in Manhattan—for the moment at least. She also booked table service at Unbridled, a high-end dance club just a few blocks away. I went to a costume shop in a neighboring suburb and got stock costumes for both of us. Nate would be a masked swordsman and I would be his damsel-in-distress.

"I don't want to wear this shit," he said as we were getting ready. He held up a tight velvet pants-suit with a cape and mask.
"Why?"
"Because this shit is gay."
"It's the 21st century. Aren't you man enough to wear velvet?"
He ignored me.
"You're worried that if you wear a velvet onesie people will think you're gay? I didn't think you were that insecure."
"Fuck you."
"It's a costume party. Please don't be that douchebag that shows up to a costume party without a costume."

He held the pants up in front of him. They were clearly the right size.
"God damn it," he said as he took his pants off. "You couldn't have gotten something more masculine?"
"I liked the dress that goes with it," I said.
"Fine. Should we take an Uber?"
"You don't want to drive? Won't it be really expensive to get a nice

car all the way to and from the City from here?" *Come on! You always want to drive. You always complain about how crappy even the Uber Blacks are in the City.*

"Yeah, you're right. I'll drive."

Phew!

We arrived at Velvet around seven and Nate valeted his car.

He went straight to the bar and returned to hand me a glass of wine, clutching a double scotch on the rocks in his other hand.

"Come say hi with me." He motioned to a few couples we knew across the room.

"I'll catch up with you in a minute, just need to go to the bathroom," I said, and disappeared to the back of the restaurant.

As I came out of the bathroom, I hung back and watched him work the room with complete control. He was truly artful and always impressive to watch. I hated that I admired his confidence, but I did. It was intoxicating to be in his orbit. He took control with ease and could captivate an entire room. *Why does he have to be such a monster?* I realized that this would probably be the last time I would be in public with him. It was strange and exhilarating to think that I had the power to end it all. His confidence, his swagger, his bravado. I alone could finally knock him down to where he belonged.

He grabbed my hand and pulled me toward a photo set-up, complete with an assortment of elegant, gold-colored props and a gorgeous hand-painted banner that read:

A Carn(iv)al Celebration!
Happy 27th Birthday Julia!

Nate and I posed in front of a black backdrop. Martina, Julia's assistant, began to snap photos. I posed with my hands clasped in front of me and my head tilted back. Nate scooped me up in his arms and twirled me around. He kissed me playfully for the camera.

A few hours later, I watched as he finished his third double on the rocks and I went to the bar for a drink. I brought him another.

"Oh, thanks, but I think I need to slow down a little. Could you get me a water?" he said.

"Sorry, just trying to be polite," I said. I handed him the scotch and headed back to the bar. He held onto the scotch for a little while, cupping it in his hand like a prop. Eventually he began to sip.

A little after eleven he sauntered over to me. "I think I'm done for the night. Need to get up early to get some work done," he said.

"You look a bit tired," I said. He tried to stifle a yawn in response.

He pushed his face toward mine trying to kiss me. The sweet smell of booze on his breath was overpowering. I turned to the side and he snuggled his face into my neck and pulled at my waist. "Come home with me?"

"It's pretty early. I think I'll hang out for a while."

He looked up at me and I saw the disappointment on his face. I realized immediately that he knew that Julia would be out late tonight and wouldn't be available, so he was relying on me instead.

"I really want to go to the club for a little bit," I said. "All this hanging around the house is starting to make me restless. I think I need a night out to get my spirits up. Don't worry about me. I'll get a ride home."

He grumbled but nodded. "Fine, I'll stay."

Yes, come have another drink!

Just as he said it Julia stood up and yelled, "Okay, it's time to party." She grabbed her purse, finished off the remainder of the glass of white wine that was in her hand, and headed for the door.

We walked to the club and were immediately waved past the line and into a VIP balcony on the mezzanine level. There was another group in the balcony, but there were enough bartenders that there wouldn't be much of a wait for drinks.

"Want anything?" he asked.

"Rob Roy," I yelled back.

He nodded.

I watched at the bar as the busty female bartender handed him a Rob Roy full to the brim. He tipped her and then took the first sip so that he'd be able to carry it without spilling.

He handed me the drink and took a sip of water from a glass in his other hand.

"Oooh, can I have some?" I asked, looking at his water.

He handed it to me and I handed him the Rob Roy. I took a big sip of water and just as I was about to hand it back to him I heard my name. Candace was yelling for me from across the room. *Impeccable timing.* I took off with the water before he could hand the Rob Roy back to me.

Candace was busy telling Julia about some trip to Nantucket that she wanted everyone to take together next summer. Her family had some nine bedroom house on the ocean, although she was careful to warn us that eight of the nine bedrooms were small but that we would all fit reasonably comfortably. She added that we wouldn't want to spend too much time inside anyhow because the beach was fantastic, and so was the shopping in the historic downtown. I nodded and smiled. I watched Nate from across the room as Candace blabbered on. He tried to hide a big yawn. *Come on! Go home!*

Julia began to dance to the beat blasting from the massive speakers downstairs. "Let's go dance!" she yelled.

She dragged us downstairs to mix in with the crowd. Warm, sweaty bodies bounced back and forth. I waited until the end of the song and then looked up into the balcony. Nate was leaning against the railing on his forearms. The Rob Roy was almost gone. He was watching us and made eye contact with me. I smiled and nodded. Nate yawned, finished the Rob Roy, and motioned sleep with his hands. I held my hands to my head like a pillow and nodded. He waved goodbye and I blew him a kiss. *Yes! Finally!*

I waited until he was out of the room and made my way down a long hallway at the side of the building toward the bathrooms. There was an emergency exit door propped open by a metal bucket and just outside a few smokers loitered. I stepped into the lingering cigarette smoke in time to see Nate get into his car and begin to pull away.

"Hey, can I borrow your cell?" I asked a young guy. "It's important." I smiled sweetly.

He furrowed his brow.

"I'll buy you a drink," I offered.

"Ugh. Yeah, fine, but don't go anywhere."

"Thank you."

I took a couple of steps toward the street and turned away from him. I dialed '911' and hit "Call".

A female dispatcher answered the phone, "9-1-1, what is your emergency?"

"I was at a bar with a friend. He just left in his car after I warned him that he was too drunk to drive. I'm worried he'll kill someone on his way home. He's really drunk."

"Which direction is he heading and which route is he most likely to take?"

"From the bar, he's most likely to take FDR Drive to the Thruway. He'll be headed north from downtown to Old Greenwich."

"Okay. What's he driving? Do you know the license plate number?"

"Black Porsche 9-11," I said. "N8 GR8."

"Are those New York plates?"

"No, Connecticut."

"When did he leave the bar?"

"Just now. Maybe three minutes ago."

"Okay. And what is your name?"

"Andy," I said, for no reason other than it was the first thing that popped into my head. "I mean Andrea."

"Last name?"

"Smith."

"And what is your phone number?"

Shit, I can't give her my real phone number and I don't know this one. I rattled off seven random numbers.

"I've alerted the patrols in the area."

"Thank you."

She hung up.

I went back inside, fought my way through the crowd, and rejoined the group. I danced to take my mind off Nate. A waitress pushed her way toward us with a tray full of shots.

"To Julia!" Candace shouted.

We each grabbed a shot and threw it back. I didn't feel a burn as it went down. The bass permeated my body and time flowed. I checked my phone. An hour had passed. *Nothing yet. Did they catch him? It's been a while. Maybe he's already home. I should go home.* I passed Julia on my way off the dance floor.

"Heading out soon," I yelled. "Happy Birthday!"

She pulled me toward her and gave me a hug.

I grabbed my purse from the coat check and requested a car. I waited in front of the club and bummed a cigarette from one of a handful of smokers. My nerves were getting to me. *This has to work. I can't do this any longer.* The deep bass permeated the old brick walls of the club.

A small grey car pulled up and I climbed into the back seat and made necessary pleasantries. He hit the road and I nearly fell asleep when my phone began to ring. It was a random 914 number. *Nate?* I let it go to voicemail. *This will be fun.* Another call a few minutes later was from the same number.

I asked the driver to turn down the radio and listened to the two voicemails.

"Wyn, you're not going to believe it. It's bad. I need you to…" he was cut off.

In the second message I could hear the panic in Nate's voice; "Wyn, answer your goddamn phone!"

A guttural laugh came from somewhere deep inside me.

"Ma'am. Are you okay?" the driver asked.

"Oh, yes, excellent actually!"

I hit the green call icon next to the 914 number. The phone rang so many times I nearly hung up, but then a woman picked up; "New Rochelle Police Department."

"Yes. I believe my partner just tried to call me from this number. His name is Nathan Ellis. May I please speak with him?"

"What do you think this is, Ma'am? A hotel?"

"No, I guess not."

"I will have to see if he can be brought to the phone. Please hold." I waited.

"You'll have to wait until he calls you again," she said. "It's shift change so he can't be brought up now. If I were you I'd keep my phone close at hand and the volume up."

"Thank you," I said.

I watched the city retreat in the rear view mirror, thinking that just a couple hours earlier Nate had likely taken this exact same route.

I texted his cell phone a few times for good measure.

1:18 am: "Nate, what happened? I got your messages."

1:25 am: "Tried calling the # from ur missed calls. Got some useless bitch at the county jail. Best practical joke ever!"

1:32 am: "Getting worried now. Where r you? Whats going on?"

251

I was so exhausted when the driver finally dropped me off that I fell asleep on the couch in my 'damsel-in-distress' dress.

The ring of my cell phone woke me up abruptly at half past seven. At first, I wasn't exactly sure where I was or what was going on, I hardly ever kept my phone on ring. The caller ID showed the 914 number from the night before.

A robotic voice said, "To accept a collect call from 'Nate', please press one now. I hit one. "Nate?"

"Yeah, it's me."

"Oh my god! Where are you? What happened?"

"I got pulled over on my way home."

YES! YES! "Shit."

"Yeah, shit is right. My blood alcohol level was .250"

"What does that mean?" *It means you're fucked and I'm finally going to see you pay!*

"It's about five times the legal limit."

"Shit."

"Yeah, shit. It's an aggravated DWI. Up to a year in prison."

"Oh my God."

"I need you to call Simon immediately. Tell him to be at the Westchester County Courthouse Monday morning at ten sharp to represent me at my hearing."

"Okay." *Hmmmm, how far am I willing to go? To call or not to call?*

"Do you know where his number is?"

"No."

"Are you in the kitchen?"

"Yeah."

"It's in the drawer next to the fridge on a post-it note, I think."

"Okay."

"I'm going to get cut-off soon. Please call Simon right now. I'll call you again when I can. Love you."

"Love you too," I said just before the line was cut.

I got up and went to the kitchen. I found the old yellow post-it in the back of the drawer buried under a handful of loyalty cards, an assortment of rubber bands, and a few warranty cards. I held the post-it in one hand and my cell phone in the other. I examined Nate's nearly illegible handwriting. His future was in my hands. *Should I play fair? He certainly hadn't. What if I don't call? What if no one shows up tomorrow? He'd have to represent himself. But then he'd know something was up. He'd wonder whether I'd made the call at all. I can't let him know yet.* I figured not calling Simon wouldn't change things for Nate too much at this point. He'd find a lawyer, it would, however, reveal my intentions. I decided to call Simon. I wanted things to appear as normal as possible for now.

I dialed the number and was put through to Simon Katz, a college frat brother of Nate's who happened to be a criminal lawyer out of New York City. Nate had mentioned before that Simon was expensive: the best defense money could buy. He told me that he wasn't available on such short notice, even for Nate, but promised to send one of his very capable colleagues.

A Facebook notification popped up on my phone; "You've been tagged in a photo". Then another. Then another. *Julia.*

I clicked on one of the icons and it took me to a list of five photos from the night before. I accepted. In the top of my feed was a picture of her and Adam from the night before kissing in front of the banner with a caption that read, "Thanks to everyone who came out and made my Carn(iv)al 27th birthday party unforgettable! #JuliasCarn(iv)al27th @JWeber1". A long list of guests had been tagged. It had been posted in the early hours of the morning and already had over a thousand 'likes'.

It was only Saturday and Nate's arraignment wasn't until Monday morning. I needed a distraction, so I went to yoga, but none of the regulars were there. I texted Jenna. She reminded me that she and her husband had the weekend to themselves and were in the Catskills. *What to do all by myself in this boring suburb?* I wanted to text Adam but didn't want there to be any evidence that I'd reached out to him the same day Nate was arrested. *Too soon.* I thought. *I have to play the grieving wife to perfection right now.* I missed Ali and Vi and thought about home. I realized that I hadn't heard from Ali since she'd stayed over so I texted her again and then called Vi.

"Freddie," Vi said as she picked up.

"Hey."

"How are you?"

"Fine. How are you?"

"Good."

"How's Ali?"

"I think she's fine. Why?"

"Have you seen her lately?"

"Yeah, I saw her on Saturday. What's going on?"

"Did she say anything about me? About her trip?"

"Nope. Nothing. She and Soren came over to help me do a little painting in the new place before I finish moving all my stuff in. Is something wrong?"

"I don't know. Probably not. She just hasn't been responding to my texts. She's probably just busy and we did just see each other."

"Probably. How are you?"

"I'm okay. A bit lonely lately, but I think I'll go stop by Adam and Julia's for some company."

"Look, I've gotta run right now, but call anytime you want to talk."

"Okay, I will."

"Love you."

"Love you too."

I walked the dirt path that connected our yards and poked around hoping to catch a glimpse of Adam, alone. He wasn't there. Julia saw me and motioned aggressively for me to come in.

Julia was dressed in yoga pants and a tight long sleeve shirt. She looked like she had been working out but it was hard to tell because she had make-up on and her hair was pulled back in a messy bun that still looked perfectly styled.

"Hi," I said.

"Oh my God, you look so good considering," she said. "It was on the local news this morning. Did you see it?"

"No. I've been trying not to watch."

"It was in the local paper today too."

She picked up the paper which was already open to the short article about Nate's arrest. She handed it to me.

"I'd rather not, thanks."

"Okay, sorry." She was clearly offended that I didn't want to gossip about it.

Adam let himself in from the garage. "Hey you two. What's up?"

I watched Julia make an espresso, add a couple heaping teaspoons full of fake sweetener, and then down it in one large gulp.

"Are you okay?" I asked her. "You look really tired." Her eyes were red around the edges with dark circles underneath, which was uncharacteristic. She also looked even thinner than usual, if that was possible.

"I'm fine, thanks. Just a little thirsty." She grabbed a bottle of water from the fridge and walked out of the room.

"Is she okay?" I asked Adam. "She doesn't look healthy."
"I think she's fine," he said, "maybe just a little hung over."
I nodded.

THE BREAKDOWN

Monday, February 19, 2018
White Plains, New York

I woke up just before my alarm on Monday morning. The sun
had just crested the horizon. I showered and put on one of the more
casual business suits left over from my working days. The taught
fabric inhibited movement in a way that felt utterly stifling. *Have
business suits always been so uncomfortable?*

The Westchester County Courthouse was an imposing, 1970s
brutalist concrete high-rise in downtown White Plains, less than a
half hour drive from the house. As I drove, I thought about the lines
that a caring, concerned wife would be expected to deliver. *I was
worried sick about you! I can't even believe this happened! You'll be home
soon, don't worry.* Anticipating that a tear or two might be appropriate
at some point, I had applied a liberal amount of make-up before I left
the house, knowing that tears resulting in a ruined face are always the
most effective.

I parked a few blocks from the courthouse and walked. I could
feel my nerves increase as I approached the building. *Will he be let out
on bail before he's DNA tested? Will he know that I called 9-1-1 on him?*
Despite all of my planning, this was uncharted territory, and I still
wasn't sure how it would end, or if I'd ever be satisfied.

The security line was long and I fidgeted with my car keys
while I waited. After security, there was a long hallway lined with
courtrooms on either side. The judge's name and the cases they
were hearing were listed outside each room. I searched each one for
Ellis, finally finding his name listed eighth in a 10am to 2pm slot.
Jeez, it's going to be a long day. I found an empty bench at the back of
the small courtroom and settled in. I'd brought Vi's diary to keep
me busy, but my attention was immediately drawn to a middle aged

couple sitting together in the front row. They looked absolutely ordinary and I wondered why they were here. *Is their son or daughter in trouble?* There were a few well-dressed men and women sitting in the gallery, ranging in age from about thirty to sixty. *Lawyers for the accused?* I wondered if Simon's associate was among them. I had never met Simon. All I knew about him was that he had handled some legal issues for Nate in the past. At some point after we moved in together, Nate had shown me the post-it with Simon's number on it and emphasized at least two or three times that if anything bad ever happened to either of us we should call Simon immediately.

Just as I picked up Vi's diary and began to read I was startled by the aggressive rap of the gavel against the large wooden podium that stretched from one end of the courtroom to the other. A clerk announced, "All rise for the Honorable Judge William Murphy."

I put the diary down and stood. The clerk bellowed, "I pledge allegiance to the Flag of the United States of America, and to the Republic for which it stands, one Nation under God, indivisible, with liberty and justice for all. Court is now in session."

The first defendant was accused of aggravated battery while on probation. The judge read out the charges. There was little dispute about what seemed to be the facts and the man's lawyer argued primarily that his client was young, misguided, and extremely remorseful, which his demeanor mostly supported. He was given a stern lecture, time served, and treatment in an anger management program. A few other cases were relatively straight forward and seemingly easily resolved.

It was late morning when a young guy, 19, who was accused of his fourth DWI in three years was called. This time he had crashed into another car, badly injuring a young woman in the passenger seat of the other vehicle. I felt bad for his lawyer because there wasn't much he could do or say. It made me wonder, given the improbable odds of getting pulled over while drunk, how many more times had Nate driven around wasted and not been caught or ruined someone's life. The judge read out a statement from the young woman who had been injured in the crash about the three surgeries and the months of intensive rehab she would need to regain the use of her right arm. *So much of life is just about being in the wrong place at the wrong time.* Of course, the fault lay with the young man, but his lawyer began to describe an abusive home, a life full of expectations derailed by The Great Recession, and a series of near misses that left him grasping for a hand up, to no avail. There wasn't a dry eye or much sympathy for a drunk driver left in the room when Nate's case was called.

"Case number 91564. Westchester County versus Nathan Patrick Ellis," announced the Bailiff. A smartly dressed man seated a few rows in front of me jumped to his feet.

"Counsel requests a moment to confer with his client," he said.

Nate was escorted out in an orange jumpsuit and handcuffs and was seated at a long desk that faced the judge.

"Granted, Mr. Simms," the judge replied.

The young lawyer walked over and took a seat at the desk beside Nate. They whispered back and forth. Their exchange lasted a few minutes before Nate's lawyer turned his attention to the judge and nodded.

"Mr. Simms. While this is your client's first DWI in the State of New York, it is Aggravated DWI and it says in his file that he has prior DUIs in Connecticut. That is a very concerning pattern of behavior if you ask me."

That's it! Nate had mentioned those when we first met but I wasn't entirely sure whether the State of New York would have access to his record from Connecticut. This just keeps getting better.

"Understood, Your Honor."

"Did your client consent to a Blood Alcohol Concentration test in the field?"

"Yes, Your Honor."

"And what was your client's BAC level when tested?"

"According to the police records, it was .25, your Honor."

"Is your client planning to contest that result?"

"No, Your Honor."

"Your client is aware that in the State of New York, a second offense within ten years is a Class E Felony, punishable by up to four years in prison."

"Yes, your honor. However, since this is only his first DWI arrest in the State of New York, and the mandatory minimum is only five days, of which he has already served two, we are hoping that you will take these and other key factors into account."

The judge turned slightly to look directly at Nate. "How do you plead, Mr. Ellis?"

Nate spoke confidently into the microphone, "Nolo contendere, Your Honor."

What the hell does that mean? I discreetly Googled it. *No contest in Latin. He's essentially pleading guilty without actually saying that word. That's how it always goes with him, doesn't it? Even when he knows something is his fault he won't take responsibility.*

I realized at that moment, just how badly I wanted to hear him say it; *guilty.* I had a strong feeling that there was no way he'd ever say he was sorry, which meant *guilty,* coming from Nate's lips would be the closest thing to closure, resolution, amends.

"Your Honor, my client understands that he has a problem. He is prepared to do whatever it takes to rectify the situation, and will of course comply with all of the standard requirements, such as a one-year license suspension, however we ask that Your Honor consider that Mr. Ellis runs a health and wellness business that employs approximately 500 full-time staff and that he is also the sole support for his lovely wife, Wyn, who has recently learned that she is carrying their first child."

What?

The young lawyer turned toward the gallery and the Judge's gaze followed. I nodded instinctively and did my best not to look completely taken aback by the news. *This must have been Nate's sick idea!*

The judge acknowledged me and Nate's lawyer continued, "Your Honor, we request mandatory completion of a rehabilitation program, the maximum fine allowed under the law, supervised probation, community service, and of course my client will comply with all legal requirements including license suspension and use of an ignition interlock device."

"Mr. Simms, I assume that your client has already been through an alcohol education and treatment program after his first offense, as well as community service, which is standard for first offenses. If so, it didn't seem to do much to change his behavior. If the program did not work then, why should we believe that it will work now?"

"Your Honor, Mr. Ellis was younger and less mature. Given his wife's condition, Mr. Ellis understands the gravity of the situation and the importance of changing his behavior."

"Hmmm, I do wonder whether Mr. Ellis has the maturity now to learn from his mistakes and adjust his behavior appropriately.

However, I do believe in second chances, and his wife will need a partner for support over the next year."

Fuck. After all of this I'll be the reason he gets let out? I shouldn't have come today. If I wasn't here, Nate's lie wouldn't have been nearly as effective.

"Your Honor, your point is not taken lightly, however, the news of Mrs. Ellis' pregnancy has had a significant impact on Mr. Ellis and he is ready to reform himself and change his behavior now that he will be a father."

I'm not Mrs. Ellis.

"Mr. Simms, if Mr. Ellis was behaving recklessly on Saturday evening, am I to believe that he has had a complete change of heart in the span of less than forty-eight hours?"

"Yes, sir," he replied. "Because he only found out about Mrs. Ellis' pregnancy this morning, Your Honor."

The Judge turned to look at me again. I buried my face in my hands.

"Mr. Ellis. Your behavior is inexcusable. I sincerely hope that you were able to hear the proceedings that came before yours today, and if not, I hope that Mr. Simms and Mrs. Ellis will convey what occurred, because it is an apt example of where you are headed if you do not learn from your mistakes. You have a choice. You can change your ways and be a responsible member of this grand society, a good husband to your wife, and a good father to your child, or you can continue on the path you are on, which will inevitably lead to the destruction of your family and everything you have worked so hard for. I sincerely hope that up to this point, you have only harmed yourself. In the future, I guarantee that any ill-advised actions you take will result in the harm of others, potentially irreparable harm. While I am moved by the news of your wife's condition and therefore I do not pass this sentence lightly, I cannot ignore the severity of this offense in light of your past behavior. You will submit to a DNA test immediately and will not be released from custody until the results of the test are received by this court. You will pay the maximum fine for a misdemeanor Aggravated DWI. Upon release, your license will be suspended for one year and you will be required to complete 100 hours of community service during your probation. Once your probation has ended, and for a period of three years, you may not operate any vehicle that does not have an ignition interlock device installed and operational. You will also complete an inpatient alcohol treatment program immediately upon your release by the Department of Correction. You are dismissed."

I wept audibly into my hands to hide the smile that accompanied my tears of joy. An older gentleman came over to offer a packet of single-use tissues. I obliged, thanked him, and wiped the black mascara from around my eyes.

Nate was escorted out and the young lawyer walked over to console me, shepherding me out of the courtroom and back into the main hallway.

Once outside he turned to me and said earnestly, "I'm so sorry, but I think that actually went as well as could have been expected."

"Yeah, I guess." *Thanks to your lie.*

"I know, the mandatory minimum is only five days and we didn't get that, and it may take a few weeks to get the DNA test results back, but he will be home to you soon. Certainly before the birth. Hang in there."

"Yep. Thank you."

"Of course."

"You know I'm not pregnant, right?" I said.

The look on his face was all the confirmation I needed: he was Nate's pawn too.

"I'm so sorry."

I nodded, playing along. "Thank you."

"Do you want to see him now?" he asked.

"I'm exhausted," I said. "I think I'll come back tomorrow. I can visit whenever I want, right?"

"Well, not exactly. There are visitation hours. They should be posted online or you can call."

I nodded.

"You okay?" he asked.

"Yes, I'll be okay. Thank you."

As I walked back to the car, I worried about what the future might hold. *Will the DNA test come back a match to my rape kit? Will he be released on bail even if it is a match?* I knew that playing the role of Nate's distraught wife would be difficult, but he had made it even more difficult with his lie. I laughed nervously about the suggestion that I was pregnant with his child, as I thought back to how that had felt. I felt the empty void inside me where hope should have been. *Will this ever be over?*

THE BREAKDOWN

Friday, March 16, 2018
Old Greenwich

Almost a month and no word on the DNA test. *How long can a DNA test take?*

I'd visited Nate in prison the week after the hearing, but hadn't been back since. Putting on the show, even for Nate, was exhausting. It had been hard enough under normal circumstances, but having to play sympathetic to my rapist's current plight was too much, even for me. Not wanting to give too much away, I sent Nate notes of encouragement on the backs of completed pages ripped out of my coloring book. In the white spaces on the front of the pages, I reproduced passages from Sun-tzu's *The Art of War* that Nate had carefully underlined. Things like, "Ultimate excellence lies / Not in winning / Every battle / But in defeating the enemy / Without ever fighting" and "The difficulty of the fray / Lies in making / The crooked / Straight / And in making / An advantage / Of misfortune." and "Anger / Can turn to / Pleasure; / Spite / Can turn to / Joy / But a nation destroyed / Cannot be / Put back together again; / A dead man / Cannot be/ Brought back to life." At some point in his life these nuggets had no doubt motivated him, but under the current circumstances they were sure to confound.

Movement in the backyard caught my eye. It was Adam. He came in the back door and walked over to the chair next to me.

"What's up?" I asked.

"Came over to see what you're up to tonight. I'm on my own again," he said. "I thought maybe we could have dinner. Watch a movie."

"Adam, Nate's in jail."

"For raping you."

"I know, but we can't be together right now. It won't look good if I'm seen with another man while my husband's in jail." *The last thing I need right now is someone accusing me of cheating on Nate while he's in prison. I've been the perfectly faithful wife for this long. I just need to be patient, at least until I hear something about his DNA test.*

"What's going on?"

"I can't tell you yet. Soon. I promise." *I can't tell you until I know the plan has worked and I'll be free and safe.*

"You're always full of secrets. I don't get it."

"This is all part of the performance. I need you to help me right now by staying away. We can't be seen together at all. Please."

"You sure you're okay? I know this has been a difficult time but you seem a little paranoid."

"I'm fine," I said. "You'll understand soon enough. Please just go." He frowned but stood up. "Fine."

"It has nothing to do with you," I yelled as he let himself out.

I felt a little bit bad and would have enjoyed his company, but I knew he needed to stay away. *What if the Evanston Police never had my rape kit tested? What if it's just sitting around in a warehouse somewhere collecting dust? The whole plan would be ruined. I can't believe I haven't heard anything yet. Maybe there's just a backlog on testing.*

I needed to stay busy to avoid getting impatient and doing something I would regret. I flipped through the channels but there was nothing on t.v., so I picked up Vi's diary.

April 4, 1989

Shreveport, Louisiana. I went to the only clinic in town for pregnant women. The nurse did some tests and then I asked her about an abortion. She turned almost white and said that I should never say that word again as long as I live. She asked where I had even heard about that. I didn't tell her. She said that my baby has a normal heartbeat and that I am probably going to go into labor around the middle or end of August. I will be in Chicago by then. I have no idea where or how I will have the baby. I'm really starting to get nervous! Ruth and Elizabeth said that they will help me raise the baby and we will be like the Three Musketeers but moms. I don't think they understand.

April 19, 1989

Shreveport, Louisiana. It was her! She did it! Now I understand what he meant when I visited him in the jail. She was bothering me again about marrying him. I told her to lay off and that I don't want to marry him. She said I was ungrateful and should thank her for everything she has done for me! I told her I had no idea what she was talking about. She said that she was the one who called the police and told the cops that he had sex with a minor. She's the reason he's in jail at all and she was trying to guilt trip me the whole time! She says that the only way to save myself, my child, and my child's father is to marry him, then it wouldn't be rape. I asked her why she did it and she said that she did it for my own good. Because if she didn't I would be ruined and she would have no choice but to kick me out of the house. She said she did it to save me. She thought that if he was in jail and Father Connelly agreed to lie about our marriage that I would agree to it to get him out of jail. She thinks it was an honorable thing to do. She set this whole thing up. I don't even understand why she would want me to marry him. I thought she hated him after the awful names she called him. I won't marry him, but I think I'm also too far along to have an abortion. I guess I'll have to take care of myself and the baby alone.

Holy shit! So that is why she never talked to her mom again! It all makes sense now. How sad! She was betrayed by her own mother. Just when she needed her mother's help the most, her mother turned on her and let her down. And to think, I never even asked Vi for help when I needed it most, because I didn't want to burden or disappoint her. Maybe I should have told her what happened.

The next morning I indulged myself and stayed in bed. I was reading the news on my phone, when my cell phone rang. I recognized Simon's number. *Have they done the DNA test and finally gotten the results? Is that why Simon's calling early on a Saturday? It must be! Do they know it's my rape kit?*

I hesitated and then answered, "Simon?"

"Wyn, thank God!"

"What's wrong?"

"I have some bad news. Are you sitting down?"

"Yeah, of course."

"I just got a call from the State Police. There was an offender hit in CODIS."

Hallelujah! "Oh my gosh! What does that mean?"

"Nate's DNA came back a match to evidence collected in an unsolved rape case in Illinois."

"What? How is that possible?"

"Well, DNA from a rape kit done in 2012 matches Nate's DNA profile. Mistakes are occasionally made, which means we will petition for a reexamination of the evidence. If it's a mistake, which Nate says it must be, then he will be released."

Of course he says that! "And what if it isn't?" *It means he's finally on the hook for what he did!*

"If the DNA in the rape kit really is a match, he would be charged in the State of Illinois with a felony. That would mean a trial, unless we can strike a plea deal first."

"Would he go to jail if he's convicted?"

"For the more serious of the charges he could be facing it's a minimum of six years mandatory incarceration, but we will fight it. I believe that because he has no prior history of this type of offense and the criminal complaint is old and charges were never pressed, combined with his excellent standing in the community and as an employer, we should be able to work out a plea deal with better terms. He may be able to plea to a lesser charge that is probationable, which would mean he could be released from prison as soon as the deal is finalized."

That's it? Jesus Christ. All of this for a year in prison? "Did they say who the victim was?" *Obviously they don't know it was me or he wouldn't have called.*

"Not yet, the accuser's identity will be withheld until a trial."

"Oh my god, this is bad isn't it?" *Not bad enough.*

"It's definitely not good, but I think we have a few things working in our favor at this point, so I'm optimistic. Like I said, it's been a long time since the incident occurred and the victim chose not to press charges initially. Also, the prosecutor said something about the victim not being a very reliable witness."

"When will we know whether there will be a trial?"

"It could be a while. We've just started discussions with the Prosecutors team. The negotiations could take some time," he said. "I will, of course, call you as soon as I have more information about the charge and the potential plea options."

"Will Nate be able to come home? I mean, can we bail him out?"

"Unfortunately, no. Given the seriousness of the charges and Nate's resources, the judge has denied bail. Wyn, I can't imagine how difficult this must be for you. I'm so sorry. I know Nate is just ready for this whole thing to be over and get home to you."

"Uh huh."

"He keeps asking about you. He mentioned that he was surprised that you haven't come to visit again."

"Oh, yeah, I meant to, but I've been busy. I'll try to get up there this week."

"Great, I know that would really cheer him up. I will keep you posted."

"Thank you so much, Simon. That's very kind of you."

"I'll be in touch, Wyn," he said. "Take care."

"You too." I hung up.

I felt like celebrating. I knew it was too early, but I couldn't help thinking that things were finally going to change.

I cut through the backyard and let myself into Adam's through the back door. He was in the kitchen making a sandwich.

"I thought we weren't supposed to see each other, at all," he said.

"I have some good news."

"What's up?"

"They did a DNA test," I said. "There was a positive match to DNA in a national database for the rape. It looks like Nate's going to be charged with a felony for what he did to me."

Adam turned and looked at me, his eyebrows raised. A wide smile crossed his face. "So that was it? That was the plan all these years?"

"Well, not exactly, it was Plan B. But when Plan A didn't work out it became the plan." I smiled.

"So, what next?"

"Not sure exactly. I would think that the prosecutor should contact me, but I don't really know how this stuff works."

"Does Nate know it was you?"

"I don't think so. Not yet," I said.

"Will he find out?"

"Apparently he might not if he strikes a plea deal with the prosecutor to avoid a trial, which will probably be in his interest."

"Do you want him to know?"

"I'm not sure," I said. "I guess, I think so, but not until I'm ready."

He nodded. "Well, congratulations, I think."

"Thank you."

"Keep me updated," he said.

"Will do."

I went home, left my phone on the kitchen counter, and went upstairs to take a hot bath. I turned on a meditation soundtrack and tried to relax, but my mind raced. *Will Nate find out it was me? Will the prosecutor tell Simon? Is he allowed to? If he chooses to go to trial can they force me to testify? How could I talk about what he did to me in front of him and a jury? He would find out how much he hurt me. He would know that it devastated me. I would have to relive every painful moment all over again, he would have all the power again.*

As I laid in the bathtub it occurred to me that the video that I was so afraid of before could now be evidence, if it even still existed. *Does he still have it? Where would it be if he did have it? I have to find it!*

THE BREAKDOWN

Monday, March 19, 2018

Old Greenwich

My cell phone rang around noon. It was a number I didn't recognize with a 312 area code: *Chicago*. I answered.

"Wynafreda Laurent?"

"Yes, who is this?"

"My name is Detective Wilshire from the Cook County State's Attorney's Office."

"Hello."

"Wynafreda, I would like to speak to you about a witness statement you gave in June 2012."

"Yes . . ."

"There's been an unexpected break in the case and we are wondering whether you would be interested in pressing charges?"

"Oh, wow. That's amazing. Yes, I think so."

"I understand you live in Connecticut now."

"I do."

"We would like to have you meet with a local detective to answer a few questions. You'll need to go to the State Police Department in Bridgeport."

"Okay. I have one question," I said.

"Sure."

"I would like to speak to the prosecutor assigned to the case."

"He is very, very busy. It's not likely, but I will see what I can do."

"I would really like to understand how this whole process works and what my options are."

"I understand, Ma'am, but typically the prosecutor will reach out to you once we have gathered all of the evidence and determined what charges can be substantiated."

"Oh, okay. I would still like to talk to him sooner than later. I would appreciate any help you can provide."

"Of course. In the meantime, Detective Donaldson from the Connecticut State Police will contact you. He will conduct the interview in Bridgeport for us."

"Okay."

"Thank you. Good bye."

I hung up.

My cell phone rang a few hours later. It was another number I didn't recognize. *Local this time.* I answered.

"Wynafreda Laurent?"

"Yes."

"My name is Detective Donaldson, Connecticut State Police."

"Hello."

"We need you to come in for an interview," he said.

"Okay."

"Can you come in on Thursday around 2pm?"

"Sure."

"Great. The address is 149 Prospect Street."

"Okay." I jotted down his name and the address.

"Just ask for Detective Donaldson at reception," he said and hung up.

What to do now? Do I need a lawyer or will I look more innocent if I show up alone? Yeah, I think alone is best for now.

The State Police Department was in a cheap-looking building made of grey cinder block with a periwinkle roof, right off the highway exit. I pulled into the parking lot and walked into a brightly lit entryway with a glass barrier that separated guests from the receptionist.

"I'm here to see Detective Donaldson. He's expecting me."

"Name please?"

"Wynafreda Laurent."

"Please have a seat. I will let him know you're here."

"Thank you."

That day in the Evanston Hospital six years earlier started to come back to me. I immediately felt the emotional exhaustion of that experience all over again. The desire to be home and not here, anywhere but here, under the bright white lights, surrounded by concrete and never ending questions. *Do I really want to go through with this? A trial would be exhausting. Is it really worth it if he only gets a year or two in jail?*

I looked around the empty room; there was another young woman, maybe early twenties, sitting across from me. *No other woman should have to go through this. He should be behind bars, even if only for a year. He should have to register as a sex offender. I have to do this, for all of us.*

"Ms. Laurent," the detective said. He looked to be in his early to mid-forties, with dark brown hair, and a bit of a baby face.

I stood up and offered my hand.

"Detective Mark Donaldson," he said as he took my hand. "Please follow me."

He escorted me down a long white hallway with scuff marks on the walls, and showed me into a stark room with a simple wooden table in the middle and two chairs. There was a one-way mirror on the long wall facing me. I wondered who was behind it. *Could Nate's lawyer be back there?*

"Wynafreda," he said.

"Please call me Wyn."

"Wyn, do you know why we've asked you to come in?"

He had a way of talking to me that was extremely patronizing, but was also a little bit flirtatious, which made him extremely hard to read. My gut told me not to trust him.

"The detective I spoke to on the phone earlier said that there was a DNA match to my rape kit," I said.

"Yes, that's correct."

"Who is it?"

"I think you already know who it is," he said.

I tried to look as perplexed as possible without overdoing it. "What do you mean?"

"I'm confused, Mrs. Ellis."

I'm not Mrs. Ellis!

"You signed a criminal report in 2012 alleging that you were raped. Correct?"

"Yes."

"And at the time, you said you were drugged and unconscious for the entire rape. Correct? You said you have no idea who raped you."

"Yes."

"Then how is it that six years later you are married to your rapist and living with him in Greenwich, Connecticut?"

I shook my head. "It's complicated. I didn't know who to trust," I said. "I was so scared."

He took notes on a pad of legal paper and scrutinized the notes, as if looking for a clue.

"You mean, you didn't know who to trust when you figured out who raped you? You mean you figured out who it was on your own and you didn't report him to the police once you knew?"

"I knew what he would say…that it was consensual sex and I wanted it, which I didn't. I was convinced he would get off easy and then come after me. I couldn't bear to go through a trial and have him walk away without any punishment. I was sure if he did he would find me and ruin my life. Maybe even kill me."

"You were scared of him and so you began dating him?"

"No, not right away. I thought about going to the police. I really did. And I tried to forget about him and move on, but I couldn't. I was haunted. I couldn't sleep; I couldn't eat; I couldn't be touched. I relived it in my nightmares and when I was awake. If I heard any of the songs that were playing while he did it, I lost it. I started having panic attacks. I went to therapy, but nothing worked. Eventually, I decided I had to see him, so I tracked him down. After I'd seen him, well, watched him really, I realized I had to talk to him. I had to see if he remembered me. When he didn't remember me, I became fascinated with understanding him. Understanding who he was and what would drive a person to do what he did to me and then not even recognize me. I needed to know what was wrong with him, how fucked up he really was. I got closer and closer to him, until we were dating. The more time I spent with him, doing things that made him happy, things that made him love me, the more dependent I became. I know it sounds completely fucked up, but he's confident, handsome, and charismatic. He's easy to be around when he's happy, and I realized that as long as he got what he wanted, he was harmless."

"What do you mean, you became dependent on him?"

"I became dependent on him, emotionally and financially. He made me believe that I was nobody without him. Over time he made me believe that without him I would have nothing and couldn't survive."

"Are you saying that he brainwashed you?"

"My therapist says it's called trauma bonding. It's like Stockholm

Syndrome, except that the abuser isn't a stranger."

He made a few notes and I waited in silence. Then he looked up and stared right at me.

Does he think I'm bullshitting? Will he believe me?

Finally he broke the uncomfortable silence. "You said you were surprised when he didn't recognize you, but this is what you looked like the day he raped you." He laid a photo on the table in front of me. It was a photo of Krista and me, all dressed up, at the frat party the night of the rape. I remembered the headband and the blue eyeliner. It must have been posted on Facebook. My blonde hair was perfect, my smile, innocent. *I miss that naïve girl who had no idea how her life was about to be turned upside down.*

"So I started dying my hair a few years ago. Lots of women dye their hair. I was starting to go grey early."

"And change their names too?"

"I didn't change my name, I just asked to be called a different nickname when I started working. Freddie isn't exactly the kind of name a woman puts on her business card when she wants to be taken seriously."

"Okay," he said. "Did you two have any kind of prenuptial agreement?"

"I don't see what that has to do with the rape?"

"Please just answer the question."

"I think instead I'd like to invite my attorney to join us."

"Wynafreda," he said, "there's nothing to get upset about."

"It's Wyn," I said.

"Wyn, I was just about to get to my questions about the rape."

"I have to go. I'm sorry." I stood up and showed myself out of the room and back down the hallway.

I walked out into the glaring sun and immediately dialed Vi. *I need a lawyer! A really good lawyer.*

"Hey Freddie," she said.

"Hey Vi."

"How are you?"

"I need a favor."

"What's up?"

"I need a lawyer," I said. "The best criminal lawyer in Illinois."

"Freddie, what happened?"

"I'll tell you later."

"Are you okay?"

"Yeah, I'm fine. I just need help figuring out who I should hire."
I'm finally in over my head. I need to understand what is possible now and what isn't. I need to understand so that I can plan my next move.

"I'll get contact info to you a.s.a.p."

"Thank you. As soon as possible please."

"Of course."

"Gotta go. Thanks."

"Love you."

"Love you too."

I got in the car, plugged in my phone and selected a hits radio station. I turned up the dial and sang along as I drove home.

Vi texted me just as I pulled into the driveway. "Asher Morgan, III, Esq. 312-345-6789. Tell him Professor Adams gave you his #"

I pulled into the garage, and dialed the number. "Asher Morgan." Beep. I was caught completely off guard, expecting he'd have a secretary. *How did Vi get his direct number?*

"Mr. Morgan, I got your number from Professor Adams. I need your assistance with an important legal matter. It's urgent. My name is Wyn Laurent. Please call me as soon as possible at 847-362-8934."

I turned the ringer on my phone all the way up, made a cup of tea, and grabbed my coloring book. I settled in on the couch and tried to forget everything.

My phone rang. It was the 312 number I had called earlier.

"Asher Morgan."

"Mr. Morgan," I said. "Thank you for calling me back so quickly."

"Wyn?"

"Yes."

"Look, I'm really busy but I've had something open up on tomorrow morning at nine. Are you available?"

"Oh, shoot, no. I'm in Connecticut."

"How about Monday?"

"Yeah, sure."

"Monday at 11am then."

"Great. Thank you so much."

"See you then." He hung up.

I bought roundtrip airfare to Chicago.

The afternoon dragged on. It was cloudy and drizzling, so I turned on the fireplace in the back den and picked up Vi's diary.

May 5, 1989

Shreveport, Louisiana. I went to the police station today. I told them that I don't want to press charges because he didn't rape me. I told them it was all a big misunderstanding. I signed a piece of paper that they prepared that said that I thought he should be free to go. I don't know what will happen to him but I did what I could to get him out. I hope he's okay, but I have bigger things to worry about now, like getting to Chicago and having a baby.

May 28, 1989

Shreveport, Louisiana. I didn't even go to graduation. I took my last test and went straight home to pack. She was out of the house when I got home, which was perfect. I hate her so much! I packed the biggest suitcase I could find and then Ruth took her mom's car and drove me to the bus station. Ruth cried as she hugged me and watched me get on the bus.

I'm on the bus now and can't sleep. All I can think about is this baby growing inside of me and the new life that awaits us in Chicago. I'm watching the scenery out the window. There are signs along the road for towns with names like…

LOUISIANA
Audrey Park
Vivian
Mira
Ida

ARKANSAS
Hope
Emmett
Curtis
Joan
Donaldson
Shannon Hills

We just stopped in Little Rock and I got off the bus to go pee and everyone stared at me. I'm sure they're wondering why a pregnant girl is travelling alone, but I don't care. They can all go to hell!

ARKANSAS
Crystal Hill
Beebe
Alicia
Portia
Pocahontas

We just stopped in St. Louis. We're in Illinois now. It's funny the further north we drive the less it seems the towns are named after women and the more men's names there are: Troy, New Douglas, Raymond, Andrew, Williamsville. I wonder why.

Chicago is so big! The buildings are sooooo tall and there are cars and people everywhere! There are buildings made of stone, and metal, and brick. I didn't know that buildings could be so tall. I took the subway from the bus station downtown to Evanston, the town where the university is. When I finally found the dorm where I will be living, there was a young woman with a baby sitting in a lounge area near the front entrance. The dorm is for families only. The young woman was very nice and explained that I needed to go to a different building to check-in. I walked across campus and signed a few forms promising to follow all the various rules and I was given a key to my room. It is really just one big room, but it has a small kitchen with a fridge and a stove and its own bathroom. The campus is beautiful. I'm so much happier here already...in my own place!

THE SEND

Monday, March 26, 2018
Old Greenwich

I flew to Chicago on Monday morning and went directly to the offices of Morgan, Staunton, and Moretti. The receptionist asked me to have a seat. I waited for a few minutes and, just as I was beginning to get impatient, a frosted glass door opened.

A well-dressed man in his early sixties appeared. "Ms. Laurent?"

I stood up. "Yes."

"Good morning," he said and held the door open for me.

"Good morning."

I followed him down a long wide hallway into a corner office. He turned and offered his hand. "Asher Morgan, pleased to meet you."

"Wyn Laurent. Nice to meet you."

"Please have a seat," he said.

I took a seat opposite his desk.

"Wyn," he paused. "You mentioned that you have a problem of a criminal nature."

"Mr. Morgan, my husband violently raped me years ago before we were married. I had a rape kit done at the time, but decided not to press charges for various reasons."

"Hmmm."

"He was arrested about a month ago for drunk driving and they took a DNA sample. It came back as a match to my rape kit."

"I see," he said.

"A detective from Illinois called me on Monday. The rape occurred in Evanston, when I was in college. He asked me to go meet with the Connecticut State Police to discuss the rape with a detective. I went to the station in Bridgeport on Thursday thinking that they just wanted to do due diligence, you know, talk to me, since I was the victim in the case, but he began asking some questions that made me uncomfortable."

"Sorry, why were you in Bridgeport?"

"Oh, that's where we live now. That's where Nate was arrested."

"Nate?"

"My husband," I said. "And my rapist."

"And you're sure that *your* rape kit was the hit on your husband's DNA in the system?"

"Well, I'm assuming it was. The officer I spoke with implied that it was."

"Hmmm. Please tell me more about the rape."

"We met at a frat party on campus. I guess he was in town visiting for the weekend because he didn't go to my university. He raped me in the room he was staying in, while the party was raging outside."

"I'm so sorry," he said. "Can you tell me more about what happened? The details are important."

"I hardly knew him at all. I didn't even know his last name at the time."

"Okay," he said. "What else? What exactly happened that night?"

"It was my freshman year of college. He was a high school friend of my roommate's boyfriend. He was extremely charismatic and I thought we were falling in love. He said he was a Christian. I told him I was a virgin and was planning to wait until marriage."

He nodded.

"We were drinking together and dancing at the party. I was attracted to him." I paused and tried to keep my composure. "It was getting late and we were walking down a long hallway in the house and he grabbed me and pulled me into his room. At first I thought it was romantic. I thought he wanted to steal a kiss in private, but that wasn't his plan."

Mr. Morgan handed me a tissue.

"He tied my wrists together and threw me on the bed. I begged him to stop. I told him no. He gagged me and pulled my clothes and my underwear off. I tried to scream, but the music was so loud. He forced himself inside me. It was extremely painful. The next day I needed twelve stitches inside my," I paused, "vagina." I still felt awkward using that word in front of a man his age. "He finished inside. I was relieved at the time because it meant it was over, but it was actually only the beginning. He kept me tied up in his bed all night. I cried until I fell asleep."

"I'm so sorry," he said.

I nodded. "When the sun came up he told me that he had videotaped the entire thing and that if I told anyone he would dub porn audio over the video and put it online with my real name. He told me he would ruin my life. That no one would hire me or ever want to marry me. I was scared."

"Do the police know about the video?"

"No, I didn't tell them very much when they interviewed me at the hospital because I was in shock. He had threatened me, so I might have given the police incomplete information. I don't remember exactly, but I know I didn't tell them everything when they interviewed me that day."

He scribbled furiously on his note pad.

I continued, "I only had the rape kit done because I'd been told how important that was, and honestly I was worried that he had done permanent damage to me, so I knew I needed to go to the hospital."

"But you didn't press charges?"

"No. I didn't even tell them his name or who he was. Everyone I knew at the time warned me that I wouldn't be taken seriously. Like I said, Nate wasn't enrolled at my university. He lived in Philadelphia and I was told that even if he had been, the university administration was likely to give him the benefit of the doubt and not do anything. I was warned that my accusation could hurt me more than him."

He studied his notes.

"So how on Earth did you come to be married to him?" he said.

"I found him."

"I don't understand?"

"I did some searching on social media and figured out his last name and where we was living. I moved there and went to the places that he frequented. I knew because he had checked-in and liked some places. Eventually, I saw him and we talked. We matched on a dating app and started seeing each other. A few years later, we were married," I said. "Well, we had a wedding but he didn't send in the forms, but it doesn't really matter."

"Why did you want to marry him?"

"Like I told the police, he haunted me. He haunted me in my sleep, and while I was awake, I saw him everywhere. He ruined my life without ever posting the video of the rape. The attack played over and over again in my head. If I heard any of the songs that were playing while he did it, I lost it. I couldn't trust anyone. I began having panic attacks. Eventually, I figured that the only way to make him go away was to see him. So I tracked him down. After I'd seen him, I knew I had to talk to him. I had to see if he remembered me. When he didn't remember me, I became fascinated by him. I needed to understand what would cause someone to do what he did to me. I needed to know what was wrong with him, and what made him tick. I guess I wanted to understand him so that I could have some closure, but the more time I spent with him, doing things that made him happy, things that made him love me, the more I needed him. He was confident, handsome, charismatic. All the things that had first attracted me to him were still there, and as long as he got what he wanted he was harmless. I know that this will sound crazy, but eventually I think I even began to love him, in some way. I tried to remind myself that he was a monster," I said. "He is a monster. But only when he doesn't get exactly what he wants. Only when he's told 'no'. As soon as he knew he could have me whenever he wanted, he didn't need to hurt me and in fact he lost interest and moved on eventually."

"Wow," he said.

I nodded.

"I have to ask you something, and you must tell me the truth. You must tell me what you would tell a judge and a jury of your peers under oath," he said, staring directly at me. "You have to tell me the truth so that I can advise you accurately."

I nodded.

"Did you marry him to get revenge?"

I shook my head. "That was never my intention," I lied. "My therapist says I exhibit classic signs of trauma bonding."

"Hmmm."

"It's like Stockholm Syndrome," I said. He jotted "Stockholm Synd?" down on his notepad.

"So you said that he orchestrated a fake marriage. Why do you think he did that?"

"Honestly, I don't know. Especially since he made me sign a prenup."

"Do you have a copy of the prenup?"

281

"I do."

"Can you send me a copy, just in case?"

"Yeah, of course."

He continued, "So what else did the detective say?"

"He told me he thought I already knew who the match to my rape kit was, even though he hadn't told me. Then he asked a bunch of questions."

"Like what?"

"Why I didn't report him when I figured out who raped me, and something about the prenup."

"Yeah."

"Will I have to testify? Will he have to know it was me?" I said.

"Wyn, this is serious stuff."

I nodded. "I understand."

"Do you?"

I nodded again.

"The Sixth Amendment of the U.S. Constitution guarantees the right to confrontation, which means not only the opportunity to cross-examine witnesses, but also the right to face-to-face confrontation. So if the case went to trial, his counsel would have the right to cross-examine you in person. You could request an exception on the grounds that you would be harmed by testifying in an open court, but I do not believe that your request would be granted in this case. Exceptions to the right to confrontation are typically reserved for minors."

Shit.

"If he strikes a plea deal with the state to avoid a trial your identity as the victim may be withheld. As for a trial, your rape kit and your testimony will be helpful, but he could still get off with the minimum sentence or possibly less if he has a really good lawyer, and even if he does serve time, he might be able to get out early for good behavior. You said there was a videotape of the rape, right?"

"Yeah, I saw it and he said he filmed it."

"Do you have it?"

"No, but I think I might be able to find it."

"Did you tell the detective about the videotape?"

"No. It's hard to remember, but I don't think I told the police about it when they first interviewed me."

He nodded and scribbled on his legal pad.

"To your knowledge, have you been charged with any crimes at this point?"

I shook my head. "No. I don't think I've committed any."

He studied his legal pad carefully and made a few more notes.

"Wyn, I would advise you to find that videotape. If you find it, let me know. We'll figure out whether the prosecutor has it and make sure he gets it. Otherwise, lay low. Don't talk to the detective again, or any other police for that matter, without me. Call my direct number immediately if they want to question you."

He continued, "Also, this guy sounds dangerous. You might consider getting a restraining order."

"Okay, thank you." *It's cute that this guy thinks a restraining order will stop Nate from coming near me if that's what he wants.*

As if he could read my mind, he said, "The restraining order is a good idea, even just to demonstrate on the record that you believe he is a threat to your safety. You might install a high grade security system too and change the locks."

"I understand."

"Do you have any other questions?"

"What do you think are the chances that he'll serve any time?" I asked.

"He'll serve a little time, but not much unless you find that videotape and we can develop a rock solid story that a judge and a jury will believe about why you were living with your attacker. That won't be easy."

"Thank you," I said. "Will they extradite him to Illinois?"

"Eventually, yes. Timing will depend on whether there is a trial or he pleas and if the latter, then whether his plea deal includes additional time in prison."

"Hmmm. Oh, and what is your fee?"

"For you, just $350 an hour, moving forward."

Jeez, is that the family and friends discount? I thanked him. He declined to charge me for the consultation and I left his office and went straight back to the airport.

THE SEND

Monday, March 26, 2018
Old Greenwich

I got home late and ran upstairs to Nate's office, pulled the blinds shut, and began searching for an old laptop I remembered seeing in a drawer after we first moved in. I had no idea how old it was or what was on it, but all I could think about now was how vital it would be to have video evidence.

Rummaging through drawers, pulling folders and papers out, looking for a laptop or old data storage device, I noticed that the bottom left drawer of his desk was locked. *I've never noticed that before.* I found a small set of keys hidden in the back of the top drawer. *Yep, perfect fit.* I pulled open the drawer which turned out to be nearly empty save a black case. I pulled it out and popped open the clips holding it shut. A handgun was packed neatly into a foam mold. *Holy shit! That psychopath had a gun in the house the entire time and I didn't know. What would I have done if I'd known? He could have killed me if he'd found out what I was up to.* I sat for a few minutes just staring at it, not sure what to do.

After a bit more searching I found a laptop in a cardboard box underneath an envelope filled with old pictures and other college mementos. I put the computer on the desk and pushed the power button. *Nothing.* I plugged in an old charger that was in the drawer. It booted up slowly and then asked for a password. *Damn it!* I thought for a minute. *What would Nate's password be?* That was a difficult enough guess now, but he would have created this password in college. Despite how long we'd been together, he'd never shared a single password with me. *Shit! I need help. It's too late today. First thing tomorrow.* I grabbed the laptop, the charger, and an external hard drive that was shoved under a bunch of loose papers in one of his drawers. I put everything in my biggest purse. The gun was still in its box, open on the chair. *Maybe I should learn how to use it, for protection.* I had fired a rifle at a summer camp when I was young. It had been years, but I could learn again. I picked it up. It was heavier than I'd expected. How such a cold, lifeless metal object could cause so much destruction was unfathomable. I engaged the safety and put it in my purse.

The next morning I drove into Manhattan, paid to park, and went into a little hole in the wall I'd passed a million times and never thought twice about called 'Hackers'. Below the name, a sign promised they'd be able to solve my most difficult computer problems.

Inside, every wall was painted black and covered haphazardly with decals advertising everything from computer equipment to skateboards.

"What's up?" A young guy with nearly invisible eyeglasses asked.
"I need a copy of everything that's on these." I pulled the laptop and hard drive out of my purse. "I forgot my password."
"Okay. When do you need it?"
"Yesterday," I smiled, but he didn't smile back.
"Sorry, not possible. We're busy. And the password thing can take time."
"I understand, but I have to have this as soon as possible. Price doesn't matter."
He perked up and took his eyes off the motherboard he was fidgeting with. "Five thousand," he said cautiously, as if testing the water.
"Three thousand."
He shook his head. "Like I said, we're really busy."
I looked around the empty shop. "Thirty-five hundred."
"Four thousand."
"Okay."
"You may want to come back. I can call you when it's done."
"I don't live close by," I said. "I'll wait."

I sat down in a chair near the front door. *I can't charge this to my credit card or write a check, and I can't just go take four thousand dollars out at a bank. I have to make sure that it can't be traced back to me.*

I texted Adam. "You at your office today? I've got an emergency."
He replied, "Yes. What's wrong?"
"Need to stop by now. Ok?"
"Of course."

I gathered my purse and sweater.
"I'm gonna go for a walk," I announced to the young hacker.
He didn't acknowledge me.

I left the shop, turned left, and walked up to 5ᵗʰ Avenue. I walked down 5ᵗʰ to 37ᵗʰ, and took the elevator up to the 30ᵗʰ floor of Adam's office building. The receptionist nodded as I walked past.

Adam was on his cell phone when I walked in. "Yeah, but I told you that I wouldn't be home until late tonight. I don't know why you're mad at me. It's not like I'm cancelling on you. I never agreed to go!"
He turned around and saw me.
"I have to go. I'll see you later." He slammed his phone down on the desk.
"Sorry," he said. "What's up?"
"I need money."
"Is this about him?"
"You said anything."
"Of course. I just didn't expect you to ask for money," he said. "How much?"
"Four thousand. I'll pay you back of course. But I need cash, now."
"You need four thousand dollars in cash right now?"
"Yes."
"Freddie, what the hell is going on?"

I stood up and closed the door to his office.
"He videotaped it," I said.
"The rape?"
"Yep. That vain bastard videotaped it and I need to find the footage for the case against him. In case it goes to trial."
"Why do you need four thousand dollars to find it?"
"I found Nate's old computer but I don't know the password. I've

got a guy working on it, but I need it today, so he's charging me premium to crack the password."

He nodded.

"I need to pay cash so that he doesn't have my name, and obviously I can't take a bunch of cash out right after my husband was arrested. They might think I'm planning to disappear or do something crazy."

"Are you?"

"No, of course not. I just don't want to attract any unnecessary attention."

He shook his head.

"Okay, let's go to the bank," he said.

"Can I wait here?" I asked. "I don't think we should be seen going to the bank together."

"But you've been seen coming in here and then I'll be seen leaving and coming back."

"Yeah, I know. I didn't think ahead. Just go. Please," I begged.

He picked up his wallet and phone off the desk and slid each into a pocket. He walked around the desk and stood in front of me. I stood up. He wrapped his arms around me and pulled me against his chest.

"I'm sorry about all of this," he said.

"I know. Thank you."

After he left I fought the urge to snoop around his office. *I need him to trust me.* I waited alone and watched out the floor to ceiling window.

Where is he? I looked at the clock. *Half an hour already. Come on Adam.* I paced around his office for another five minutes until I heard the door knob turn.

"Relax," he said. "I got it."

He walked in, closed the door behind him, and put a plastic bag with the bank's logo on the desk. The familiar smell of his aftershave and cologne was comforting. *I love the way he smells.*

He took his coat off, turned to me, and pulled me toward him.

"It's going to be okay," he said. He held my face in his hands and kissed me. His tongue lingered in my mouth. I kissed him back.

"I love you," he said. It should have been another glorious moment in our story. It should have lifted me up. Instead it felt like just another complicating factor in an already fucked-up situation.

"I know," I looked up at him. He pulled away, clearly offended that

287

I hadn't reciprocated.

"I love you too," I said. *I need him on my side now more than ever.*

He pulled me closer and I felt his erection against my stomach.

He looked at his watch and then fumbled for the end of my sweater and pulled it over my head. I kissed him. *Sure, why not? For all I know, this thing with Nate may never end.*

He took off his suit coat and began to undo his belt. His pants dropped to the floor. He was naked. I glanced at the door.

"It's locked."

"You sure?"

"Yep."

He unbuttoned my pants and pulled them off my hips, fidgeting with my bra as I slipped the straps off my shoulders. He pulled my thong down and I kicked it off.

He lifted me up onto the desk and began to kiss my neck, collarbone, and chest. I grabbed his hips and pulled him toward me. I was already wet and I wrapped my legs around his waist, as he worked his way deeper inside. After so many years of anticipation the pleasure was intense. I laid back on the desk and held on to the edge. He put his hands on my hips and held me in place as he rocked back and forth rhythmically.

"Oh my God!" I said quietly. Waves of pleasure spread through my body and I let go. The climax was so intense that I had to muffle my own screams. He began cumming and I felt him let go and hit me in just the right spot. My body convulsed again. We came together. Slowly it passed and he leaned over me and kissed me tenderly.

"I've only ever loved you," he said.

A tear rolled down my cheek. He wiped it away with his thumb.

"I know," I said, as he gathered me up in his arms. I cried and cried and he just held me and rubbed my back.

"I'm sorry," I blurted out. I looked up at him and saw the tears streaming down his cheeks. There was a depth of sadness in his eyes that broke my heart all over again.

"I'm so sorry," he said. "I'm so sorry all of this happened to you. I'm so sorry that 'we' didn't happen earlier. I'm so sorry we fucked things up all those years ago."

I nodded. "I know. Me too," I said. "But it's not worth dwelling on now. It is what it is. What do we do now?"

"Whatever we need to do."

I nodded and he kissed me.

"Shit, my meeting is starting," he pulled his pants back on and buttoned his shirt. "Good luck with the video thing." He wiped his cheeks. "Let me know how it goes."

"I will. I'll stop by tonight."

"Great."

He pulled his suit coat on and grabbed a pen off his desk. He looked back at me before he opened the door. A huge smile crossed his face.

"Love you," he said.

I smiled. "Love you too."

He squeezed out the door and closed it behind him. I got up and got dressed quickly. I checked my hair and makeup in the reflection of my phone. I put the plastic bag full of cash in my purse, and slipped out past the receptionist.

THE SEND

Tuesday, March 27, 2018
Old Greenwich

"Long walk," the hacker said when I walked in the door.

"Are you done?"

"Yep. You got lucky. Password was pretty simple, so the algorithm cracked it fast."

"You got everything?"

"Yeah, I copied everything there was on both onto this." He handed me a new external hard drive.

"Okay. Thanks."

"How do you want to pay?"

I pulled the plastic bag out of my purse and put it on the counter.

"Oh! O-kay then," he said. "Thanks."

"Also, I need the laptop and the old hard drive back." *Can't have evidence laying around here.*

"Whatever." He pointed to his desk. I walked over and grabbed both.

"Thank you," I said, and walked back out into the cold, fresh air.

Back at home, I ran upstairs to get my laptop, plugged the new external hard drive in, and began searching through the folders. There were two folders, the first called "Laptop" was full of his college applications and essays, scans of important documents: his birth certificate, his condo mortgage documents, and his first life insurance policy. There were photos of him when he was younger with his mom and sister, and his friends from childhood. There were, of course, folders full of pirated music from the late 90s and early 2000s. *Not helpful.*

I navigated back to the second folder, "hard_drive", and clicked on a folder labelled only "Graphics". There were about thirty video files in the folder, each named in the same way: location and then date. *Bingo?* I clicked on the first file, "dorms_03-18-11". It was dark and hard to tell at first what was going on. Then the voice of a woman could be heard.

"Yeah, that's it. Just like that."

Nate's voice was clear in response, "You make me so hard."

Getting closer! I watched for a few more seconds, but the sex seemed to be consensual, so I closed the file and moved to the next, "sigchi_06-11-11". The light was better. He was kissing a tall, thin woman with dark hair, but his face was not turned toward the camera. At first she seemed to be into it, but then she began to resist. Her efforts were futile. He threw her onto the bed. *Rape?*

I scanned the dates, realizing that they spanned from early 2011 all the way to 2016. My stomach turned. *Holy shit, he's been doing this to other women the whole time.* I didn't want to keep looking. I didn't want to see him hurting other women after me. *Could I have stopped this if I'd reported him right away? Saved these other women from the same fate? No. Nothing would have stopped him. I just have to find my video.*

I remembered that Nate kept a few really expensive bottles of wine in the cellar and grabbed the one that Nate had been saving. I got a juice glass from the cupboard, and filled it to the brim.

As I skimmed the files I saw, "phi_psi_NU_06-09-12", and my heart began to beat faster. I took a big sip of wine. Another darkly lit room filled the screen. It was hard to tell, but the room looked like the one that had filled my nightmares over and over again for years.

The camera was further from the action and it was nearly impossible to see what was happening, except for the outline of Nate's body which was slightly illuminated by what I could only guess was the hall light coming through the crack under the door. Unlike in the other videos, there was no audible dialogue, but there was music. He walked over to the bed and reached down. He appeared to struggle for a few seconds and then threw an item of clothing across the room. Then the bass became louder and he began to shift his weight back and forth and I knew. The pain came back to me and the aggressiveness of his rhythmic movements sent shivers up my spine. I could almost feel him again, tearing his way into me uninvited. The beat of the first song began to transition and I already knew what song came next. The playlist had been permanently etched into my memory. The beat was a little bit faster and Nate sped up his rhythm to match.

As I sat and watched, my body completely tense, I began to realize that despite the pain that I knew was being inflicted, to anyone else in the world this would just look like a really bad sex tape. So far, the resolution and angle made it difficult to even discern for sure that there was another person in the frame, let alone who. He had started the camera after the handcuffing, gagging, and my vocal protests. I kept watching, hoping that he had forgotten to hit stop and that some of the aftermath would be caught on film, but I glanced at the progress bar and saw that the entire video was only twenty-two minutes long. *Had it really only been twenty-two minutes?* In my memory it had gone on forever. I had always assumed that what had felt like forever had been at least an hour.

I resisted the urge to skip ahead, afraid I might miss something important. At about the eighteenth minute, just as I remembered it, his body began to convulse and he started cumming inside me.

Once he was done he could be heard saying: "Crying I see. It was *that* good for you too?" Then he laid down on the bed next to me. *Certainly not proof of rape.*

And then I could just make out: "That wasn't bad at all. You were pretty good for your first time. Being tied up really suits you." *Again, not proof of rape. Just proof that I was a virgin. At least that corroborates the story I told the cops.*

The video was nearly over. His face was out of the frame as he got up and walked toward the camera, his limp penis swinging from side to side as he walked. His face was still off-frame as he hit stop.

Fuck. Will that help at all? Is it evidence of a rape or just evidence that Nate, or someone who resembles him, likes kinky sex? It's hard to tell. It's certainly not irrefutable evidence that Nate raped me against my will, or that I said no. And it's not even clear that it's me.

I gulped Nate's exquisitely smooth wine as I clicked through a few more videos. Most of them were dark; a bit grainy. Many of them unfolded the same way that mine had. Each of the videos was difficult to watch but I couldn't help myself now. I wanted to see if there was damning evidence among the videos. I nearly gave up and in my distraction I let one of them continue playing. It had begun the way they all had, with passionate kissing and foreplay, but about three minutes in it took a different turn.

"Hey, can we slow down?" The blonde woman whispered just loud enough to be picked up by the small laptop microphone. He continued to grope her, in fact, the suggestion that he slow down seemed to embolden him.

"Hey, I said slow down," she said, louder than before. Again, it seemed to only encourage him and he pulled at her pants.

"What the fuck?" She was angry.

He responded in kind and pulled the same move on her that he had on me, throwing her to the bed, he grabbed what looked like a tie and bound her hands behind her back. She began to scream and he grabbed a pair of socks off the floor. You could hear her struggle.

"Shut the fuck up, bitch!" he said. She continued to try to make noise but it was clear he'd been successful. He walked over to the computer, although he seemed to intentionally stay mostly off-camera. He fidgeted with the mouse for a minute and heavy metal with a lot of bass began to play. His anger was palpable. He turned back to her and went to work pulling off her clothes. He forced himself inside her and pounded as aggressively as he had me. *This video is so much better!* I realized that the clear audio in it was key to understanding what had transpired. While the victim still wasn't completely visible or clear in the images, it was clear what was happening. *This is rape caught on tape. Proof! But not my rape. She is blonde though, and it's not that clear. Would they even be able to prove that it isn't me in the video? What do I do now? Do I hand this over to the investigator? What if they still drop the charges or he gets off easy despite this evidence? It certainly wouldn't be unprecedented. What if they fail to bring him to justice? Then I'll have nothing. No leverage or card to play. I can always turn it over to the DA later and say that I just found it, but if I hold onto it for a little bit, maybe it will prove more valuable. Patience!*

I changed the name of my video to "NU_06-09-12" and the file name of the better video to "phi_psi_NU_06-09-12".

THE SEND

Friday, March 30, 2018
Old Greenwich

I paced around the house after yoga. *It's been two weeks! What is going on? I haven't heard anything from the prosecutor or Simon about the charges against Nate or the negotiations. Is that a bad sign? Are they going to let him off entirely? Should I put that video online?*

I was nearly worried sick when my phone rang. *Simon!* I hesitated for a second and then picked up.

"Wyn! Good news!"

"Simon?" *Does he know it was me yet?*

"Things went pretty well this morning. It looks like they're open to a plea deal."

"That's great," I lied. "What does that mean for Nate? Would he have to go to jail?"

"The formal charge is criminal sexual assault, which is a Class 1 Felony, but the plea deal would see him plead no contest to a lesser charge of aggravated criminal sexual abuse, which is probationable."

He'll never admit he's guilty, will he?

Simon continued, "Aggravated criminal sexual abuse is punishable by a minimum of three to seven years' incarceration. We proposed three years of probation. It looks like some of it might have to be served as home detention, although he'd get credit for time served and could be released from home detention early for good behavior. Obviously it's not ideal, but he'd probably be able to leave the house to go to work. The prosecutor knows that this case rests entirely on the DNA evidence, which only proves they had sex, not that it was rape. Well, and her testimony, of course. I think they know that they have a pretty weak case against Nate, given how old it is. He would have to wear a GPS tracking device at all times."

So they still don't know it's me. His punishment would be to live at home and go to work? Unbelievable! Someone would have to take care of him, at home! His punishment would be my living hell. He would expect me to wait on him hand and foot! I won't do it. I won't let that happen.

"That's great!" I lied. "What about the woman? Would he have to compensate her?"

"Criminal trials usually don't result in financial compensation for victims, and the no contest plea means that it would be really difficult for her to sue him for damages in civil court because he isn't exactly admitting guilt."

Of course. He'll never admit he's guilty. "Oh, that's good," I lied. "She?"

"Yeah, we don't know anything more at this point, just that she had a rape kit done in 2012 right after she says it happened and it was a match to Nate. Which, as I said, doesn't prove that she was raped, just that they had sex."

"Got it. Thanks for the update. It looks like it might work out for Nate." *Not if I can help it!*

"I knew you'd be happy. This whole ordeal is finally going to be over."

No really, it's just begun. "How's he doing? I wasn't able to get up there again."

"He's doing okay. I think he's finally learned his lesson. He's ready to move on."

I shook my head. *He will never learn.* "Gotta run. Thanks again." I hung up.

How is this possible? How can he get off with living at home, in his mansion, after what he did to me? What kind of justice is that? How in God's name? I paced around the kitchen.

I picked up the phone and called the Cook County State's Attorney's Office in Chicago. *Maybe Simon is lying. Maybe it's not as far along as he makes it sound. Maybe there's still a chance he'll go to trial or get a harsher sentence.*

A woman answered the phone.

"I need to speak to Detective Wilshire."

"What is your name?"

"Wyn Laurent."

"Hold on, Ma'am."

I waited in silence.

"I'm sorry, Ma'am. He is not available. Can I take a message?"
"I really need to talk to someone about my case. The district attorney. I need to speak to the district attorney."
"Ma'am, there are a number of district attorneys in the office. I would need a name, and I doubt they are available. It's best if I take a message."
"Never mind." I hung up.

Looks like my sorority sister was right all those years ago. If I'd left things up to the system and put my faith in the men in charge I would have been let down long ago. I'd had my doubts over the years. Wondered whether taking things into my own hands was wrong. *Had I tried to play God?* I'd questioned whether I should have had more faith in the system, but it was becoming clearer than ever that Elisa was right. *This is just further proof that the system protects the powerful, not those who need protecting. I'm going to have to finish this thing off myself if I want to make sure he pays for what he did. He may be in custody now, but that's no guarantee of anything. There's no money, and no guarantee that he'll spend any real time in prison. All he has left is his business and his reputation. Fuck the plea deal! If they won't deliver justice then I will. I have no choice. House arrest doesn't fit his crime. He must pay. Life for life, eye for eye, tooth for tooth, hand for hand, foot for foot, burn for burn, wound for wound, stripe for stripe. If they won't hold him accountable, I will.*

I created a new post on Facebook and embedded the video of the blonde woman being raped by Nate. I added, "When I was just nineteen and still a virgin, planning to wait until my wedding day, I was introduced to Nathan P. Ellis at a frat party in college. We danced and I told him that I was a virgin and was waiting for marriage. He plied me with alcohol, forced me into a bedroom, and tied me up against my will. I said no and fought against him, but instead of listening, he forced himself on me, so aggressively and violently that the next morning I needed stitches inside my vagina. He raped me until he was satisfied and then held me hostage overnight. When he woke up he threatened me. He told me that he had videotaped the whole thing and that if I told anyone about what he'd done he would dub the video with porn audio and post it online under my full name. He said he'd make sure that no one would ever hire me and I would be ruined. Everyone I talked to said that even with a rape kit, he could just deny that it wasn't consensual, and so even if I pressed charges, he would just lie and there was a good chance that his word would be taken over mine (a couple of my friends had had that exact experience). DNA evidence recently linked him to my rape but after finally getting caught, the Cook County State's Attorney's Office has agreed to let him serve out his sentence at home in his Greenwich mansion, where he will be waited on hand and foot. The prosecutor didn't even contact me as they negotiated his punishment. There is no justice for rape victims! #metoo #exposed @NateTheGr8"

I reread it once. *Should I talk to that lawyer first? He said to contact him if I found the video. But he'll probably just advise me not to put it online. He doesn't understand how Nate operates and what he's capable of.* I thought about it for a minute. *What are the odds that the State's Attorney's Office will take the video and use it against Nate if I give it to them first? On the other hand, what harm could posting it online do to a case against Nate? It's not really even my video. But will they be able to tell?* I reread the post again. *It doesn't ever even say that it's the video of Nate raping me. It just tells the truth about what he did to me. I need to destroy his reputation the way that his legal team would destroy mine if this thing went to trial. I need to control his public image before he does, before his legal team has a chance to paint him as a successful entrepreneur and doting husband who can do no wrong. I have to control the narrative before he does. His reputation is my only shot at justice if the prosecutor is going to let him off so easily.*

I hit share, and watched as the post immediately began to garner 'likes', 'hearts', 'angry faces', and outraged comments.

I walked to the kitchen and poured myself a glass of wine. When I got back to the screen I had 35 reactions and 15 comments. *Come on! Go viral!*

An hour later I had more than 2000 reactions and 400 comments. *This is the only way. He has to be exposed for who he really is!*

I got a message from a Facebook group dedicated to women's equality and fighting sexual assault, asking for permission to repost my post to their membership.

"Please and thank you!" I replied.

That did it. As I made dinner I watched the reactions climb past 3,000. There were nearly 500 comments, all from complete strangers. I read a few:

"I am so sorry this happened to you. You are so strong. We believe you. #metoo"

"Don't stop until you get the justice you deserve. Sharing to spread the word about Nathan Ellis @NateTheGr8 #metoo"

"Stay strong and keep fighting! You deserve more!"

"I believe you!"

As I read through them my eyes filled with tears. *Maybe there is hope. Maybe this will work!*

Then I saw the first negative comment: "Rot in Hell, Bitch!"
And then the second: "You will pay for your lies!" *I will pay, for what he did to me?*
An email notification popped up on my phone. The subject read "All sluts should die!" I swiped right to delete. *How did they already get my email address? It's not on Facebook.* I double-checked the info and settings on my account.
I read a few more notes of support. *I am the victim. He is the monster.*
Another email notification popped up; "Why'd you wait so long? LIAR, LIAR, PANTS ON FIRE!" Swipe, delete.

I rolled over in bed the next morning and checked Facebook: over 15,000 likes and 6,207 comments. There were also about twenty private messages. I opened one from a podcast host asking for an interview. I wrote back and agreed.

On Monday morning, as I was indulging in a cup of my favorite tea, my phone rang. It was a local number I didn't recognize. My heart beat a little faster. *What if someone is calling to harass me? What if they are calling because they don't believe me? How would they even have my number?*
I swiped right to answer.
"Wynafreda Ellis?" a woman asked.
"Who is this?"
"My name is Tina Sherman, from ABC 7 New Haven. We saw

your post on social media about your husband and we'd like to have you in to the station tomorrow for an exclusive interview. You'll be featured on our investigative journalism program at night, but we'll film it earlier in the day."

"Of course. Absolutely."

She gave a few instructions on when and where to go and then hung up.

I called Asher Morgan.

"What about media? Can I give an interview?" I asked.

"I would advise against that," he said. "Anything you say in public related to the case could be used by the defense in court, but if you haven't been served a gag order, so legally you can do whatever you believe to be prudent."

"Got it." *So, if I don't talk to the media now and the State's Attorney declines to press charges down the road then I've wasted my only chance to expose Nate, because a lack luster plea deal that doesn't result in an admission of guilt or jail time doesn't exactly make for exciting day-time television and will only further diminish my credibility, but if I do talk to the media, then Nate's lawyers will already have my side of the story.*

I didn't tell him about the video evidence, but thanked him and hung up.

An hour later I stood in my walk-in closet, agonizing over what to wear to the interview. I knew how important it would be to look reliable, trustworthy, and believable, not too self-confident, stuffy, or pretentious, and definitely not too attractive, and of course not sexy. I pulled at least five combinations out and went back and forth between a black sweater with a high neck, a merlot-colored crew neck, and a bright blue button up cashmere sweater. *Don't they say that red makes people angry? If I wear black will people think I'm depressed? Does wearing a lot of black imply you're trying to hide something? Who knew that the thing that was never a simple task for a woman, picking out the perfect outfit, would be so much more difficult when defending a rape accusation?*

I fell onto the bed, exasperated. *I think I need help! Professional help. Is there even such a thing when it comes to preparing for a talk show interview? There must be. There are professional consultants for everything today.* I stared at the options in front of me. *No matter what I wear, some people will love me and some people will hate me.* I did a Google search and found a few publicity consultants in New York City specializing in preparing the average person for television. I made a few calls and hired the only one who was available with such short notice.

A gorgeous middle aged woman, who looked much younger than her resume suggested, arrived after noon. I invited her in and offered her refreshments. She declined and began to pepper me with questions: What was my background? Where had I gone to college? Why was I appearing on television? If she was shocked by the last answer she didn't let on. I figured she'd probably heard crazier stories given her line of work.

She ran through a list of seemingly obvious recommendations: speak slowly, chin up, shoulders back, imagine gossiping over coffee with a girlfriend, be polite, and whatever happens do not let your emotions get the better of you. She told me to memorize the definitions of Stockholm Syndrome and trauma bonding and led me through a few role playing exercises, where she bombarded me with difficult questions about my background, motives, and intentions. Then we moved on to my wardrobe.

She quickly vetoed a few options and then selected a few that she thought were appropriate. We talked make-up, hair, and she gave me a feel for what would happen when I arrived on set. She encouraged me to rehearse my answers to questions that the hosts were most likely to ask.

When she was finally gone I texted Adam; "you home?"
His reply came a minute later; "Yes."

I walked next door and let myself in. Adam was in his office.
I pulled my Facebook post up and handed him the phone. I watched as he read the full post and his expression shifted.
"Do you think he's seen this?" he asked.
"I don't know. I haven't heard anything from him or his lawyer since I posted it, but I'd be surprised if they don't know by now."
"Yeah."
"I got invited to appear on a local news show. They want to interview me because of that post."
"Are you gonna do it?"
"Yeah, I don't know if I will ever get any justice," I said. "In court

or otherwise. But if there's no justice, and no alimony, then there's only one thing left, and that's his reputation."

"What are you gonna say?"

"I'm going to tell the truth about Nate." *And hold nothing back, because I might only have one shot.*

He pulled me toward him and held me close. "I'm so proud of you."

"Thank you," I said. "Thank you for believing me and supporting me."

THE TOUCH
Tuesday, April 3, 2018
Old Greenwich

I arrived at the studio just before noon. A young woman showed me back to a room lined with hair dresser booths.

"I'm fine, actually, I think," I said.

"Just sit," she demanded and then disappeared.

Another woman dressed entirely in black appeared.

"Do I need more make-up?" I asked.

"Oh, honey, guests are on their own," she said. She flicked the switch on a bright light. "I'll take a quick look though."

She examined my face under the light.

"Not terrible," she said. "I've seen a lot worse."

"Thanks."

"Your eyes are a little understated but leave them alone now. Trust me. You'll probably just need to reapply powder and a little lip gloss before you're called up."

"When do you think that will be?"

"Your guess is as good as mine. I don't think the host is here yet. It might be a while."

I nodded. "Thanks."

I pulled Vi's diary out of my purse.

May 29, 1989

Evanston, Illinois. I went to the health clinic for students today. They seemed surprised that I am pregnant and asked me to wait for a while until I could be seen by a special nurse who could do some

tests. The nurse was nice enough and did the tests pretty quickly.
She said everything looked fine and she told me that it's a girl. I
asked her about an abortion but she said that it's too late. She said
that no one would do an abortion for me now since I am more than
27 weeks pregnant. I guess I have no choice now. I will have to have
the baby. She gave me some papers that have information about
adoption. I guess I'll read them tonight.

July 12, 1989

Evanston, Illinois. I'm huge! They say I have another month of
this and I really can't believe it! I can only sleep on my side now
and everything is getting more difficult and uncomfortable. I met
a woman named Adrienne, who is a junior and lives down the hall
from me. She is married and lives with her husband. She offered
to help me with some things when I need it. She brought me a few
groceries the other day. She is very sweet. Today she told me that she
is also pregnant, although she's not as far along as me. Maybe our
kids can be friends. I think we will be great friends!

At least an hour had passed before a young woman appeared.
"Follow me!" she said.

I grabbed my lipstick, applied it quickly in the mirror, and turned
to follow her down the hall. She showed me to a set with two chairs
and a black backdrop.

"Sit here," she said, pointing.

I waited and watched the shuffling of the camera crew and the
whispers of the staff just out of view.

The female anchor walked in, commanding attention. She sat in
the chair next to me and leaned forward to shake my hand. I was
surprised by how different she looked in person than on t.v. The
layers of make-up caked on to hide the fine lines around her eyes
reminded me of the painted-one-too-many-times window frames in
our historic Cape Cod.

"How are you doing?" she said.

"Fine, thanks." I looked wide-eyed at the cameras. *Here we go! Soon*
everyone will know what a monster he is! This is going to work!

"Just remember to smile and relax," she said and I sat up a little straighter.

Another command signified that the cameras were rolling.
"Wyn! So glad to have you here today."
"Thanks. I'm really glad to be here."

"Let's talk about that 'me too' bombshell you just dropped," she said. "Why did you turn to social media to expose your husband, Nathan Ellis?"

"I did it because I felt like I had no other choice. I did it after I found out that he probably wouldn't serve any real time in prison for what he did to me. I lost faith in the justice system when I heard that and so I turned to social media because I felt empowered by the stories that other women have been sharing."

"This is a little bit different than many of the other allegations coming out now though, isn't it? You posted a video of the assault, right?"

"There's also DNA evidence linking him directly to the crime. I don't know what more a woman needs to get a fair shake these days. Maybe a live confession?"

She nodded. "Right. But seriously, some people are saying that the video could have been staged and it's difficult to tell if it's even you in the recording."

"The video is authentic. I told him no. I barely knew him, we were at a party and I told him no, but he didn't listen. If you listen closely you can hear it on the tape. No means no," I said. "Nate Ellis raped me."

"Wyn, what would justice look like for you now?"
"That's a great question. I just want him to be held accountable for what he did. I want him to be locked up so that he can't do this to other women," I said.

"Wyn, how long has it been since the rape and why didn't you come forward sooner?"

"It was six years ago, and I did come forward right away. I filed a police report and provided evidence the day of the assault."

"Why was he never arrested then or charged?"

"I don't know. The police said they would investigate my claims but I never heard back from them. I told them everything I knew at the time," I lied.

"Wyn, are you saying that the police neglected to investigate your claims?"

It was completely silent in the studio. Eyes watched me from behind cameras and curtains, and tucked out of sight, off stage. The silence and the weight of the unwavering attention made me feel exposed, isolated, and alone. I knew that in going public I would open myself up to the entire world, and would no longer be operating under the radar. I knew that the stakes would be much higher moving forward and that everything I did from now on would be scrutinized in the public domain, but I didn't realize how quickly I would feel completely alienated. I had given up my anonymity and privacy to get even, and as I sat there, I prayed that I wouldn't come to regret my decision.

"I don't know what the police did or didn't do. I just know that I never heard back. I didn't get the feeling that they believed it was a serious, credible accusation, or that Nate was a real threat. They kept asking me how much I'd been drinking that night and whether I had led anyone on."

"Oh my," she said. "Wyn, I think the question that everyone is really dying to ask is why you ended up married to your rapist years after you filed that report and why you didn't get the police involved earlier?"

I looked down at my hands and then back up at the host. "I couldn't eat. I couldn't sleep. I had nightmares. I saw him everywhere. In my sleep, in my dreams. He haunted me and ruined my life. The rape played over and over again in my head, and yet I was so ashamed that I couldn't talk about it. I couldn't tell the people I loved for fear that they would blame me. I retraced every moment of that evening over and over again, wondering if I hadn't done just one thing differently, if I would have been spared. I wondered if it was my fault that he raped me. When I heard the songs that were playing when it happened, I lost it. I couldn't trust anyone. I began having panic attacks. I needed some closure, but I didn't know how to get it."

"What do you mean by closure?"

"At first I just wanted to know more about him. More about this person who could do such a thing to me and then just disappear from my life. I needed to make sense of it. I needed to understand why he had done it. Maybe I wanted to know that something was wrong with him, so that I could forgive myself. Let myself breathe deeply again. Find a reason to let the guilt and shame go. I tried therapy first but that didn't work, so eventually, I figured out who he was and tracked him down."

She nodded. "Wow."

"I wasn't sure what I was going to do once I found him, I didn't have a plan. I just knew I needed to get close enough to understand why he did what he did and what was wrong with him. At first I just observed him, but then we began to interact."

"Did he recognize you?"

"No. He didn't recognize me and he didn't seem to have changed at all. I was devastated and weak from what had happened and he seemed totally unaffected. Strong and confident even. We began spending more time together, which was really difficult for me at first, but the more time I spent with him the easier it was and the more dependent I became actually. He is a very charismatic guy. I don't want to say manipulative, but he definitely knows how to get what he wants, and when he is happy, he's actually incredible to be around. He only gets aggressive or violent when he is told 'no', so I just did whatever he wanted. I felt like I had to in order to get what I needed, which was an understanding of why it had all happened. I consistently felt like I was close and would find the key to what had happened and then I'd be able to walk away."

"Really?" Her look conveyed skepticism.

"Yes, there's actually a name for when a person starts to have feelings of trust or even affection for an abuser. It's like Stockholm Syndrome, except it's called trauma bonding when it's someone you know. I spent enough time with him trying to understand what had happened, that I grew comfortable. And then slowly, over the years, he took away everything that made me confident, self-sufficient, and independent. I didn't know how to be those things anymore and I was scared of leaving or going to the police. I felt trapped, and I know it sounds a little crazy, because I put myself in that situation, but I really never thought it was possible to become so dependent on someone who hurt you."

She shook her head.

"Wyn, it still begs a question about your intentions. Some people would say that on top of being married to your rapist, it looks very suspicious from the outside that you've come forward now that he is a highly successful businessman who has a lot to lose?"

"I understand how it might look, but I was really scared when it first happened. I was young and I had a lot to lose. He used that to silence me. The morning of the rape he threatened me and told me that if I ever went public he would destroy me. I knew other young women who had been broken trying to get justice the right way and came out the other end with nothing but open, public wounds, and spoiled reputations. I wasn't ready for that. I felt all alone and I didn't think I could handle going through public scrutiny at the time. He would have just said that I was a slut and that I got what I wanted. It became clear to me that a victim doesn't win when they go through the formal justice system."

"Wyn," she said. "What about now? What is your intention now?"

"Look, I've been a Christian from a young age, and I want to be able to forgive him and move on, but no matter how much I've prayed, I just haven't been able to, so the only thing left is justice. I want the world to see him for who he really is and I want everyone who meets him to be able to judge him fairly for what he has done."

"Wyn, have you given up on the judicial system entirely at this point?"

"No, I hope that the prosecutors change their mind and he gets the sentence he deserves, but I have to admit I'm not very optimistic at this point."

"Well, thank you Wyn, for sharing your story with us today. We know it is difficult for you to talk so openly about what happened."

"Thank you."

A young woman removed my microphone and escorted me back to the dressing room.

A few hours later, as I was preparing dinner, my phone rang. *Hmmmm, 312 is Chicago.* I hesitated but decided to answer.

"Hello?"

"Wynafreda Laurent?"

"Yes."

"My name is Scott Weiss. I'm calling from the Cook County State's Attorney's Office."

Interesting timing. Did they hear about my interview? "Hello."

Maren Foster

"You signed a criminal report on June, 22, 2012 regarding an alleged rape that occurred on June 9, 2012?"

"Yes, that's correct."

"As you are aware, a new lead has prompted us to reopen that case."

"Yes!"

"I see that you spoke with Detective Wilshire on March 19th and then you met with a Detective Donaldson in Connecticut a few days later."

"Yes."

"There is a note in your file that you requested a meeting with the prosecutor."

"Mmmm hmmmm."

"We would like to meet with you to gather more information for our case and discuss our process."

"Sure. Yes. Does that mean the plea deal isn't final?"

"I can't comment on that at this point, Ma'am. Would you be willing to come to Chicago for an interview?"

"Yes. Absolutely."

"Great. I have some availability on Tuesday afternoon, the 10th. Does that work?"

"Yeah sure, that should work."

"Two p.m. Daley Center."

"Okay. Thank you."

He hung up.

I texted Vi, "Need to be in Chicago next week. Can I stay with you?"

I flipped open my laptop and looked for flights.

Vi replied, "Of course! Can't wait to see you. When do you get in?"

"Tuesday morning. Fly out Thursday."

"Great. You'll have to take a cab in from the airport though. I'm tied up at work on Tuesday morning."

"No problem. Thanks"

THE BREAKDOWN

Thursday, April 5, 2018
Old Greenwich

Simon called early but I didn't answer and he didn't leave a message. *He must have seen the show or my social media post. Either way, he has to know by now, which means Nate knows.* I wasn't about to call him back to find out.

After noon my phone rang again. It was a New York City number. I answered.

"Wyn Ellis?"

"Yeah."

"Megan Helmsley with the CBS Morning Show. We want you to come in for an interview. We're doing a show devoted to the impacts of the #metoo movement on ordinary women."

"It's Wyn Laurent actually, but yes, of course. Just let me know when and where to be."

"Be at 30 Rock tomorrow morning at 6:30am. Just check in with security. Your name will be on the list."

"Just make sure you list me as Wynafreda Laurent. L-A-U-R-E-N-T."

"Got it. Thanks!" she said and hung up.

National news! This will be the nail in the coffin!

The next morning I applied what I thought was an appropriate amount of make-up, and put on one of my 'I'm a credible rape victim' outfit. I made an espresso and hit the road.

The traffic was still surprisingly light heading into New York City, but it was only a matter of time. I pulled into a parking garage off 50th, checked my make-up and headed out into the fomenting chaos that was a weekday morning in Manhattan; dodging distracted professionals, gaping tourists, and hawkish street vendors on my way to 30 Rock.

I checked in with a security guard at the front desk.

"Follow-me young lady," he said and tapped his key card on a turn style behind a long bank of elevators. I walked through and looked back expecting additional instructions but he was gone. I wandered down the hallway aimlessly until I heard my name. I followed a runner to the guest waiting area, where a few other young women were already sitting. As I applied a little more make up some of them began to chat. It was clear, as I listened, that they were meeting for the first time, but they seemed to already know each other's stories. Eventually we were all led backstage.

"Up next, a group of young women who have all used the 'me too' hashtag to expose powerful men," one of the hosts announced. *They didn't say this was a group interview. I guess it's better than nothing.* The crowd clapped and a few women in the audience even cheered.

During the commercial break we were led on stage and told where to sit. The live studio audience applauded on queue. I sat up straight and smiled, trying not to look nervous.

"Ladies, we're so glad to have you on the show this morning."
We all nodded. "Glad to be here."
"Of course, we wish you were here under different circumstances. You have all been victims of sexual assault or rape. Correct?"
We nodded. "Yes."
"And you have all used the 'me too' hashtag to expose your attackers."
We nodded again.
"Let me start with you, Megan."

The hosts took turns asking each of us questions about our specific experiences. It became clear as the women shared snippets of their stories that we each represented a different phase in the process of exposing our assailants. One woman was among the early wave of women to use the hashtag but had run into resistance and setbacks trying to get her claims taken seriously by authorities. Another woman had a more recent story of success, and her use of the hashtag had resulted in an arrest.

"Wyn, you recently posted a video that you say is evidence that your husband, Nathan Ellis, raped you. Why did you decide to go public now and what do you hope will come of your use of the 'me too' hashtag?"

"I posted the video right after learning that he was negotiating a plea deal with the District Attorney that would see him released from prison in the coming weeks. Obviously, posting a video that personal is extremely difficult, and I wish I didn't have to do it, but I also didn't feel like I had any other choice. House arrest doesn't seem like it fits the crime."

"Wyn, of all the women here today, you have one of the longer gaps between when you say your rape occurred and when you used the 'me too' hashtag. Why did you wait all these years to come forward and do you worry about how that might look to skeptics?"

"I can see now that by waiting to publicly accuse him I gave people reason to question the authenticity of my claims, but I did come forward when it originally happened. I filed a police report immediately. I had a rape kit done. I just wasn't ready to risk my future back then. I was young and scared. I was in college and needed to get a job. I had so much to lose, but I still had the rape kit done and talked to the police, so it's not like this is the first time I'm accusing him. I didn't show up out of nowhere, claiming that he raped me for the first time. There's a police report, there's DNA evidence, and there's video evidence."

He nodded and let me continue, "The truth is that some people will never believe us, no matter how much evidence there is. They just want to tear us down at any cost because they're afraid. They're afraid of what is happening. They're afraid that they won't be able to hide anymore behind excuses, and victim blaming, and slut shaming. They're afraid that for the first time in history we are really being heard, and not immediately discounted and swept under the rug. For the first time, women are being taken seriously, and treated like people whose experiences matter." My voice waivered as I fought back tears. I finally understood the feelings that had, for so many years, motivated Vi and Ali.

Another host spoke up. "But Wyn, some people would argue that if we are too quick to believe every woman who comes forward accusing a guy of rape then we put too much power in the hands of women who may be lying, be it for money, or fame. Some people say that this might fundamentally change the dynamic between men and women, doing harm to the trust that exists in our society today, and destroying reputations that do not deserve to be destroyed. What is your take on that?"

Now we are scared of the changes that may come to a system that has historically treated women like property, undermined their ability to be self-sufficient at every turn, and placed the burden of proof on them when they are victimized?

I shook my head. "I'm not advocating that we take at face value everything every accuser says. I'm asking that we listen and ask the tough questions about the accused that we haven't even asked before. There will always be people looking to take advantage of an opportunity, but the more open we are, the more transparent as a society, and the more supportive we are of victims, the more victims will be willing to come forward immediately. That will mean that we can collect the evidence and ask the tough questions right away, when memories are still fresh, and evidence is still obtainable. If this happens, it will actually be harder for someone to accuse someone else falsely years later, because there will be no excuse for not coming forward immediately. If victims can trust in the justice system and the process, and believe that they will get a fair shake if they report assault or abuse immediately using the appropriate channels, then we will know that anyone who puts forth an accusation years after an alleged assault, whether through the news media, or on social media, is a fake. In my opinion this is the only way that we can protect victims while also safeguarding our society against false accusations."

The host turned back to one of the other women and continued asking questions.

After we were ushered off stage, I grabbed my purse and thanked the runner, who pointed me to a back exit. I emerged onto West 50th and made my way down 50th toward the parking garage.

I heard the ping of a new text message as I popped the car into reverse. The text flashed on the screen on my dashboard. It was an unfamiliar number: "You fucking cunt. I will tie you up for the last time and fuck you to death as your screams for help go unnoticed. You think your husband is a bad guy? Just wait until I get my hands on you."

Holy shit. What kind of sick person? I should report this to the police, not that they'll do anything about it.

I turned on the radio and tried to stay calm.

Vi called while I was sitting in traffic on my way home.

"Freddie."

"Hey."

"I saw it," Vi said.

"Oh, yeah? I didn't think you watched morning television."

"I don't, but Adrienne does and she texted me to turn it on."

"Oh."

"Why didn't you tell me?"

"I thought you'd be ashamed. I didn't want to let you down," I said.

"I've been through more in my life than you know. I could have helped you."

"You would have told me to fight him but I wasn't ready."

"You don't know that. I could have helped you even if you decided not to press charges," she said.

"I wasn't sure you'd understand. You've always been so strong and I was so weak."

"I've been through my share of adversity too, you know."

"I didn't know that then. I just couldn't see how the woman who raised two children alone was going to help me get an abortion?"

"You had an abortion? Alone?" Vi said.

"Yes."

"I'm so sorry, Freddie." She paused but I knew instinctively not to interject. "I wish the world wasn't such an ugly place, but sometimes it is. I guess we just have to look for the silver linings and support each other through the bad times."

"Yeah, I guess so."

"Do you want me to come out there now?"

"No, thank you. Remember I'm coming home next week. I'll see you on Monday," I said.

"Okay. You know I'll get on a plane tonight if you need me."

"Thank you. I really appreciate it, but I can stay with Adam and Julia if I need to."

"Really?"

"Yeah, I'll be fine. Gotta go," I said.

"Okay. Love you."

"Love you too."

I checked my phone: ten new voicemails. Some were agents who wanted to represent me. Some were t.v. or radio shows calling directly to schedule interviews. A couple were prank calls. One was a literary agent wondering if I'd consider publishing a memoir. *A memoir? Another opportunity to get my side of the story out there first and direct the narrative? With some tweaks, maybe the diary entries I wrote for my therapist could become the basis for a damning expose. The more attention I can throw on Nate's immoralities and monstrous character the better. A memoir would do just that and might even allow me to support myself while I figure out what I am going to do. My savings is beginning to run out.* I called the agent back and left a message with a secretary.

My phone rang about a half hour later. "Wyn, my name is Kristin Jones. We've been playing phone tag it seems."

"Hello."

"Wyn, I represent writers, specifically memoirists. I'm interested in your story. I think a memoir about your life and experiences would be a big hit, given what's going on."

"Really?"

"Yeah, I have a writer who I think is perfectly suited to write it if you're interested in selling your story."

"Kristin, I'm glad you called. I've actually been writing already and have something I think you could work into a memoir."

"Oh, great. Why don't you send me what you have so that we can take a look and develop some samples and marketing materials?"

"Sure, but I have one question before I send it."

"Yeah, sure."

"What is your commission?"

"Of course. Seven and a half percent of print royalties and thirty percent for digital is standard. That includes audio and e-books. We'll reserve all film rights. No advance."

Hmmm, not sure I have time to shop around at this point.

"I want to donate some of the proceeds to charities that assist victims of sexual assault. I'd like to maximize that donation. Do you think you could negotiate a higher percentage of print royalties based on that?"

"That's really sweet. I'll do what I can. You do have some name recognition already and your story has been in the news in New York every day for the last week, but even that doesn't guarantee sales, especially in other markets where it hasn't gotten as much publicity, and publishers aren't very flexible."

"Got it. Let me think about it."

"Of course, I understand. Why don't I send you a sample contract to review as you think about it?"

"Sure."

"Great. What is your email address?"

I rattled off my email address.

"Thanks. I'll be in touch soon," She said and hung up.

Back at home, I threw a bag of popcorn in the microwave and ate at the kitchen island while I flicked through Instagram. The top post was a photo of Julia at the gym, wearing only a black sports bra and knee length spandex tights. The caption read, "Getting sweaty in style thanks to @lululemon for the fabulous gear! #ad". She was the skinniest I'd ever seen her. She didn't look like she belonged (or had ever been) in a gym. She had absolutely no muscle and looked like she might snap in half if she tried to do anything that could be considered a workout. Unlike in the past, when I had been admittedly a little jealous of her physique, I now felt genuinely sorry for her. There was clearly something wrong. She looked frail, sick, malnourished actually. The post had 39,877 likes. Apparently, 39,877 people disagreed with me.

THE TOUCH

Saturday, April 7, 2018
Old Greenwich

On Saturday morning, as I walked past the front door on my way to the kitchen, I noticed a single, plain white business envelope on the floor with no postage or return address. I cut it open neatly with a paring knife. A single sheet of paper fell out. "We know where you live, LYING WHORE! Drop it now or you'll be sorry." *Who the hell would have brought this here? Nate? Simon? Can't be. Weird. Maybe I should have a security company out and have the locks changed while they're at it, just in case.* I called and made an appointment and then went next door.

Through the back windows of the Hart's sun room I could see Adam and Julia sitting together on the couch. I waved and Julia motioned me in.

"Wyn, how are you?" She didn't pause to let me answer. "You must be so sick about the stuff with Nate."

"Why would she be?" Adam said. "He's a bastard who deserves to rot in jail for the rest of his life."

"Oh come on."

"Do you live on Mars?" he continued. "She had to have an abortion. He's a complete douchebag and they are going to basically let him off with a slap on the wrist." The anger in his voice was unmistakable.

"But he's her husband."

"They weren't really married," he said. "I mean, they were, but it was never real. Don't you get it?"

"What if it's all been blown out of proportion?" she said.

"You think someone being held accountable for violent rape is blowing things out of proportion?" Adam said.

"How do I know that it wasn't consensual sex? Maybe she's a gold digger. Maybe all the women in the videos consented too. Maybe they were just role playing."

"All of them? Are you kidding? He's a monster," I said. "And just because you're his consensual fuck buddy of the month doesn't mean he isn't a rapist. He's been raping other women the whole time, probably while you two were already having an affair."

I looked at Adam and mouthed, *sorry*.

"Get the fuck out!" she yelled.

"Gladly!" I got up and walked out.

I heard her yelling at Adam as I walked across the lawn. Her voice got a little louder for a few seconds as the sun room door opened and then slammed shut behind him.

I kept walking until I was back in my yard, and then turned to see him walking briskly toward me. He reached out and pulled me into his arms.

"I'm so sorry. Forget her," he said.

"I'm surprised you're still with her after what she did with Nate."

He shrugged. "I wasn't that surprised, honestly. I don't love her anymore."

"Run away with me," I said.

"Of course." He squeezed me tighter. "When?"

"I have a business venture in the works. I want to be sure that I can support myself in case I never get anything from Nate."

"It doesn't matter," he said. "Let go of it. We don't need his money. We can move home. We know enough good people there who will help us. We can both get jobs, settle down, keep a low profile, maybe have some kids."

I squeezed him tight. "Mmmm hmm."

"That's it? 'Mmmm hmm'?"

"I mean, yes, of course. I want to be with you. I've always wanted to be with you."

"You have?"

"Of course. I just had to deal with this shit first," I said.

"You mean Nate?"

"Yeah. I guess I mean my shame, my anger, and the nagging sense that it wasn't fair."

"You've been planning this since the day it happened, haven't you?"

"Something like that. I didn't know what to do at first, but when I realized that accusing him would be awful for me and he would probably walk away unscathed, I knew I had to do something else. I began dreaming of how to make him suffer the day I decided not to press charges. The plan changed over time, of course. It evolved as it had to, but the goal was always to get even. I want to see him broken, like I was broken."

"How did you do it?" He looked me directly in the eyes. "How could you be married to him and have sex with him after what he did to you?"

"It was the hardest thing I've ever done, in my entire life. There were days I thought I couldn't go through with it, but the thought of him getting off scot-free kept me focused. I wanted him to pay for what he did," I said. "You probably think I'm insane, don't you? Maybe I am. I don't know anymore."

"Look, what you've done is crazy, but I can't pretend to understand what he put you through or how you felt. I trust you, so I trust that you did what you did because you thought it was the only way. I wish you would have told me earlier," he said, never losing his focus on me. "I wish you *could* have told me earlier. I wish I could have done something to help you."

"I couldn't tell you. I was worried you would kill him."

He nodded. "I know. I love you."

"I love you, too."

We held each other tight.

"Now what?"

"Divorce, I guess." I said.

"Yeah." He seemed lost in thought.

"Are you sure you want to leave Julia?"

"Yes, I want to be with you."

"Then you know what you have to do," I said.

"Yeah, I'll take care of it. Don't worry about her," he said. "And you'll file for divorce too then?"

"Yeah, I guess I might actually need a divorce since technically I am married under Connecticut law. I don't know though. I'll need to talk to a lawyer."

He leaned down and looked me in the eyes. His look was intense. I wasn't sure what he was thinking. He leaned forward and kissed me.

"I can't wait," he said.

"I know. Me too."

He turned and walked back toward his house. I watched him until he disappeared.

Will he tell her today? Will I finally get my happily ever after? Are things going to work out?

I went to church on Sunday. I was feeling lost and needed motivation to keep going. I tried a new church down the road. It was Episcopalian. I didn't know much about Episcopalians but it was close to the house and it had the most beautiful chapel. As I sat listening to the sermon my mind wandered. *Is God just? Will His will be done?* Will *His* will be done? I guess I knew instinctively, but I had never really thought very hard about why Vi and Ali were agnostic. I figured it was because they were lawyers who believed in evidence and proof... beyond a doubt. This explanation had always made sense to me, but as I wondered and prayed to *Him* for justice it struck me as obvious. It seemed ridiculous that it had never occurred to me before. *How could two Feminists believe that He was their salvation? That He would guide their way and provide comfort in times of distress?*

On my way out of church I picked up my cell phone. *One missed call. A local number I don't know.* There was no voicemail.

The calls for interviews kept flooding in. It was overwhelming and exhausting, but I returned a few of them assuming that any publicity was good publicity at this point, and would increase sales when my memoir was released. I didn't want to answer any more questions about why I did what I did, or what it meant for women around the world or the future of our justice system. It was amazing how quickly I'd become a trusted expert on law, psychology, and women's rights with zero formal training or education. I kept thinking that I should be happy that people were finally listening and seemed to be valuing what I said, but I couldn't help feeling like an imposter.

I called Asher Morgan, the criminal lawyer I had talked to before and asked for a referral to a divorce lawyer. He provided a name and direct number. If he'd seen the news he didn't say anything, which surprised me. I called and spoke with a paralegal, who confirmed that I could seek alimony through a divorce settlement even though our marriage certificate was never filed. *I can't believe I still need a divorce. I wonder if Nate will contest it. Given the circumstances it shouldn't be difficult to get a divorce granted, but what about a settlement? How long will it take to negotiate? Does it even matter anymore? I've exposed him for who he really is. Isn't that enough?*

I kept busy around the house as much as possible. I refused to admit that I was getting bored and was even beginning to miss work a little bit, but it was true. *If I had a child to look after, things would be so different. Our baby would have been almost six years old now.* I wondered whether it was a boy or a girl and felt guilty thinking about the life that never was even if it was his.

I looked at my phone. I'd missed another call. *Simon again? Nate must be furious.*

My phone rang while I was making dinner. It wasn't Simon but the number was local. I answered.

"Wyn!" There was an urgency to Nate's greeting.

"Nate?"

"Yeah. It's me."

I didn't say anything. *Why is he calling me now? What does he want?*

"What's going on? Are you okay? You haven't come to visit at all."

What? There's no way he doesn't know already? He must be faking.

"Um, yeah, I'm okay I guess."

"I need to talk to you. There's a bit of a problem. It's about the company and the mortgage. I don't want to talk about it over the phone. Can you come here to talk?"

Is he lying? What's his angle? He has to know by now. Maybe he wants to talk about a financial settlement.

"Look, I need your help. There's some financial stuff I can't take care of from in here and it's important. I need you to come here so I can tell you what's going on with our finances, so that we won't have to worry about money when I get out."

Hmmmm, if there is a problem and I don't help then there won't be any alimony. "Sure."

"Good. When will you come?"

"I'm not sure. I'm out of town. After I get back."

"Great. Thank you."

"Okay." *What does he want? Is this some kind of trap? He has to be lying, right?*

"Okay, I have to go," he said.

"Alright."

"Bye."

"Bye."

He hung up.

Does he want to strike a deal with me? Maybe he wants to pay me to stop giving interviews. Maybe he thinks he can pay to make this whole thing go away. I just want this whole thing to be over. I want to move far away with Adam and try to forget that any of this ever happened.

THE SEND
Tuesday, April 10, 2018
Chicago

My morning flight to Chicago was annoyingly full, mostly businessmen and women. Even before take-off the guy next to me got out his laptop and switched on his overhead light. Clearly I wasn't going to get a nap, so I asked the flight attendant for a cup of coffee and opened Vi's diary.

August 25, 1989

Evanston, Illinois. I started to feel a little weird in the morning.
By early afternoon I was having contractions. I went to the clinic
and they sent me directly to the hospital. I didn't feel very well and
they said my heart rate was elevated. She came out feet first which
I guess is a bit of a problem. I pushed as hard as I could and it hurt
so badly that I just remember screaming and wanting it to be over.
Nobody prepared me for how hard it was going to be. I kept telling
myself that once it was over everything would be fine ... life would
go back to normal ... ha, what is normal? Nothing will ever be
normal again. I named her Alicia. It was my favorite of the names
of the towns we passed on the drive up here from Louisiana. They
brought her back to me and she laid peacefully on my chest for a
long time, and then we were allowed to go home. I fell asleep on the
couch with her in a bassinet next to me. Eventually I was woken
up by her crying. I tried holding her in my arms, but she just cried,
well, screamed really. I tried to feed her but she wouldn't take and
just kept on crying. I felt like she was the devil incarnate, trying to

tell me that I had made a grave mistake, having a baby by myself. It might be a sign, but I have to make the best of it now, she is here and that is it.

I got a car from the airport to Vi's new address downtown. It was my first time staying at her condo. The stately gothic limestone and red brick mid-rise overlooked the Museum of Contemporary Art, and was just down the street from a quaint neighborhood park near the lakefront.

I parked on the street and grabbed my small overnight bag. An older gentleman behind a desk buzzed me into an ornately decorated, oak paneled lobby.

"Good morning, young lady," he said.

"Good morning. I'm staying with Vi Laurent. Number 1201."

"Oh yes. She mentioned you on her way out this morning. You're her youngest daughter, right?"

"Yes, I'm Wyn."

"Wyn! Nice to meet you Wyn," he said with a warm smile.

"Nice to meet you too." I paused hoping he would offer his name, and he did.

"Jeremiah," he said.

"Jeremiah," I repeated. "I'll be leaving tomorrow afternoon."

"Not staying for the weekend, Miss Wyn?"

"No, not this time."

"Elevator's on the left. Key is under the doormat."

"Thank you."

I hit the button for the 12th floor. The old gilded elevator had once been manually operated and still had relics from its prior life. A large bronze wheel no longer turned and the back of the automatic door had the old metal cage built into it. I walked down the cream colored hall, with its elegant crown molding, to the door labeled 1201. I found the key under the mat and let myself in.

Vi's condo was on the southwest corner of the building, surrounded by much taller modern high rises, but the four-story museum in the park across the street afforded her unit a nice view of the soaring skyscrapers of the downtown Loop. Her simple furniture from the Queen Anne fit in perfectly with the vintage interior. I put my bag on the couch and poked around in the fridge for a snack.

Just before two, I ordered a car to the Daley Center. The driver stopped mid-block at the entrance on Clark Street. The Daley Center's modern, rusty colored steel frame and clear glass looked dull and artless in contrast to Chicago's City Hall, a beautiful 11-story classical revival, complete with monumental Corinthian granite columns, across the street. I got out, checked in at the front desk, and was directed to the fifteenth floor.

"I have an appointment with Scott Weiss," I told the receptionist.

"Thank you. Please have a seat and I will let him know you're here."

"Thanks."

I picked up a copy of Crain's Chicago Business and unfolded the half-sized paper. Just as my mind began to wander a man in a navy blue business suit appeared in front of me.

"Wynafreda Laurent?"

"Yeah, call me Wyn," I said, stood up, and took his hand.

"Scott Weiss. I'm an Investigator in the Trial Support Command."

"This is Emily," he said. "She's an assistant on the case." A young woman shook my hand enthusiastically. They turned and I followed them to a small conference room with floor to ceiling windows.

"Please take a seat," he said.

He put a thick file folder down on the table in front of him and pulled out a stack of papers. The police report with my victim statement sat on top. The young woman set up a laptop and began tapping away at the keyboard.

"Wyn, I need to ask you a few questions so that we can determine what kind of case we have and whether we think it should go to trial," he said.

"Okay." *So they haven't accepted the plea deal yet.*

"We need you to be completely truthful and forthcoming so that we can make the right decisions about how to proceed."

"I understand."

"Great."

We went through the same old set of questions that everyone asked: how had I come to be married to my rapist whose name I

wasn't able to remember the day after the assault? Why hadn't I
turned him in to the police when I figured out who he was? What
was my motivation for marrying him and did I have any other
evidence that proved that it was rape and not consensual sex, besides
the grainy video and the DNA sample? Had I seen a therapist or told
anyone about the rape in the days and months after it happened? Had
the rape resulted in a pregnancy? Could I provide evidence of the
pregnancy or its termination?

I held it together and answered their questions the best I could
without incriminating myself. As the investigator said pregnancy I
broke down crying. I tried to suppress my tears at first, but I was so
exhausted from the questioning that it was no use. I began to sob.
The paralegal handed me a box of tissue.

"I'm sorry," she said, as I struggled to pull tissues from the box.
I nodded and blotted the tears running down my cheeks.

I took a deep breath. "Do you think the case will go to trial?" I
asked.

"I'm not the prosecutor, just the investigator. The prosecutor will
review our notes from this interview and will make a decision on
whether to take the case to trial," he said.

"I heard that there may be a plea deal in the works."

"I'm not authorized to comment on any ongoing negotiations,
Ma'am."

"Please," I begged, wiping my eyes with the tissue. "I'm a nervous
wreck waiting for a decision. I can't take it anymore."

"There have been discussions," he said quietly, as if he was being
surveilled.

"I can't sleep at night thinking that he might get off easy."

"I can assure you Ma'am that we will do our best to bring him to
justice."

"What about that Brock Turner guy? Do you think he got off
easy?" I said.

"This is a very different case, Ma'am. There were witnesses to the
crime in that case."

"And he still got off easy!"

"This is an older case, which makes it more difficult to get a
conviction from a jury in the first place. Add on top of that the fact
that you were married to and living with your rapist for years before

you posted videos of his alleged abuse online." He shook his head in disbelief.

"I don't understand. There's DNA evidence and a video," I said.

"Again, I'm not the prosecutor, but to be honest, the video is of low quality and the DNA evidence only proves that you had sexual intercourse."

After everything I've been through, justice is slipping away again.

"He threatened me, yesterday. If you don't lock him up permanently he'll come after me. Please," I begged.

"Thank you for your time, Ms. Laurent," he said.

As I stood up to leave the door opened. A tall man in a dark grey business suit blocked the doorway.

"Ms. Laurent, my name is Connor Donoghue, I'm the District Attorney assigned to your case."

"Great, great to meet you."

"I need you to stop talking to the media. You are only hurting your case. Help me help you by keeping your mouth shut," he said.

"Ah," I stammered. "I did have a few questions for you."

"Thanks for your help, Ma'am," he said and turned to leave.

Are you kidding?

"What are the terms of the plea deal?" I shouted after him, but he was already out the door and down the hallway.

So much for protecting the victim!

The young woman led me back down the hall.

"I'm so sorry," she said. "Please take care."

"Thank you."

I decided to walk back to Vi's condo to clear my head. It was a clear, windy, albeit unseasonably warm spring day and the sun bounced playfully off the waves in the main branch of the Chicago River. *There won't be any justice through the system. No one believes me. I was right to do everything I've done to this point. They'll let him off easy. I can't let that happen.*

Once back at Vi's condo, I went straight to the fridge and grabbed her special French cognac from the freezer. I poured a double helping and flipped on the t.v., grabbing my laptop and external hard drive, which I now kept in my purse at all times. I uploaded all of the videos of Nate's conquests to my file sharing account on the web and labeled it "Nathan Ellis". I made it public, copied the link to the folder, and posted it on Facebook. I created a tweet with the caption, "Nathan Ellis is a monster and a serial rapist and there is video evidence to prove it. Nathan Ellis has done this before and will not stop until he is locked up for good. He is a threat to public safety." I sat at the kitchen counter and watched the 'likes', 'shares', and 'retweets' begin to accumulate. A smile of pure satisfaction crossed my face.

By the time Vi came home I was on my second cognac and beginning to feel quite tipsy.

"How'd it go today, Freddie?" she asked.

"Not as well as I hoped."

"How come?"

"Well, the prosecutor basically told me to shut up and mind my own business. He wouldn't even talk to me about the plea agreement when I asked."

"Really?"

"Yeah, he only came in for a minute at the end, but I asked about it and he refused to talk to me."

"You know, there's a thing called the Crime Victim's Rights Act. It guarantees a crime victim the right to talk to and be consulted by the State's attorney for the case, and to be informed in a timely manner of any plea bargain or deferred prosecution agreement. You might talk to that lawyer of yours about what happened today."

"Thanks, I will." *Doesn't really matter now. I've made my next move already and if I'm right, the D.A. will be forced to do a lot more than talk to me.*

She gave me a hug and then set about making dinner.

"Oh, hey, are you here tomorrow night as well?" Vi asked.

"Yep."

"Great. I invited Ali over for dinner. Thought it'd be nice for you two to catch-up."

"Yeah, of course. Thanks."

THE SEND
Wednesday, April 11, 2018
Chicago

The next day I met up with an old friend for lunch and did a little sightseeing downtown.

Vi and Ali walked in together around dinner time.

"Ali! How are you?" I said.

"Thanks for letting me know you were gonna be in town," she said.

"Sorry, I thought you were mad at me when you didn't text after you stayed over a few months ago."

"Vi told me what happened. I'm really, really sorry. He's a really bad guy. Even worse than I thought." Ali said as she helped Vi prep dinner.

"Thanks, he is," I said. *Not even an 'I told you so' from her?*

"Since when is there a t.v. in the kitchen?" I asked. Vi had always had a strict limit on t.v. time, and the kitchen and dining room were her most sacred spaces when we were growing up.

Vi shrugged.

"I think she gets lonely while she cooks now, since we are both gone," Ali whispered to me.

The local news came on. The newscaster struck a somber tone, "Breaking news tonight. A Greenwich man who was arrested for drunk driving has been charged with criminal sexual assault, a Class 1 Felony in the State of Illinois. A spokeswoman for the Cook County State's Attorney's Office says that Nathan Ellis, originally of Westport, Connecticut was a match to DNA evidence collected in a rape case in 2012. The State's Attorney held a news conference this afternoon asking any other women, who believe they were raped by Nathan Ellis, to come forward."

The frame cut to a woman in a business suit in front of a white wall with a seal framed by the words "Cook County, Illinois".

"We believe that Nathan Ellis may have raped other women and we are asking any woman who believes that she may have been his victim to contact my office and report the incident."

A reporter yelled out, "Do you believe that Nathan Ellis is a serial rapist?"

"We have evidence that supports that theory."

She's talking about the videos that I uploaded yesterday! It worked! I nodded, smiling.

"Oh my God," Ali said.

"This is fabulous," I said. "The more victims that come forward, the more likely he is to be ruined forever."

Ali was silent as the newscaster moved on to the next story.

"He tried to rape me too. In your house. While you were sleeping upstairs," Ali said.

"What?" *What the fuck? Is she kidding?*

"That night I stayed over, in January, when I was in town for business."

"Oh my God. What happened?"

"I was lying in bed in your guest room, catching up on some emails after you went to bed. He came in and locked the door behind him. He smelled like booze. I asked him what was up, thinking at first that he was just confused and in the wrong place. Then I saw the belt in his hand and the smirk on his face and I knew something was wrong."

She shook her head and paused. I waited for her to continue.

"He got on top of me and grabbed my hands, but he was just drunk enough that his movements were clumsy, so I was able to push him off me. He fell onto the floor and I grabbed the belt and used it to fasten his arms behind him. I told him that if he ever hurt you or me I would kill him, and then I left."

"Oh my God. I'm so sorry," I said.

"He's a monster."

"I know."

"Why did you marry him?"

"I couldn't let it go."

She shook her head. "I can't believe you did that."

"I know. I'm so sorry."

"I'm sorry for you," she said.

"I never meant for him to hurt anyone else."

"Then why didn't you turn him in immediately?"

Here come the usual questions.

I shook my head. "It wouldn't have mattered. I guess I thought I could satisfy him. I meant to control him but I was naïve. Obviously, I couldn't. Why didn't you tell me sooner?"

"I didn't know what to do. I agonized over whether I should wake you up and tell you what happened, but I didn't want to cause trouble. I was worried that he'd be mad and hurt you, but I also knew he'd be embarrassed. I left. I didn't know what else to do. I checked into a fleabag motel off I-95. I couldn't sleep all night and it was all I could do to get myself to work the next morning for my client meeting and then go home."

That's why she didn't text. "I'm so sorry, Ali."

"I've been having nightmares. I'm twitchy and irritable. I don't feel like myself and he didn't even rape me," she said. "I can't understand how you've survived all these years."

"God damn it. I never would have done what I did if I'd known how many women he would assault after me. I didn't realize at the time how evil he was. I thought it was just me. I thought I did something to provoke him. I know nothing I say now can make it right or undo what's been done, but please let me at least explain. I realize now how selfish all this seems," I said.

She looked up and nodded through tears.

"In some ways it was completely selfish, but I was also terrified. He threatened me and I was warned by everyone I trusted that he would ruin my life. I am so sorry that I wasn't stronger, that I didn't fight against him earlier, and that I put you and other women in danger."

"Why didn't you tell us? You could have warned us so that we would know to stay far away from him," Ali said.

"I'm sorry. I didn't want you to know what happened to me. I didn't want Vi to know either. I was ashamed and embarrassed. You have both always been so strong. I was ashamed. I didn't want you to know how weak I was, and honestly I never thought he would do that to you, of all people."

"But we could have supported you."

"I didn't think you'd understand. I thought you would tell me to press charges, but I wasn't ready. I was so weak," I said.

She shook her head. "Stop it. He hurt you badly and you survived alone. You were strong. I just wish we could have been there for you."

"Thank you," I said. "He got me pregnant too."

Vi shook her head, listening as she finished preparing a salad.

"Oh my God! What happened?" Ali asked.

"I got rid of it. I couldn't keep his child."

"Of course not, but that must have been so hard."

I nodded. Ali pulled me toward her and wrapped her arms around me. "I'm so sorry. I wish I could have protected you from him."

I shook my head as tears began to well up in my eyes. "It was my fault for falling for his act in the first place. I let my guard down. I trusted someone I never should have trusted."

My tears became sobs and my body wretched in pain.

"He's a monster. It's not your fault," she said.

I cried into her soft sweater.

"I understand now," Ali said.

I clenched her even tighter. "Some days I hate myself for what I've done, but it really seemed like the only way," I said.

"All we have is each other. I will support you, whatever you feel you need to do," she said.

It's already done.

We sat down for dinner and Vi poured us each a glass of wine. She raised her glass in the air.

"I'm so sorry for what you've been through, but I'm so grateful that we have each other. À-ta santé."

Ali and I raised our glasses and nodded in agreement.

"So, anything positive going on lately amidst all this stuff with Nate?" Vi asked.

"I think I'm in love," I said.

"Really?"

"Yep."

"Not with your husband, obviously," Vi said.

"Obviously not."

"Who?"

"It's Adam," Ali said.

"Thanks for ruining my surprise."

"That's not a surprise," Ali said.

"I always knew you two would end up together," Vi said.

"Then why did you forbid me from dating him in high school?"

"I didn't want you to date anyone in high school because I didn't want you to get pregnant in high school," she said.

"Like you did?" I said.

She looked at me, shocked.

"I understand now, because I took this." I pulled her diary out of my purse. "I read it. I shouldn't have," I said. "I'm sorry."

"What is that?" Ali asked.

"That's my diary," Vi said tersely.

"I had no idea," I said.

Vi nodded and I saw a sadness in her eyes that I'd never seen before.

"I'm so sorry," I said.

"Sorry for what?" Ali asked.

"She's sorry because now she knows my secrets."

"What secrets?"

"Ali, do you remember how I told you that your dad and I were married and moved to Chicago together just before you were born?"

"Yeah."

"We weren't. We were never married. He was my first crush. I got pregnant the first time because the only sex education I ever had was abstinence," she said. "I mean, I would never choose to go back and not have you, but it wasn't easy. My mother accused him of rape just to have him thrown in jail, so that she could use that to try to force me to marry him. She said that if I married him they would let him out of jail and everything would be fine, but I didn't want to be married. I was so young. I didn't know what I wanted, but I knew I needed more. I didn't want to get stuck in that town, so I left home and came here all by myself. When I had you I was all alone."

Ali leaned forward and took Vi's hand over the table. "I'm sorry.

I'm sorry it was hard for you, but you did an incredible job. I love you so much."

Vi began to cry and Ali hugged her. I walked over and they pulled me into their embrace.

"I get it now," I said and they began to laugh.

"About time," Vi said.

As we sat finishing our drinks Ali mused, "I wonder what happened to him."

"I don't know," Vi said. "I tried to get him out of prison. I told them I didn't want to press charges and that he didn't rape me, but I really don't know. I wouldn't be hurt if you want to try to find him."

"Thanks. I don't know. I'll think about it," Ali said.

The next morning Vi drove me to the airport before work. We drove in silence for a few minutes before she said, "Did you really marry him for revenge?"

I didn't answer right away and time passed silently in front of us in the form of bumpy gray asphalt.

"Why else would I marry him?" I said eventually.

"Look, Freddie, no one is disputing that what he did to you was atrocious," she said, "but it's still hard for me to understand why you didn't just turn him in and let the authorities deliver justice."

"Really? I thought you, of all people, would understand. You're smart enough to know that it doesn't work like that in the real world. It might work out nicely in Hollywood movies for the heroine who goes through hell and fights the system, only to be elevated in some grand redemption scene. But in real life the system is run by men, who set policy and weigh evidence—which is itself biased—against reputations, preconceptions, and established value systems. *They* decide what they are comfortable believing and affirming."

"I'm sorry," she said quietly. "I know."

We rode the remaining half hour in silence. I wasn't angry, but I didn't have anything to say either. Vi pulled up to the departures curb and I grabbed my leather duffle bag from the back seat.

"Thanks for the ride," I said.

"Love you, Freddie."

"Love you too."

"Have a good flight."

"Thanks."

THE SEND

Thursday, April 12, 2018

Old Greenwich

Visitor's hours at the Westchester County Correction center, where Nate was being held, were from six to eight on Thursday night. I found a parking spot in the large lot behind the jail. There was no line. I filled out the paperwork to request visitation and took a seat.

About fifteen minutes later a guard opened a large door.

"Wyn-a-freda Laur-ent," he called.

I stood up and he motioned me back through the doorway.

The visitation room reminded me of the cleanest middle school lunchroom in the world, without a serving counter. There were a few different plastic tables for various sized groups of visitors. He motioned for me to sit down at one of the smaller tables. I sat down and clutched my purse in my lap. It was a few more minutes before Nate was brought in. His hands were cuffed and he had shackles around his legs. He looked defeated, which made me feel emboldened.

He sat down and nodded to the guard, who looked at him and said, "I'll be watching."

I smiled at the guard.

"So that was it? Quite the scheme you've pulled off," Nate said.

I didn't react but watched him steadily. *He doesn't actually seem that angry. Why not? What's he up to?*

"Simon told me about your allegations and the police report you filed in 2012," he said softly. "And all the interviews you've been giving. I've seen all of them."

I nodded.

"I'm impressed," he said. "I still can't believe you pulled any of it off."

I studied his expression with skepticism.

"What do you want?" he asked.

"What do you mean?"

"Is it still money you're after?"

"There is no money, right?" I said. "I want justice."

"What does that mean?"

"Justice for all of the women you've hurt," I said loudly.

"I'm not going away for this. I did nothing wrong," he said. "I only gave you what you wanted."

Unbelievable!

"You gave me what I wanted?" I said.

"Yeah, don't pretend I didn't. You wanted me that night. I'm sure you did. They all do."

Wow! He can't really believe that, can he?

"And since then I've done nothing but take care of you. I gave you the life of luxury you wanted, the ability to stay home. You had everything."

I shook my head. *So that's it. He'll never change. I should have known.*

"Let it go," he said. "Drop the charges, apologize publicly for lying about what happened between us in 2012, and tell the world that you've been lying the whole time because you were jealous. Say that you were wrong to lie about it, that we only ever had consensual sex. If you do that, you'll never have to worry about anything else, ever again. Forget about whatever you think happened all those years ago. Come back to me and we will move on. You win."

Ah, so he's after a reconciliation again, like after the party. But this time, I'm the one with the upper hand. He must know that. Why on Earth would I apologize this time? No, he hasn't given me any good reason to reconcile this time. "How the hell do I win?"

"Oh, come on. Living with me hasn't been all that bad, has it?"

Hah! He really believes that I enjoying living with him all those years and thinks that's enough to get me to stay! "I hated every minute."

"Even all those orgasms I gave you?" he said loudly so that everyone in the room could hear.

"I faked every single one," I replied as loud as possible.

"You fucking bitch," Nate said. All of a sudden his anger was unmistakable, scary even. "Liar!" He yelled.

The guard cleared his throat loudly.

I shook my head. "You're the liar and you'll pay for what you did to me."

"I will fight you every step of the way. Give up while you're still ahead."

"Never. I want justice and I'll do whatever it takes to get it."

He laughed out loud. It was a deep, full-bodied laugh.

I waited.

"You won't get that. I won't let you. You're nobody. Come back to me. Come back now and you'll be forgiven, but you better crawl back on your hands and knees. You better make sure everyone knows that you know just how wrong you were to ever accuse me and how much you regret ever filing that erroneous police report. You better grovel on your way back. I think a public apology tour might do the trick."

I shook my head. "Never!" I growled as I stood up to leave.

"Fucking whore!" he yelled after me. "You'll be sorry! I promise."

A small smile crossed my face as I walked out the door, but back in the safety and silence of my car I broke down. I began to shake uncontrollably.

I drove home in silence. *So that was it. He was lying about the stuff with the business and our finances. It was just bait to get me to go see him so that he could try to reel me back in and threaten me.*

I pulled up to the house on the water, where I had lived with my rapist, and played the game for so long. The sun was just setting and there were three cars parked near our house, which struck me as odd, given that there was never anyone parked on our street. As I got closer, I saw the white news vans in our driveway with their antennae up. *Fuck.* There were at least three camera crews standing at my front door. *What are they doing here? I'm too tired to tell the story again, plus the D.A. just told me not to talk to the media.* But as I pulled up to the house I reminded myself that any publicity was good publicity. *How can I spin this to my advantage?*

I pulled into the driveway and navigated through the very narrow space between their vans to the garage. I hit the garage door opener and watched as they began to follow me in on foot. I killed the car, rolled down my window, and yelled in my loudest voice possible.

"If you want an interview GET OUT NOW! Get out!" When they didn't move I yelled, "I'm calling the police now. You're trespassing!" They backed off and I closed the garage door.

I checked my face in the mirror in the front hall and refreshed my lipstick. Then I engaged the security lock on the front door and opened it a crack.

"I would like to give you all an interview but I need you to be civilized. I am going to come out onto the porch on the condition that not one of you sets foot in my house or touches me, and when I say the interview is over, it's over."

I shut the door, removed the security latch, and slipped outside. Shutting the door quickly behind me, I moved over to the side of the front porch, in front of a big planter, making sure that the house number next to the front door wasn't in their shot.

"Okay."

They began shouting questions over each other: "What was it like to be married to your rapist?"; "Will you be getting a divorce?"; "Did you love him?"; "Was it all about his money?"

I held my hand up, commanding them to stop. I looked up at the clear, rosy sky and took a deep breath. "Nathan Ellis raped me violently when I was eighteen years old. I was still a virgin and was saving myself because of my faith and because I believed in happily ever after. I didn't come forward earlier because he threatened my life and because the people I trusted told me, based on experience, that his word would be taken over mine because he was young, handsome, and successful. I was naïve and scared."

"Where did you find the videos?"

"In our house. They were right there, under my nose for years and I had no idea."

"Do you regret not pressing charges when the rape occurred?"
No.

"What made you decide to post the videos online?"

"When I realized that I wasn't alone. That he'd been doing the same thing to other women for years. I decided to post the videos so that those women wouldn't feel alone like I did."

"If you had turned him in earlier he might not have raped those other women. Do you feel responsible?"

"Women who are raped," I paused for effect, "assaulted, abused are kept silent by the fear that they will lose even more than they have already lost. Imagine being harmed, and having something dear ripped from you, and then imagine that to get any sense of peace about what happened, you will have to go through a process that will expose you to the world, rip you open again, lay bare the most painful experience of your life in front of total strangers, only to be told that the perpetrator's future success is more important than your healing. That his potential shouldn't be stymied on account of your pain. For too long I was a victim of this fear and, by allowing myself to be a victim, I did allow it to happen to other women too. I enabled him to keep doing what he was doing, ruining the lives of other women, and for that, I am so sorry. I didn't know about the other women until I discovered the videos. I've put them out there so that together we can end the culture of victimization and fear that surrounds rape."

"Are you worried that circumventing the judicial process by putting evidence online will undermine your case?"

No.

"The Cook County State's Attorney's Office has all of the videos now. They know that he is a serial offender and they have evidence, so it is up to them to do the right thing and hold him accountable. I've done all I can. Thank you."

"Do you know who the other women are?"

I shook my head as I turned and slipped back into the house. The shouting continued, and just before I pulled the door shut I heard, "Are you having an affair?" *What? Do they know about Adam? How would they know?* My heart raced. *I'll have to be even more careful.* I slammed the door shut and locked the deadbolt quickly behind me.

I turned on the nine o'clock local news as I got ready for bed. "A business mogul from Greenwich, Connecticut says his wife has framed him for aggravated rape."

339

What? I spun around. A mugshot of Nate was on the screen next to a picture of us at our wedding.

The news anchor was talking about the statement I had given all those years ago at the hospital. They had apparently gotten ahold of a transcript. She read excerpts of my statement and then talked about two new women who had come forward to accuse Nate in response to the State's Attorney's request. One was a lawyer at a big-name law firm in New York, the other a partner at a consulting company. Both said that they had met Nate online on some dating app, that he had told them he was married, but was unhappy and planning to get a divorce. They both said that they were sure he had videotaped the assaults, plus he had threatened to ruin their careers if they ever told anyone. *Hasn't changed a bit. Just took his game to the big leagues.* When asked what had prompted them to come forward they said they had seen my appearance on the morning show and been inspired to follow suit.

The host continued, "In response, the accused's lawyer released the following statement: 'I deny these latest unsubstantiated allegations. They are patently false. I have never forced myself on anyone. Ever. I have only engaged in consensual sex. I demand a full investigation into these claims, which I am confident will clear my good name.'"

The newscaster cut back in, "Breaking at the top of the hour, we will hear from Mrs. Ellis herself on what it was like to live with a rapist all those years and why she posted all of the videos online! Stay tuned."

Ugh, it's not Mrs. Ellis! I'm not his property. He doesn't control me anymore.

THE TOUCH

Wednesday, June 6, 2018

Old Greenwich

I indulged in a lazy morning, reading the rest of the Sunday paper in the back den with a cup of tea. My phone rang just as I was finishing the paper.

"Kristen. Hi."

"Wyn! Just checking in."

"Oh, great. How's it going?"

"Good. We're making progress on your memoir. Do you want to know the title?"

"Yeah."

"*At all costs: A memoir.*"

"Really?" I said.

"Yeah, you don't like it?"

"Does it matter?"

"Of course," she said.

"If I don't like it will it be changed?"

"Um, it's a little late, but I'll see what I can do."

"Yeah."

"Look, Wyn, I have to run, but I'll be in touch about promotional events. Keep talking to the media, and get back on social media for God's sake!"

"Yeah, will do. Take care."

"You too," she said.

It was just after four-thirty in the afternoon when Adam texted. "Watcha up to tonight? Wanna hang out? You know who will be out at some event." It was as if he read my mind.

I took a shower, did my hair, and put on a little bit of make-up.

As the sun was beginning to dip below the treetops I poured myself a glass of wine. I got comfortable in the back room where I had a view of the Hart's sun room. I figured I'd wait for the lights to go on.

Finally, he's home! I polished off the rest of the glass in my hand. Just as I was about to leave the thought crossed my mind that it was possible that it was Julia, not Adam, who'd turned the lights on. *Didn't he say she was going to some event?* Regardless, I didn't want to go over there empty handed. Just in case, I grabbed a Tupperware from the cupboard that didn't match any of the others in our collection, and let myself in their back door.

I took a few steps into the house and realized that the only light was coming from a lamp next to the couch. Otherwise the house was quite dark. *Is that light on an automatic timer?* I tried to remember whether it was always on at night. *I should have waited in front until I saw his car.* I thought about turning around and going home but then looked at the Tupperware in my hand and felt stupid. *That bitch he's married to would barge into my house for less any day of the week. Well, before Nate was arrested she did at least.* I walked toward the kitchen.

As I got closer I saw a few pieces of glass on the kitchen floor. I took another step forward. More broken glass including the severed stem of a wine glass, and then I saw her. Julia was lying on the floor in the dark, her eyes were closed, her right hand was extended out toward the broken glass and her fingers were open, pointing toward a small puddle of liquid. She was wearing a beautiful, long black evening gown, gorgeous diamond earrings, and her make-up was picture perfect.

"Julia?" I said. She didn't move. *Holy shit!*

"ADAM!!!" I yelled, hoping he had gone directly upstairs when he'd gotten home and just hadn't seen her yet. No response. I ran to the door to the garage and opened it. Adam's car wasn't there. I ran over to the dining room and looked out at the driveway. *Not there either. Shit!*

I went back into the kitchen. *Maybe she's just passed out.* I shook her a little bit but she didn't respond. I shoved my fingers into the soft flesh of her neck, under her bony jaw. *No pulse.* I looked at her frail, disheveled body strewn out on the tile floor.

OH MY GOD! What do I do? If I leave and my fingerprints are here, will they think I killed her? What if Adam was involved? Is this what he meant when he said he'd take care of it? Why isn't he here? Did he run? He wouldn't do something like that, would he?

I steadied myself on the counter and took a deep breath. *What if she wasn't murdered? There are no visible signs of foul play. It wasn't robbery because she has diamond earrings on. God, why am I so morbid? Maybe she just died. But she's so young. Young people don't just drop dead in the middle of the afternoon!*

I grabbed my cell phone and began to dial 9-1-1. *Maybe the neighbor finding her would look less suspicious than her husband finding her like this...maybe not. The police would want to know why I was here. Maybe I should wait and he should call it in. Fuck, I don't know what to do.* I put my cell phone back in my pocket, wiped the garage door knob with the inside of my sweater, and rubbed both handles of the back door as I let myself out.

Back in my kitchen I poured myself another glass of wine and took a seat in the front living room with a clear view of their driveway. I waited.

I began to wonder what had happened to her. *Was she murdered?* I reminded myself that there were no obvious signs of foul play. *Did she kill herself? But she had so much going, why would she do that? Maybe it was the pressure of being famous. Maybe she was having an affair. Well, she was, with my husband, but he's been in prison for months now. Maybe he was blackmailing her. But for what? Maybe they were running some kind of scam together and now that he is locked up people are after her to get what they're owed. She did seem to make a lot more money with that stupid blog and her Instagram account than I'd ever believed was possible. Maybe it was just a front for something else.* My imagination ran wild. *Maybe she and Nate knew each other a lot longer than I thought. Maybe they've been playing us the whole time. But why and for what?* I pulled out my phone and clicked on Facebook. I opened Nate's profile and scrolled down to the oldest pictures of him. Maybe there was some evidence on social media. He had never deleted any of the old pictures of him and his exes. There were tons of pictures of him with busty blonde toothpick women that I remembered seeing when I first friended him. Maybe she was one of those women.

Light thrown by approaching headlights bounced across the living room. I looked up. *Finally, he's home.* I watched and waited.

About five minutes later an ambulance and two cop cars pulled up into their driveway. *I can't go over there now.* I watched as more lights went on in the back of the house, and then I watched as an officer escorted Adam to a squad car and shut the door behind him. *Did they arrest him? Oh my God. Do they think he did it?*

A half an hour later there was a loud, aggressive knock on the front door. I engaged the security lock and slid the door open a few inches.

"Who's there?" I said.

"Detective Scala," came the man's response. "Greenwich P.D. I just have a few questions I'd like to ask."

"About what, Officer?"

"About your neighbor, Mrs. Hart."

"Oh, okay," I said and opened the door. "Please, come in."

"Mrs.," he paused waiting for me to fill in the blank.

"No, sir. Ms. Laurent."

"Oh, you're the…"

"The what?"

"Never mind," he said. "I just have a few questions."

"Would you like a glass of water?"

"No thank you, Ma'am."

"Please sit down." I motioned toward the living room sofa.

"Thank you."

He sat and I took a chair across from him.

"Have you been home all day Ms. Laurent?"

"Yes."

"Did you leave the house at all today?"

"No." *Shit, I don't have an alibi!*

"And what were you doing at home all day by yourself?"

"Oh, you know, just tidying up, doing some laundry."

"And when was the last time you saw Mrs. Hart?" he asked.

"Oh it's been awhile. I think a month, maybe two."

"When and where did you see her last?"

"At her house. Her husband was there too."

"Why were you there?"

"Just to say hi. Catch up. We've been friends a long time."

"Friends?" he challenged.

"Yes. I've known her husband since I was born essentially. We grew up together," I paused and he waited. "She and my husband were friendly too," I said.

"Your husband?"

"Yes, Nathan Ellis. He's in prison now, but before that they were friendly."

"What do you mean by friendly?"

"Um, they did some business together."

"Is that all?"

"No."

"Were they having an affair?"

"Yes." *Crap, this doesn't sound good for Adam, does it?*

"Did her husband know about it?"

"I'm not sure," I lied.

"Did she have any other lovers besides your husband?"

"How would I know?"

"Did you notice any changes in Mr. Hart's behavior recently?"

"No."

"What about hers?"

"No, although she just kept getting thinner all the time."

"Do you believe that Mrs. Hart and her husband were unhappy?"

"Um, it's hard to say, but I don't think so."

"Did you ever hear them fighting?"

"No, never."

"Do you have any reason to believe that Mrs. Hart would hurt herself?"

"No."

He stood up. "Thank you for your time today, Mrs.," he stopped himself, "*Ms.* Laurent." He handed me his card. "If you remember anything that you think may be relevant to our investigation please call me immediately."

"Your investigation?"

"Into the death of Mrs. Hart."

"Yes, of course," I said.

I was in the grocery store an hour later when my phone rang. *A*

312 number I don't know. Chicago. The State's Attorney? I picked up.

"Hello?"

"Wyn Laurent?"

"Yes."

"This is Connor Donoghue with the Cook County State's Attorney's Office. Is this a good time?"

Not really, but it shouldn't really matter if you have big news, should it?

"Fine," I said as I found my way to the junk food aisle, which was usually empty at our specialty grocery.

"Wyn, we have reached an agreement with the defendant, which we believe is satisfactory to all parties."

"What is it?"

"Mr. Ellis has agreed to plead guilty to aggravated criminal sexual abuse, a Class 2 felony, punishable by three to seven years' incarceration. In this case, we have agreed to accept time served for the DUI plus probation for the remainder of the sentence. He will also have to register as a sex offender, and seek treatment for violent behavior and sex addiction. His probation will include regular psychiatric evaluations and continuing treatment if deemed necessary."

"I thought he would at least get house arrest," I said.

"Ma'am, you've been living with your rapist. Your behavior over the past six years has made this a very difficult case to prosecute."

So that's it. After everything I've been through. It's my fault of course.

"Ms. Laurent?"

Tears streamed down my cheeks.

"Ms. Laurent?"

"When will he be released from prison?" I said between gasps for air.

"Whenever the paperwork is completed and processed. It could be days or weeks."

"Will he need to be in Illinois after that, during his probation?"

"Typically yes, but in this case his attorney has requested an exception. We have agreed to transfer his probation to the jurisdiction of his domicile, which is in Fairfield County, Connecticut, I believe."

I fucking know where he's domiciled. At my house!

I couldn't help myself; "So, he just gets to go home? After everything he did?"

"Ma'am, there were a number of complex factors in this

negotiation. We feel that the accused is making a good faith effort to address his problems with this plea deal. He is an otherwise productive member of society, whose reputation will be irreparably impacted by his felony plea and registration as a sex offender."

"What if I disagree?" I said.

"With what?"

"The terms of the deal," I said.

"Well, there's really no reason to disagree. A team of professionals evaluated the case, weighed the charges and the evidence, and determined that this is the best outcome. It is final."

An eye for an eye?

"Ms. Laurent?"

An eye for an eye.

"Ms. Laurent?"

Click. He hung up. I put the phone back in my purse and stared at the wall of crackers in front of me. I closed my eyes. *Is that it? Is it really over? What will he do when he gets out? He'll be angry. Would he try to hurt me? I need to leave a.s.a.p. What about Adam? I need to talk to Adam first. It would be best if he comes with me, for both of our safety.*

The nine o'clock local news came on as I began to pack my things.

"Breaking news tonight!" the anchor said. "A local celebrity was found dead in her Greenwich home today. Blogger and social media influencer, Julia Hart, was found dead by her husband this evening when he returned home from work."

The screen filled with video footage of Adam being loaded into the back of the squad car. "Hart's husband was taken to the Greenwich Police Station tonight for additional questioning in relation to his wife's death. The cause of death is unknown at this point, but our sources are saying that there were no obvious signs of foul play. The Fairfield County Coroner's office confirmed that an autopsy has been ordered." *Crazy. I wonder what happened to her. There's no way Adam had anything to do with it.*

I'm all alone now without Adam. What if Nate gets out while Adam is in custody? Should I leave? No, I need to be here for Adam when he gets out. I can't leave without him. I do need to be ready to get the hell out of here the minute Adam is back. Will he even be able to leave the state if he's still under investigation?

What if Adam never comes back?

THE TOUCH

Thursday, June 7, 2018
Old Greenwich

I was surprised by aggressive knocking on the front door. I peered through the peephole in the imposing wooden door. It was a man in his late thirties or early forties wearing fitted black jeans and a V-neck sweater. He was holding a leather wallet with a police badge open toward the door. I turned the deadbolt and opened the door the three inches the security chain would allow.

"Mrs. Ellis?"

Ugh, it's Laurent, but sure. "How can I help you?"

"Detective Samuels. I've been assigned to the Hart case."

"I didn't know there was a *case*," I said. "I thought I saw on the news that there was no sign of foul play."

"Ma'am, you shouldn't believe everything you see. We are required to conduct a thorough investigation in every case. Isn't that what you would want if it was you?"

Yeah of course. "Sure."

"Can I come in?"

I opened the door and showed him to the living room.

"What is your name?"

"Wynafreda Laurent."

He looked at me skeptically. "You're the wife of Nathan Ellis?"

"Yes. I talked to a detective yesterday about all of this."

"I know. I'm just here to ask a few follow-up questions."

"Okay."

"How close were you to Mrs. Hart?"

"I don't know. I'd say we were more than acquaintances, but I'm not sure I'd go so far as to call us friends. We certainly weren't close."

"How did you come to know Mrs. Hart?"

"Her husband and I grew up next door to each other. He and I were good friends and dated in high school. We all lived in the city after college and then they moved in next door about a year ago."

"Do you think that was coincidental?"

"I'm not sure, honestly. We were already living here when they moved in. I never really thought about it."

"Did Julia ever talk about her weight?" he asked. "You know, did she mention that she was dieting or something?"

"Not really. She was always skinny, even when I first met her. I remember that about her, but she was slowly getting even thinner in the last few months. I did notice that. But no, she never said anything about it at all to me. I'm sure."

"Did you ever hear her and her husband talking about her weight or her dieting?"

"Not really. I think the only people I heard talking about her weight were her girlfriends. We were at a bar once and they were speculating about whether she was bulimic or anorexic. They were envious of her figure and I remember one of them saying that she wished she knew what Julia's secret was, because she seemed to eat whatever she wanted and still be so thin. I guess I just figured that she might be bulimic or something, but it was none of my business, you know?"

"And what about her husband? You mentioned that the two of you were friends. Did he ever confide in you that he was worried about her weight specifically?"

"No, not that I remember. I know he really cared about her though," I said. "He loved her, but I don't remember him saying anything about her weight specifically."

"Ms. Laurent, were you having an affair with Adam Hart before Mrs. Hart died?"

"No!" I said. *Does sleeping together once qualify as an affair?*

"If not, then what would you have us make of the text message that he sent you yesterday? The day Mrs. Hart died."

"He sent me a text message? Honestly, I don't remember. We are friends. We've known each other since we were born. We text. I don't know what you should make of a text message that I don't remember."

He looked down at the pocket notebook in his hand. "Watcha up to tonight? Wanna hang out? You know who will be out at some big event."

"Right, my husband worked late a lot and Julia had a lot of evening events for her work. Adam went along to some of them, but not all of them. Sometimes, when both of them were out for the night we would have dinner together for company. I wouldn't call that an affair."

He squinted at me and raised an eyebrow. "When was the last time you saw Mr. Hart?"

"About a week ago, I think. I stopped by to say hi."

"Thank you for your time," he said.

"Yeah, no problem," I said.

I followed him to the front door and locked the deadbolt behind him. The news vans were still parked at the end of the driveway, and a few reporters tried unsuccessfully to interview the detective as he made his way back to his car.

My cell phone rang after noon. *A local number I don't recognize.* I answered.

"Freddie, it's me. Can you come pick me up from the police station?"

"Adam?"

"Yeah. They said I'm free to go."

"Oh great! Yeah, of course. I'll be there in ten."

"Thanks," he said.

I threw my purse in the back seat. As the garage door went up I noticed a few cars and one white van parked opposite Adam's driveway. *They're back!* I waited until my garage door was completely shut and then kept my gaze locked on the road ahead as I pulled out and drove past them.

The parking lot outside the station was quiet. I let the receptionist know I was there to pick up Adam Hart. She told me to pull around back and wait.

Eventually, Adam walked out, followed by two officers. They exchanged a few words and then he opened the door.

"You might want to get in back," I said.

"What? After what just happened you don't want me to sit next to you? Do *you* think I did it too?"

350

"No, just trust me."

He muttered something as he slammed the passenger side door, but got in back and put his seatbelt on as the officers watched. I put the car in reverse and began to drive away.

"There's media at your house," I said. "It's getting late, so they may be gone by now, but you never know."

"Shit, you have a gun?" He was looking down at my purse.

"It's Nate's. I found it in his office. I've been pretty freaked out lately by myself at night in that big house."

"Be careful, please," he said. "Do you even know how to use it?"

"Sort of."

"You need to learn or get rid of it."

"Yeah, I know. Hey, when we get within a few blocks you should get down so they can't see you. I'll pull into my garage."

"Okay," he said, "but will you please stay with me tonight? I don't want you to be alone in that house anymore."

"Yeah, of course."

About three blocks from the house, Adam laid down across the back seat. As I pulled past the stake out I glanced over to see if they were watching. A young guy looked up but seemed uninterested in me. *Phew.* I drove quickly into my garage. I checked to make sure that the stake out hadn't moved before hitting the button on the garage door opener.

"Clear," I said as the garage door closed.

Adam sat up, and looked around.

"Thanks."

"Of course," I said.

"I get it now," he said, "and I'm sorry for everything you've been through."

"Thank you."

We went inside and he waited in the middle of the house until I had closed all of the window shades. Then he snuck up behind me and wrapped his arms around my waist.

"I'm never leaving you again. I love you so much! I am going to make sure no one hurts you again," he said.

I kissed him.

"You said they didn't charge you with anything, right?" I asked.

"No. They just questioned me all night and again this morning."

"You must be really tired."

"I am."

"Who do you think did it?" I asked. *Adam didn't kill her. He couldn't have. He's not capable of that.*

"Honestly, no one. I think she did it to herself. You know as well as I do that she wasn't healthy. I don't know what exactly was wrong, but she was way too thin. I told her she needed to eat more, but she seemed to eat all the time, and junk too, but it didn't seem to matter. Maybe she did that thing where women eat a lot and then throw up."

"You think she was bulimic?"

"I don't know. Maybe. Makes as much sense as anything, doesn't it?"

"She ate a lot. She would have been doing a lot of puking that went unnoticed."

He shrugged. "Can't say I was really paying attention."

"She didn't look well the last few times I saw her," I said.

"No."

"There was some big event recently that she'd been talking about a lot. She seemed to be losing weight for it."

"I bet the autopsy will show that it was an accident," I said.

"Yeah, hopefully."

"Look, I know she just died, and I understand if you are overwhelmed, but I got a call from the D.A. about Nate yesterday," I said. "He said they reached a plea agreement and that Nate could be released any day. He won't serve any more time in prison. I know that this is all happening fast, but I don't think we have much time. I don't want to be anywhere near here when he's released."

"Jeez. Yeah, we need to leave. It's not safe here. We should get out as soon as possible. Let's go back home. Leave all of this behind us and forget about it."

I smiled. "Yes. Let's go home."

"I'll need to sell my house, but I can deal with that once we're in Chicago," he said.

"What about your job?" I asked.

"I'll tell my boss I need a transfer and that it's urgent. I can't see why they wouldn't let me move and work from the Chicago office, but if for some reason they say it's not possible I'll find something else."

"Thank you."

"Of course. We're lucky to have each other. I don't want to risk that now. I'll go get started packing up essentials."

"Yeah, I started this morning, but still need to finish."

"Okay, come get me when you're done and I'll help load everything into your car. Then you can stay with me tonight and we'll put your car in my garage."

"Are you okay to leave first thing tomorrow morning?"

"Yeah, that's what I was thinking too."

"Okay." *This just might work. Everything is going to be okay.*

THE BLOW-OFF & THE FIX

Thursday, June 7, 2018
Old Greenwich

I finished filling two big suitcases with everything I valued: clothes, jewelry, the scrapbooks Vi had encouraged me to make when I was a teenager, and a few framed pictures of the three of us. My hands shook as I threw my must-have sweaters, shirts, pants, underwear, and toiletries in an overnight bag. I left everything at the top of the stairs for Adam to carry down. I went next door and got him and he helped me load everything into the back of my car, which I then drove next door.

I grabbed my passport, birth certificate, a file folder where Nate and I had kept our important documents—life insurance, mortgage, bank account info—and my laptop. I made sure to take the love lock necklace that Nate had made me, which I'd stopped wearing the minute he was put in jail. I locked all the doors on my way out.

Adam's kitchen was mostly empty, but I found enough food to put together dinner and flicked on the t.v. as I worked.

Adam came downstairs just as I was plating our dinner.

"Okay, I made some good progress packing. I just have a few more things to pack tonight and then I'll just need to grab a few things in the morning before we start driving," he said.

"Great."

The six o'clock news came on. "Breaking news tonight. The Fairfield County Coroner's office just released a report about what killed a local Greenwich woman in her own home." The newscaster's tone was somber.

He continued, "Social media influencer, Julia Hart, was found dead by her husband in their home yesterday. The cops questioned her husband, Adam Hart, extensively into the morning. He was released without charges this afternoon. A Police Department spokeswoman confirmed to ABC news early today that there were no signs of foul play, but that the Department would not close the investigation until the autopsy was complete. In the last hour the Fairfield County Coroner's Office has released their preliminary findings. We will have more on what really killed Julia Hart in a few minutes. Stay with us." The program cut to commercial.

Adam stared at the television.

"Why don't you sit?" I said and motioned toward a bar stool. He sat down.

The commercial break ended. "I'm joined by Doctor Johnson from Stamford Hospital. He is not involved in the ongoing investigation into Julia Hart's death, but he *has* read the report that the Fairfield County Coroner's office released today," she said, and turned toward the doctor, who was particularly handsome and not more than forty-five. He was wearing a white physician's coat with his name embroidered above the breast pocket.

"Doctor, what is the report's key finding?"

"Well, Karen, the key finding today from the Fairfield County Coroner is that Julia Hart died of heart failure as a result of hyperglycemia and ketoacidosis."

She looked at him very seriously. "Doctor Johnson, what does that mean?"

"Hyperglycemia means high blood sugar, and ketoacidosis is a buildup of acids in your blood. Both occur when there is too much sugar in the blood for too long, caused by a lack of insulin, which means that Mrs. Hart was a diabetic."

He continued.

"Specifically, she was probably a Type 1 Diabetic, who needed to inject insulin multiple times a day in order to live. The report notes that her body mass index at the time of death was extremely low. Critically low actually, which indicates that she may have been diabetic for quite some time and either didn't know it, or had been diagnosed and chose not to treat herself with an adequate amount of insulin over a long period of time."

"But Doctor Johnson, why would she do that?" Karen flashed him a flirtatious smile.

"This is really important. When a person's body stops producing insulin, which is the key marker of Type 1 Diabetes, their body begins to use fat and muscle tissue for energy, which means they lose weight quite rapidly. If a Type 1 Diabetic doesn't inject an adequate amount of insulin on a daily basis, the body begins to use fat and muscle for energy. When done intentionally, it is a condition called diabulimia. It is similar to bulimia, where a patient is intentionally purging calories from their body after consuming them, in order to lose weight."

Karen said nothing, and he continued, "Some of the sugar in the blood leaves the body through urine, but most of it stays in the blood, damaging critical organs like the liver and heart, as well as the eyes and nerves. This damage can lead to death, as it did in this case. It's very serious and I want to take a moment to mention that if you know someone who is Type 1 Diabetic, who is extremely thin, you may need to be concerned."

"Very scary stuff, Doctor Johnson. And especially because it can lead to such an unexpected death at such a young age, as it did in this case. Thank you for being with us today."

She looked at him with an appropriately furrowed brow and then quickly turned back to the camera and adopted a smile as she read from the teleprompter, "And we'll be back in a minute with your weather forecast and a recap of today's sports action."

The program cut to a commercial for a local car dealership.

I looked at Adam. He was staring blankly at the t.v.

"Did you know?"

He shook his head.

"Holy shit," I said.

He nodded.

"At least you're cleared," I said. "They must have been waiting for those results to release you."

He nodded.

"You okay?"

He said nothing immediately and so I just sat next to him and held his hand in mine.

Eventually he turned to look at me. "I would have done something if I'd known," he said.

"I know."

"Julia and I may have had an unusual relationship, but I did care about her. I would have been the first person to get her help if I'd known she was sick."

"Of course."

We sat in silence watching the last few leaves flutter in the setting sunlight, falling from the big oak trees.

"I love you so much. I always have," he said.

I smiled. "I love you too."

He was silent for a few minutes and then continued, "I never wished her any harm. I thought she was quite skinny, but never realized what was happening, what she was doing to herself," he said. "If I had known, I never would have..." he sat silently, his eyes were focused directly ahead of him at a spot on the floor.

"You didn't know," I said and rubbed his hand.

"But I probably should have."

"You knew she was under pressure to be thin to impress her followers and attract sponsors. Honestly, that's the world she lived in. It's what she wanted."

"Yeah, but I had no idea she loved it enough to die for it."

"Maybe she didn't know either."

"Maybe not."

He shook his head.

"Please just let it go. We have each other. We are lucky," I said.

"We are. I'm going to take care of you. I'll never let you down like that."

"Stop it, it wasn't your fault. I know you didn't mean her any harm," I said.

He pulled me into his arms and I laid back against his chest, listening to his heart beat. I felt so comfortable with him. *I can finally relax!*

"I just want to be with you," he said. "Somewhere we can be safe. Maybe have some kids and grow old together."

"Me too," I said.

I opened a nice bottle of wine and we ate dinner. He did the dishes, while I savored the moment. *A normal life together, finally!*

"Wanna watch a movie?" I said.

"Yeah, I just want to get a few more things packed first. Warm up

the couch for me and pick out a movie. I'll be there in fifteen. Okay?"
"Yep."

I sat down and leaned back into the couch. I turned the t.v. on
and scrolled through the listings in silence. *So many channels and
nothing worth watching!* Beep, beep, beep, beep. The four numbers on
the keypad at the front door sounded. *That's weird. Adam's upstairs.*
Footsteps echoed in the front hall. *Dress shoes.* The steps grew closer
until they stopped at the entry to the room. I looked up. Nate was
standing in the doorway watching me.

"A-D-A-M! It's Nate!" I yelled as loudly as I could.

Nate was wearing the Carnival costume from Julia's birthday
party. It was a bizarre sight. Despite my racing heart and sweaty
palms it was hard not to laugh.

"You changed the locks!" Nate barked.

"How did you get in here?"

"You think Julia didn't give me the code?" He chuckled to himself.
"Speaking of that, where is she?"

"Dead."

"What?"

"Yeah, she died yesterday. Simon didn't tell you?"

"No. Did you kill her to punish me? I know you're a crazy bitch,
but that's insane."

"No. I don't care that much about you anymore."

Adam walked in from the kitchen, one hand behind his back.
"Nate," Adam said flatly.

Nate ignored him and looked at me. "Keys," he demanded.

"In my purse, hold on." I got up and grabbed my purse from the
kitchen. As I walked back into the den I saw light reflecting off a
fileting knife in Adam's right hand. I put my purse down on the
dining table and threw the keys at Nate.

"Come on," Nate said and motioned to me.

"Those are the new keys to the house. It's the only set I had made.
I don't need them anymore. They're yours."

"Yeah, fine, come on," Nate said.

"I'm staying here."

"You're my wife. Come with me."

"No, I'm not. I'm staying here with Adam. This is my home now."

"So you killed Julia so you two could be together?"

"Stop it. She killed herself," I said.

"After everything you've put me through, you think I'm just gonna walk away now, let you run off with the neighbor?" Nate said.

I shook my head. "It's over. Just go. I don't want anything from you anymore. You don't owe me anything. Just leave me alone."

"That's not how it works. You're my wife and you'll make all of this up to me. You don't get to accuse me of rape, have me thrown in jail, and then sail off into the sunset."

"Yes, I will. You got off easy after what you did to me and the others. Now leave me alone. Let's call it even," I said. "You're trespassing. Get out!"

Nate began to walk toward me.

"Stop!" Adam yelled, holding the knife up in Nate's direction.

"You think this guy is the answer to all of your problems? He's no saint," Nate said.

"Get out or I'll call the police," Adam said.

"You don't know do you?" Nate asked me. "You still don't know that he's the reason you and I met in the first place. If it hadn't been for Adam, none of this would be happening right now. None of it would have happened in the first place."

"What are you talking about?" I said.

"You mean you never told her?" Nate looked at Adam.

"Told me what?" I demanded.

Nate continued, "That in 2012, when I was a senior and he was a freshman, I told him that I was going to visit a friend at NU and he told me that there was this girl I had to meet named 'Freddie'. That was you, Wyn, wasn't it? I knew you looked familiar when we met in New York but I couldn't place you."

I looked at Adam. His eyes were fixed on Nate.

Nate continued, "He knew what my reputation was and he still told me to look you up. He said you were easy."

I turned to Adam. "Is that true?"

He shook his head, but didn't look at me.

"Look at me," I demanded.

He turned toward me. "No, he's lying."

"Oh, come on, of course it's true," Nate said. "And it gets better. When I got back I told him that we'd had sex. He practically lost his mind. Something about all of the times you'd rejected him. Right?"

Adam shook his head, but I wasn't sure. *Nate is a liar, no doubt, but I did reject Adam. Maybe he was jealous, vindictive. It's possible.*

"I know you think he's your soulmate, and some devoted knight in shining armor that will rescue you from this, but he isn't," Nate said. "He's no better than the rest of us. Come on, time to go," Nate said and moved toward me, grabbing my upper arm firmly.

"No!" I yelled and tried to pull myself from his grip.

Adam lunged at Nate. Nate let go of me and they began to wrestle for the knife in Adam's hand. As I watched, Nate grabbed the knife, raised it in the air and plunged it into Adam's chest. *Oh my God! Holy shit!* He pulled it back out of Adam's chest. Adam let out a primal moan. Nate stood up, towering over Adam's body. Deep red blood stained Adam's shirt where he'd been stabbed. He clasped his chest. I froze, panicked. *What do I do now? He'll kill me.* I backed away.

Nate turned toward me. "You ruined my life," he growled.

"You ruined mine first."

"You think I ruined your life? Just wait."

"Why? Why did you do it? Why did you rape any of us?"

"Oh come on. You were so cute back then." He mimicked my voice, "'I'm gonna wait till I'm in love and married', I'd forgotten that little detail before you said it in that interview, but you were a virgin, weren't you? There was no way I wasn't going to fuck you that night, you were such a little cock tease. You just had to make it difficult. Why?"

I shook my head. "You selfish asshole."

"You wanted me. They all do," Nate said.

"It wasn't your right to take that from me."

"Why not? Someone was going to."

"Because I said 'no'."

"Women always say no, play hard to get, that's their thing, and it's what makes them irresistible."

"You're a psychopath," I said.

"Be careful or you'll be next," he said, looking down at Adam.

Adam's eyes met mine, his look pleaded: *help!*

How could you betray me too? Disappointment and anger enveloped me. *If there is repentance, you must forgive.*

I hurried to Adam and kneeled next to him, lifting his head up off the floor. He opened his eyes and looked directly into mine.

"I love you," he whispered, looking completely helpless. Memories of our life together flashed before my eyes.

I nodded, leaned down, and kissed his lips. "I love you too."

He closed his eyes and I could feel the weight of his lifeless body in my arms.

"I'm calling 9-1-1," Nate said, "I'm going to tell the police that Adam attacked me and I stabbed him in self-defense. You're going to corroborate my story. Then we're going to forget any of this ever happened and move on together. Your little high school romance is over, you need me more than ever. I'll take care of you, and you'll be a good wife. We'll move on. Rebuild our life together."

I shook my head. "No."

"You'll never have to worry about anything else, ever again," he continued. "Forget about whatever you think happened all those years ago. You're nobody without me."

"You're wrong. I don't need you, I never did, and I won't lie for you," I said.

He looked at me, "You're going to tell them exactly what I tell you to say."

I shook my head.

"You will because your life depends on it." He looked down at the bloody knife in his hand, "Why can't you just...do what I tell you?" He shook his head and began to move toward me.

I pulled his gun out of my purse, flipped the safety, and pointed it squarely at him. His look betrayed utter disbelief. I fired, pulling the trigger again and again. My heart raced. Nate fell back.

I walked over to him. He looked up at me and I could read his mind: *holy shit, she actually did it.*

I watched him. I watched the puddle of blood surrounding him grow, slowly absorbed by the area rug beneath him. I waited silently. After what felt like an eternity I checked his pulse. *It's finally over.* I walked to the kitchen, leaving a trail of little, round specks of blood in my path.

I grabbed the house phone and dialed 9-1-1.

"This is 9-1-1. What is your emergency?"

"There was a fight. My husband tried to kill me after he stabbed my friend. I shot him before he could kill me."

"Ma'am, where are you?"

I gave her Adam's address.

"Ma'am, stay calm. An ambulance is on its way."

"Thank you."

I went to the foyer and sat down on the first step of the front hall stairs. *Holy shit! It's really over.* I burst into tears and the tears became wails. I cried so hard I gasped for air. I felt every emotion that I had felt since the assault: intense pain, happiness, and sorrow, all at once. *That's not how he was supposed to be punished. That's not how it was supposed to end. He was supposed to rot in prison, all alone, for the awful things he did. He was supposed to suffer like we did. He was supposed to think about it every day for the rest of his life, like I will. He was supposed to repent. He was supposed to finally understand the weight of the word "guilty". Instead he destroyed my only hope and my best shot at happiness.* I held my head in my hands and tried to focus on each slow, deliberate breath. *I'm alive, thank God. I'm going to be okay. I have to be okay.*

The sound of sirens grew louder. Flashing lights filled the driveway. My heart raced. *Stay calm. This was not my fault.* How would I convince the police if I didn't believe it myself?

A loud knock on the door was followed by, "Mr. Hart?"

I opened the front door and pointed to the den.

A wave of uniformed bodies filed past me, quickly going to work, checking for pulses, snapping photos, and preparing stretchers.

A female detective approached me. "Come with me please," she said.

I followed her into the kitchen.

"Please sit down. Are you okay?" she said.

I shook my head, tears still moistened my cheeks.

"Can you tell me what happened?" She pulled a tape recorder out of her pocket and hit play, "February 27, 2018. Hart residence. 87 E. Vista Drive."

"I was scared. I knew that my husband, Nate might be let out of jail any day, but I didn't know when, so I asked my neighbor and friend, Adam Hart, if I could stay here. He was upstairs packing and I was watching t.v. back here in the den."

She looked up from a notepad where she was taking notes.

"Packing for what?"

"Adam and I were going back to Chicago. We were planning to move there together. His wife recently died and I was going to file for divorce. We wanted to go home to be near our families."

"Okay. Where was your husband?"

"He was in prison, like I said. He had been serving a sentence for DWI, but was held for longer because his DNA matched a rape kit. He struck a plea deal with the District Attorney was getting probation for the rest of his sentence."

"Okay, so you believe he was released today?"

"I guess so. He came in the front door. It was locked but he said he knew the code. I screamed when I saw him. Adam came downstairs. He must have grabbed a knife from the kitchen because he had it behind his back."

"Then what?"

"They began to argue. Nate said I needed to go home with him. I said no. I told him I was leaving him and staying with Adam. He demanded that I go home with him. Adam told him to leave. Instead he started to come toward me, I think he was going to try to drag me home. Adam pulled the knife out and told Nate to leave. He said he would call the police if Nate didn't go."

"Then what?"

"Nate lunged at him and they struggled for control of the knife. They were on the ground and then Nate stabbed Adam in the chest."

"And where were you when all this was happening?"

"A few feet away. It all happened so fast. I wasn't sure what to do."

"So what happened after Nate stabbed Adam?"

"Nate told me that he was going to call the police and say it was self-defense and I would have to tell the same story. I said I wouldn't lie to the police. That's when he came at me with the knife, so I pulled the gun out and fired. Several times. He was coming at me. I was terrified. I shot him. I can't believe it. I was so scared. He fell back onto the ground. I waited a few minutes to make sure he didn't get up and come after me, and then I went into the kitchen to call 9-1-1."

"Where's the gun? Is it your gun?"

"No, I assume it was Nate's. I found it in our house a couple of months ago. I decided to start carrying it around for protection. I was living all alone in that big house next door. I started getting threats from men who said I made up my whole story for attention and fame. I was scared one of them would actually do what they promised to do in their anonymous notes, voicemails, social media posts, and online rants."

"What story?"

"The rape," I said. "I didn't...make it up. I was raped. By Nate."

"Your husband?"

I nodded. "Before we were married."

"I'm so sorry. And what threats were you getting?"

"They were ugly. All kinds of graphic things I'd rather not talk about. Guys saying they'd rape me so violently that I'd be wishing they'd go easy on me like Nate had. Guys saying they would rape and then murder me to teach all women a lesson."

"Oh my God."

I let out a deep sigh. "I kept them all in case you want to see them. Some were online."

"One other thing. Were you and your friend having an affair?"

"Adam?" I said.

"Yes," she said.

"No. We grew up together. We were in love, I guess we always had been, but we didn't act on it," I lied. "We were planning to move home. He was there for me through what was a really tough time, and I guess I was there for him too. His wife had just died. He wanted to sell his house. He didn't want to stay here without her."

"Okay, we are going to need you to come down to the station to sign some paperwork, including a statement about what happened tonight. You can stop by first thing tomorrow."

"Okay. Should I call my lawyer?"

"If you want to, sure, but the statement will just be a written transcript of what you've told us tonight."

"Okay. I'll be there first thing tomorrow."

I got my cell phone, went up to my bedroom, closed the door and called my sister.

She answered on the second ring, "Hey."

Phew! "Hey, I need help."

"Are you okay?"

"Yeah, I think so, but there's been a terrible fight. Adam and Nate are both dead. I just gave a statement to a detective from the Greenwich Police Department. She wants me to come in first thing tomorrow morning to sign a witness statement. I don't know whether I need a lawyer."

"My God. Yes, you do. I'll book a flight right now," she said.

"You don't need to come out here."

"Yes, I do. I won't take 'no' for an answer," she said.

"Okay. Will you book a one-way ticket then and drive back with me tomorrow?"

"You are planning to drive home tomorrow?" she asked.

"Yes."

"Are you packed?"

"Yes. First thing tomorrow we can go to the station to review and sign the statement. Then we can hit the road."

"Oh, okay. Yeah, why not?"

"Okay, I just found a seat on the last flight out tonight. It leaves in two hours so I have to go."

"Thank you!"

"Of course. Gotta go."

"Love you!" I said.

"Love you too." She hung up.

There were still a few forensic investigators in the foyer when I went back downstairs. Now it really looked like a crime scene. A large section of the area rug had been removed, but there was still quite a bit of dried blood on the remaining section. There was crime scene tape around the front of the house and haphazardly hanging off the front hall staircase. The floor of the den and front hallway were covered in dirty shoe prints, wet from a recent summer shower.

I found the keys to the house that I had given to Nate. They were laying under the table. My purse was much lighter for the weight of Nate's gun, which had been taken as evidence. My boxes and suitcases were piled up in the back of my s.u.v. I opened the hatch door of Adam's car and pulled out the two big suitcases he had packed for himself. I squeezed them into the back of my car. *Adrienne will want these.* I put my overnight bag and my purse on the passenger seat.

I opened the garage door manually. By the time I was back in the car I could see the news crews beginning to move. I turned the key in the ignition, and drove out onto the driveway. I had to get out and manually put the garage door down. As I did, the news crews surrounded me.

The lights on their cameras lit up the driveway and the questions started: "Wyn, what happened?"; "Wyn, did you kill your husband?"; "Did he attack you?"; "Wyn, did Nate kill Adam or did you kill them both?"

Not tonight boys, it's over!

I got back in my car and slowly maneuvered past them. In the rear view mirror I watched them follow me back down the driveway.

I pulled into my garage and didn't get out until the garage door was closed. I tried to wait up for Ali but fell asleep on the couch. She knocked on the front door to wake me up. I let her in and threw my arms around her. She reciprocated and held me tight.

"Hey, are you okay?" she asked.

"I'm alive," I said.

"Yeah, wow, I can't believe Adam is dead."

"I know. It happened so fast. There was nothing I could do."

"Let's get some sleep and then we should talk about what happened and what you told that detective before we go to the station."

"Okay. I'll make breakfast before we go."

The detective led us back to an austere room, where we were asked to wait. She asked to take a look at my cell phone. Ali gave me a critical look but I nodded.

"It's fine," I said and handed it to the detective. *Anything they could use against me they should already know. There's nothing left to hide. I'm finally free. He was the monster. I did nothing wrong.*

We waited silently until the detective came back and handed me my cell phone and a sheet of paper. "Please read this carefully and if you believe that this is an accurate reflection of your statement regarding the events of February 27th, please sign on the line at the end. This witness statement can be used in a court of law. It will be entered into the file as evidence in the case."

"Thank you," Ali said and took the paper. "Please give me a few minute to consult with my client."

Ali studied the statement and then handed it to me. It was all there, factually correct but devoid of the emotion that had coursed through me as I learned that the man I loved was the reason for all of my pain, and then as my rapist plunged a fileting knife through my lover's heart. The description captured none of it, just words to describe the actions I had witnessed.

"Does that seem accurate?" Ali asked.

"Yes." In our morning preparations in the motel room I hadn't told her about the revelation about Adam's role in my original encounter with Nate. I wasn't sure I would ever tell anyone, but now certainly wasn't the time.

"It looks fine to me. Nothing in here contradicts a defense based on self-defense. I think you can sign it."

I signed on the line.

The detective made a copy of the form and put it on the table in front of me. "You're free to go," she said. "We'll call you if we have any more questions."

"Can she leave the state?" Ali asked. "She has a vacation planned soon."

"No charges have been filed against her."

"Thanks."

Ali and I got back in my car.

"There's one place I need to go before we head out," I said. *I have one last bit of unfinished business.*

"Whatever you want," Ali said.

MOM

Friday, June 8, 2018
Manhattan

We got on the Pike, drove into downtown Manhattan, and parked near City Hall Park. Ali walked with me along the promenade toward the historic bridge. Spandex-clad runners and cyclists passed us as we made our way to the tower where Nate and I had affixed the lock for a photo op. I took the lock out of my pocket.

"What is that?" Ali asked.

I opened my hand and held out the lock.

Ali pursed her lips and shook her head.

I wrapped my fist around the lock, wound up, and launched it as far as I could into the heavy morning air. *Finally free!* I lost sight of it as it disappeared into the East River. As I looked out toward the horizon and the expanse of dark grey water I began to laugh. I laughed until I began to cry. *How did it come to this?* But as I looked out at the open horizon in front of me and the world beyond the bridge, the vastness before me reminded me that my broken heart was minor in the grand scheme of things. *I'm still here. I made it. I have Ali and Vi. I'll survive this too.*

I turned to Ali, and she stepped forward and wrapped her arms around me. I hugged her back.

"Okay, we can go now," I said.

We walked toward Manhattan. Back in the car I pulled onto the highway heading out of town, and we sat in traffic until we were clear of the sprawling suburbs. We drove in silence and eventually Ali fell asleep.

I was tired but the desire to be as far away from Greenwich as possible, to feel safe again, kept me going. *There's only one place that I can feel safe now.*

We stopped only for fuel: gas, caffeine, and candy.

"Thank you for coming all this way for me," I said to Ali when she woke up.

"Of course. I know you've been through hell. Why wouldn't I do what I can to help you?" she said.

"I don't know, because it was all my fault."

"Look, at first I struggled to understand what you did, and my encounter with Nate pales in comparison to what he did to you, but the more I listened and tried to put myself in your shoes, the more I understood. I get it, or at least I respect that you made the choices you thought were best for you at the time. I love you. I forgive you. I don't want to hear anything else about it. Let's move on, together."

"Thank you," I said.

She squeezed my hand.

"How are you? How is Soren? Have you been really busy planning the wedding?" I asked.

"Soren and I broke up," she announced without hesitation.

"Oh no, I'm so sorry. What happened?"

"I called off the engagement," she said.

"What? Why?"

"Just didn't feel comfortable with the idea of being married in the end. The more I thought about it, the more anxious I became. I was dreading our wedding day."

"I'm sorry."

"Don't be," she said. "I am who I am. I don't need to be married to be happy."

"But you were so happy with him for so long. So don't get married, but did you need to break up?"

"Well, I broke off the engagement and then he broke up with me. He said he needs some space and time. We'll see. I'm not sure what will happen now."

"I understand." I squeezed her hand in mine.

Despite her best attempts, Ali fell asleep as we pulled out of the next rest stop.

I lost cell reception in the Allegheny forests of western

Pennsylvania, and began to flip through the few radio stations that
came in.

"And in the Old Testament we learned about punishment and
we learned about what we are called to do when we have been
wronged...'You must purge the evil from among you. The rest of the
people will hear of this and be afraid, and never again will such an
evil thing be done among you. Show no pity: life for life, eye for eye,
tooth for tooth, hand for hand, foot for foot.' But in the Sermon on the
Mount Jesus tells his followers, 'You have heard that it was said, 'Eye
for eye, and tooth for tooth.' But I tell you do not resist an evil person.
If anyone slaps you on the right cheek, turn to them the other cheek
also. And if anyone wants to sue you and take your shirt, hand over
your coat as well. If anyone forces you to go one mile, go with them
two miles. Give to the one who asks you, and do not turn away from
the one who wants to borrow from you'."

I turned the radio off and I drove in silence. *An eye for an eye, an eye
for an eye. It's over. Forget it. Let it go.*

An eye for an eye. In the miles upon miles of open road I saw Nate,
raising the fileting knife into the air. *It happened so fast.* Adam laying
helplessly in his own blood. *An eye for an eye.* Nate standing over
him...*I had no choice...it was self-defense...an eye for an eye.* The gun.
The explosion. The impact. The blood. *An eye for an eye leaves everyone
blind.*

As I drove toward Toledo, the sky in front of us turned a glorious
shade of pink. My cell phone rang.

"Kristen?"

"Wyn! I'm so glad you answered! I got you on The Late Late Show
two weeks from today."

"That's amazing!"

"I have a couple other speaking events in the works, too," she said,
"What does your calendar look like this month?"

"Wide open actually," I said. "Book anything, everything."

"Will do. I will let you know!"

"Thank you!"

She hung up.

"Sorry I fell asleep again," Ali said.

"Yeah, it's fine," I said. "You took a red eye to New York for me.

Sleep."

I drove through Gary, Indiana as dusk was taking hold. Rusty colored industrial behemoths stood between the highway and the vast expanse of Lake Michigan. Grey smoke billowed from chimneys, flames danced, bright blue, white, and orange amidst a grey fog. Mustard-colored clouds hung low and heavy in the sky, chimneys spewed flames. The scene was otherworldly.

I rounded the bend at the south end of the lake and saw the city glowing in the distance. Tears began to roll down my cheeks. *All of the pain and for what? How things could have been.* I imagined living near Vi in an apartment downtown. Taking a little girl with pigtails to see grandma. There was no man in the scene this time. It was just us.

We parked in a garage down the street from Vi's condo. It was late and dark and we left the big suitcases in the back of the car and walked straight to Vi's building. Jeremiah greeted us.

"How are you little lady? It's so nice to see you and your sister again!"

"I'm fine, thank you, Jeremiah. Yes, I'm back to stay for a while. We both are. How are you?" I said.

"Great, I'm doing just fine, thank you. You two just go on up."

"Thanks."

We walked down the hall to Vi's door. I paused for a minute and took a deep breath. *Yes, she will understand.* Ali knocked.

It took a few minutes, but eventually Vi opened the door.

"Freddie, what on earth are you doing here?" She asked. "Ali!"

"I'm lucky to be alive," I said and Vi seemed to understand without knowing more. She held her arms out and I practically ran into them.

"Thank god, you're safe," Vi said. "I love you."

"I love you too," I said, as the tears began rolling down my cheeks. Ali joined the embrace, clutching Vi and me from behind.

"I'm so glad you are both safe," Vi said.

"Me too," I said through tears.

Vi let go. "Well, come on in. You are welcome to stay as long as you'd like, of course."

"Thank you," I said.

I picked up my overnight bag and carried it to the guest room. Ali came in behind me and closed the door. "Are you going to tell her what happened?"

"Yeah, I will. I'm just so tired right now. I think I need to get a good night's sleep first."

"You know it will be on the news soon."

"Yeah, I know."

"And you know as well as I do that keeping an unbearable secret will eat you up inside."

"Mom did it for all those years."

"And I think she regrets it now. It didn't make her happier," she said.

"Yeah, I know. I'll tell her. Just please keep it to yourself for now."

"Okay, it's your story to tell."

The next morning Vi made tea and we sat on the couch and talked.

"So, how long do you think you'll be in Chicago?" she asked.

"Not sure, probably a while. I have no reason to go back anytime soon."

"What's your plan while you're here?"

"Not sure. I wrote a memoir about everything that happened with Nate. It should be released this spring. My agent is going to try to line up some promotional events before the release."

"Oh my gosh, that is wonderful," she said. "I'm so happy for you."

I heard approval in her voice in a way that I had never heard before. Her support was sincere.

She's finally proud of me!

I nodded, "Thank you, Mom. And Mom, there's something else I need to tell you."

Did you enjoy **THE VIRTUOUS CON?** Please take a moment and leave a review on Amazon, Goodreads, or your social media platform of choice. Your support means the world.

ACKNOWLEDGEMENTS

This book would not have been possible without the encouragement, guidance, and constructive criticism of many wonderful women and my beloved husband.

To my earliest readers, Rebecca Geissler and Connie Magnuson, you slogged through shit and came out the other end with smiles on your faces and invaluable insights, and for that I am grateful. Thank you for your perseverance and willingness to focus on potential!

A huge thank you to my talented editor, Susan McBride, whose attentive editing was critical to the story and the final result. I am incredibly grateful to my beta readers who stuck with me and provided invaluable feedback and moral support, just when I thought it might never be quite complete: Bonita Sen, Julie Montgomery, Martha Spaulding, and my very best (and toughest) critics, Vesna Rogulja and Martin Rogulja.

For early feedback and direction: Eva Hershaw, Amy Seeboth, Laura Gilbert, Mary Penn, Jessica Albers, Leanne Fox, Natalie Cahill, Meridith Aiello, and Victoria Solomon. A big shout out to my style consultants, Anne Gilbert and Nora Massey. For instrumental guidance on the industry and this business of storytelling and publishing: Kate Colbert and Leslie McLean.

Finally, a big thank you to my parents and my husband, without whom nothing is possible.

ABOUT THE AUTHOR

Maren Foster is a former management consultant turned author. She is an alumna of the University of Washington in Seattle with degrees in English Literature and Psychology. Maren is interested in what drives human behavior and motivates every action and reaction. She writes fast-paced thrillers with empowered female leads, and lives in Chicago with her husband and two cats. This is her debut novel. For more information and to stay up to date on new stories by Maren please visit:

www.marenfoster.com

Notes

The sermon on forgiveness in The Put-Up (Sunday, June 28, 2015)is adapted from *What Does the Bible Really Say about Forgiveness?* by Maria Mayo, M.Div., Ph.D. in the Huffington Post, published on 07/29/2011 and updated Sep 28, 2011. It was accessed online on 8/15/2020.

TWO TAILS PRESS
Reading Group Guide

THE
VIRTUOUS
CON

Maren Foster

Note: In order to fully explore the central themes and issues of
The Virtuous Con, it is necessary to describe key aspects of the plot
and ending. It is recommended that the questions that follow be
reviewed only after you have finished reading *The Virtuous Con*.

Questions and Topics for Discussion

According to the largest anti-sexual violence organization in the United States, RAINN (Rape, Abuse & Incest National Network), there are, on average, more than 400,000 victims (age 12 or older) of rape and sexual assault in the United States each year.[1] Among undergraduate students, 23.1 percent of females and 5.4 percent of males experience rape or sexual assault through physical force, violence, or incapacitation.[2] Yet, only 20 percent of female student victims, age 18-24, report the assault to law enforcement.

1. Why do you think so few female college students report sexual assault and rape to the police?

2. What factors influenced Wyn's decisions to get a rape kit done and then lie to detectives?

3. What do you think you would do in Wyn's particular situation? Do you think you would report the rape or not? If not, why?

According to RAINN, 37 percent of victims of sexual violence experience problems with family and/or friends after an assault. These can include getting into arguments more frequently than before, not feeling able to trust their family and/or friends, or not feeling as close to them as before the assault.

4. How does Wyn's relationship with her sister change after the assault?

5. How does the reaction of her roommate, Krista, at the time of the assault, impact Wyn's decision about whether or not to report Nate to the police?

6. Why do you think women, in the past, have been so hesitant to support and believe other women when they come forward to report sexual assault?

The 'me too' movement was founded in 2006, by Tarana Burke, to help survivors of sexual violence, particularly Black women and girls, and other young women of color from low wealth communities, find pathways to healing. The 'me too' movement continues to focus on helping those who need it to find entry points for individual healing and galvanize a broad base of survivors to disrupt the systems that allow for the global proliferation of sexual violence.[3]

7. How do you think the #MeToo movement has changed how women view victims of sexual assault? Has it changed the way that men and/or individuals with power view victims of sexual assault?

8. How do you think high profile verdicts—such as the Harvey Weinstein and Brock Turner verdicts—have impacted or will impact the way that victims are treated when they come forward with accusations of sexual assault now and in the future?

9. What still needs to change in order for the victim and the accused to be treated fairly and for justice to be done through the legal system?

10. Wyn makes a difficult decision not to provide the police with critical information that would help them solve the case of who raped her, effectively stalling the investigation and allowing Nate to walk free and continue to rape and assault other women. Is Wyn culpable for the assaults that Nate commits after her rape? Are Wyn's actions justified? What would you do if you were in Wyn's position?

11. Wyn's actions conflict with her religious beliefs. How does Wyn's view and understanding of forgiveness change over time? How does she reconcile her actions with her faith?

12. Wyn finds and reads her mother's diary without her permission. How does what Wyn learns about her mother's life experiences influence her own decisions and behavior? How does it impact Wyn's relationships with her sister and her mother?

13. Throughout most of Wyn's relationship with Nate, she

believes that she has the upper hand. What does Wyn's marriage to Nate, and his revelation about the state of their shared finances highlight? How does her memoir figure into her ability to exact justice?

14. Wyn uses DNA evidence from the rape to ultimately deliver Nate to the authorities. As of 2017, all fifty states had post-conviction DNA collection laws, but only thirty states had enacted pre-conviction DNA collection laws.[4] Pre-conviction DNA testing differs in these thirty states, with some states testing the accused upon arrest, and some upon arraignment. Pre-conviction DNA testing has led to some high profile convictions for past crimes committed, however, opponents argue that this practice circumvents a detainee's right to a presumption of innocence until proven guilty. Do you believe that pre-conviction DNA testing should be allowed?

15. The title of the book, The Virtuous Con, makes clear that this is the story of a confidence artist at work. Which characters can be considered con artists at which points in the story? Is Wyn's con really virtuous? Why or why not?

16. What did you think of the ending? Is justice achieved in the end? Do the means justify the ends?

Notes

1   Department of Justice, Office of Justice Programs, Bureau of Justice Statistics, National Crime Victimization Survey, 2018 (2019). Note: RAINN applies a 5-year rolling average to adjust for changes in the year-to-year NCVS survey data.

2   David Cantor, Bonnie Fisher, Susan Chibnall, Reanna Townsend, et. al. Association of American Universities (AAU), Report on the AAU Campus Climate Survey on Sexual Assault and Sexual Misconduct (September 21, 2015).

3   https://metoomvmt.org/

4   Hu, Xiaochen, et al. "Pre- and Post- Conviction DNA Collection Laws in the United States: An Analysis of Proposed Model Statutes." Journal of Criminal Justice and Law, vol. 1, no. 1, Jan. 2017, pp. 23–42., www.uhd.edu/academics/public-service/jcjl/Pages/Journal-of-Criminal-Justice-and-Law.aspx.

1-3   RAINN. Accessed online (18 July 2020). https://www.rainn.org/about-sexual-assault

Read on for a sneak peak at Maren Foster's new thriller

I AM ASHLEY CLARKE'S MOTHER

Available for pre-order Spring 2022

Sign up to receive additional sneak peak content and be the first to order your copy at www.MarenFoster.com

The kitchen was quiet, eerily quiet compared to the night before. I tiptoed toward the coffee maker as if on eggshells, even though A.J. was still in his room upstairs. Picking up a stray piece of broken picture glass from under a bar stool, I remembered the sound it made as A.J. smashed the picture frame of the three of us against the granite counter. It was supposed to be my night. The best night I'd had in years, and it was, until I got home.

"A.J., time to go!" I yelled.

I miss my happy, sweet little boy, I thought as I picked up what was left of the photo of us: a two-year-old A.J., with idyllic curls, between me and his father Dustin, dressed in his army fatigues. *I wish it wasn't like this too.*

"Come on!" I yelled. "You'll be late."

"I'm ready," he said standing in the hallway, dressed entirely in black, with his guitar case strung over his shoulder.

I still love you, even if I hate this rebellious phase you're in.

"Oh, there you are. Okay. Don't forget that I have a PTO meeting tonight after work. There's a meatloaf in the fridge for dinner. Help yourself when you get home."

"Sure."

"What are you doing with your guitar? You know I don't want you going over to John's house after school anymore."

"He's in the band and we have nowhere else to go to practice."

"It's a band now? Who else is playing with you guys?"

"No one."

"Can it really be called a band if it's only two people?"

He followed me into the garage.

"Local H, I Set My Friends on Fire, Middle Class Rut?"

"What are you talking about?"

"Bands with two guys."

"I've never heard of them."

"That's because you're old and lame. How about Simon and Garfunkel?"

"Oh, yeah."

"Uh huh. But we're not a band, right?"

"Get in the car," I said. "Please."

We drove towards the high school in silence.

"Stop here! I told you to stop here!" he yelled as we approached the corner of Oakwood and 3rd.

I pulled over quickly. *I can't handle another fight right now.*

"Love you. Don't forget about the meatloaf," I yelled as he jumped out of the car to catch up with John, who was halfway down the block, walking toward the high school.

I don't like that kid but I guess I'd rather he have a friend than no friends at all. I had encouraged A.J. to join a sports team when we first moved to the neighborhood, but he'd never been very coordinated and was still scrawny, even for a sixteen year old.

I drove the mile across town to work, clutching my coffee mug. My new job at the insurance company already felt old, although it had been almost a year since we'd moved to the large suburb outside of Kansas City. I had read that it was one of the best places to raise a family, and we had to get away from that girl. *He's such a good kid. Why does he always seems to attract bad apples? At least he hasn't talked about enlisting to follow in his dad's footsteps yet. I can't bear losing him too.*

"Tammy!" I said on my way to my desk. "You're not gonna believe what happened last night!"

"Morning Sweetie! What happened?"

"This!" I said, holding out my left hand proudly.

"Oh my God! He did it!" she squealed.

I nodded and grinned as she admired my engagement ring.

"Oh my God, congratulations!"

"Thank you."

"Oh Sweetie, I'm so happy for you!"

She hugged me and I held on tight.

"Ooooh, tell me all about it," she said, settling back into her chair.

"He took me to Magnolia for dinner and then we walked over to the carousel as the sun was setting. They were closing up but he begged for one ride and the guy let us on. He helped me up onto the most beautiful horse and then got down on one knee in front of a glorious pink sky. It was really beautiful."

"Wow! I knew it was only a matter of time!"

"I guess so."

"And?" she asked.

"He said I'm the love of his life!"

"Oh my God!" she squeeled. "That's amazing!"

"I know. I love him so much."

"Did you tell A.J.?"

"I did."

"And?"

I shook my head. "Not great."

"Oh, I'm so sorry."

"Morning," our boss offered sternly from across the room.

"Yeah, morning." I said and powered on my computer.

I finished off my cup of coffee and settled in, trying to find motivation to dig into the pile of receipts on my desk from our President's last business trip.

"Oh my God, Dee!" Tammy yelled. "There's been a shooting. At the high school."

"What?"

She was in front of my desk, cell phone in hand, reading out loud, "Reports of shots fired at Fairview High. Emergency services arrived on the scene at 10:35am."

"Are you sure it's Fairview?"

"It says 'Fairview High'. Says it's ongoing."

Oh my God. A.J.!

"Go!" she urged. "Do you want me to come with you?"

"No, it's fine," I said and grabbed my purse.

Speeding toward the high school, traffic began to back up on Front Street, about three blocks away.

A uniformed police officer was directing the line of cars into an overflow parking lot about two blocks from the high school. I parked behind another s.u.v. and realized that my hand was shaking as I popped the car into park. *This can't be happening. Not here. We came here because it was safe.*

Parents emerged from their cars with looks of shock, stubborn disbelief, and confusion. I watched from my car as they formed little groups, huddling close together and nodding as they exchanged intelligence and reassurances. News crews descended on the faded parking lot and began to approach the groups of parents.

Maren Foster

I hesitated to join them, fearing what they may or may not know, but as I sat alone my thoughts ran wild: A.J. alone in the school somewhere; A.J. injured; or worse yet, A.J. dead. *I can't bear it.* I got out and floated tentatively between groups of parents that I recognized, but none of whom I knew personally.

A younger woman was in the center of one group, reading social media posts and messages from students inside the high school, the parents around her frozen listening: "I can hear them shooting down the hall. I don't want to die." "I love you Mom and Dad. I love you Teeny." One of the moms broke down in tears and was comforted by her husband. A woman screamed across the parking lot, letting out a howl that sounded animalistic. Panic engulfed the anxious crowd. Parents comforted each other as word of their childrens' fate reached them.

A woman pulled out her cell phone. "Oh my God! It's a text from Nicole! She's okay." Tears of joy overwhelmed her and provided a momentary calm for those around her.

I pulled out my smart phone and pretended to pull up A.J.'s profile. He'd given up on social media years ago as a preteen, when online bullying had reduced him to tears for the third or fourth time. Instead I pulled up the local news station's feed: First responders on the scene, reports of two shooters, students at the high school. Multiple casualties. At least ten reported dead on the scene. *Jesus Christ! The shooters go to school here.* I looked up at the high school and saw a few young people running toward the parking lot. *A.J.?* I wondered, but he wasn't in the group.

I watched as more students streamed from the school toward the parking lot. As they got closer I could see their tear stained cheeks. They began to locate their parents in the now full parking lot. The camera crews invaded their euphoric reunions with microphones and spotlights.

The reunions were more than hugs and kisses, they were a sort of rebirth of children into the safety of their parents' arms. They had survived, and as the realization of how lucky they were washed over them, they entered the world anew, although they would never be the same. They shook with the shock of knowing.

Where is A.J.? Is he hurt? Or worse? I remembered yelling 'I love you' to him as he got out of the car less than three hours earlier. *At least I said 'I love you' this morning. Oh God. Stop it. I don't know that he's hurt.*

My fatalistic train of thought was interrupted by a girl a few feet away, in her mother's arms saying, "It was them. You know. It was the two of them. I can't believe they did it, but I guess if anyone would, it would be them. I hope they're dead now."

Them? Who?

"Dee! Oh my God! Dee!" Krystal Jenkins yelled from across the parking lot, as she made her way toward me. Krystal was on my PTO committee. She was the kind of mom that thinks she can solve every problem, no matter how large or whose privacy may need to be invaded in the process. Overbearing would be polite.

God, not now!

I forced a smile and nodded.

"What about A.J.?" she asked.

"I don't know," I said.

"Oh my God. I'm sure he's fine."

Are you? Why are you so sure? Innocent children are dead. Mine might be one of them.

"What about Eliza?" I asked.

"She texted a little while ago that she was okay but we haven't seen her yet," she said, clearly worried.

"She's probably on her way out now," I said, as I looked toward a line of high schoolers walking toward us, hands raised above their heads.

"Yes."

As the students made their way across the fields that separated the parking lot from the school I thought about A.J.. *I know I haven't always been a perfect mom, but you're all I have. Please be okay. I need you.*

Emotional reunions played out again and again around me. As I watched the tears of joy, fear, and relief, I thought about my husband, Dustin, and the tears of sorrow and fear that I had shed on that cool autumn day when the news came that he'd died honorably, serving in a vast, lonely desert half a world away. A.J. was too young to understand what had happened, so I lied at first. His dad had been away on one tour after another since he was born, so for my innocent five-year-old son it was just another day, but it broke my heart every time he asked when his daddy was coming home. As he got older I would find him staring at a framed photo of his dad in the desert in his army fatigues and camo helmet, with a rifle perched against his chest.

Made in the USA
Middletown, DE
18 October 2022

13029337R00234